No Return

CHRISTINE POPE

Dark Valentine Press

This is a work of fiction. Names, characters, places, and incidents are either the product of the author's imagination or are used fictitiously. Any resemblance to actual events, places, organizations, or persons, whether living or dead, is entirely coincidental.

NO RETURN: A CONTEMPORARY PHANTOM TALE

ISBN: 978-0615656557
Copyright © 2012 by Christine Pope
Published by Dark Valentine Press

Cover design and interior layout by Indie Author Services

To learn more about this author, go to
www.christinepope.com.

For the real Erik...

Chapter One

SOMEONE IS WATCHING ME.

The feeling of wrongness had been there awhile, tickling the back of my mind for several days, but this was the first time I could remember the sensation taking any kind of coherent shape.

The thought that immediately followed, naturally, was, *Of course someone's watching you. You're a singer, for God's sake.* But I somehow knew the wrongness hadn't come from the intent eyes of the watching directors for whom I'd auditioned, or even from the patrons at the restaurant where I worked part-time as a waitress and was occasionally required to stroll between the tables and sing popular opera to give the place "atmosphere" (George, the owner's words, not mine).

I paused, key still in the lock to my front door, and gave an uncertain little glance over my shoulder. The street was quiet, baking in the heat of the usual October onslaught of the Santa Ana winds. The gales had subsided some time earlier that afternoon, but the heat remained, implacable, solid as a hot wave from an open oven door. It was too early for the neighborhood children to be home from school, and too warm for the usual Spanish chatter at the mailboxes that was usual for the stay-at-home mothers on my street at this time of day. The air hummed with the sound of overworked air-conditioning units.

I turned the lock and went inside the bungalow. It smelled of overheated Murphy's oil soap and a faint lingering trace of patchouli, underlaid with what I always thought of as "old house smell": the scent of aged wood and generations of perfume and smoke. The bungalow had been built in the early teens—was in fact located on a historical landmark—and made up in charm what it lacked in conveniences. I couldn't run the bathroom heater and the toaster oven at the same time without blowing a fuse, but the bungalow had lovely oak floors, built-in bookcases in the living room, and a real stone fireplace.

I laid my few pieces of mail—the dreaded electric bill, a flyer from the theater department at school—on the coffee table and pulled the chain on the ceiling fan. The blades moved slowly at first in the hot air, but at least the draft they created broke up the oppressive heat somewhat. At this point a room air conditioner was something I dreamed of when reading the sales circulars that got deposited in my mailbox every Tuesday.

Luckily, I'd already formed the habit of keeping my shades drawn, more to keep out the heat and light of the hot weather than for privacy's sake. I sat there in the warm semi-darkness, feeling alone at least for the moment.

There were no watching eyes here, as far as I could tell.

The bungalow was tiny, one small bedroom, an even smaller bathroom, and a kitchen that was more of an afterthought than anything else. The living room alone was a decent size, although it was crowded with my loveseat (I'd found out very quickly that a sofa was out of the question), a drop-leaf table against the far wall, and my grandmother's ancient spinet tucked into a corner next to the table.

"Not a lot of places for a serial killer to hide," I said out loud, then smiled, mocking myself. It was just stress. Stress could cause feelings of paranoia—at least I had a vague recollection of reading something to that effect in a freshman psych course. Not to mention that carrying a full course load while working thirty hours a week and going to auditions on the side was probably enough to make anyone crazy.

The message light on my answering machine was blinking. I reached over to the file cabinet that doubled as an end table and pushed the button.

Meg, of course.

"Christine, I know you're at class right now, but is there any chance you could take my shift tonight?"

I wondered why Meg even bothered with a part-time job—half the time I picked up her shifts anyway, which was why a gig that had started out as fifteen or so hours a week had slowly mushroomed into closer to thirty. Meg didn't really need the job but had taken it to "give her more practice singing in public." She had a good voice but was lazy about showing up for class and even worse about work; during the year I'd had known her, Meg had been on academic probation the entire time, and even now, with graduation looming (at least for me), Meg seemed airily unconcerned about the whole process. Of course, if she had to go a fifth year it would not be the end of the world—with an architect father trying to assuage the guilt over his divorce by piling money on his daughter and a mother who worked as a producer at a local television station, the cost of the whole thing was a non-issue. Whereas I was scraping by on a patchwork of scholarships and grants that covered tuition and some books but certainly not necessities such as a place to live and something to drive, even a car as makeshift as my battered but still breathing Honda Civic.

I had a paper on mid-nineteenth-century Romantic composers due on Monday, but today was only Wednesday, and I didn't have to work until Saturday night, so I knew I could take Meg's shift without too much trouble. It meant yet another day of delayed practice, but my next recital was still two weeks off, and the electric bill just happened to be due next Tuesday. It wasn't much of a contest.

Besides, I thought, as I picked up the phone to leave a message on Meg's cell, if I were at the restaurant working I wouldn't be here, startling at every noise and certain that a whole gang of serial rapists was lurking out on the front porch.

He picked up the photo, certain that the girl couldn't be everything Jerome had reported, but the image was promising. Just a quick, surreptitious shot from his assistant's iPhone, it was a little blurred, frustratingly dim, but it showed enough. The subject had apparently paused as she left the restaurant, stopping to push a stray strand of hair away from her eyes—the winds had been strong two nights ago. Her face was illuminated by the street lights and the heavy wrought-iron light fixture that hung above the entrance to L'Opera. She was fair, her oval face surrounded by a cloud of curly dark hair, the features in the photo grainy but obviously regular: large eyes and a full mouth separated by a straight nose. She wore a plain white shirt and narrow black pants that outlined her slender body.

"And her voice?"

Jerome straightened even more, if that were possible. "Classically trained, coloratura. Very lovely."

He set the photo down on the leather blotter at his desk. How long had he waited for this chance, this one fulfillment of dreams and desires he could no longer explain even to himself? He ached to hear her, to see her delicate features before him, unblurred by an unfriendly camera. He took a breath. Not yet.

"Anything else?" Of course he knew that Jerome had more to report, but he also knew that his assistant preferred the give and take of question and answer, not a simple regurgitation of facts.

"She's a senior at USC." Jerome paused, tapping away on his iPhone. "Twenty-three; she had to wait a year to start because her scholarships weren't all in place, so she worked as a waitress. Orphaned—her parents were killed in a car accident when she was fifteen, so she lived with her paternal grandmother after that. The grandmother passed away a few years later, and Christine had to sell the house they lived in to cover medical expenses."

"And where is she living now?"

"Still in Pasadena." Jerome wouldn't allow himself to smile, but it was apparent he was somewhat amused by the irony of it all. "Less than two miles from here."

Two miles, he thought, and felt his own lips twist in the closest approximation of a smile he could make. Two miles in terms of geography, but it might as well have been two hundred when it came to economics. Her shabby little bungalow was in a heavily ethnic working-class neighborhood where one could go blocks without hearing a word of English; his home stood in a world of faux Norman chateaux, replicas of Mediterranean villas, and substantial Craftsman homesteads that bore as much resemblance to Christine's tiny bungalow as her battered Honda did to the sleek new S-Class parked in the driveway outside. To think that she had been here all this time…

"I need a recording, Jerome," he said finally. "I want to hear her."

"Of course, sir."

He knew that a recording would only give a blurred, half-accurate impression of her, much like that one indistinct photograph, but it would be a start. Jerome could be trusted with certain things, but while not completely ignorant he was unaware of certain subtleties of the vocal art.

"Not at the restaurant, though," he continued. "There would be far too much background noise. Perhaps from one of her classes, or a recital, if she has one coming up."

Jerome typed something into his iPhone. "Very good, sir."

For quite a while he'd been under the impression that Jerome could do perfectly well without his newest electronic toy, but he'd refrained from comment on the matter. If it helped Jerome feel that he was something more than a glorified errand-boy, so be it. At least he could trust the man to be completely discreet, and discretion was needed here above all else. Of course, Jerome was paid very well to carry out his duties seamlessly and quietly, but it was still something to feel that he had at least one person in the world he could trust.

"That's all," he said finally, and waved his hand.

Jerome nodded, secreted the phone in the breast pocket of his suit jacket, and left the room.

He pushed the heavy antique chair back from his desk and stood, then went to the damask draperies that framed the window and pushed one aside. Outside, the gardens wilted under the heavy autumn heat, despite nightly soakings by a carefully orchestrated sprinkler system. A few brave roses still clung to their stems, bright flashes against the green of lawns and shrubs. He squinted at the light that poured into the room, then shook his head, letting the drapery fall from his fingers. Better to stay in the dark, in these carefully climate-controlled rooms, where, if he never looked outside, he could believe it was winter, or nighttime.

The heavy antiques in the room had come to him with the house, and he had never had the slightest desire to change any of them. They suited him, suited the shadows and dark to which he clung, shrouded from the outside world. To his neighbors and the few family members who remained, he was practically a ghost. And since his world had formed itself around him so perfectly, barricaded behind his wealth the way his home was barricaded behind high stone walls, he had never bothered to alter any of it.

Until now.

Chapter Two

"CHRISTINE."

I looked up, not wanting to meet my professor's eyes. Dr. Green was watching me carefully, voice mild, expression calm, but those dark eyes of his were disappointed.

"Do you really think a performance like that is up to recital standard?"

Thank God this had been my one hour of private tutoring for the week. I would have been mortified if I'd sung like that in front of the other students in my senior class. As it was, I found it difficult to stop beating myself up mentally long enough to reply, "No, Dr. Green. It's just that I had to work double shifts—"

He held up a hand, forestalling any further explanations. Most likely he viewed them only as excuses. "I know that most students these days need to work to make it through school. But if you allow a part-time job to take over your life, then you have no business being in this class—or pursuing a career in music."

The words were cruel, but true, I knew. If I only had the discipline, I'd be practicing far into the night, after I returned home from work. But exhaustion usually drove me straight into bed after my shift was over. That familiar choking feeling rose in my throat, and I swallowed, hard. If I dissolved into tears in front of Dr. Green, I knew I might as well pack it in and give up on my dreams of singing forever.

"I'm sorry, Dr. Green," I said at last, after I was reasonably sure that my voice wouldn't betray me—at least any more than it already had. "I'll tell them I can't do more than twenty hours a week. I'll be ready."

He studied me for a moment, the worry lines between his brows seeming deeper than they had a few minutes ago. "Christine, I know this has all been difficult for you—"

"I'm fine, Dr. Green," I said, knowing that the last thing I needed right now was words of sympathy. I admired Dr. Green greatly and knew that he was genuinely concerned about me, but sometimes compassion was harder to bear than cruelty.

"Mmm." He hesitated, appearing to pick through the words he wanted to say and finding them all lacking. "I don't say this to many students, Christine. You have one of the finest pure instruments I've heard. But talent isn't enough. Without practice, dedication, hard work, all you have is potential. And that's not what casting directors are looking for."

There being no real reply to that, I said only, "I know, Dr. Green."

Again he was quiet for a moment. Then he said, "I

think that's enough for today. Concentrate on the middle section, and we'll see how you're doing tomorrow."

I took the dismissal as gracefully as I could and nodded, then retrieved my canvas satchel and shoved my score into it. "Thanks," I said, and turned to the door without looking at him. I wasn't particularly thankful, and I knew he knew it, but there didn't seem to be anything else to say at that point.

A glance at my watch told me that I'd only used up half of the hour-long practice time I'd been allotted. Funny, it had felt much longer than that.

This was my last class of the day, so it was time for the murderous slog up the 110 Freeway through downtown L.A. back to Pasadena, and I wasn't looking forward to getting into the crunch at five-thirty instead of six. Even a half-hour could make a huge difference in the chimerical beast that was the Los Angeles freeway system. At least it had cooled down somewhat over the past couple of days. Sitting in bumper-to-bumper traffic in ninety-degree heat with no air conditioning would have been enough to push my already frayed nerves over the edge.

I had barely looked up from my watch before I almost collided with a man who stood outside the rehearsal studio. He was studying a small tabloid-size poster someone had tacked up to advertise the senior master class autumn recital. "Sorry," I said automatically.

He looked at me swiftly, eyes sharp behind a pair of dark glasses, and I almost took a step back. That stare was far too penetrating, and as unexpected as it was unwelcome. Then it seemed as if a shutter closed down over his features, and he smiled. "No problem."

"Well, as long as I didn't smash your foot or anything…"

"All intact." He continued to smile, but I was not reassured.

Eager to keep moving, I manufactured a smile of my own, gave a little nod of acknowledgement, and hurried off down the sidewalk, not wanting to look back.

The strength of my reaction surprised me a little. Sure, the guy "creeped me out," to use one of Meg's favorite phrases, but I couldn't exactly say why. He did look a little out of place—I would have put his age at around forty, probably—but schools were full of "nontraditional" students these days, whatever that meant. He didn't look like a student, though. His air was too polished, his clothes too good. Possibly a grad student, although they usually had an even worse air of poverty than the undergrads.

I shook my head. *Jumping at shadows again. Like you don't have enough to worry about already.*

George, my boss, was going to flip out when I told him I could only work twenty hours a week. And how I was going to make expenses on that amount of money, I had no idea. I had a small, tightly guarded hoard of money in a savings account, all that was left from the sale of my grandmother's house, but it probably wasn't enough to get me through the rest of the school year. I'd thought about getting a roommate, but my place was so small I didn't even have room for a cat, much less an actual person.

"Christine! Hey!"

I turned. Randall again. This was starting to get awkward.

"You still haven't scheduled that practice time with

me," he continued, planting himself in my path so I had no choice but to stop.

"Well…" I hedged. Things were complicated enough already. Even though I might admit to myself—deep down—that he interested me, I knew a relationship should be the last thing on my mind right now.

Randall was a graduate student who sometimes worked as an accompanist for the senior master class. He was also, as Meg liked to put it, a "hottie." I wanted to pretend I was immune to the charm of his hazel eyes and ready smile, but I knew better than that.

While I tried to play it cool, he made no secret of his interest in me, much to the disappointment of several other girls in the master class. And although I thought for sure my hard-to-get act would wear after time, he showed no signs of calling a halt to his pursuit. It would have been a lot easier if he'd been someone who didn't interest me at all.

He smiled, that easy grin which probably could have melted harder hearts than mine. "The recital's only two weeks off—"

"I know that!" I snapped, my tone sharper than I had intended it to be. I was still smarting from that painful session with Dr. Green.

Randall seemed unfazed. "So why would you turn down hours and hours of free practice time?"

"I've been working a lot of shifts at the restaurant."

His eyebrows lifted. "Uh-huh."

Despite myself, I had to smile. "Okay, so now you've succeeded in making me sound like an idiot."

"Never that." He fixed me with those hazel eyes of his. "So what are you doing right now?"

I was caught. This was my one night off from the restaurant, so truthfully all I had planned to do was go home and slog through that paper. I still had the weekend, though. And while the music history class was important, my marks in the senior master class would actually determine whether I'd get accepted into the master's program. How I'd ever be able to afford it was a worry for another day.

I smiled back at him, surrendering finally. "Looks like I'm practicing."

"Good answer."

I let him take my satchel as he directed me to follow him to the staff parking lot—being a T.A. had at least a few perks, it seemed—so we could drive to his place. Apparently the practice studios on campus were all booked up, he explained ingenuously, and I had to keep from laughing. He was probably right, but his enthusiasm about my having to go practice at his home was all too transparent. Well, if he thought I planned to do anything more than practice, he was going to be sorely disappointed.

His home turned out to be a well-appointed Spanish-style duplex in the mid-Wilshire area, about fifteen minutes from campus. Although it appeared to have been well decorated in the not-too-distant past—the velvet slipcovered couch and curtains were straight out of the Pottery Barn catalog—right now most of the casually bohemian chic was buried under music scores, empty pizza boxes, and copies of L.A. Weekly.

"Sorry about the mess," he said, grabbing a couple of pizza boxes with one hand as he dumped my satchel on the floor next to the piano. "I haven't been here all that much lately."

"Just long enough to order pizza," I said, and he grinned.

"Well, it's fast and easy. My microwave's on the blink."

"And God forbid you'd have to cook something—"

"Like on a stove?" He gave a mock shudder. "You're kidding, right?"

I thought of my lone toaster oven and tiny apartment-sized stove, and decided not to mention the fact that I'd had to get along without a microwave for the past two years after mine self-destructed while nuking a bag of popcorn.

"Right." I waited in the living room while he disposed of the boxes and rustled around in the kitchen, doing who knows what.

It was really a lovely place. Los Angeles still has some amazing architecture, despite the developers who seem determined to raze anything more than twenty years old. Randall's duplex, probably built in the 1920s, had charming arched doorways, art niches, hardwood floors, and a fireplace that looked as if it actually still worked. And it had been furnished intelligently, which led me to believe the decor was probably the work of an ex-girlfriend.

The living room was dominated by the grand piano, a gorgeous carved behemoth in walnut, not the standard black Yamaha or Steinway I had come to expect. At least this room was big enough to accommodate the thing; at my bungalow I had been hard-pressed to squeeze in my grandmother's tiny spinet.

I stepped around the curve of the piano to look at the name emblazoned in gold leaf above the keys, which, believe it or not, were apparently the original ivory. "'Baye,'" I read aloud.

"Never heard of them, right?"

I shook my head. "I'm not an authority, but—"

"No, that's a really obscure reference." Randall came back into the living room, a glass of red wine in each hand. I opened my mouth to protest, but he just handed the wine glass to me, smiling, daring me to say something, and I took it meekly. He sipped some his wine, waited until I had followed suit, then continued, "Baye was actually the company that made the guts—you know, the sounding board, the strings, all that good stuff—for Steinway back in the 1920s. Then they decided to strike out on their own and start their own company, but their timing was lousy; the Great Depression hit about a year later, and the company folded. But they made some amazing pianos before they went bust."

The wine was good. Probably a cabernet, but past that my uneducated palate couldn't distinguish much except that I liked it. I hadn't allowed myself to indulge for a long time—couldn't afford it—and I took another sip. "That's too bad."

He nodded. "It happens. I'm just glad my grandfather actually bought one. Probably because it had the sound of a Steinway without the price tag."

"Was he careful with his money?"

At that Randall laughed, but he didn't seem all that amused. "Christine, he made Ebenezer Scrooge look like a party animal."

"Well, Scrooge was a party animal by the end of the story," I replied.

"Touché. But not Grandpa. Still, he did have the good sense to pick up property all over L.A., hold on to it, and then leave it to his grandkids."

I lifted my wine glass in a gesture meant to encompass the living room. "And so you're here?"

"Did you really think I could afford this place on a T.A.'s salary?"

I'd secretly been wondering about that but wasn't going to admit it. "Well, even a T.A.'s salary looks pretty good from where I stand."

His smile faded. "I'm sorry about that, Christine—"

I cut him off. "Why should you be? As if any of it's your fault!" I bent and picked up my satchel and pulled the sheet music from it. I handed the photocopied pages to Randall. "We did come over here to practice, right?"

His eyes met mine for a moment, and I sucked in my breath. Under the easy smile and the friendly demeanor I suddenly got a glimpse of the desire underneath, and I felt a tremor go through my body. This could be dangerous, then, probably more so than I had guessed. After all, I'd never really had a serious relationship or experience with anything more than a few awkward dates.

He took the score from my hand, and the moment passed as he seated himself in front of the keyboard. His fingers brushed mine as he took the music, but the touch was so fleeting I wasn't sure whether it was by accident or intention.

Then there was no time for worries about his intentions or my reactions to them, because Randall launched into the opening notes of the aria, and the music stole me away with the first trill.

"Ah, je rit, de me vois si belle en ce miroir," and I felt the rush, the warmth of the music flowing over me and welling up from somewhere deep inside, the notes coming out pure and strong, my voice clear, unmarked this time by worry or doubt or fear.

I didn't know whether it was Randall's presence, the half a glass of wine I'd just consumed, or a desire to prove Professor Green wrong, but whatever the case, I had never felt in truer voice. And I could tell, as the last few notes of the aria died away, that Randall felt the same.

After a moment he finally lifted his hands from the keyboard and looked over at me. "You blow them all away. You really do."

I made some sound of demurral, but inside me was a tiny, fierce triumph, because I knew at some level he was right.

Randall kept his gaze locked on mine, and I could see a sudden shift, just the slightest twinkle in his hazel eyes before the corner of his mouth twitched. "But that doesn't mean we can't try to improve perfection, does it? From the top, then—"

And we launched into it all over again. Then again, and again, until two hours were spent and I was limp with exhaustion and euphoric at the same time.

Finally Randall closed the piano lid and said, "Well, I think you've earned an Italian dinner."

I opened my mouth, but he didn't even give me time to let the protest cross my lips.

"And a bottle of chianti, I think," he added, daring me to argue.

"Sounds decadent."

"Absolutely."

That was the end of the argument. He whisked me off to a lovely restaurant only a few miles from house, an intimate little place called Cucina, where we had entirely too much pesto and chianti and amazing fresh-baked bread, and all sorts of conversation. We were both that rarity, natives of Southern California, but his tales of his extended family and growing up in Larchmont Village with his well-to-do but domineering grandfather, lawyer father, writer mother, and apparently teeming hordes of brothers, sisters, and cousins were as foreign to me as if he'd grown up on the other side of the continent. Nothing could have been further from my quiet childhood in Pasadena, where I had been the only child of an only child, and my mother estranged from her own family back in Wisconsin. Certainly there had been no visits from her relatives, and I had grown up knowing only one set of grandparents.

Randall and I talked about so many other things, of course, of music and art and all the seemingly endless distractions of student life, comparing professors and fellow students and pointless papers and the whole crazy mess of it, until we were the last couple in the restaurant—it was a weeknight, after all—and we finally emerged into the cool night air. We both shared a guilty glance at our watches, and he bundled me into the passenger seat of his older-model but meticulously maintained BMW while apologizing for the hour.

"I do tend to run off at the mouth," he said. "Youngest child syndrome—always looking for attention."

"It's okay," I said, somewhat dreamily, enjoying the luxurious warmth of the wine in my stomach and the happy afterglow of a good meal. "My first class isn't until ten tomorrow."

"Well, that's something."

We finished the rest of the drive back to the parking lot in silence, broken only by my giving brief directions as to where my car was parked. At that hour only a few cars remained, and Randall pulled up in the space next to my shabby Honda.

I climbed out a little awkwardly, pausing to collect my satchel from the back seat, then rummaged through my purse to find my car keys.

Randall followed me to the driver's-side door, where we both paused. The yellowish light from the sodium vapor street lamp overhead cast odd shadows on his face, bleaching the color from his eyes, making him suddenly a stranger.

The words—"thank you for a lovely evening"—didn't even make it to my lips before his mouth was on mine, his arms encircling me in an embrace that was both shocking and expected. How else, after all, could this evening have ended?

I hesitated for the slightest fraction of a second—so slight it was hardly a hesitation at all—then let myself surrender to the pressure of his lips, the warmth of his body against mine. The adolescent fumblings I had suffered in the past were nothing compared to this, nothing to the heat I could feel rising in my own body as I kissed him back, let his tongue explore my mouth as I tasted him, tasted the chianti on his lips.

We pulled apart finally, and for a moment we were silent, watching one another.

"You have no idea how long I've wanted to do that," he said finally.

I touched my swollen bottom lip. "I have some," I said, and managed a shaky laugh.

"Oh, God, Christine, I didn't mean to—"

"It's all right," I interjected hastily. It wasn't as if I had tried to stop him, after all.

"Well—"

"Well," I repeated. "It's almost midnight. I really do need to get home."

He stood by silently as I turned the key in the door lock, but spoke when I tossed my satchel on the passenger seat.

"I hate to see you go."

Deliberately, I sat in the driver's seat. "I know, Randall, but I'm not ready for that yet—"

"Of course not," he said immediately, and I was gratified to see that he actually meant it. "I'll see you in senior seminar tomorrow, though—I'm accompanying."

I smiled, and held his gaze. "I'm glad."

He smiled, too, and then let me shut the car door. Thank God the car started. Lately I'd been given to uttering an invocation to whatever powers may be that the damn thing wouldn't strand me twenty miles from home. But after a little introductory cough the Civic kicked right in, and I was able to navigate my way through the empty parking lot with whatever calm my rattled nerves would allow me.

Crazy or not, ill-timed and ill-advised as it might be, I knew, even after one evening together, that I was dangerously close to falling in love with Randall Cagney.

"Impossible," he said, pushing the envelope with the 8x10 photographs inside away from him.

"I'm afraid so, sir." Jerome shifted his weight almost imperceptibly from one foot to the other, the only betrayal of his discomfort. "I thought it suspicious that she would leave her car there for so long, so I waited—"

Waited with the patience of a spider, and captured the evidence he had so long feared. Nothing in Christine's life had borne any evidence of a lover or even a casual boyfriend, and now this, this—

"Randall Cagney," Jerome supplied. "A graduate student and teacher's assistant. More importantly, a talented pianist who works as an accompanist for the vocal program."

He could feel the anger growing, the sinuous beast that was already tightening his innards into knots. Rage, and the impulse to kill, to remove any obstacle in his wake. Under the desk, his hands clenched, bitter fists eager to reach out and destroy.

"Get out," he said, and was only slightly gratified to see Jerome immediately turn and practically flee for the door, moving more quickly than he had ever seen him do so before. Apparently his rage was visible even behind the mask.

Alone again, he returned his focus to the object of his fury, the photographs shoved carelessly back inside the manila envelope. He pulled out the first one; it showed an almost-empty parking lot with two nondescript cars parked next to one another. A man and a woman stood next to the driver's door of the smaller vehicle, and it was obvious what they were doing. His arms were around her, as hers encircled his torso; their mouths were locked, her face almost obscured by the back of the man's head. But he would have known that fall of curly dark hair anywhere, that graceful curve of cheekbone. Christine.

How could she? How could she, when he was so close to having her?

A sudden violent gesture, and the photographs flew off the desk to scatter on the Persian rug. He didn't need to see more—they were all variations on a theme.

Why now? Why, after a youth of apparent solitude, a college career where she had carefully avoided any sort of romantic entanglements, had she finally succumbed?

Randall Cagney. His mouth lifted—the side that could lift, anyhow—in a grimace. He didn't know much about him, other than what Jerome had just related, but he would soon know much, much more. Everything, really, from the amount in his bank account to the brand of underwear he wore.

Soon, very soon, Randall Cagney would be in for a series of most unpleasant shocks. Perhaps he would be forced to reconsider his connection with a certain Christine Daly.

He pressed the speaker button on the intercom. "Jerome, get back in here. I have another assignment for you."

Chapter Three

HE AWOKE, SCREAMING, FROM A NIGHTMARE of blinding pain, the flash of sharp blades, restraining hands. His breath came in loud tearing gasps, and he slammed a hand down on the empty space in the bed next to him. Of course there was no one to comfort him as he lay alone in the darkness. There never had been.

A moment passed before he felt steady enough to stand. Despite the absolute blackness of the room, he had no problem navigating his way from the bed to the table by the window where he kept a decanter of cognac and a few Waterford snifters. With a hand that shook only a little, he poured himself several fingers of a rare vintage from an ancient French label, then drank deeply, with utter disrespect for the quality of the liquor.

"God damn it," he said aloud finally. His voice—his one beauty—was ragged. He pulled out a chair and sat down, closing his eyes, even though he was surrounded by merciful darkness.

The nightmares had begun in early childhood, just after he had stolen the first fleeting glimpse of his face. That one look was allowed by a careless nanny who had left him unattended just long enough for him to wander into his mother's bedroom—his parents had taken separate quarters not long after his birth—and peek into the elaborate Venetian-style mirror that hung over her dresser. One shocked look started him screaming, and he had been quickly scooped up and carried out by the butler— but the damage was done.

The surgeries started soon after. His clearest memory of the years between three and six was of masked surgeons bending over him, the lowering of the oxygen mask over his nose and mouth, the weeks and months of pain that followed. He always recuperated at home, never at the hospital—too many prying eyes—and never was he allowed to want for anything. Anything except peace, of course.

At some point during that evil time his mother left, never to return. Since he had hardly seen her anyway, he did not miss her that much, but he heard voices raised, doors slammed in distant hallways, then brooding quiet. Her infrequent visits ceased. His father would make an obligatory stop every evening, when they engaged in stilted conversation regarding his lessons, but he never stayed longer than ten minutes; you could time his visits by the clock.

Other than that, his only personal contact had been Ennis, the butler, and a steady stream of nannies, nurses, and doctors, all of them paid extremely well to never speak of their young charge or his lamentable condition. Some of them never saw his disfigurements at all—up until the age of fourteen, his face had been perennially swathed in bandages and gauze from the unending surgeries. He supposed the procedures would have gone even longer than that, had it not been for the outspoken young plastic surgeon from UCLA.

He closed his eyes. The man's voice and face were as clear to him as if they had last spoken yesterday, but more than twenty-five years had passed since then. That doctor had been the only one with the strength or integrity to stand up to his father, the only one in a long parade of distinguished surgeons from Beverly Hills to Pasadena.

Doctor Santos. Not so long out of his fellowship, new on the staff at UCLA, but already famed for his skill at reconstructive surgery for those with birth defects or disfigurements caused by accidents. He was a slight, dark man with piercing eyes under straight, expressive brows and the fine hands of a concert pianist. Apparently he spent his summer vacations doing pro bono work in South America, repairing burn scars, harelips, and cleft palates, even performing amazing reconstructive work on those suffering from neurofibromatosis, commonly known as "Elephant Man's disease."

Even now the irony struck him. Perhaps Dr. Santos could have helped John Merrick, but he himself was beyond the doctor's skill.

He'd gotten very good at hiding in corners, skulking in shadows. So it was no problem to lurk in the hallway outside his father's office, listening to the conference between his father and Dr. Santos. He had noted that even the earnest doctor had made the long drive from Westwood to Pasadena for this meeting, instead of having them come to his own offices for a consultation.

"Enough," Dr. Santos said. "I won't be a party to any more butchery on that poor boy's face."

He couldn't see their faces, but he knew that his father would allow no betraying expression. He'd inherited a massive fortune, but he also had the killer instincts to build on it in his lifetime. "If not you, then someone else."

"Quite possibly," Dr. Santos replied. "I have no doubt that you could find someone else to take on the task—although it appears you've already run through most of the reputable plastic surgeons in the Los Angeles area. But all that would do is drain more from your bank account."

His father was silent.

After an awkward pause, Dr. Santos continued, "And it's apparent that's of no real concern to you. How much have you spent over the years? A million? Two? A drop in the bucket, maybe, but if no one else will be honest with you, then I will. There's just no more that can be done."

"Your opinion."

"Yes, my opinion, and a damn good one. I've read the boy's history. Forty-five surgeries—forty-five, and the kid's not even fifteen yet! For God's sake, there's nothing left to operate on!"

He could hear the shift of his father's body against the leather desk chair. "What do mean, nothing?"

Dr. Santos paused. Then he said, "There is so much scar tissue, so much damage to the underlying bone struc-ture, that you risk creating wounds that will never heal.

Do you want him to run the risk of infection for the rest of his life? At least now he has half a face. Better that than nothing."

"I see. And that is your final opinion?"

"Yes. The boy needs to learn to live with what he has. It's a tragedy, but causing further disfigurement or risking death would be much worse."

A long, heavy silence. Then his father said, "Thank you, doctor. You may leave your bill with Ennis on the way out."

A short laugh from Dr. Santos. "This one's on me, Mr. Deitrich. Consider it to be part of my charitable work."

"We don't take charity, Dr. Santos," his father replied, his tone frosty.

"Guess you don't need it, do you, Mr. Deitrich?" A pause as he gathered up his briefcase. "Then consider it an early birthday gift for Erik."

The doctor's imminent departure necessitated a hasty retreat down the hallway before his eavesdropping could be detected, but Erik had heard enough. Although it was disconcerting to hear that nothing more could be done, as he'd been fed false hopes for years, at the same time he felt liberated. No more surgeries. No more nights of pain where he stubbornly resisted the opiates they'd left for him, afraid even then of what they could do to his mind.

Erik lifted the cognac to his lips and drank. Yes, the surgeries had finally stopped, but the nightmares continued. Not every night, of course, and of varying intensity, but he had soon come to view sleep as an enemy. At least the pain had finally subsided, and he'd been able to live a somewhat normal life—as normal as a life completely bounded by the walls of his father's estate could be. He had tutors and music instructors, even a fencing teacher who was paid very well to not question why his pupil never removed his fencing mask.

The music lessons were his favorite; by the age of five he could master original scores as if he had written them himself, and after a whispered suggestion from Ennis, who had heard Erik singing to himself when he thought no one could overhear him, a vocal coach came twice a week. No comment was ever made about the bandages, or later the mask, although they both interfered with his singing, but Erik had learned very early on that those who questioned or commented were soon dismissed, their dismissal accompanied by subtle threats if the Deitrich boy's physical condition were ever mentioned again. And it never was. No one had the courage, it seemed, to take on the Deitrich fortune.

His father had died when Erik was just eighteen, of a sudden thrombosis after one of his frequent business trips to New York. There wasn't even enough time to call Dr. Maddox, the family physician, although all the proper steps were taken, paramedics appearing by magic to transport his father to Huntington Memorial, where he was declared dead on arrival. A flurry of activity followed, ending with the discovery that, with the exception of minor bequests to a few distant relatives and ten million to his mother—he suffered a mild shock when he realized she was still alive—Erik was the sole possessor of a fortune that totaled almost three-quarters of a billion dollars.

That was more than any eighteen-year-old could be expected to handle, and of course he wasn't. An army of lawyers had been appointed to manage the money, and the household continued to be run by Ennis, and in a way, very little changed. He dismissed his tutors and decided to earn his degree in history through correspondence, which he did easily and in fewer than three years. He chose history simply because it seemed mildly more interesting than any of the other choices. Then, because he thought it might be a good idea to know more about money and how to manage it, he got another degree in accounting. Since he had a monthly allowance equal to most people's yearly incomes, he toyed with the stock market, earned a considerable fortune, then socked it away in a separate account, unsure what to do with it. On a whim he donated a large amount to the charity for which Dr. Santos did his pro bono work, thus ensuring many more corrected harelips and cleft palates, but truthfully, he was bored. What good was it to be able to play a huge classical repertoire from memory if no one was there to hear it? What difference did it make that he had the voice of an angel, if the only living beings he could serenade were the squirrels that inhabited the trees outside his bedroom window?

His eyes now adjusted to the darkness in his room, Erik looked over at his bed, the heavy carved four-poster rising blackly in the dimness, and one corner of his mouth twitched. At least not all his memories of that bed were evil…

At twenty-one he had made the unexpected and pleasant discovery that there were women in the world who would overlook all sorts of physical limitations if enough money were involved. Apparently the request that the act take place in total darkness and that there be no touching of his face was routine, even tame compared to what some of these women had experienced. But his first—a lovely redhead named, appropriately, Amber—had introduced him to lovemaking skillfully and even tenderly, and what could have been a tawdry experience became instead a night of revelations. She was with him that night, and several more over the next few months, until she told him—with possibly a trace of regret in her tone—that she was about to take the bar and was going to, as she put it, "quit the business."

Even now the recollection made him shake his head. Only in Los Angeles, he thought, could a sharp-thinking redhead with amazing legs put herself through law school as a $1,000-a-night call girl. Amber had been replaced by Sheila, and Kelli after her, until he could no longer remember all their names. Of course he had been careful to be moderate—only seeing them once or twice a month—but even so the parade of faces and bodies became blurred as the years passed.

Then, only a short time later, he suffered a shock in his carefully managed universe. Although he was necessarily cut off from any form of public entertainments, he still liked to amuse himself by reading the arts sections of the national magazines, if only to give him ideas of what he could use to expand his massive library of recorded music. And what he saw there, along with one photo, was a review of Andrew Lloyd Webber's latest musical to cross the Atlantic, *The Phantom of the Opera*.

He was familiar with the story, of course, and had caught the original silent version with Lon Chaney on late-night television more than once, along with the less distinguished remake starring Claude Rains. He had been moved by the story—considering his situation, it would have been odd if he hadn't—but he had never particularly identified with the character. Disfigured he might be, but at least he was able to hide from the world in the mansion his grandfather had built, not in the damp cellars of an opera house.

The photo in the magazine, however, showed a very different image from Lon Chaney's gruesome, if remarkable, death's head makeup, or the smooth curved mask that had covered almost all of Claude Rains' face. This Phantom wore a mask that covered only half his face.

Only half his face. He could remember the shock of that moment as if it had happened just minutes before instead of more than two decades ago. With a shaking hand he had reached up, fingers spread, to encompass the ruined right side of his face. Of course. How perfect, how elegant. Up until then he had worn an altered surgical mask that covered him from cheekbone to jaw on that one side—a mask that still exposed the scarring on his forehead and the mess that was his right eye socket—but as he never went out anyway and the only person to ever see him was Ennis, the butler, its shortcomings were overlooked in favor of the comfort factor. But this mask—

A few carefully placed phone calls to New York resulted in a box of gleaming masks arriving on his doorstep only days later. Of course he was unable to have a life cast taken of his face to ensure the most perfect fit, but he had compromised by requesting a copy of all of the masks made for the New York production, including Michael Crawford's and all of the understudies' masks. The Crawford mask didn't fit, unfortunately—it was a touch too broad—but one of the others suited him well enough, with a little extra padding on the sensitive brow and upper cheekbone areas.

That was the beginning of an obsession that soon consumed him, devoured almost every waking moment for more than five years and still had its grip on him even today. One cast CD was played into scratched ruin, then another. Efforts were made to procure recordings from around the world, even before they were commercially available. His library soon burst with bootlegs—both audio and video—of the show. He collected press clippings, books, sent to New York for every souvenir the show offered, wired to London for the ones he couldn't procure in New York, went so far as to have an unused back parlor gutted and fitted with a small pipe organ and ornate candelabras in an effort to duplicate one of the sets from the show.

If he had stopped to think about it, he supposed he would have shocked himself with the depths of his obsession, but it all seemed perfectly natural and, if anything, at least a constructive outlet for his energies. The compulsion at least allowed him to think of something besides his isolation, his utter loneliness.

And then the show came to Los Angeles.

Up until then he had resigned himself to never being able to see it in person. There was no way a trip to New

York would be feasible; he couldn't allow himself the vulnerability of being that far from home. But with the show only a little more than ten miles over the hills to downtown Los Angeles, the thought of not seeing it was pure torture. The terror of facing crowds was nothing compared to the agony of being deprived of the one thing he had desired for so long. Still, the planning took some time, and it wasn't until the show had entered the last year of its run that he finally got to see it.

With Ennis and a handsomely compensated LVN as his companions, he had ventured out, face well-covered by a surgical mask and dark glasses, a wheelchair as his excuse for the mask and the nurse, to a Saturday evening show. Unfortunately, the subterfuge of the wheelchair forced him into a slightly less desirable chair-accessible seat, but that was a small price to pay. The lights went down, the first chords of the overture were struck, and the magic began.

Afterward he was shaking, and immediately replaced the dark glasses so his companions could not see the tears that stained his cheeks. They were forced to wait until the theater had mostly emptied before they could wheel the chair out to the street where his limousine waited. He remembered being angered by the delays, wanting nothing more than to return to his home, to the comfortable dimness of his suite. To be alone again, away from prying eyes.

His wish was granted soon enough, even though at the time the wait seemed interminable. Once he was safely in his chambers, he flung the dark glasses into a corner and sat huddled in a chair by the window, utterly spent. Finally his loneliness had been given a shape and form. Finally he was unable to deny any longer what he had been craving for so many years.

"Christine…" he had whispered, finally raising his eyes to the moonlit gardens beyond the mullioned windows. What was it like, to burn for a woman in such a way, to descend into hell, only to be redeemed by her kiss?

He had to know. It seemed as if until this night he had only been half alive, haunted by something that should be there. Those brief encounters with the women he had paid over the years suddenly disgusted him. What were they but only bodies, bodies paid well to satisfy an animal craving that had nothing of soul behind it?

That night he made a vow. Until he had his Christine, he would never know the touch of another woman. Until he could find the soul that answered the emptiness inside him, he would not rest.

Little had he known, he thought now, just how long that search would take. She had to be perfect, the modern-day embodiment of Christine Daaé. It was not just the voice, but the face, and not just the face, but a certain innocence, an attribute not as easy to find these days.

A few years down the line he hired Jerome, who came with sterling recommendations from several of Erik's lawyers. A former private investigator, Jerome was more than happy to abandon his practice for a far more lucrative exclusive contract with a mad multimillionaire. If said millionaire made the odd request that he locate a local voice student with dark curly hair, fair skin, blue eyes, and a pure coloratura, and then dig up every fact about her, well, he was being compensated handsomely enough that he was more than happy to find out everything he could. It also caused Jerome to do more loitering around college campuses than he probably would have cared to do otherwise, but a man could put up with a lot when he was being paid in the low six figures to do so.

There had been a few near-misses over the years. One time the girl was physically perfect but was, unfortunately, a mezzo. Another had a lovely voice and was quite beautiful, but she was a flaming redhead, and apparently that wouldn't do at all. Yet another had a notable voice and a head of gorgeous brown curls, but the presence of a long-time boyfriend and a penchant to smoke the occasional joint on the weekend combined to make her completely undesirable.

And then, after Erik had almost given up hope, Christine Daly was found. It was unfortunate she hadn't been located earlier, since she was now in her senior year at USC, but apparently she had transferred in midway through the junior year, and Jerome had missed her. Since he traveled amongst a huge number of campuses all over Southern California, it wasn't completely surprising that she had been overlooked—Jerome had paid someone to hack the music department's records, and her name had appeared on the list said hacking produced, but her student photo was missing. It wasn't until he visited the campus himself and saw her leaving a class that his interest was caught. From then it was a simple matter to gather all the information he could about her, from her orphaned state to her precarious financial situation, her utter aloneness in the world. Now all Jerome had to do was get her voice on tape, to prove finally that this was the girl Erik had been seeking for so long.

After that, well—Erik lifted the cognac and drank deeply, this time savoring the aromatic warmth that caressed the back of his throat and tickled his nostrils. If her voice truly matched her looks, then she would be his, even if she didn't know it yet. As for Randall Cagney—he was an irritant, a nuisance, nothing more. He could be dealt with. But it was important to procure Christine, and soon, before hers and Randall's relationship could progress much further. The thought of her untouched beauty was deeply arousing, and he did not want it sullied by Cagney's common gropings.

After all, if the Phantom could steal Christine out from under the Vicomte de Chagny's nose, then it shouldn't be that difficult for him to do the same thing to Randall Cagney. The Phantom, however clever, certainly didn't have the immense resources that he, Erik Deitrich, had at his disposal. Very soon Cagney would realize he had crossed the wrong person…and then the true fun would begin.

Chapter Four

I STOOD IN FRONT OF THE BULLETIN BOARD in the break room at work and groaned silently. A new flyer highlighted yet another one of my boss George's fabulous ideas, something designed to lure in more patrons and give me yet another headache to deal with.

"So who are you coming as?" Meg asked, leaning over my shoulder to read the announcement for herself.

"A starving college student?"

"Oh, come on!" she said, her brown eyes crinkling at the corners as she grinned in anticipation. "How many people get paid to dress up on Halloween?"

"Apparently a few more this year," I replied. Great— huge Halloween party this year, since we were lucky enough to have the big day fall on a Saturday. All staff on board, special buffet, costume contest, the works. No doubt it would be a big success.

Of course George couldn't make it easy, either— the flyer tacked to the bulletin board specified that all restaurant employees dress "in theme," which, since the place was named *L'Opera*, made it fairly obvious what sorts of costumes he was looking for. No simple ghost sheet or leotard with bunny ears was going to do—not that I would have ever worn something like that out in public in the first place.

"I think I'll go as Carmen," Meg said dreamily, twisting a strand of dark hair around one finger as she considered her costume. "Some sort of off-the-shoulder blouse, one of those fun waist corset things, red flower in my hair—it'll be totally cool."

It would be, too, since Meg's mother was from Venezuela and had given her daughter a warm olive skin and glowing dark hair and eyes. She would be perfect.

I, on the other hand—

"Ooh, do something from *Aïda*," Meg urged. "Egyptian stuff is awesome."

"Yeah, because I look so Egyptian!" It would be even worse than trying to dress as Carmen, although luckily Meg had already chosen that role.

"Violetta!" she proclaimed.

"Right, and it'll be too fun to watch me navigate between tables in a big old hoop skirt," I said.

She laughed. "Oh, yeah, hadn't thought about that." Then, apparently noticing for the first time my troubled look, she added, "Oh, it's not that bad. You've got almost three weeks to figure it out."

Meg was so airy in her unconcern, I almost laughed as well. No problem for her—she'd collect her costume bits from funky shops in Old Pasadena and possibly even make a foray downtown into the Fashion District for the finishing touches—but I didn't have the luxury of such largesse. Still, she was right. I did have three weeks…barely. Something would work itself out before then.

Of more pressing concern was the autumn recital for the senior master class, now only a week and a half away. Thanks to my continuing practice with Randall—on campus only, since I'd had to work every night since that one time we'd had dinner—I felt in command of the aria, charged and energized and ready to perform. Certainly Dr. Green hadn't had cause for disappointment since then. But although I was confident in my voice and my mastery of my performance piece, there was always the faint unease that came with performing in public. I knew I wasn't alone—even seasoned professionals could get butterflies—but as much as I was looking forward to the recital, I'd be equally glad when it was over.

Well, as my mother used to say, if it wasn't one thing, it was another. Our break time was almost over, and I nodded significantly at the clock. "Back to the salt mines," I said.

She grimaced. "Yeah, I am so over this!" But still she dropped her order pad in her apron pocket and headed back out.

I wondered when she was going to be "over" it enough that she actually quit. Certainly she didn't really need the money, but she'd made noises about how her parents considered it "character building," whatever that meant. I hoped she'd make it through the rest of the school year. I'd miss her if she quit, although we'd still see each other at school. Even during the most difficult shifts, times when I could have cheerfully strangled a few of my customers, Meg was breezy and relaxed. Of course, her casual attitude might simply stem from the fact that she could walk away whenever she felt like it.

As I left the break room I wondered, idly, what it would feel like to have that kind of money…

It turned out that Randall had the perfect solution to my Halloween predicament. "Go as Marguerite," he said simply, after he let me vent for a few minutes about George's crazy ideas and last-minute schemes.

"Marguerite?"

"You're doing the aria for the recital. I think it fits."

"Maybe, but if you think I can just whip up a fifteenth-century gown in the next few weeks—"

He laughed. "Of course not. The drama department did *Romeo and Juliet* last semester. They've still got the costumes lying around. I've got contacts over there—I'm sure they'll let me borrow one for a while. I can give it to you the night of the recital."

Randall looked so serious about his "contacts" that I almost laughed myself. But, limited though my experience of men might be, I knew better than to make a comment that he might think was mocking. And I was grateful, after all. "That would be great, Randall. This has been driving me nuts!"

He smiled at me. "Couldn't have you worrying over that when you've got the recital coming up—" and he glanced significantly at the score resting on the piano.

"Ready when you are." I took the usual singer's stance, tucked in the curve of the Steinway grand, and we were off once more, and there was nothing in my mind except the music.

As promised, Randall delivered the dress to me the evening of the recital as I waited backstage at Alfred Newman Recital Hall, the usual venue for smaller-scale performances on campus. More than once some prankster had changed the name on the building to the "Alfred E. Neuman" Recital Hall after the *Mad* magazine icon, but of course that's not really who the hall was named for. I'd found myself hoping several times that the hall's namesake had departed this world before he discovered he was being confused with the gap-toothed spokesman of a humor magazine.

I unzipped the garment bag just enough to reveal the glory of white and gold brocade inside, then murmured, "Wow…"

"Nice, huh? Guess it was from the scene at the ball where Romeo and Juliet see each other for the first time. I think Teresa is about your size, but you might have to hem it a little. She's pretty tall."

And I, at just barely five foot five in my stocking feet, was anything but. "A hem I can handle," I said. "Thank you, Randall. I can't tell you how much this helps me out."

He waited until I had hung up the garment bag on one of the hooks in the dressing-room area, then said, "Maybe it can help you imagine to be her—Marguerite."

I had a brief image of myself wrapped in flowing white and gold, hair streaming down my back, and shivered. Was that how Marguerite had first felt when she lifted up the mirror and beheld the glittering jewels at her ears and throat, the pearls entwined in her hair? Suddenly I felt glowing, regal, despite the simple black recital gown I wore.

Randall must have noticed something different in my aspect, because he smiled suddenly and said, "Well, that seems to have done the trick."

"I think it did."

He opened his mouth to reply but was interrupted by Dr. Green, who stuck his head in the door and said, "Five minutes, Randall."

He held up his hand in acknowledgment. "No prob—" and Dr. Green's head abruptly disappeared, something like a jack-in-the-box retreating into its container.

We both grinned. Then I said, "You need to get going. I'll see you out there soon enough."

He surprised me with a quick kiss on the cheek. "Break a leg."

"I hate that expression," I replied, but he had already turned and was hurrying down the hallway to the stage.

My aria was at the end of the program, and I tried to reassure myself that the unfortunate placement had something to do with saving the best for last. I didn't have much to do except cool my heels backstage for most of the evening, although I was able at one point to peek out past the curtain to see what kind of audience we had.

Not bad for a Thursday night. The auditorium was

probably a little more than two-thirds full, with the usual row of overeager parents with camcorders on tripods taking up residence toward the back. I tried to ignore the now-familiar pang as I realized there wouldn't be anyone out there carefully recording my performance...

I narrowed my eyes suddenly. It was hard to tell, what with the dim lighting, but one of the figures in the back row looked oddly familiar. I recognized a couple of the onlookers—in fact, there was Meg's father, over to the left, hunched over a camera so complicated that it looked as if he had borrowed it from his ex-wife's television station—but I didn't think it was a parent who had caught my attention. No, now I was sure of it—the brown-haired man who stood almost at dead center in the back row of videographers was the same man I had almost knocked over several weeks earlier, when I had run from Dr. Green's classroom in disgrace.

Who the hell was he? He didn't really look old enough to be the parent of a senior-class college student. Also, as I stared at him, I noticed something odd. He might be standing with the rest of the parents in the back, but unlike most of them he wasn't paying any attention to his camcorder. From time to time he glanced at his watch, then at his program, and then, faintly, I could see his chest heave, as if he were sighing with boredom or annoyance. It seemed as if he were waiting for something.

He's waiting for you, came a treacherous little thought in my head, a thought I clamped down on immediately. Rampant paranoia was the last thing I needed right now. He could be anyone—someone's older brother, an uncle, whatever—and very possibly he didn't see the value in recording the whole program if he were really only there to see one performer.

"Spying?"

I jumped a little. It was Carrie Gustafson, the only person in the senior master class whom I genuinely disliked. She had a decent voice, but from the way she paraded around the class, you'd think she had already inked an exclusive contract with the Met.

I swallowed my anger. "Just wanted to take a look."

"I can't imagine why," she drawled. "It's not as if anyone's out there to see you."

Taking a deep breath, I reminded myself of the legal consequences of assault and battery. Still, as much as I would have liked to snap back with something witty and yet pejorative, the only rejoinder I could come up with was, "Whatever…" before I dropped the curtain and slunk away. Carrie was one of the few people who could make me feel as if my IQ had suddenly dropped by fifty points. My only satisfaction lay in the fact that she had obviously been interested in Randall and was now doubly spiteful because he had made it plain that not only was he not interested in her, he was in fact already seeing the hated Christine Daly.

"Ten points to me," I whispered as I waited in the darkness backstage. Then my name was called, and I walked out into the blinding spotlights.

I could still see myself—see Marguerite—robed in white and gold, shimmering with jewels and precious pearls. I took that image with me as the music welled up from inside, wrapping everyone in the hall, including myself, in its glorious spell. And I rode the waves of golden sound until the hall burst into applause like booming thunder and I stood alone in the spotlight, tears rolling down my cheeks as the audience erupted into a spontaneous standing ovation.

Erik took the disk from Jerome with a hand that shook only a little. Now past twelve, it was still the early watches of the night for him. Besides, he knew he couldn't have slept knowing that he was so close to hearing her.

"Thank you, Jerome," he said.

The man was obviously bursting with news, but Erik did not want to hear his assistant's version of the night's events. He wanted to see and hear for himself.

Even though Erik had meant his last words as a sort of dismissal, Jerome still lingered.

"That will be all, Jerome," he added, putting extra emphasis on "all" just in case the man really was too dense to understand that he wanted to experience her alone.

Jerome blinked. "Of course, sir."

Finally. Erik stood and went to the armoire that housed his audiovisual equipment, then slipped the DVD in the player. The LED screen powered up and he stepped back, watching.

The image came on abruptly, as the audience was still applauding the previous performer. Christine walked to the center of the stage, heartbreakingly lovely in her simple black dress, her luxuriant dark hair pulled back from her face with a silky ribbon. She had a faraway look on her face, and he sucked in his breath, his thoughts running in an incoherent little prayer: *Please...please...please...*

Then she opened her mouth to sing, and it was all he could do to not fall to his knees there and then, hearing the glory of it, the utter bell-like perfection, the sweetness and purity and strength. There was not a single false note, not a single hesitation—she sang as if the music had come to her directly from God. Perhaps it had.

It ended with a tumult of applause and then the sound of everyone rising to their feet almost simultaneously, as if directed by a power as far beyond them as her talent. Erik stood there in shock for a moment, staring at the blank blue screen, as the tears ran down his ruined face and the remote dropped from suddenly nerveless fingers.

He had hoped for—what? Of course, a lovely voice, a true coloratura, but he had never imagined this. Long ago he had abandoned the thought of God, save as possibly some cruel entity who existed only to inflict torment on hapless souls such as he, but surely only God could have been the architect of such beauty.

For a second he wavered. Who was he to presume to take such perfection from the world, to keep it only for his own pleasure? Was he really so desperate, so low, that he could only think of himself when the whole world deserved to share in her beauty? Better to abandon his plans now, before he could debase himself any further. He could still worship her from the shadows, make sure the way was smoothed for her so she could quickly become the dazzling star she deserved to be.

The indecision lasted only a moment before he

reached up angrily to brush away the tears on his one uncovered cheek. The world didn't deserve her. She was everything that was good and pure, and the world was all too harsh to women such as she. No, she should live in sheltered luxury, surrounded by music and art, nurtured in love and unending passion, never to want for anything again. She should be his.

He turned away from the television screen and noticed for the first time that Jerome had laid a piece of folded paper on his desk. Picking it up, he unfolded it, scanned its contents, then felt a slow fire kindle in his chest. He could see her, be with her in her own world, if only for a night. The only night of the year where no one would question his mask.

On Halloween, the Phantom would definitely be in attendance at *L'Opera*...

Chapter Five

Halloween in Southern California was always unpredictable. One year the area could be scoured and dry under the fierce winds of a late-season Santa Ana condition; the next year trick-or-treat could be cut short by unpredictable rains. This year, unfortunately, the evening threatened to be one of the latter type. I threw a wary glance at the lowering skies, blood-colored to the west with the last traces of sunset, and prayed that if it was so inconsiderate as to start pouring down rain, it would at least wait until I had arrived at work. One of my windshield wipers was starting to disintegrate into long ribbons of black rubber, and it was hard enough driving in the bulky Marguerite dress without having to deal with wet streets and drivers who seemed to lose their last few brain cells when a few drops of water fell from the sky.

Luckily, though, I pulled into the parking lot of *L'Opera* without incident, although a few scattered drops had hit the windshield on the way over. The rain looked as if it was about to start any minute, so I gathered up my heavy skirts and hurried in to the employees' entrance at the back of the restaurant. I hoped that it would let loose soon and get it over with—I was pulling an eight-hour shift tonight and wouldn't be off until two in the morning, so it could happily rain away while I was safely inside.

The break room looked like an explosion in the costume closet at the Met. Everyone appeared to have taken George's instructions seriously, and there wasn't a cheap satin-draped Dracula or bunny-eared leotard in the bunch. Probably a lot of people had done the same as I had—called in favors from the drama departments of their respective schools, since most of the wait staff were struggling students like myself.

"Wow," Michael, one of the waiters, said at my ear. "Who are you supposed to be?"

"Marguerite," I replied, then added, at his blank look, "From *Faust*."

"Ah. Better watch out, then, because I think George is dressed as Mephistopheles."

"Great…" It made sense, though. George resembled Goethe's dapper version of the devil even in street clothes, with his carefully groomed goatee and slicked-back dark hair.

Michael himself was wearing some fancy toreador-style outfit that looked as if it had come straight from Olvera Street. It went well with his dark hair and olive complexion, but he didn't look very comfortable in it; he kept hitching his shoulders under the heavy embroidered jacket and pulling at the tight collar of his high-necked shirt.

"Don José?" I asked, and he nodded.

"I couldn't think of anything else, and then when I heard that Meg was dressing as Carmen…"

Poor boy. Meg probably couldn't remember his name from one day to the next, but I wasn't about to tell him that. I smiled and said, "Well, just remember that Don José ends up knifing Carmen at the end!"

He looked stricken. "Are you kidding?"

It was amazing how many people worked at *L'Opera* without knowing anything about the real thing. Michael was a musician, but strictly of the rock variety, and didn't seem to be too concerned about furthering his college career, since he was now in his fourth year at Pasadena City College.

"It's okay, Mike," I said. "We're just supposed to dress like them, not act like them."

"Oh, right, yeah."

I looked up at the clock. "Oh, heck, I need to get out there. If I make it through tonight without spilling a plate of marinara on this gown, I'll be totally shocked."

I picked up a menu pad and a pen—George had told us it was all right to go without the aprons tonight—and went on out into the dining room. Looking around, I had to admit that George and the staff who'd been on earlier in the day had done a nice job of decorating the place. Cobwebs festooned the heavy wrought-iron chandeliers, candelabra flickered on the tables, and interesting gargoyle fixtures had been placed at strategic spots around the restaurant. It wasn't overdone, but the additions definitely made the restaurant—already highly atmospheric, with its stone walls and floor, iron light fixtures, and mural of the façade of La Scala on the far wall—look gloomy and haunted.

The real festivities wouldn't start for another hour or so, but we had early diners who were grabbing a bite before moving on to their own parties or concerts. Some were in costume, but not all. Everyone seemed to be in a cheerful mood, however, and I hoped the evening would continue to run smoothly.

Not for the first time, I found myself wishing Randall could have come. He had a paying gig to play at a private party in Bel Air, though, and I hadn't been about to ask him to turn down five hundred dollars just so he could watch me wait tables all night. He'd wanted to see me in the Marguerite gown, but I'd promised to take lots of pictures—a promise I was miserably failing to fulfill right now—and we had made tentative plans to go to the Day of the Dead festivities in Olvera Street in two days as a sort of compensation for not being together on Halloween, since neither of us had ever been.

I'd always loved Halloween growing up; we'd lived in a quiet family neighborhood where kids could roam safely in search of treats, and my mother, a talented seamstress, had always delighted in coming up with something new for me to wear each year. Usually it had been some variation on a "princess" dress, because I'd always been fascinated by fancy gowns and historical costumes. So the Marguerite dress was really the latest in a long line of pretty Halloween costumes for me, although I hadn't had much desire to dress up even for private parties the past few years.

These days it seemed as if more and more adults were
getting in on the fun; I supposed the relentless marketing
of the holiday made it easier for those of us who missed the
good old days of "dress-up" to keep throwing on the costumes year after year. At any rate, the array of fancy dress
that started arriving soon after seven o'clock was truly startling, since I hadn't done anything much for Halloween
the past few years except stay at home and hand out candy
from the dollar store.

True, George was sponsoring a costume contest with
a $500 grand prize, as well as a discount of ten percent off
the bill to anyone in costume, but I was still amazed at
the effort some people had put into their get-ups. A party
of four at one of my stations included a pretty creditable
Scarlett O'Hara in her famous green velvet "curtains"
gown, a fairy princess complete with fancy airbrushed
wings, a man dressed as either a Ringwraith or the Grim
Reaper (I guessed from the absence of a sickle that he
was probably supposed to be a Ringwraith), and George
Washington. Or maybe he was supposed to be Thomas
Jefferson, but it was hard to tell.

I took their orders and more from an assortment of
nuns, flappers, vampires, and zombies before I returned
with a tray full of drinks and discovered there was a new
arrival, seated at the far edge of my station next to a
pillar.

Jerri, the hostess, leaned in and whispered in my ear
as she was heading back to her station at the front of the
restaurant. "You've got a live one there."

"What?"

"That guy just tipped me two hundred bucks so he could sit in your station. What's up with that?" Then she grinned, rubbed her first two fingers and thumb together in the universal sign for big bucks, and hurried off.

Two hundred dollars? Just to sit in my station? *L'Opera* wasn't really the sort of place where people usually dropped that kind of cash. True, there was no way I could afford to eat there myself, but still it wasn't exactly Spago or something. I looked back toward where he sat, half-shrouded in the dim lighting next to the pillar, and took in a quick breath.

The Phantom of the Opera...

Or at least, I told myself quickly, a damn good version of the character. The fedora, the white half mask, the impeccable tails, the dark cloak that glittered with beading on the shoulders—he'd definitely done his research. He looked as if he'd walked straight off the Broadway stage.

I'd always loved the show. My parents had taken me to see the touring company at the Pantages when I was about twelve, and I had been completely smitten. I loved the music, loved the fact that the lead female character had the same name I did, loved the whole sweep and romanticism of it, even though at that age I had been unaware of some of the more passionate and sensual undercurrents of the musical. At the same time, though, it had awakened feelings in me that I had never experienced before. But I had to say that it was a little disconcerting—to say the least—to see the real-life embodiment of my first exposure to adult passion sitting at one of my tables.

Still, if he'd been willing to tip two hundred dollars

just for the privilege of sitting at my station, I could only imagine what my own tip might be if I played my cards right.

"Happy Halloween!" I said to him in that sprightly "customer service" voice George insisted on and I hated with a passion. "What would you like this evening?"

He looked up then, and I had to keep from catching my breath. The half of his face I could actually see was just on the interesting side of handsome—high cheek-bone marred by some sort of scar I couldn't see clearly in the dim restaurant lighting; strong eyebrow over hooded dark eye; mobile, beautifully sculpted mouth that never-theless had that taut look at the corner which indicated some sort of chronic pain.

Quite the Byronic hero, I thought, purposely keeping the thought ironic and light. The costume was enough of an attraction without the fallen angel looks underneath.

"The veal milanesa," he replied, closing the menu and handing it back to me. Even in the noisy restaurant I could tell his voice was a clear, pure tenor, warm and vibrant. "And a bottle of the '99 Banfi, I think."

I scribbled hastily on my pad, hoping he hadn't noticed my raised eyebrows. Just the most expensive wine we offered! We probably sold a bottle a month if we were lucky, but George liked to keep a few of the high-end labels around just to prove we were a cut above the chain restaurants that were our direct competition.

"That's a very elegant gown—" He paused delicately, apparently noting my lack of a name tag.

"Christine," I supplied.

"Ah. Fortuitous, it would seem." He regarded me for a moment, and for some reason I felt a thin fingernail of chill run down my spine. "*Faust*, I believe?"

"Excuse me?" Had I ever sounded like more of an idiot?

"The gown. Marguerite?"

I let out a breath. "Yes, of course. I'm doing the 'Jewel Song' in my master class at USC, so—"

He smiled—or rather, the right side of his mouth lifted. "And do it very well, I might think."

I started to make a self-deprecating gesture, then realized, damn it, I did do it well. "People tell me I do." Then, feeling suddenly awkward under his dark, half-masked gaze, I added, "Let me get your order in—I'll bring your wine straight out."

I got the feeling he was amused by my discomfort, but he said only, "Thank you, Christine."

And I fled to the kitchen, feeling more relieved than the situation probably warranted. George caught me pulling out a bottle of the Banfi—I had paused to dust it off—and gave me an unexpected and totally uncalled-for smack on the cheek.

"Someone bought a bottle of my baby?"

"Yes, George." I dropped the clean towel I'd been using to wipe off the dust. "And he ordered veal."

"You are my star, Christine!" he said with a dramatic flourish, and I just had to laugh—he looked so silly standing there in the kitchen, making grand gestures in his red Mephistopheles doublet and short black cloak.

"Who knows, if I play my cards right, I might get a

tiramisu and some espresso out of him, too!" I gathered up the now-clean bottle and a corkscrew and headed back out into the dining room, but not before I gave George a wink.

Well, he had every reason to feel good this evening. The restaurant was packed, and I could tell from the crowd in the lobby area that it was at least a forty-five-minute wait to get a table.

The Phantom—I had to think of him that way since naturally I didn't know his name—looked up and smiled when I approached the table.

"Was there much celebrating in the kitchen when that bottle was brought down?" he asked, his tone sly, and I couldn't help laughing.

"Hosannas and everything," I replied. Then I had to turn my attention to gently slicing the top of the label to reveal the cork and even more carefully pulling it out. The damn thing was hard to pull, too, and I uttered a brief prayer that it wouldn't break during removal. That had only happened to me once or twice, but it was equally mortifying each time it happened.

"Allow me," he said, and reached for the bottle.

"I couldn't—really, it's almost there—"

Silently he ignored my protests and took the bottle and corkscrew from me. His right hand brushed mine in the process, and I couldn't prevent the shiver that passed over me. Whoever he was, something about him seemed to resonate in my very soul.

He deftly removed the corkscrew. I noticed that his hands were beautiful, too, long and very slender, although quite pale, as if he did not spend much time out of doors. An onyx and gold ring gleamed on the pinky of his right hand.

"There," he said, and handed the now-open bottle to me. "You may pour, if you like."

I took the bottle and carefully poured him a glass without spilling anything, thank God. I hoped he wouldn't notice that my hands shook a little. "Your meal should be out shortly."

"I look forward to it."

And then I tore myself away, soon absorbed in bringing out plates to the patrons who had been seated before him, refilling drink orders—in short, buried in the minutiae of any busy shift.

Once I paused in the kitchen to gulp down a glass of water, and Meg popped in and grinned.

"I hear you have a secret admirer."

"What?"

"Oh, come on, Christine!" She paused for a moment to readjust the red silk rose she wore tucked into the bun at the back of her head. "I haven't had too many guys plopping down two hundred bucks for the chance to sit at my station."

"Oh, that."

"Yeah, that." She reached out and readjusted a curl on my forehead, looked at me critically, then said, "You probably need to put on more lipstick."

"Oh, come on, Meg—"

She produced a tube from a pocket hidden somewhere in her skirt. "Girlfriend, if there was ever anyone who needed a sugar daddy, it's you. So pretty up already."

I took the lipstick from her and dabbed a little on. "I'm sort of seeing someone, Meg."

"Yeah, and?" She reached out and flicked away a little excess lipstick from my lower lip with her pinky. "You've gone out with Randall what, once? Plus a couple of practice sessions? I wouldn't exactly call that an exclusive relationship."

"Meg, the guy's a customer—"

"So what? Women meet rich men on the job all the time."

"Who says he's rich?"

She gave me an unbelieving, "you are so stupid I'm not even going to comment on the fact" look. "Last time I checked, poor guys don't tip two hundred bucks to sit at a particular waitress's station, and they don't order hundred-dollar bottle of wine, either."

"Okay, so he's rich. Does that matter so much?"

At that, all Meg did was lift an eyebrow. "You of all people should know the answer to that one, Christine."

And she left me with that, picking up a tray of food and sailing back out into the dining room.

That's really unfair, I thought. Did being poor automatically render you vulnerable to the first guy with a big bankroll who came along? I didn't think so. Besides, compared to me, Randall really was comfortably well off—his home was paid for, and he made a decent stipend as a T.A., not to mention the private gigs and studio time he took on the side. Not exactly Donald Trump, of course, but certainly a lot farther up the economic scale than I was at present.

But I didn't have a lot of time to ruminate on the value of a rich boyfriend, or whether what Randall and I had so far constituted a "relationship"—the Phantom's dinner was ready, and I had to take it back out to him.

Unfortunately, my promise to him that it would be out "shortly" had, well, fallen short. It was pretty common on busy nights like this, and we were just about the busiest I had ever seen. By the time I got back to his table, it was well after eight o'clock, and the music had been turned up a click to accommodate the people who were starting to filter onto the dance floor George had set up at the far end of the restaurant.

"Sorry about the wait," I said, placing his plate of veal before him. "We're sort of maxed tonight."

"No bother," he replied. "I've been people-watching."

There was definitely plenty of that to be had. The group seemed to have grown even wilder and more diverse as the evening progressed. But he sat in a sort of dark eddy away from the crowd, observing but not really a part of it.

"Is there anything else you need?" I asked.

He turned then and looked up at me, and again I could feel my breath catch in my throat. Something about the gleam of those eyes behind the mask made it hard to think straight. But he said only, "If I think of anything, I'll be sure to let you know."

I managed to muster a smile. "You know where to find me."

"Indeed I do."

The exchange seemed innocuous enough, but again

I found myself searching for a suspicious subtext in his words. Still, it was enough of a dismissal that I could make my escape and go on to tend the other customers at my station. But even as I went about my tasks I could feel his eyes still on me, watchful behind the half-mask that hid everything save what he cared to reveal to the world.

Christine...

He finally was willing to believe in the mercy of God. Finally, tonight he had seen her, spoken with her, even managed to touch her delicate hand as she struggled with the bottle of wine he had ordered.

The photos were nothing, liars that had done nothing to convey the luminosity of her fair skin, the hidden auburn gleam in her dark curls, the subtle dimple at the corner of her cheek. Even less had they been able to convey her quiet wry humor, the gleam of intelligence in her blue-gray eyes, or the pretty lilt of her voice. That he had been able to sit here, conversing with her in the merciful half-darkness of L'Opera, seemed nothing short of a miracle.

He was able to watch her as she bustled about, expertly removing dishes or placing steaming plates of food in front of her patrons, all the while gleaming like a princess in her white and gold gown, ropes of pearls glimmering in the dusky glory of her hair. She reminded him of some of the old fairy tales he'd read when he was a child, of the princess in exile, forced to do menial chores but still retaining her innate nobility and grace.

It was all he could do not to take her from this place,

here and now, but of course that was not feasible. No, he could only sit and make himself enjoy the truly excellent wine and quite passable veal, when all the while his true nourishment came from watching her.

He watched as more couples took to the dance floor at the rear of the restaurant. God, what he would give to hold her in his arms, feel her body pressed against his! But that had to be impossible—she was working this evening, and surely that would be a heinous breach of protocol?

She appeared to remove his empty plate, and asked if he would care for dessert or perhaps a cappuccino or espresso?

What he wanted was for her to sit at his table and share the last glass of wine from his bottle, but of course that was even less likely than taking her on to the dance floor. Still, anything to prolong the evening—

"An espresso, and a tiramisu," he said in response to her question. He actually did not care much for dessert as a rule, but it was a good way to pad the bill.

She took the order and disappeared into the kitchen, collecting a few additional requests for coffee and drink refills along the way. He admired the easy, casual way she was able to work with people, as if it were perfectly natural for a being with the looks and voice of an angel to wait on others like a common serving girl.

More than ever he was convinced that what he planned was the only true, right way for Christine. She was too good for this world, and if fate had been cruel enough to force her into servitude, then it was his place to combat fate and take her where she would be utterly secure and protected, where her enormous gifts could be nurtured and cherished.

In her absence the costume contest commenced, with a man who appeared to be the restaurant owner acting as master of ceremonies. He was dressed as Mephistopheles and certainly looked the part, right down to the spade beard and pointed eyebrows. Still, his costume was unimportant, and Erik had to admit he was somewhat amused by the eclectic group that paraded across the temporarily emptied dance floor.

Since the winner was chosen by audience appreciation, it was no surprise that the one chosen was a woman in a very scanty—if gorgeously beaded—devil costume. He shook his head, amused and disgusted at the same time. There were many more costumes in attendance that deserved the prize, but none of them had legs that went on forever and an amazing amount of gravity-defying cleavage—no doubt surgically enhanced.

Still, the costume contest was of very little interest to him, since he had decided not to participate and Christine, as an employee, was of course ineligible. He knew that his costume was correct in every detail, down to the ring on his little finger and the diamond-patterned $200-per-yard fabric that made his dress suit. He certainly had not come here to put himself on display, however, and would not have done so even if he had needed the prize money, which he certainly did not.

Christine arrived with his espresso and dessert just as the dance floor began to fill again. He allowed her to set both before him, but then he leaned forward impulsively and said, "Would you care to dance?"

She took a step backward, obviously shocked. "But—I'm working!"

"And have you taken a break yet this evening?"

From her hesitation, the answer seemed to be "no." He wasn't surprised, considering how busy the place was.

"Indulge me," he said and stood, offering her his hand.

For one long, frightening moment he feared she was going to refuse. Then she laid her hand in his and said, lifting her chin valiantly, "I don't think I'm breaking any labor laws."

He smiled at the defiant sparkle in her eyes and the sheer loveliness of her. Hardly daring to believe this was really happening, he led her to the dance floor.

Luckily, the restaurant's owner (and presumed arbiter of the evening's playlist) was something of a traditionalist. Instead of some hard-pounding techno or completely undanceable rap, the song playing was Andrea Bocelli and Sarah Brightman's duet, "Time to Say Goodbye." Of course, at the moment Erik hoped this was anything but goodbye, but at least the song gave him a chance to really hold her, to sweep her along with the melody.

Being a singer, of course she was attuned to the rhythm of the music, but she also did not seem to fear being held by him, to let him clasp her one hand and cradle her slender waist in the other. God, the sensation of her body against his, the intoxicating scent of roses that came from somewhere in the dark masses of her hair! Her fingers twined with his, and she moved gracefully despite the heavy skirts of her costume, which he could only assume was none too easy to dance in.

He had experienced a few moments like this in his life. The first time he had heard Beethoven's Ninth. The first time a woman touched him. Of course the first time he saw "Music of the Night" performed on stage. But the difference here was that the embodiment of all those passions, all those dreams, he held now in his arms.

All too soon the song was over, and Christine pulled away almost immediately. Her cheeks were flushed, but she would not meet his eyes.

"I really need to get back to work—"

He had to let her go. As much as he wanted to hold her forever, he did not want to cause trouble or call too much attention to himself. He had probably done too much already.

"Of course. Thank you very much for the dance."

She shot him a quick, uncertain smile but still would not look him directly in the face. Murmuring something about getting his bill, she disappeared among the crowd.

Was it unreasonable that he could still feel the touch of her hand in his, still smell the scent of her hair? His body ached for her even as he made his way back to his table, sipped at his now-lukewarm cup of espresso, and wished that the evening would never end.

But, as with all things, of course it did. Christine brought him his bill, but at least now she seemed to have recovered herself enough to meet his eyes and smile.

"Thank you for coming this evening—"

Of course he couldn't tell her that he'd give up all his useless millions just to hold her again. "This has been a memorable Halloween," he replied instead, and was amused to see the quick blush rise in her cheeks.

"Yes, it has," she said, and looked as if she wanted to say more, but she was interrupted by a drunken hail from the next table over.

"Waitress—hey—another round over here!"

She turned, distracted, and he took the opportunity to drop five hundred-dollar bills on the table and sweep himself away outside before she could notice. The air outside was cold and smelled damp, bringing with it the unmistakable scent of wet asphalt. It had obviously rained hard during the hours he had spent inside the restaurant, but now the pavement was merely slick with rainwater, the sky mottled with hard-driven clouds that were charcoal-gray against black.

The valet brought his S-Class around promptly, obviously giving him preferential treatment even though several other people had been out there waiting for their cars before Erik had arrived. He tipped the young man—obviously another college student—with a twenty before taking the wheel and driving off into the night.

He had actually learned to drive at a fairly early age, although it had been Ennis, who had taught him, certainly not his own father. Erik enjoyed the isolation he could experience behind the tinted windows of his car, and although he never drove during the daytime, he liked to take the car out at night, when he could drive through the meandering roads that crossed the arroyo and feel as if he were somehow part of the world, if even for only a short time.

Tonight was no different. Tonight, if anything, he felt more kindly disposed toward the human race than he had in a long time. He had spoken with her, seen her face with his own eyes—even, incredible as it seemed, held her in his arms. And she had not recoiled—if anything, he could sense her attraction to him, even though she tried to hide it, even though he knew even now she was probably telling herself that it was just a silly response, that she was truly only interested in Randall.

Well, she could tell herself anything she wanted. He had held her, felt her breathing quicken as he touched her, and he knew that, deep down, she had wanted him.

That, of course, would make things much easier. Possibly she would be resistant at first, but he felt certain that once she understood everything he had to offer her, she would surrender to him completely. After all, her current life had so little to give her, and he was willing to lay the world at her feet, in exchange for so little. Such a small thing, really.

All he wanted was her heart.

Chapter Six

IN THE DARKNESS I COULD FEEL the heat of his body next to mine, the strength of his hands as he cupped my face in his fingers and brought his mouth against my lips. His lips were warm and strong, and I felt myself open willingly to him to let his tongue explore my mouth. There was no strangeness, no hesitation as I lay back against the pillows, felt his strong yet sensitive fingers move over my body, cupping my breasts through the thin material of my nightgown. I moaned, arching my back to press myself more closely against him.

His voice was the merest whisper in the black night. "Christine…"

My only response was a soft moan. Then I could feel his hand moving lower, pushing my nightgown aside, touching me where I had never let a man touch before. But somehow this seemed right. There was no awkwardness, no hesitation. His fingers caressed my most intimate places and I moaned again, abandoning myself to the waves of pleasure that rolled over me, one after the other, until I could no longer distinguish where one stopped and the other began.

"Randall," I sighed at last, reaching up to caress his face. But instead of his firm cheek, my fingers brushed against a surface of smooth, cool plastic, and suddenly I could see the glimmer of the mask in the darkness.

"Not exactly," he replied, and at that I felt myself sit bolt upright in bed, gasping as I looked around and realized that I was alone in my narrow daybed, no company save the soft tick-tock of my old wind-up alarm clock from across the room.

It took a few moments for my breathing to settle down, for me to overcome the last remnants of the dream. I had never before had a dream that explicit, that overtly sexual—and to be dreaming of that stranger from the restaurant, instead of the man I was supposed to be in love with! Though the night was cool, I could feel my cheeks burning with mortification. Was I so weak that only a few hours with that man could poison my subconscious desires?

With a sudden angry gesture I pushed the bedclothes aside and went to the bathroom, where I poured myself some cold water and splashed some on my face before I turned off the faucet. Then I stood for a long moment, regarding my face in the soft half-light cast by the night-light in the corner of the room. How much of the residual flush in my cheeks was due to embarrassment, and how much by mental arousal caused by my dreams?

I would never know, of course. All I could do was

vow to keep my thoughts under control from now on. My life was complicated enough without allowing myself to brood over a mysterious man I would probably never see again. As I climbed back into bed, I tried to ignore the small pang of regret that last thought had caused me. Why should I even care about someone I had only seen for one evening, whose name I didn't even know? Why should the thought that I might never seen him again cause me that sudden flash of pain?

"Get a grip, Christine," I whispered fiercely into the darkness. "You've got Randall. Anything else is just asking for trouble."

Then I closed my eyes, willing myself to sleep, to take myself back into a blackness without thought, without dreams.

Without desire.

Randall did not look happy.

We'd agreed to meet at a restaurant at the western end of Olvera Street at four-thirty, since he had class until four, but it wasn't until almost five o'clock before he rounded a corner, looking grim. I was just glad he had shown up; all sorts of horrible possibilities had presented themselves, ranging from a simple standing-up to a multi-car wreck somewhere along the 110 Freeway. Aside from his expression, though, he looked none the worse for wear, so I thought maybe the traffic had just been especially bad—nothing unusual for Los Angeles at rush hour, even though campus was only about five miles or so from the historic pueblo near Union Station.

"Hi," he said briefly. "Let's go inside. It's freezing out here."

Nice of him to notice, especially when I'd been sitting in the chill for the last forty-five minutes. Although the rain of Halloween night had gone, the cold air mass still hovered over the city, and it was unseasonably chilly.

"Bad traffic?" I asked, hoping that my tone was neutral.

"Sucked," he replied. "They're still tearing up part of Main for something—pipes, I guess."

The hostess seated us in a dark booth toward the back of the restaurant. It was fairly crowded, no big surprise considering that the Day of the Dead festivities were still going on outside. At least I'd gotten to see a parade of folkloric dancers while I sat waiting for Randall, although I wished I had a proper coat instead of the thin denim jacket I had thrown on over my sweater.

"Do you drink beer?" he asked, after we'd been seated and were looking over the menus.

"Not usually, but I do kind of like it with Mexican food."

"God, I'd kill for one right now."

I raised my eyebrows, but luckily Randall wasn't forced into homicide, as the waitress appeared at my elbow and asked what we'd like to drink.

"Two Dos Equis," Randall said. "Stat."

The waitress—her name badge announced that her name was Lupe—blinked, then smiled. Up until then she had been looking somewhat tired and even sour, but when she smiled she was an entirely different person. "That kind of day?"

"You have no idea."

"In that case, I'll make sure you get a double order of chips and salsa. And I'll get those Dos Equis—stat," she added with a grin as she left us.

Randall ran a hand through his hair. "Sorry," he said. "I'm being an ass."

"Hey, if you've had a bad day—" Seeing him like this was harder than I had thought. After my evening with "the Phantom" and the dream that had followed, I'd been feeling more than a little guilty. I knew I was being silly—all I'd done was dance with the man for five minutes, after all, and I certainly couldn't control my subconscious—but I didn't think it was right for me to have felt the attraction I had experienced, not if I cared about Randall.

The problem was that I knew nothing about love and attraction, really. After our first date, I had thought I was falling in love with Randall, or at least seriously in infatuation if nothing else, but what was my basis for comparison? A few high school crushes that had amounted to nothing? I wanted to be with him, thought of him when he wasn't around, felt my heart speed up a little when he sought me out with those gorgeous hazel eyes of his and gave me a quick smile during class, but was it really love, or just an extension of my not wanting to be alone any longer? Surely if I were truly in love I wouldn't have felt the touch of that stranger's hand on mine for hours afterward, or shivered at the look in his dark eyes as he spoke with me. As for that dream…I didn't know what to think.

Randall's voice brought me back to the present. "Even if I've had a bad day, I shouldn't be taking it out on you. I just had some bad news this morning, that's all."

"Do you want to talk about it?"

He hesitated, and then we were interrupted by the arrival of Lupe with our drinks. She set them down, along with the promised chips and salsa.

"Ready to order?"

Randall and I looked at each other, guilty. We had barely even glanced at the menus.

"Give us a couple of minutes," he said.

"No problem," she replied, and left again.

He lifted the beer to his lips and drank deeply. I took a more cautious sip, then helped myself to a chip with some salsa. The beer tasted okay in combination with the chip, but it wasn't something I would have sought out on my own.

"Guess we'd better figure out what we're having before we get into anything else," Randall said, and for the next couple of minutes we busied ourselves with perusing the menus, preparing ourselves for Lupe's return.

Eventually we decided on carnitas for him and chicken molé for me, gave our orders to Lupe when she returned, then looked back at one other.

There was an uneasy pause.

"If you don't want to talk about it, it's okay," I said at length.

He waved a hand. "No, that's all right. I'm just simultaneously pissed off, frustrated, and confused, none of which are fun, especially all together."

"So what happened?"

"Stupid bureaucratic screw-ups is what." Randall took a more reasonable swallow of beer before continuing. "The duplex is paid for, and it's in my name, but of course

I'm responsible for paying the property taxes. They're kind of hefty, but I just put the money away each month like I'm paying rent until it's time to pay the tax bill in the spring, and I send it all in in one big chunk." He frowned. "So this morning I pick up my mail, and there's a notice from the county assessor's office that I'm delinquent in my taxes and that the property's going to be put up for auction in ten days unless I pay all the back taxes plus some seriously major fines!"

"Oh, my God!" I exclaimed. No wonder he was in such a foul mood. "Did somebody screw up?"

"Of course somebody screwed up—they'll just never admit it. I spent most of the morning on the phone with a series of dipshits—sorry—bureaucrats who all swore up and down that my taxes this spring hadn't been paid and that I was seriously delinquent."

"But don't you have a canceled check or something to show that you paid?" I asked.

"Not exactly. I let my stupid bank talk me into doing the whole electronic check storage thing, so now I have to go in and request my records back six months, locate the check, and get a facsimile made. No problem—except that that process is going to take fourteen business days, which is four more than I have."

Next to this, my recent problems seemed fairly insignificant. "So what are you going to do?"

"I'll keep fighting it, but in the meantime I'm probably going to have to borrow the money from my parents." He scowled, then took another pull at his beer. "That's going to be a real fun conversation."

"I am so sorry, Randall," I said, and I meant it. Having spent the last five years of my life fighting with various financial-aid organizations, I knew that dealing with the random stupidity of government bureaucracies was about as much fun as having a root canal.

"Yeah, so am I."

At that point the food arrived, and we were silent for several moments as we took a few bites.

Then he said, "I really didn't mean to dump on you, Christine—"

"If you can't dump on me, then who can you dump on?" I replied, and was gratified to see some of the warmth return to his eyes.

"Yes, but we were just supposed to have a fun evening together—"

"And we can," I said firmly. "Don't you feel better that you told someone what's going on?"

"Actually, yeah, I do," he replied, looking a little surprised at himself.

"Well, then," I said, and was gratified to see him smile.

"Okay, next topic." He helped himself to a bite of carnitas, then asked, "How was the Halloween gig?"

I forced myself to swallow, even though the food seemed to stick in my throat. "It was all right. Busy. I made some good tips." That was the understatement of the century—upon my return to the Phantom's table, I had discovered that he had dropped five hundred-dollar bills on top of the check, giving me a tip of approximately three hundred and fifty dollars. The relief I felt at what that extra cash could do to help me out the next month was almost overwhelmed by the guilt I experienced at how little I had really done to earn that money. Still, I couldn't exactly give it back, and I just made sure I was very generous in the percentage I had shared with the busboys and kitchen staff that evening. "How was your gig?"

"Fine. Bunch of annoying Hollywood types. Still, there were a lot of agents and producers there, and it never hurts to get heard. I actually got a couple of business cards, so we'll see what happens."

Ah, the sordid side of the business. I supposed it was all about schmoozing and who knew whom, but at the university I was still sheltered from much of that. Of course I had gone out on auditions, but they were usually for local productions and just summer stock at that, since I simply didn't have time during the regular school year to perform in a full production unless it was something being staged on campus. I'd been lucky enough to play the role of Pamina in last spring's production of *Die Zauberflöte* but had held off auditioning for the autumn opera, since they had chosen *Norma*, which had never been one of my favorites. Also, breaking into opera was not exactly the same as trying to break into Hollywood—not that Randall was trying to become an actor or something. He had admitted to me that he knew he was never going to be a concert pianist, but he did have a gift as an accompanist, and being a full-time studio musician was not a bad way to go.

"You're dreamy tonight," Randall said, and I was brought back to myself.

"Oh, I was just thinking that I wish they'd chosen something else for this semester's opera besides *Norma*."

He laughed. "It is a little heavy for your voice. You were stellar as Pamina, though."

"Well, thank you." I smiled back at him, and the conversation drifted on to a more musical direction as we discussed the merits of various operas. I was glad to see that much of the angry, distracted look had disappeared from Randall's eyes and made sure to keep the rest of the conversation light.

After dinner we drifted out to the main plaza, where a band played some lively Latin dance music. Even though neither of us really had a clue as to what we were doing, I let Randall swing me out onto the pavement with the rest of the dancers as we moved to the intoxicating beat. Luckily the crowds of dancers around us were forgiving of our missteps, and really it was more about moving to the rhythm than being technically perfect. It was also a really good way to stay warm, because I could see the breath of the dancers as white smoke in the cold evening air. I would have been freezing in my thin jacket if it weren't for the fact that I was moving fast.

Since it was a weeknight, the dancing ended at seven o'clock, but we'd had enough by then anyway—I don't recommend salsa dancing on a full stomach! The crowd began to disperse, and we paused by the statue of King Carlos to one side of the plaza, trying to decide what to do next. Most of the shops and restaurants at the monument closed early in the evening, so if we wanted to continue, we'd have to decide on a change of venue.

I was tired, though, and usually I tried to go to bed early on Mondays because I had an eight o'clock class on Tuesday mornings, as well as a five-hour shift at the restaurant in the evening. Still, I hesitated—it didn't seem fair for me to cut the evening short when Randall had had such a nasty shock.

He seemed to notice my diffidence, though, because he said, "Are you ready to pack it in?"

"I'm sorry, Randall—" It didn't help that the cold was starting to really bother me now that I was standing still again, and I began to shiver.

"Can I persuade you to come back to my place?"

That would be treading on dangerous ground, I knew. I was pretty sure Randall had a good idea of how inexperienced I was, but he was, after all, a man, and of course he'd be wanting the relationship to progress physically. And I—well, I didn't really know what I wanted. It didn't help that my thoughts continued to be muddled by that dream I had had the night before. Surely some part of me was eager to experience the physical side of a romantic relationship. I just worried that, for some reason, some part of me didn't want it to be with Randall.

Dancing with him had been exhilarating—we had moved together easily, and I had felt the familiar leap of my heart as he held me, but I did know that I wanted things to move more slowly than he did. But how to express that delicately without offending him—

"Not tonight, if that's okay." I wrapped my hands around my elbows, trying to persuade myself that I wasn't as cold as I thought I was. "I have an early class, and then I have to work—"

The only real betrayal of his disappointment was a subtle tightening of his jaw. "Oh, right."

To both our surprise, I stood on my tiptoes and kissed him full on the mouth. He hesitated for a second, and then he put his arms around me and pulled me in closer, his mouth opening to mine. When we broke apart, he was smiling, and I felt considerably warmer.

"Rain check?" I asked. "I don't work on Thursday, and I don't have class on Friday."

"Deal," he replied.

Then we walked arm in arm over to Union Station—I had taken the light rail from Pasadena, since it was actually cheaper than paying for parking—and he kissed me goodnight, thoroughly and well, before I climbed on the train and headed back home. I'm sure it wasn't the first passionate goodnight kiss shared in the station, nor would it be the last, but the memory of it was enough to keep me warm until I lay myself down in my narrow, lonely bed, to a sleep unhaunted by any Phantom.

The room was dim, lit only by the four candles mounted in the candelabra that sat on the right side of the massive gilded organ. Erik sat in the semidarkness, mechanically moving through the third Brandenburg Concerto. His thoughts were not on the notes, as much as he had admired them in the past for their pure mathematical complexity. Things had finally been set in motion, and so far everything seemed to be going well, but still he felt vaguely uneasy. Jerome continued to track Christine's every movement, and his report that she had spent another evening with Randall was disquieting. One would think that she had felt nothing when she had danced with Erik on Halloween. He knew in his soul that was untrue—he had sensed her heart quickening in her breast, watched her soft lips part as they had moved together. But apparently that brief attraction was not enough to distract her from that annoying young man.

And Randall, damn him—one would think going out on a dinner date would be the last thing on his mind, considering he was in very real danger of losing his house. That had been an elegant stratagem. Really, it was so easy to have those records hacked and altered, and since one of the basic tenets of survival in a bureaucracy was never admitting you had made a mistake, it would take Randall quite a bit of maneuvering to keep the lumbering beast of government from swallowing his pitiful little property whole.

His distorted mouth pulled to one side as Erik grimly remembered the last time he had been crossed. That time the fools had been his own neighbors, the family who had owned the property that shared the block with his mansion. He had always disliked their home, mostly because it was an uninspired piece of mid-century mundanity that offended his artistic sensibilities, but it wasn't until they had decided to build a pool in the piece of their property that backed up to his own gardens that indifference had flared into hostility.

It wasn't the pool so much as the fact that it became a haven for all the members of the family, including a pair of very noisy seven-year-olds, as well as seemingly every other child within a five-block radius. The sounds of their screaming laughter echoed off the walls and rendered that portion of his property completely unusable.

In self-defense, Erik had a row of closely planted Italian cypress placed there in an attempt to buffer some of the noise. Instead of settling back into uneasy coexistence, however, his neighbors promptly sued him for blocking their view of the mountains. He immediately countersued for loss of property usage as well as emotional distress.

The legal bickering went on for quite a while, during which time he had some carefully placed bribes at city hall unearth problems with the permits that had been given to build the pool in the first place. The owners of the property were then hit with more fines in addition to the ever-mounting legal fees from their lawyer. The final blow was the recession, which caused the owner of the property to lose his software company along with any hope of paying off his enormous legal bills. Bankruptcy soon followed, and the home was sold at auction—to Erik, of course, who promptly razed the house, knocked down the wall dividing the two properties, and extended the stone wall that encircled his own mansion to include the new acreage. The hated pool was dug out, and he had a lovely neoclassical gazebo erected there in its place. It was still one of his favorite haunts.

Homelessness and bankruptcy were not really his plan for Randall, however. No, the boy would probably pull it out by appealing to his parents for money, but the whole process would be humbling at the very least, not to mention a colossal waste of his time. And that was what Erik wanted all along—to make life difficult for him, to distract him from Christine by any means possible until she literally disappeared out from under his nose.

The disappearance, though, was the most difficult part. As isolated as Christine was, she still went to school and had a job, and so there were people who would quickly note her absence if she turned up missing. But he could not wait forever—obviously, Christine and Randall were still seeing one another, and things would progress naturally unless she were taken away, and soon. Within the month, if possible.

His fingers stilled on the keyboard as a sudden thought struck him. Of course. He had been stupid not to think of it earlier. In less than four weeks, the perfect opportunity would present itself. In less than a month, it would be the Thanksgiving holiday, and she would not be expected at school for at least four days. He knew that she did not work on Mondays, and very probably no one would think it strange that she missed school the first day after a long weekend.

Yes—very soon, for the first time in his life, Erik would finally have a reason to give thanks.

Chapter Seven

THE ENVELOPE LOOKED INNOCUOUS ENOUGH — just a slim ivory piece of paper with my name neatly laser-printed across the front. But then I looked at the return address, read it again to be sure, and dropped my books down on the dining room table. The letter appeared to be from the Long Beach Opera, and I was pretty sure it wasn't a flyer advertising their latest production. They sent out slick brochures for that sort of thing.

"What the—" I said aloud, then ran my finger under the flap to tear it open. The envelope contained a single piece of matching ivory paper with the Long Beach Opera logo embossed at the top. Unfolding it, I quickly scanned its contents, then read over them again, slowly, at first unbelieving, then with my heart beating faster and faster.

"Dear Ms. Daly," the letter read, "as you may know, our organization is always on the lookout for new and promising young talent. I was privileged enough to attend the master class recital several weeks ago and hear you sing. I was very impressed by your performance and would like to extend an invitation to you to come audition for our production of The Rake's Progress, which is scheduled for next April. Our next auditions are scheduled for Monday, November 9, at 4 p.m. Please bring two prepared pieces, one in English, one in the foreign language of your choice. We look forward to hearing you then."

The letter was signed "Andreas Mitisek, artistic director." I'd never heard of him, but I wasn't that familiar with the staff of the Long Beach Opera. I did know that they tended to specialize in less-performed operas and avant-garde pieces, leaving the more mainstream works to the L.A. Opera company.

"Monday, November 9," I repeated, then groaned a little. Only five days away, and awkward timing, too, since I was done with class on Mondays at one o'clock and then usually headed straight home for Pasadena. So I had to decide whether to hang around campus for an extra few hours—not very appetizing—or drive home, and then turn around and make the slog all the way down to Long Beach just a few hours later, at the very beginning of the afternoon rush, which was even less appetizing. Still, you didn't argue with audition times. You either showed up or you didn't, in which case your slot would be promptly filled by at least ten other hopefuls eager to take your place.

I knew even then I'd just wait at campus—I'd have my laptop with me and could work on the paper for my comp. lit. class if nothing else. I just couldn't afford to waste the gas it would take to go up to Pasadena and then all the way back down to Long Beach. Then I stopped for a second and shook my head at myself, just a little. Here I was, being handed an amazing opportunity practically on a silver platter, and all I could do was worry about the gas it was going to take to get to Long Beach!

The phone startled me then, and I picked it up on the second ring after placing the letter down on the love seat next to me.

"Hello?"

"Hey, Christine."

Randall, probably calling to confirm our date for the following evening. Oops. In my excitement over the letter, I'd forgotten for a moment that George had called me in to work unexpectedly on Thursday night—and this time it wasn't even Meg I was having to cover. Two of the other waitresses had called in sick with a nasty stomach flu that was making the rounds, and George really had no choice but to ask me to take their shifts. I knew Randall would be less than thrilled to hear that our date was canceled, so I opened with the unexpected letter from the Long Beach Opera.

"You will not believe what I got in the mail today," I said.

"What?"

I explained about the letter, let him give me his congratulations, then said slowly, "Um, Randall—about tomorrow night—"

Even through the phone line, I could hear him tense up. "What about it?"

He was not making this easy. "It turns out I can't make it. George needs me to come in."

A silence. "George, huh?"

Well, if he was going to be that way about it—I continued, sounding defensive even to myself, "Look, Randall, it's my job. Two of the other waitresses are out with the flu, and he needs me to help cover for them. It's not like I volunteered or something."

Another pause. God, I hated telephones. That was how I first found out about my parents' deaths—the hospital called the home number the O.R. staff had found in my father's wallet. They didn't know that the only person at home to pick up the phone was a frightened fifteen-year-old girl who waited alone, wondering why her parents were taking so long to come back from that dinner party...

Randall said, "Okay, fine. It's not as if I'm not going through something over here or anything—"

I felt a little flame of anger then. Guilt was the last thing I needed to deal with right now. "I'm not doing this on purpose, Randall!"

"Of course not. You never do anything on purpose if you can help it, do you, Christine?"

That came right out of left field. I glared at the phone for a moment, then snapped, "What the hell is that supposed to mean?" I was angry enough that I didn't bother to hide that fact. "If you really think I'm some passive-aggressive victim type, then fine! Think what you want—it doesn't change the fact that I have to work for a living!"

"And I don't?"

Possibly I had gone a little too far, but at that point I didn't much care. "Well, at least you've got some kind of safety net. You can always count on your parents to bail you out, right?"

Silence again, this time so long I wondered whether he had hung up on me. Finally he said, "Well, at least now I know your opinion of me. Talk to you later." And with that he did hang up.

Crap. I sat there for a moment, holding the useless receiver in my hand, until the dial tone changed to the angry busy signal of a phone left off the hook for too long. Then I did replace the receiver in its cradle, not sure whether I should be angry or hurt. The truth was, maybe Randall had hit a snag in his perfect little world, but even as upset as he was over the whole property-tax mess, he did have resources that I didn't. His parents were very comfortably well off and could probably afford to help him out without too much effort. Whereas I —

Well, that way led to self-pity, and I'd been there often enough in the past that I really didn't feel like revisiting the territory. If Randall wanted to be angry, then let him. Either we'd make up or we wouldn't. I felt a pang then, wondering if he really were angry enough to call everything off, but I wasn't about to play the needy girlfriend and call him with apologies I really didn't mean.

As far as I was concerned, he really was overreacting. We hadn't been seeing each other long enough for him to be quite this possessive — or at least, I didn't think we had. Not for the first time, I wished I had just a little more understanding of how guys' brains worked. I didn't know if this sort of behavior was normal, although something told me most guys probably wouldn't be as upset over the situation as Randall seemed to be. Maybe I should have talked to the whole thing over with Meg, since she had a lot more experience with men than I did, but I was already strapped for time. I couldn't afford to get sucked into a lengthy conversation about my trust issues.

I told myself that if Randall truly wanted to be with me, then he'd have to understand my current situation and work with it. It wasn't as if I had lied about my job or the hours I had to put in to keep myself afloat.

In the meantime, I had work to do. I knew that I could sing the "Jewel Song" again for my audition, but I also needed a good English language piece. After a bit of thought, I decided that "Glitter of Waves and Glitter of Sunlight" from Peter Grimes would be a good choice. I had done it my sophomore year, and it was not something the other candidates would probably choose. The last thing I wanted was to blend in. It had been several years since I had worked on the piece, though, which meant I had a few days of hard practicing in front of me. And since apparently Randall and I weren't speaking right now, I'd have to rely on my own shaky accompaniment to prepare for the audition. Not exactly a promising start to what could possibly be the most important audition of my life so far, but I didn't have much of a choice.

The sheet music was still stored in the piano bench, thank God. I pulled it out, set it on the piano, and got to work, thankful that at least I had the music to pull me away from thoughts of Randall and the worry of how angry he really might be with me. Music had been my escape so many times in the past that I had lost count, and I tried to take refuge in it now, hoping, even as I tackled the difficult modalities of the aria, that Randall hadn't quite given up on me yet.

So they were arguing. Erik switched off the tape recorder and smiled to himself. Good—very good. If they kept at each other's throats for the next few weeks, he wouldn't have to worry about the progression of their relationship, and whether Christine would find herself attracted enough to Randall to give herself to him.

The tap on her phone had actually been Jerome's suggestion, but up until now the tapes of her phone conversations hadn't been of much use except to keep track of her schedule, since the majority of the time she spent on the phone she was either talking to Meg about picking up shifts or planning time with Randall, which didn't appear to happen very often. The paucity of personal conversation was in itself illuminating. More than anything it seemed to highlight her utter aloneness in the world. Erik had imagined that most girls her age would spend a great deal of time on the phone talking with friends or calling home to family members, but of course Christine had no family to call, and her circle of friends seemed quite limited. Oddly, she seemed to use the land line far more than her cell phone, which Jerome informed him was the type where you apparently paid as you went. It seemed she couldn't even afford the sort of plans that most cell phone companies offered these days.

The situation frustrated him, as he would have liked a little more of the personal information he could have gleaned from listening to her speak with her peers or by reading her text messages to friends. In so many ways, she was still a cipher, even though he had at last finally met her, spoken with her, even touched her. Her conversations with Meg were usually work-related, although he could sense at times Meg was trying to draw her out, with Christine politely resisting. She seemed to have none of the current generation's self-fascination that led to endless posts on the various social networks; in fact, she didn't even have a Facebook account. Jerome had observed that she seemed to be well-liked—with the notable exception of that bleached, strutting mezzo in her master class—but she did not appear to have any close friends except for Meg.

Even an examination of her transcripts back to high school did not reveal much. She had been an excellent student, and of course had participated in choir and musical theater in high school, but those seemed to be her only extracurricular activities. Her grades had suffered a dip during her sophomore year of high school—naturally, since her parents had died on a frosty New Year's Eve that year—but she appeared to have recovered and gone on to graduate with high honors. She should have gone straight to a four-year university, but the death of her grandmother set her back both financially and emotionally, with the result that she had not been able to attend USC until midway through her junior year.

Erik would have dearly loved to have seen the personal essay she had to submit with her application, but Jerome was having a hard time getting his hands on it. No matter. The paperwork would probably be procured soon enough, and, if not, then he would have the real thing in his possession within the month. Then he would be able to learn everything about her at his leisure.

At least his plans on that front continued to progress well. Really, it was a simple enough matter, and Jerome already had several promising leads as to whom to hire for the actual operation. No, the real frustration lay in waiting for the time to be ripe, for the Thanksgiving holidays to be upon them, that blessed four-day stretch where she could be missing for some time before anyone really noticed her absence. Her room was already waiting for her, an enchanting little jewel-box of a chamber ready to address her every comfort.

He flipped the pages of his desktop calendar from today's date to the 25th. Twenty-one days. It seemed like such a narrow sheaf of paper when he held it like this, measuring from one date to the next, but he knew so much could happen in such a short span of time. Twenty-one days. Wars had been fought and lost in less time. People had met, fallen in love, and gotten married in fewer days than that. Lives had ended, and begun.

Still, the last few months of Christine's life seemed to have followed a fairly set routine, and all he could do was hope and pray for it to continue in such a way. That, and pray as well she really had wounded Randall's sensibilities to the point where he wished nothing more to do with her. Of course, Erik himself knew that it would take much more than a few stinging words to give up on a woman such as Christine—actually, he had been pleased to see her show that much spirit—but Randall appeared to be made of weaker stuff. At least, that was what Erik hoped. The boy had probably never suffered a major setback before in his life, and now he was faced with a huge financial obstacle as well as a girlfriend who apparently wasn't the doormat he had thought her to be. What Randall did next would do much to prove his worth as a man.

Even if Randall did surprise him by admitting to Christine that he had been in the wrong, Erik wasn't worried...much. The spat had at least set the relationship back a few significant steps, and that would take up more time—time that neither Randall nor Christine knew was running out.

The development with the Long Beach Opera was interesting, but not of much concern. High time someone paid real attention to Christine's remarkable vocal gifts, and he was interested to see how the audition turned out.

Curious on a purely intellectual level, of course. By the time the opera was cast, let alone staged, Miss Daly would have disappeared from the scene, much to the bemusement of her friends and colleagues. Perhaps one day she might be able to return to the opera scene, but first of course she had to prove her loyalty...prove her love.

Yes, Christine would have to prove she was completely his before she could ever be allowed to return to the world.

Chapter Eight

THE OFFICES OF THE LONG BEACH OPERA were located in the heart of the city in an area of gleaming high-rises and expensive-looking restaurants. Of course there was no street parking to be had, so I pulled reluctantly around to the back, where I took a ticket from the attendant with a silent prayer that they would at least validate.

It seemed a little odd to be holding auditions here, in what clearly were administrative offices, but perhaps they had a recital chamber somewhere on the premises. After a quick glance in the rearview mirror to make sure my lipstick was still intact and my unruly hair no more than usually mussed, I gathered up my purse and the worn briefcase that held my musical scores, took a deep breath, and headed toward the elevators.

The building lobby was impressively bland, with slick polished travertine on the floors and walls and a security guard who sat at a desk half-hidden by a series of potted palms. He gave me a bored look, and I returned a slight smile even as I hoped that he wouldn't read my nervousness as suspicious behavior. Apparently not, for he looked away almost immediately and returned his attention to the newspaper spread out before him.

Between the two elevators was a building directory that showed the Long Beach Opera offices as being located on the fifth floor. I pressed the button, started to bite my lower lip, then stopped, realizing that all I'd accomplish was to chew off my carefully applied lipstick.

Before I really wanted it to, the elevator reached the lobby, its doors opening. I had to pause to let a brittle-looking woman with over-streaked hair exit the elevator, but then I had it to myself.

As luck would have it, no one else had called for the elevator, so I rode smoothly to the fifth floor, all the while trying to keep my breathing calm and unhurried. I don't know what it was with auditions, but I tended to let them get to me more than they should. It always seemed as if they were vitally important to my continued existence as a singer, even though I knew intellectually that not even the most gifted performer won every role and that my voice, good as it was, was not perfectly suited to every role for which I tried out.

Meg once tried to feed me some psycho-babble about fear of rejection stemming from the loss of my parents, but I hadn't let the conversation get very far. Who knows—maybe she was even right. Over the years I had resisted the efforts of well-meaning school counselors and psychologists to get me into therapy, thinking it all a waste of time. No amount of talking was going to bring my parents back, and in the meantime I'd had papers and tests and concerts to worry about. Even Meg had finally given up once she'd realized that particular topic of conversation was a guaranteed dead-end.

The elevator doors slid open, and I stepped out directly into a reception area. It was furnished with considerably more personality than the lobby downstairs; the couches were covered in a vibrant if tasteful modern print in jewel tones that matched the posters advertising various Long Beach Opera productions on the walls, and a gorgeous orchid bloomed on the receptionist's desk. She looked up as I entered, her gaze friendly if a bit curious.

I approached the desk with what I hoped was a confident and professional smile. "I'm Christine Daly," I offered. "I'm here for the auditions."

Behind her fashionable rectangular frames, the receptionist's dark eyes widened a bit. "The what?"

"The aud—" I began, then trailed off. Of course. How could I be so stupid? This was an office building, not a theater or rehearsal hall. But maybe only the address on the letter was wrong, or the information as to the actual audition site accidentally omitted. "Just a sec," I added, when I saw her start to open her mouth to speak. "I can show you the letter."

I set my purse down on the floor and scrabbled through my briefcase, looking for the envelope I had tucked in with my scores. Of course it was buried at the bottom, but eventually I dug it out, although it was a bit the worse for wear. Then I unfolded the piece of ivory paper and handed it to her.

She took it from me, the frown line between her brows deepening as she looked it over. "I think someone's played a pretty mean joke on you," she said at last.

I just stood there, staring at her, as my heart began to pound in heavy, anguished strokes against my ribs.

"This is our stationery," she went on, and I could tell she was trying to help me out by explaining further. At least she looked sympathetic. "And we are doing The Rake's Progress in the spring. But the production was cast two weeks ago. I don't know who sent you this letter, but it didn't come from us."

I said, in a voice not entirely my own, "I see."

"I'm very sorry," she said, and, to her credit, she actually did look sorry. Then she handed the letter back to me.

Because it was the polite thing to do, I took it—why? so I could burn it later?—and shoved it back inside my briefcase. Then, because I couldn't think of anything else to say, and because I knew I had to get out of there before I made even more of a fool of myself, I said, "Thank you," managed a watery smile, maintained enough presence of mind to gather up my purse and briefcase, and then had to endure the excruciating wait for the elevator to return.

She watched me with concern as I stood there and wondered to myself what kind of moron had designed an elevator that opened directly into an office suite. Wasn't a proper hallway with a discreet door good enough for them? Finally, after several eternities, the elevator arrived and I fled inside.

You will not cry. You will not cry, I scolded myself during the long ride down. Of course, my ignominious retreat had to be attended by the unwelcome addition of elevator riders from the fourth and third floors. I burrowed into a far corner of the elevator, my briefcase and purse clutched against my chest like a shield. Luckily, no one really seemed to pay any attention to me—it was the end of the work day, and all anyone seemed concerned with was getting the hell out of there. In that way, I had a lot in common with them.

Of course, when I got to my car I realized that I hadn't gotten my parking ticket validated—no surprise, considering the circumstances—and had to pay for my lovely little episode in the offices of the Long Beach Opera. Price of humiliation, $6.50, thank you very much. Not to mention all the gas this pleasant trip had cost me.

Not until I had peeled out of the parking structure, popping the clutch from first directly into third and almost stalling the car in the process, did I allow the tears to flow. By that point the quick-falling dusk of late autumn had already come to the city, and it was dark enough that no one could see me weeping as I pointed my battered little car northward for the long drive home.

Erik had been expecting Christine to make at least one phone call when she returned home from her audition, so he was poised by the listening equipment instead of just waiting for Jerome to give him the digital files for review. The apparatus had been set up in a smaller secondary office that had once been a bedchamber, but of course it was furnished in the same discreet opulence as the rest of the house. Because the evening was already chilly, a small fired burned in the rose marble fireplace, lending a subdued light to the otherwise darkened room.

The green light indicator for an outgoing call began to flash, and he immediately picked up the headphones and settled them over his ears even as the red recording light turned on.

"Meg?" came Christine's voice. She sounded shaky and faint. Then a long pause. "Okay—I guess you're out. Can you give me a call if you get this tonight? I don't care how late it is." Another pause. "Talk to you later."

He sat, considering, not bothering to remove the headphones. That hadn't sounded good at all. The audition hadn't gone well, then. He couldn't comprehend anyone not recognizing what a marvelous instrument she possessed, but perhaps Christine was one of those unfortunate performers who choked at auditions. It happened.

The outgoing call light began to flash again, and he sat up straighter, wondering if perhaps Christine were trying to reach Meg by another number. It was a male voice that answered, however, one which Erik immediately recognized and despised.

"Randall?" Again that frightening little hitch in her voice.

"Yeah—Christine?" Even as a disembodied voice heard through a set of headphones, there was no mistaking the sharpened concern in his tone. "What's the matter?"

A muffled sound in return.

"Are you hurt? Christine!"

A ragged breath. Then, "No—I'm not hurt. I just—I needed to talk to someone."

"What's wrong?"

Almost unconsciously, Erik's hands clenched into fists. How he longed to be the one Christine had called in her despair, the one she instinctively sought for comfort.

She took another one of those halting breaths. "Oh, God, Randall—that audition was just a fake. Someone set me up!"

"What do you mean, 'set you up'?"

"I mean that I thought I had an audition and drove all the way down there, and then—then—" For the first time she broke down into weeping, not loudly, but little wrenching cries that were somehow more painful to listen to than outright sobs.

To do him credit, Randall did not try to cover up the sound of her pain by murmuring platitudes or telling her to hush. There was silence for a moment on the line, broken only by the agonized sound of Christine's weeping, a horrible moment in which Erik waited, hardly daring to breathe until she spoke again.

Finally she said, "I'm sorry."

"You don't have to be sorry. You're upset. It's okay." A pause. "Do you want to tell me what happened next?"

"Oh, God, Randall, it was so humiliating! I go to their offices—their offices, like a complete idiot! Who holds auditions in their offices?"

"Well," he said reasonably, "you'd never auditioned for them before. How were you supposed to know?"

"No one holds auditions in their offices, Randall. A rehearsal hall, even the theater where the production is going to be held, which I should have known, if I'd stopped to think about the whole thing logically."

"Well, we can argue about that later. What happened?"

"So I walk in and tell the receptionist I'm there for the auditions, and she gives me this look, like I don't know what I'm talking about. So I show her the letter, and then—" Christine paused and took a breath. "Then she tells me that it had to be some kind of joke, that they'd cast *The Rake's Progress* two weeks earlier!"

"Jesus." Even Randall sounded shaken.

"Yeah. Exactly."

Then Randall said, "Do you want me to come over?"

Erik tensed, waiting for her reply. If Randall went to comfort Christine, there was no telling how things might end up. Certainly their previous quarrel seemed to have been forgotten for the moment.

"No," Christine said at length, and Erik closed his eyes, expelling a breath he hadn't even noticed he was holding. "I really appreciate it, but I'm okay. I just needed to talk to someone."

"Just someone?"

"I wanted to talk to you." Another pause, but not as long as the ones before. "I'm sorry we argued."

Interesting comment, Erik thought. She'd admitted regret for the quarrel but not guilt.

Apparently Randall didn't notice the distinction. "I'm sorry, too. I was being a jerk."

She made some sort of protesting sound, but Randall cut her off.

"No, really. Probably I bit your head off because I had just borrowed the money from my parents."

"So your house is safe?"

"It is unless someone else in the assessor's office screws up again—which I kind of doubt, since my dad has a friend of his in the D.A.'s office who's offered to look into the matter. We'll probably get the money back in the next month or so."

This was news to Erik, but he hadn't bothered to follow up on the matter of Randall's delinquent taxes for the past few days. He'd been too busy with his preparations for Christine's arrival in the house. Still, the outcome of the matter didn't surprise him all that much. He'd assumed that Randall would be able to extricate himself from the situation without too much difficulty, and at any rate the object had been to throw some frustration the boy's way, not to actually render him homeless.

"Thank God for that, at least," Christine said.

"Well, I have to admit that I'm glad to not have that hanging over my head anymore. But this audition thing— this is just somebody being cruel."

A brief silence. Then she said, her voice small, "Why would anyone want to do something like this?"

"Not 'anyone.' Someone. And I have a pretty good idea who."

"Not—"

"Yeah, Carrie Gustafson. It's not as if she's made any secret of the way she feels about you."

"But why? And don't tell me it's jealousy—she's a mezzo—it's not even as if we'd be up for the same parts!"

Randall sighed. "Christine, I have to say I'm touched by your faith in the goodness of humanity, but since when have feelings ever been logical? Of course she's jealous—you can sing rings around her, you're much prettier than she is, and it's obvious to everyone that you're Dr. Green's favorite student. That's enough to piss off a spoiled brat like Carrie. I know her better than you, anyway—she's been at USC for four years, and I've had to put up with her crap the whole time."

"Okay, so let's say I agree with your version of 'why.' But how?"

"Well, it's pretty easy for Carrie to get her hands on official letterhead from the Long Beach Opera—" and here Randall paused for a second— "considering that her father's on the board of directors."

"Oh."

"Exactly 'oh.' And God knows her father wouldn't deny his precious spoiled darling anything she asked for."

Then Christine said, with some heat, "What a bitch," and Erik smiled to himself. He was always pleased to see flashes of the spirit he knew burned beneath her calm exterior.

"With a capital B," Randall replied, and for some reason that made them both laugh.

"So I suppose," Christine said, obviously considering her words, "that the best thing for me to do tomorrow is to walk into class like nothing happened."

"Absolutely. It'll drive her nuts—and she won't be able to come out and say anything directly to you, because then she'd just be giving herself away."

A small, wry laugh. "This actually might be kind of fun."

"That's the spirit. You know, I wasn't going to be accompanying the master class tomorrow, but I think I'll see if I can switch with Susan. I don't want to miss the expression on Ms. Gustafson's face!"

"Sounds like a plan," Christine agreed. Then her tone grew more sober. "Thanks, Randall. Now I feel like I can actually sleep tonight."

"That's what I'm here for," he replied, the quiet intensity of his voice belying the flip words. "Take care of yourself, Christine."

"I will," she said. "Good night, Randall."

"'Night, Christine."

And with that the line went quiet. The red recording light on the listening apparatus stayed on for a few seconds longer, then dulled to black.

Erik sat in the warm semidarkness of the office, unmoving for a moment, then slowly lifted the headphones from his ears. Unfortunate that the two should have patched up their differences so quickly, but he knew he would have been fooling himself to think they would hold a grudge for any length of time. Neither one of them had the darkness of spirit for that sort of behavior.

Whereas he, on the other hand—

Discarding the headphones on the desk, Erik punched the intercom on the phone. At this hour Jerome would most likely be in the capacious apartment over the garage that was one of the perks of his employment. Sure enough, the man responded to the intercom's buzz almost immediately.

"Yes, sir?"

"Jerome, I need everything you can find on a Carrie Gustafson. She's a senior at USC."

"'S-o-n' or 'S-e-n'?" Jerome asked.

"I'm fairly sure it's the former. I don't know if Carrie is short for something else."

"I'll check on it, sir. Anything else?"

"That's all. I want her address especially."

"Right on it, sir."

Not bothering to reply further, Erik pushed the intercom button again, disconnecting the call. He had no doubt that Jerome would have the information for him by the time breakfast was ready. And then —

Then Ms. Gustafson would have every reason to regret the day she made Christine Daly the target of her spite. Yes, it would be most pleasant to give Carrie instruction in shame and humiliation. She would find that Christine was not quite so alone and friendless as she thought. It was a lesson she would remember every time she looked in a mirror.

Erik laughed softly. It was not a pleasant sound. *Thank you, Ms. Gustafson*, he thought. *Thank you for giving me the opportunity to become Christine's avenging angel!*

Chapter Nine

IT WAS IRONIC THAT ONE OF CALIFORNIA'S most prestigious schools was located in L.A.'s most notorious slum. Only a few blocks from USC's graceful stone and brick architecture and carefully manicured lawns stretched South Central, spawning ground of the 1992 riots, drive-by shootings, and gang warfare that continued despite the police department's best efforts.

Not that Erik cared much for any of that. What did bother him was the fact that USC's proximity to South Central caused the streets around the campus to be crawling with campus police and LAPD patrol cars.

He sat in the front seat of his rented Ford, a big white Crown Victoria that itself looked like an unmarked police car, waiting for the last light in Carrie Gustafson's house to go out. It was now almost one o'clock in the morning; apparently one of her flatmates was a night owl.

The house was a carefully restored two-story Victorian in a street of gentrified homes that just bordered on the campus. It had been broken up into two flats, one up, one down. Luckily for him, Carrie Gustafson lived in the bottom flat. Alone.

Still, even though her lights had been out for almost two hours now, he had to wait until all was dark in the entire building. He could not risk being heard or seen. What he had planned would take only a few moments, but he was not going to take any chances.

There—finally, the last light had been extinguished. He glanced at his watch. One-fifteen. It would be at least fifteen minutes before it was safe to go in.

A pair of headlights turned down the street, moving at a leisurely pace. Erik quickly slumped in his seat, waiting as the car moved by with agonizing slowness. Had to be some sort of patrol car, although he didn't dare sit up to take a look. The sound of its engine trailed off, and he raised his head cautiously, catching a final glimpse of red taillights before it turned the corner and headed down Jefferson Boulevard.

He sat up all the way then, pulled up the hood of his dark sweatshirt to cover the black ski mask he already wore, and drew on a pair of thin black leather gloves. His lock-pick set had already been stowed in the small black duffle that also carried a small pink plastic bottle. One last check of the time—one-thirty. Good enough.

Although he had parked across the street and partway down the block, he was still careful to shut the car door quietly and lock it with the key rather than using the remote lock. Those things were just too noisy, especially on a residential street after midnight.

Moving quickly without seeming too hurried, he crossed the street and then, when he got to the edge of the big Victorian's property, he headed up the driveway, which was partially blocked by a dusty 4Runner and a robin's-egg-blue New Beetle convertible—Carrie's of course.

He resisted the impulse to stop and slash the tires, or at least let the air out of them. That wasn't the objective here, and if nothing else his father had ingrained in him a love of German engineering, even if in this case the object in question looked more like a piece of Easter candy on wheels than an actual automobile.

The gate into the side yard had only a simple latch without even a padlock. Erik reached over the fence, lifted the latch, and let himself in, hoping at the last minute that the girls in the house didn't employ a Rottweiler or pit bull as their own form of burglar protection.

No snarls or startled barking met his intrusion onto the property, however, and he continued to the back door that opened on to a service porch. Jerome's thoroughness had resulted not only in Carrie's address, phone number, academic records (spotty at best), bank accounts (impressive for a girl in her early twenties), credit cards (mostly maxed but all paid for by daddy, apparently), and DMV record (better than she deserved), but also the actual blueprints for the house, unearthed in some archive that dated back to the gentrification of the neighborhood in the late 1980s. It was always better to go to the back door if possible; not only was it was less visible from the street, but people were usually less careful about what sorts of locks they put on their back doors.

As appeared to be the case here. He hadn't approached the front door, a handsome oak affair with a stained-glass inset, but it had a handsome newish-looking brass latching handle, probably with a matching handsome deadbolt. The back door, however, looked as if it could use a new coat of paint, and while it too had a deadbolt, it was only a Kwikset, something Erik could probably pick in his sleep.

Picking locks was something he had taught himself when he was in his early twenties, bored beyond belief and looking for something to occupy his mind. Lock-picking seemed interesting, something that would challenge his mind and his manual dexterity—and he was equally attracted by the slightly subversive nature of the skill. So he acquired a fancy lock-picking set, several books, and a variety of locks to practice on, and went at it nonstop until he could pick even a difficult Schlage in less than two minutes.

He set the duffel bag down on the back step and pulled out his lock-picking set, a fancy seventy-two-piece kit that had come in its own leather case. It seemed like overkill for the lock he was facing right now, but of course he hadn't known exactly what he would have to deal with when he came here.

First, using his left hand, he inserted the tension wrench, a thin, flat piece of metal, and turned it slightly. Then he drew out the two picks that he'd used on Kwiksets in the past and leaned close as he inserted the first one, lifting, lifting—

Click. There went the first pin. Good. He tried again for the second pin. It too clicked into place, and the next three were a matter of less than a minute. Using a cam, he was able to turn the plug as easily as if the correct key had been inserted, and the door swung inward.

Moving quickly, he removed the picks and tension wrench from the lock and tossed them inside the duffel bag. There would be time enough to put them in their proper places after he was done here.

The service porch was dimly lit by the sickly salmon glow of the sodium-vapor street lights outside, its only occupants a washing machine and dryer and an empty laundry basket. It opened onto the kitchen, which was likewise dimly lit and also empty, its counters littered with what looked like empty containers of Chinese food and several stacks of dirty dishes.

He frowned in fastidious distaste. Of course the kitchen in his own home had never been anything but spotless, its counters and floor gleaming under the watchful eyes of Ennis and his attentive staff, and he'd certainly never had to shift for himself beyond the odd midnight snack. But in those rare instances he'd at least always cleaned up after himself, unlike Ms. Gustafson, who apparently could add "slob" to her long list of undesirable qualities.

However, once he reached it, the bathroom wasn't as bad as the kitchen had led him to expect. Despite an unfortunate preponderance of pink in the decor, it was reasonably tidy, although cluttered with a frightening assortment of hair products and styling tools.

Under the ski mask, Erik's mouth twitched. Very soon she wouldn't have much need for those items…

The shampoo bottle sat in a plastic caddy that hung from the shower head. He took it, carefully poured a little over three-quarters of its contents into an empty plastic bottle that he'd also brought with him in the duffel bag, then lifted the pink bottle he'd carried along with him and drained it into the larger shampoo bottle. Then he placed the empty pink container back into the bag.

He lifted up the ski mask just long enough to take a whiff from the open shampoo bottle. Luckily Carrie favored a shampoo with a heavy floral scent, a scent that did a fairly good job of masking the underlying chemical smell of the product he had added. Very probably she wouldn't notice the difference until it was too late.

Excellent. He zipped the duffel bag shut, looked around quickly to make sure nothing else in the bathroom had been disturbed, then exited down the hall, moving with quiet haste. After returning to the service porch, he pulled the door shut behind him, double-checked to make sure it was locked once again, then made his way back to his car.

Once inside the vehicle, he threw back the hood of his sweatshirt, turned the key in the ignition, and pulled quietly away from the curb. It was not until he was safely cruising up the 110 Freeway back toward Pasadena that he also pulled off the ski mask and started to laugh. He could drive through the darkness without anyone seeing his face, and he could no longer tolerate the itchy knit against his skin.

It had all worked out perfectly. His only regret was not being able to hide there until morning, to see Carrie's rage and despair when she lifted her eyes to the mirror and saw what the Phantom's revenge had done to her.

Yes, Ms. Gustafson, he thought, *very soon a mirror will be your enemy as well!*

Meg grabbed me almost the moment I walked out of my comparative lit class on Wednesday afternoon. "Oh, my God, Christine!"

"What?" I stopped, catching my breath, certain from her tone that she'd just had a car accident, a fight with one of her boyfriends, or something similarly earth-shattering. "Are you okay?"

I must have sounded sufficiently worried, because she stopped for a second, then shook her head and laughed. "No, I'm fine. Didn't mean to freak you out there. Haven't you heard?"

"Heard what?"

Meg looked around, almost as if she didn't want anyone else to hear her gleeful tones. "See what happens when you avoid Facebook? You haven't heard what happened to Queen Bitch of the Universe!"

She could mean only one person. "Carrie?"

"Yeah, Ms. 'look at my perfect two-hundred-dollar highlights' Gustafson. Well, now those highlights are down the drain—literally!"

"What?"

"Oh, yeah. I heard it from Jessica Montalvo."

Jessica, I recalled dimly, lived in the upstairs flat in the house she shared with Carrie and another girl, Lisa Keneally, a pre-med student.

Meg practically glowed with unholy glee. "Well, I guess earlier this morning Carrie was getting ready for class and got in the shower first, which Jessica really hates because Carrie uses up all the hot water. So Jessica was already pissed because she was running late and Carrie was going to probably make her miss her first class. Then a little while later, after the water finally stops running and Jessica starts calculating how long it's going to be before the water heater makes enough water for her shower, all of a sudden Carrie starts screaming bloody murder."

"Screaming?" I repeated.

"Screaming," Meg said, obviously relishing the word. I was starting to wonder whether I should have told her the whole story of my abortive trip to the Long Beach Opera and Carrie's involvement with it. She was enjoying this way too much. "So Jessica starts freaking out, like should she call the police or should she go down and see what's wrong? After all, knowing Carrie, it could have been just a big spider or something, and then Jessica said she would have felt really stupid if she'd called the cops. So she goes downstairs to see what's going on, and there's Carrie, standing in the bathroom, screaming and bald, with huge chunks of hair on the floor and coming out of her hairbrush."

"Oh, my God," I said, even as I started to think, *Could Randall…?*

"Oh, yeah," Meg replied. "And okay, she wasn't totally bald, but she might as well be. Jessica said it was one of the scariest things she'd ever seen—there were still strands here and there, but everywhere else it was just white scalp."

"So what did Jessica do?"

"Well, Jessica can hold her own in a crisis. Maybe

it's because she's got five younger brothers. Anyway, she managed to get Carrie to wrap her head in a towel, found some Xanax in the medicine cabinet—it figures that Carrie would have some of that on hand—made her take some, and then called her parents. She stayed with her until Carrie's mom came to pick her up." Meg grinned. "Of course, Carrie's mom started freaking out, too, but she hung on to it long enough to look at Carrie's shampoo bottle, smell it, and then realize what had happened."

"Hair remover, right?"

Meg grinned. "You got it. Apparently Carrie's mom went really ballistic then—called the cops, had them come over and dust the whole house for fingerprints, even though there wasn't any sign of forced entry or anything like that. The only fingerprints they found were Carrie's, though, and a couple from Jessica and Lisa. Of course Carrie's mom started saying Jessica or Lisa had something to do with it, which is just stupid, because even though neither one of them were big fans of Carrie's they still had to live with her, for Chrissake. Jessica got all pissed, naturally, but I guess the cops finally managed to quiet Carrie's mom down and got her and Carrie out of there, supposedly to make a statement at the police station, but probably more to get them away from Jessica than anything else. Jessica talked to Lisa an hour or so ago, and Lisa said that while Jessica was out at class, Carrie's mom came back and got a bunch of her clothes and stuff, so I guess she'll be staying at home for a while."

"Wow," I said finally, once the flow of words had eased. Certainly I wasn't exactly sorry that someone had targeted

Carrie for such a trick, but it was horrible—and really hit Carrie where she lived. She'd always been insufferably vain.

"Exactly." Meg gave me a considering look. I knew exactly what she was going to say next. "Christine, you didn't—"

"Right," I said. "Because I really know how to pick someone's locks, break into their house in the middle of the night, and doctor their shampoo. All this singing stuff is just a front for my real life as a master criminal."

At that she had to laugh. "Okay, well, you're right. Of course you didn't do it. But you're not sorry that it happened, are you?"

"Take a wild guess!"

"Thought so." She paused for a moment, then added, "All the same, you do have an alibi, don't you?"

"Well, I was at work until eleven-thirty, if that helps any." Then I added, "And Jeff next door saw me come in a little before midnight, because he was just leaving for work." Jeff, my neighbor—our bungalows shared an adjoining wall—worked the graveyard shift at a local call center. It made for a nice neighborly arrangement, since we hardly ever saw each other unless we happened to do the ships-passing-in-the-night thing as I came home and he left.

"That's probably good enough." Her dark eyes narrowed a bit. "You'd better check with Randall, though. Yesterday I was pretty sure he was going to back his Beemer over Carrie's head. Did you hear what he did to her aria?"

Since I had been sitting next to Meg in the master

class the day before, of course I had heard. Carrie was already a little bit off, because when she'd come flouncing into class, she'd probably been expecting to see me a miserable, cowed heap. Instead I had just flashed her a bright smile, then continued chatting with Meg as if nothing had happened the evening before. She'd frowned for a moment, looking as if she were searching for something pointed and snotty to say without revealing her culpability. Her wits hadn't saved her before Dr. Green asked us all to stand for the warm-up session.

Things had soon gone from bad to worse for Carrie. When she'd gone to practice her aria with Randall, he altered the tempo, coming in a half-second late in some places, and then early in others, just as Carrie had caught up with the first series of misplaced beats. The result had been, well, a mess, with Carrie getting more and flustered and Randall smiling beatifically throughout the whole process. It ended with Carrie looking daggers at Randall while Dr. Green sat there, bemused, trying to figure out what exactly what had just happened.

"Oh, yeah, I heard," I said finally, smiling a little at the recollection. "But I'm pretty sure that was the extent of Randall's revenge." But even as I was upholding Randall's innocence, I was thinking that I'd better call him as soon as I got home. Not for the first time I wished I could afford to use my cell phone for anything besides dire emergencies, so I could call him right away.

"Well, you know him better than I do." Then she glanced at her watch. "Crap—I'm going to be late for my psych class. I'll talk to you later."

I waved as she took off, heading across the quad. Time for me to get moving, too, if I wanted to beat the traffic home. But even as I headed to my car I wondered about Randall. Could he? And if it wasn't Randall, then who?

"No, not me," Randall said with some regret. "I wish I'd thought of it, but I don't think I could have gotten past the lock-picking part."

"Hmm." I cradled the receiver between my ear and shoulder as I bent down to slide on one of the ugly but comfortable black loafers I wore to work. I'd called Randall as soon as I'd gotten home, but he hadn't answered his cell at the time. Now he was returning the call just as I was getting ready to leave for the restaurant.

"Who else hates Carrie Gustafson?" A pause. "Maybe that should have been, 'who doesn't hate Carrie Gustafson?'"

"Oh, come on, Randall. Not everyone hates her."

"Uh-huh." He sounded unconvinced.

"Okay, I'll admit that she doesn't do much to make herself popular. But she's got friends, and while she's irritating, this was a pretty drastic sort of revenge for someone who's just irritating, don't you think?"

"True. Unfortunately, you're the only person I can think of who has a real reason to do something like that. Of course you didn't do it—but I'm glad that only you, Meg, and I know about the whole Long Beach Opera fiasco."

I hoped that was everyone who knew about it. I'd sworn Meg to secrecy, of course, but Meg had a tendency to run off at the mouth in the heat of the moment. All I could do was hope she was distracted by something else and wouldn't mention it to anyone.

"Maybe you have a guardian angel."

"An avenging guardian angel?" I retorted. "Nice try."

He laughed. "Okay, that was a long shot, I admit." Then he continued, "I've got a good alibi, anyway. I was at a studio session until past midnight. Seen by tons of people, with audio evidence to back me up."

"How's that going, anyway?"

So we drifted off into talk about his budding career as a studio musician until I absolutely had to hang up and run, knowing that I would probably be late for work even as it was.

Still, the thought nagged me as I jumped into my car and sped off to work, praying that the god of street lights would at least grant me decent through-put so I'd only be five minutes late to work instead of ten. If it wasn't Randall who had put the hair remover in Carrie's shampoo, then who? More importantly, why?

And if I really had a guardian angel, as Randall had joked, it was definitely an angel of the Old Testament sort—vengeful, righteous, and dangerous. All I could hope was that, if he really did exist, there would be no more reasons for anyone else to call down his wrath.

Chapter Ten

I STILL COULDN'T SHAKE THAT FEELING of being watched, and more than once found myself pausing in odd places—the grocery store, the school parking lot, even my own front porch—and stopping to glance over my shoulder. Invariably there was no one, nothing that should have caused my disquiet, but it remained, a faint ghost of doubt that seemed to follow me wherever I went.

Otherwise, the days slipped by, a blur of classes, work, and far too infrequent dates with Randall. He managed to keep a good face on the situation, even joking that two people with schedules as crazy as ours had no right to be seeing one another, but we both kept at it, unable to deny the attraction. Better to have a few stolen hours together here and there than nothing at all.

Carrie Gustafson had withdrawn from classes for the rest of the semester, and her house mate Jessica seemed fairly sure she wouldn't be back for the rest of the year.

"It's kind of awful," she said one day, only a few days

before Thanksgiving. She and Meg and I had managed to get together at lunch for a sandwich and some Starbucks.

I sipped at my guilty pleasure, a chai latte, and wrapped my hands around the cup for warmth. Whoever said California didn't have any seasons had obviously never lived here. Most of November had been chilly and damp, one storm after another pushing in off the Pacific.

Meg took a sip of her own coffee. She prided herself on drinking only the real thing—no frou-frou cappuccinos or mocha lattes for her. Today it was a double shot of espresso. "So she really moved out?"

"Oh, yeah." Jessica shook her head. Like Meg, she was darkly pretty, an exotic blend of Spanish blood and Native American genes. "Thank God her parents were nice enough to pay her part of the rent through the end of the year or we would really have been stuck. There's no way we could have found someone to rent the bottom flat so close to the end of the semester."

Regular classes ended the week after Thanksgiving, and I had to say I was looking forward to the Christmas break. Not the holiday so much—that had been pretty bleak the last few years—but at least the prospect of having some time off was exciting.

"Her hair just isn't growing back very well," Jessica continued. "You know how those hair removers advertise that the new hair will grow in sparser and lighter? Well, that's exactly what's happening to Carrie's head."

Both Meg and I flinched, and I put up a protective hand to my own hair. As much as the unruly curls might drive me crazy from time to time—especially now, when straight, sleek hair was the style of choice—the thought of it being completely gone made me appreciate it all the more. At least it was long and thick and healthy.

"So now they're on to Rogaine. Carrie might be back next semester, but I wouldn't count on it. Her parents told Lisa and me to go ahead and rent out the bottom flat."

Meg turned to me, the gleam in her eyes telling me she had just had what she considered a brilliant idea. "Why don't you rent out the bottom flat, Christine?"

I gave her a sour look even as Jessica said, "Hey, that's a great idea!"

"What's it going for?" I asked in quelling tones.

"Eight-fifty."

Ouch. My own rent in Pasadena was only six hundred. "Too rich for my blood," I said, taking a sip from my latte.

"Well, you could always get another roommate," Meg said. "Carrie had it to herself because no one could stand to live with her in such close quarters."

"It would make more sense for you to live closer to campus," Jessica added.

"And you'd be closer to Randall," Meg chimed in.

I put up my hands in mock defense. "Was this premeditated?" I wouldn't put it past Meg to get wind of the opening in Jessica's house and arrange for us all to have lunch together.

"No," they both said simultaneously, and then started to laugh.

"Well, as much as I'd like the two of you to arrange everything for me so neatly, I really like it where I am. Besides, I'd have to get another job if I moved down here."

Despite its inconveniences, Pasadena was safe, Pasadena was *home*—I'd lived there all my life and didn't feel like uprooting myself in the middle of my senior year, even though there was a pretty good chance I'd be going on to graduate school at USC.

"Well, Christine, as much as George loves you, I'm pretty sure *L'Opera* would survive if you left." Meg gave me a considering look. "But I can see you've got that so-attractive stubborn-mule look going right now, so I'll shut up."

"Thank you." I took a bite of my sandwich. "I hope you're not offended, Jess."

"No prob. I've got three people interested in it—I just thought I'd give you the first shot in case you wanted to move." She drained the last of her frappuccino and said, "Well, gotta run. Dr. Leinert has been on the rampage lately—if I'm late I might get my head nailed to the wall. See ya."

Meg and I both waved, then settled back in to finish the rest of our lunch, since our next class didn't start until two.

"So what's the deal with you, anyway?" Meg asked.

I blinked. "What?"

"I thought you'd jump at the chance to dump that crappy commute—and be closer to Randall. Or is that not working out?"

"It's 'working out' as much as it can right now. I work nights, he's working more and more nights with all this studio stuff he's doing—plus squeezing in a little something called a master's thesis on the side."

Not for the first time, I found myself wondering exactly how Randall viewed our relationship. I assumed he considered me his girlfriend, for lack of a better word, but we hadn't made it much past the dinner-and-a-movie stage, aside from a couple of fairly intense make-out sessions on his couch. We'd both emerged from them strangely satisfied yet hungering for more, but I still wasn't ready to go on from there. My lack of experience frustrated Randall, I knew, and I wasn't sure what to do about it. As much as I enjoyed our physical contact and the time we spent together, I couldn't help but be nagged by a sense that I should be feeling more. Maybe it was just me. I'd never been in love before—what exactly was it supposed to feel like, anyway?

Meg sat for a moment, watching me carefully. Sometimes one could forget the sharp intelligence she hid behind the run-on chatter and trendy clothes, but it was always there. She didn't miss much. "Okay, you like Randall a lot, but you're not really sure he's Mr. Wonderful. Something like that?"

"Maybe." I sipped my latte, then said, "Actually, I'm pretty sure he's Mr. Wonderful. I'm just not sure if I'm Ms. Wonderful."

"Well…" She gave a very Latin shrug. "There's no law against just having fun. It's not as if you have much basis of comparison, right?"

"Absolutely none." I laughed. "Pretty pathetic, huh?"

She smiled at that. "I've seen worse." Then she sobered a little and said, "There's something else, though. Something's bothering you."

I tried to look nonchalant. "What do you mean?"

"I don't know. You just seem…jumpy. Always looking over your shoulder."

Caught, I said, choosing my words with care, "I don't know, Meg. It's just kind of a feeling, an uneasiness. Like someone is watching me, but when I turn around, there's no one there." I shivered a little and pulled my jacket closer around me. "I'm probably just getting paranoid in my old age."

She frowned. "I don't know. You never struck me as the paranoid type. If anything, I'd say you were too trusting."

I would have said the same thing about myself a few months ago. I said, picking my way through the words as if I were negotiating a mine field, "This whole thing with Carrie—"

"Do you know something?" she asked, leaning forward eagerly.

"That's the whole point! I don't know anything. But I can't help feeling as if somehow it was connected with me. Everyone agrees that Carrie was an annoying bitch, but no one had any real reason to do something that horrible to her. No one except me, that is."

"But you didn't do it."

"But I didn't do it. Exactly. So what if someone decided to enact the revenge I wouldn't take myself?"

She slumped back in her seat, absently biting her lower lip. "Maybe that's true. But who?"

"How would I know? I don't know many people who can break into an occupied house, mess around in a bathroom, and then slip back out without being caught or leaving any sign of forced entry, do you?"

"Not too many, no."

"So there we are." I shook my head. "Maybe I'm just being egocentric. It probably doesn't have anything to do with me at all. But it just keeps bothering me, nibbling at the back of my mind." I shut my eyes for a moment, thinking. "And then there was that guy at the autumn recital—"

"What guy?" She sat up then and leaned her elbows on the table, fixing me with a stern gaze. "You didn't say anything to me about any guy at the recital."

"Because it was so stupid, Meg!" Frustrated, I pushed the remains of my sandwich away and met her stare. "There was this guy at the back of the audience at the recital, you know, standing in the back with everyone else who was there to tape their kid's performance. But he wasn't taping anyone. He was just standing there, waiting. Like he was waiting for me, since I was on last."

Meg sat very still, watching me. She obviously could tell there was more.

"If that had been the first time I'd seen him, maybe it wouldn't have been such a big deal. But I literally bumped into him a week or so before as I was leaving class. He was reading the poster for the recital, for Chrissake!" I shook my head. "I thought it was sort of weird at the time, because he looked out of place, but I didn't think much about it until later, at the recital, when I saw him again."

Meg frowned. "What did he look like?"

"God, I don't re—" I began, and then, catching Meg's glare, amended what I had been about to say. The truth was, I did remember, or could if I tried. "Okay, probably late thirties or early forties. Brown hair. He was wearing sunglasses the first time I saw him, and it was too dark in the recital hall for me to tell then what color his eyes were. Not tall or short. Nice build—he looked like he might work out. And fairly nice-looking. Not drop-dead or anything. But—" I paused.

"But you wouldn't kick him out of bed for eating crackers," she said, and at that I had to smile.

"Something like that."

"Well, as stalkers go, you could do worse. At least he's not a gargoyle."

I gave her a pained look. "Meg, that's not even remotely funny."

"Sorry." She actually did look somewhat contrite.

"Besides, he could be anybody. He didn't look old enough to be a parent, but he could be a brother or uncle, or a grad student from another school...who knows? I just thought that it was a strange coincidence."

Tapping a manicured fingernail on the table top, Meg was quiet for a moment, thinking. "It's not much," she admitted, "but I'm glad you told me. I'll keep an eye out, too." Then she looked past my shoulder, smiled and waved, and said, "Here's Randall. Probably time for me to duck out."

"You don't have to go—"

"No, it's cool." She grinned. "Got to keep watching for your mysterious stalker. And if he's as cute as he sounds, maybe I'll just ask him out!"

She bounced away from the table before I could say anything in protest. I sat there, shaking my head, even as Randall came around the table and pulled out the chair Meg had just vacated.

"You look like a gaffed fish," he said amiably. "Meg up to her usual tricks?"

"You have no idea," I replied. Just when I thought she couldn't shock me anymore—

"I'm glad I found you," he continued. "I wanted to ask you something."

Immediately I sat up a little straighter. His tone was serious, his hazel eyes intent.

"Don't look so worried." He grinned. "I just wanted to see if you would come with me to my family's Thanksgiving dinner."

That came out of nowhere. For over a week we had danced around the holiday, never really mentioning it. I'd been wondering whether he was going to ask me to come over, or at least to go out for the evening, but nothing. I had tried to convince myself that it really didn't matter, that perhaps his family wasn't open to having strangers at their family dinner, that he was obligated to spend the holiday with them even if he'd rather spend it with me—anything except what I feared most, that I just wasn't important enough to him for us to be together over the holiday.

Still, I wasn't going to jump on his invitation like a starved dog on a bone. "Well…"

"Oh, come on," he said. "I promise we don't bite. Most of us, anyway. I can't vouch for my nephew. He just turned three, and he's definitely the spawn of Satan, even though he does look just like my oldest brother."

"Wow, that sounds really inviting!" But even as I made the protest I couldn't help smiling.

"I'll make my brother tie him up for the night. And I promise that we won't be relegated to the kiddie table." He grinned back at me, and I couldn't help but be struck by how good-looking he really was, how open and winning his smile. "What, would you rather sit home with a Lean Cuisine? Or do you really splurge on Thanksgiving and get yourself a Marie Callender's frozen dinner?"

If he only knew how close to the mark he was. "Okay, you win. As long as you promise that the demon spawn really will be tied up."

"I'll do my best. I'm not sure my mother has fully recovered from the mashed-potato incident last year, so I'm sure she'll back me up."

"Mashed-potato incident?"

"Yeah—Brian thought he'd discovered a new form of stucco and was eager to try it out on the dining room walls." Randall paused and took in my clothes with a worried look. "You'd better wear something washable."

"I think I can manage that." Frankly, if it had to be dry-cleaned, I couldn't afford to own it.

"Great. I'll pick you up at three."

"I could just meet you there—"

"Absolutely not." Although he still smiled, I could tell he was serious. "You think I'm going to put you through the whole meeting the parents thing without doing it properly? 'Meet me there'—I'd never hear the end of it from my mother, even if my slightly misplaced sense of chivalry would let me get away with it in the first place."

"Well, okay. Just to keep your mother off your back." I kept my tone light, but I was suddenly very glad he'd offered to pick me up. All other considerations aside, at least I wouldn't have to worry about my car breaking down on me on Thanksgiving.

He smiled. Then he leaned over the table and kissed me quickly on the cheek. "It'll be fun. I promise."

"I'll hold you to that," I replied, and we went on to chat about a few other things, the abnormal psych paper that was giving me so much trouble, the unusually damp weather, the exciting news that he had been invited to play with the studio orchestra for a new medium-budget action film, anything but the concerns I had just discussed with Meg. Somehow I knew that Randall would not react well—to put it mildly—to the news that I might have a stalker, and again I tried to tell myself it was nothing. Besides, Meg had said she'd keep an eye out for me, and I believed her. If nothing else, I was sure she was dying to catch a glimpse of the mysterious stranger for herself.

Soon we both had to leave the café to get to our respective classes on time, and I couldn't help but take a quick glance over my shoulder as I left. The only person I recognized was Randall, who caught my gaze and who waved and smiled in reply. I smiled back, if a little hesitantly. Good thing he didn't know that it wasn't he for whom I'd been looking.

Restless as a wind-driven shadow, Erik drifted through the darkened hallways of his home, his night-sharp eyes not needing the unnecessary illumination of electricity. The staff had long since retired, but he, as had been his custom for many years, remained wakeful through the

long watches of the night, shunning the harsh day and its
unforgiving light.

Drawn there without realizing until he stood beside
the door, he paused outside the chamber that had been
prepared for Christine's arrival. *Three days*, he thought,
and laid his unmasked cheek against the cool, smooth
mahogany of the door frame. Three days until she slept in
the canopied bed inside, until she breathed the same air
as he, until she was his.

Every part of the plan had been gone over in obsessive
detail, so much so that even Jerome had begun to lose
patience. Usually so controlled, he'd finally lost his temper and snapped, "You pay me a lot of money to handle
this stuff so you don't have to. So let me handle it."

Angry as he had been, Erik had had to admit that
Jerome was right. Jerome had been Special Ops and FBI
before he'd ever hung out his shingle as a private investigator; he knew whom to contact, how to cover his tracks,
which loopholes to plug. No, the plan was perfect, as far
as he could tell. It was the waiting that was wearing him
down, since once they had finalized the plan there was
no altering it at the last minute. No amount of money in
the world could make the days pass any faster than they
already were, and so Erik was left to wait, his temper growing shorter and shorter as the final days approached.

He'd watched the digital file of Christine's recital
appearance over and over again until he had every
nuance memorized, every gesture, every slightest movement, down to the one curl that had escaped the ribbon
which bound her luxuriant hair just at the moment she

sang *"c'est la fille d'un roi"* —and truly she had looked like a princess, even in her simple black dress. And she had sounded like an angel.

Her voice over the listening equipment had been his only other connection to her, the simple conversations with Randall and Meg and a few other friends from school his only means of knowing her. It was with some spite he saw that many of her talks with Randall consisted of rescheduling dates, since both of their schedules seemed to grow increasingly more hectic. All the better.

Even this last, this family Thanksgiving of Randall's that she had discussed with Meg earlier in the evening, did not give him much cause for worry. So he wanted to take her home to meet his parents. How sweet. He hoped they would get an eyeful of her that evening, because after that they would never see her again. After that, she would be truly lost to the world, lost to everyone.

Except Erik.

Chapter Eleven

RANDALL'S PARENTS LIVED IN LARCHMONT VILLAGE, a lovely area of vintage homes north and west of downtown Los Angeles. As we drove away from the 101 Freeway along Beverly Boulevard, a gorgeous parade of houses passed by outside the car window—lovingly restored Craftsmans, oversize English cottages, stately Spanish-style mansions. We turned right just past Larchmont Boulevard itself and then parked in front of a stunning Spanish hacienda, complete with turret in front and a porte-cochère over the driveway.

I gave Randall an anxious look.

He smiled, reaching over and giving my hand a reassuring squeeze. "It's okay. They're all going to love you."

That may have been true, but at the moment I was feeling more than a little intimidated by the neighborhood and the house in particular. I tried to remind myself that at least the home had been in the family for years and years and hadn't been purchased during the last housing boom.

How much was the place probably worth, even now with housing prices deflated? One million? Two?

I took a deep breath. "All right. Let's do this."

At that he gave me a quick glance. "You sound like someone about to jump out of an airplane."

"Then let's go before I ask the pilot to turn the plane around."

That got a laugh out of him, as I had hoped it would, and we got out of the car and walked up to the house. The front door was unlocked, and Randall led me into a long hall that opened onto a large living room on one side and an equally large dining room on the other. The hacienda theme was carried throughout the interior architecture, as far as I could see; the walls were painted white, set off by dark exposed beams along the ceilings, with heavy rustic antique furniture and gorgeous rugs on the hardwood floors. I could hear the lively sound of conversation coming from the end of the hall, where a combination family room/kitchen area seemed to be located.

"We're here!" Randall called out, as I followed him into the family room.

My first confused impression was of a large group of attractive people, all apparently talking at once. Then the hubbub died down a bit as they turned to greet us, and a pretty blonde woman with Randall's laughing hazel eyes stepped forward.

"Mom," he said, and the pride was evident in his tone, "this is Christine."

I stepped forward, hoping I didn't look as awkward as I felt, and that no one would notice how beat-up my black ankle boots really were under the layer of shoe polish I'd carefully coated them with earlier that morning. I started to extend my hand for a polite shake but instead was clasped to her in a quick hug. Taken off-guard, I stumbled a bit, but then she released me, smiling at the two of us.

"So glad to meet you finally!" she said. "I'm Denise. There are quite a lot of us, but don't worry—there won't be a quiz at the end of the evening."

"'Hey you' is always fine," added the tall gray-haired man standing just behind her. "I'm John Cagney." He extended a hand and I took it, glad that he seemed to regard a hand shake as a perfectly acceptable form of greeting.

Then it was on to the other people standing in the family room and the kitchen, Randall's older brothers and sister and their respective spouses. I knew I wouldn't be able to keep them all straight, but I did manage to remember that his oldest brother was Colin and his sister, Theresa. They all seemed to be very pleasant people, attractive, well-dressed, relaxed.

From somewhere Randall produced a glass of wine and handed it to me. I accepted it gratefully.

"So Randall tells me you're majoring in voice?" his mother inquired.

"Yes…Denise." I'd been about to call her "Mrs. Cagney," but she'd introduced herself by her first name, so I assumed that was how she wanted to be addressed. "I'm trying to decide whether to go on to graduate school or just get out there and go for it."

She smiled. "From what Randall tells us, you should take the opera world by storm."

I hoped my blush wasn't too apparent. "Randall might be a little biased."

"No, I'm not," he protested. "Even her voice teacher is bowled over by her. She just needs to get out and be heard."

"Anyway," I said, "having a masters would be a good idea, because then I could teach at the college level if the whole opera thing doesn't work out."

"Not to pontificate," Randall's father said, joining in, "but furthering your education is almost always a good thing. Don't opera singers have a fairly long professional life compared to most performers?"

"Yes," I replied. It was true—many classically trained singers performed well into their fifties and even their sixties. It was often said that the classical voice didn't truly mature until a singer's late thirties or early forties. Against that sort of time frame, another two years spent in graduate school would not exactly jeopardize my professional career. "I think Randall's just anxious to see my name up in lights."

"Well, there's more chance of that with you than with me," he said, his tone deliberately light.

I could see Randall's parents share a significant look; this was obviously a somewhat sore point in their household. He'd told me his parents had been less than thrilled when he had switched from the concert performance track to USC's fledgling accompanist program, one of the first in the country. Best to know one's own limitations, he'd said, because as good as he was, he knew he wasn't concert pianist material. He was, however, a skillful and intuitive accompanist and had decided it was wiser to focus on his strengths and try to make a living for himself doing something for which he was much better suited.

I could sympathize, since my mother had faced her own set of challenges when she decided to abandon her own rewarding career as a pianist to marry my father. They had met at USC—one of the reasons I had decided to attend the school, since I was eligible for special scholarships as the daughter of two alumni. Apparently it had been love at first sight, and they'd married within six months of graduation. Her family had been furious, though, and apparently the rift the marriage caused was so deep that my mother dropped all contact with them. I was never sure whether they even knew I had been born.

At any rate, I could never understand what they found so objectionable about my father. True, he was nothing terribly glamorous, but I always found his job as a systems engineer at the Jet Propulsion Labs to be fascinating, especially when he'd come home and turn on the television news and point to the hardware for the lab's latest space venture. "See that, Christine?" he'd ask. "Your daddy helped build that satellite." Or that deep-space probe, or rover, or whatever the flavor of the moment was. Certainly he'd earned enough for us to be comfortable without being rich, while my mother taught piano part-time so she could be home with me. It had been a safe, secure, nurturing environment—all the way up to that horrible New Year's Eve when my life had changed forever.

Randall's mother looked a little strained around the mouth, but, to do her credit, she forbore from making any pointed comments. "Well, it does sound very exciting. I'm not sure where Randall gets it from—neither his father nor I are at all musical. Were your parents musicians?"

Were. She had used the past tense, so I knew Randall had told her I had lost my parents, and I hoped there wouldn't be any awkward questions in that regard at least. It was always a conversation-killer when someone asked me politely what my parents did and I had to reply that they were no longer alive.

Luckily I was saved from any more discussion on the topic by a series of screams that erupted from beyond the French doors which led out to the backyard.

"Well, that's a record," Randall's brother Colin said, setting his wine glass down on the kitchen counter and heading out to discover the cause of the commotion. "I think they made it an entire half-hour this time before somebody got scalped."

Randall's sister and her husband followed after him, apparently to provide additional backup if necessary. Randall had told me that his sister had four-year-old twins who were usually quite well-behaved. But throw Colin's son Brian into the mix, and it was only a matter of time before the combination of the three provided the pre-school analog to TNT.

In the general hubbub that followed, I was able to retreat somewhat out of the way to a couch off to one side of the family room and watch as the twins were led off to an upstairs bedroom where they could be pacified with a DVD, while Brian was given a stern lecture on the evils of trying to get his cousins to eat dirt. As an only child, I hadn't been around small children very much, and I was a little amazed by the amount of disruption such small beings could create.

With things brought somewhat back to normal—with the exception of Brian's continuing whine in the background—the conversation picked up again, but I was able to take my favored role of observer, since Randall's siblings were talking about all the minutiae of child-rearing—discipline, the problem of the right preschool, and God knows what else. Randall himself took a seat next to me on the family room couch and was mostly quiet except for a few pointed remarks here and there about his nephews and niece, remarks that his brothers and sister mostly ignored.

I was glad to see that it wasn't long before dinner was ready, and Randall's mother commanded everyone to vacate the family room so she could get everything out of the kitchen without tripping over someone. My own feeble offer to help was met with a polite demurral, and so Randall and I went to take our places at the dining room table, which was large enough to accommodate all ten of us adults with room to spare. In the corner of the dining room a small table had been set up with plastic cutlery and paper plates for the children—Randall's dreaded "kiddie table." Of course there hadn't been any such thing at my own family's holiday gatherings; my father had been an only child as well, so it had always been my parents, my grandmother, and myself, since my paternal grandfather had passed away before I was even born.

Randall has once described his mother to me as "Martha Stewart without the mean," and once I saw the spread she laid out for us, I could see why. The table itself had a festive centerpiece of warm autumnal flowers and gorgeous place settings of fine china, sterling flatware, and crystal wine glasses, while the food seemed to be of an infinite and dizzying variety—the turkey of course had the place of honor, but there was also smoked salmon and both mashed and roasted potatoes, homemade spiced cranberry sauce and two kinds of dressing, salad, and fresh-baked breads and rolls. Certainly I had never seen anything like it outside the pages of a magazine, but then I remembered that Denise was a food and entertaining writer for a variety of magazines, so I supposed for her this sort of spread was only normal.

Food is a great icebreaker. Whatever awkwardness I had felt at the beginning of my visit was soon forgotten, as we all talked of normal things, film and current events and everyone's jobs or school, all the while helping ourselves to the truly prodigious mountain of food Randall's mother had provided. The flow of conversation was broken up once or twice by a commotion at the children's table, but the problems were quickly smoothed over—even the kids seemed more interested in shoveling down Thanksgiving dinner than in torturing one another.

Randall had been right. I felt happy, welcome; there were no awkward questions, no probing remarks. For the first time in I didn't even know how long I had an overwhelming sense of belonging, of content. I could have been a part of his family all along. And from the gratified looks Randall gave both me and the rest of his family, I knew he was feeling the same way.

Before I knew it, however, the evening was over, all of us so torpid with food that Randall and I could barely muster the energy it took to drag ourselves out the front door. The hug Denise gave me in farewell was much more welcome than the one she had given me in greeting. It seemed she was very pleased with me, both for Randall's sake and for my own, and I was inwardly relieved that I had made such a good impression on her.

The drive back to Pasadena was quiet, both Randall and I so full that even speech was an effort. He laid his right hand on mine for most of the trip, though, as he navigated the twisting Pasadena Freeway up through the arroyos and I listened to the soft melodies of a string quartet on the car radio. I felt at peace, drifting with the music and the slight lightheadedness caused by my last glass of wine, savoring the pressure of his hand on mine.

My street in Pasadena was quiet, the homes sleeping under a dreamy cloud-flecked night sky barely illuminated by a fingernail moon. We paused on the porch as I unlocked the front door and opened it, letting out a narrow bar of golden light from the lamp I had left on in the front room.

"I had a wonderful time," I said, knowing that he was about to kiss me

"So did I," he replied, and brought his mouth to mine, warm and welcome.

We stood like that for a long moment, until at last I broke away, still feeling the pressure of his lips.

"It's late," I said, knowing even then the words were inadequate.

"I know." He reached out, traced the curve of my lower lip with his forefinger, then said, "I'll call you tomorrow."

I smiled, then gave him a second kiss, this time not as lingering but just as intense. "Good night."

And with that I slid in through the open door, into the familiar shabbiness of my living room. The afterglow was still with me as I deposited my purse on the drop-leaf table and went on to wash my face and climb into a ratty but comfortable USC jersey and yoga pants, my usual sleeping attire during the cold months. Tired and full as I was, just a few moments passed before I dropped into dreamless sleep…only to be wakened either a few seconds or an eternity later by a pair of dark forms that seemed to coalesce from the blackness to place implacable hands on my throat and mouth. I bucked up in my bed, at first not sure whether I was experiencing a very realistic nightmare, and then there was a sudden sharp pain as a needle pricked my arm, and I fell again into blackness, swirling down into nothingness.

There was so much that could have gone wrong, even though he and Jerome had tried to plan for every contingency. So many things that could have disrupted his careful plots, but, in the end, all his worries were for naught. Even Jerome said it had been absolutely textbook.

As much as Erik had wanted to be the one to take Christine from her bed, he knew that it was utter folly to risk himself in that way, and so had allowed the task to be carried out by the men Jerome had hired, men who had been paid extremely well to execute the kidnapping and then disappear afterward.

They had waited until a little after two in the morning, a time when Christine's neighbor had long since departed for his graveyard shift and the rest of the street slept, unaware of the crime taking place in the shabby little bungalow at number 572. An unexpected piece of good luck had come their way when the two girls who lived next to Christine on the other side of her home had packed up late Wednesday night and departed for destinations unknown. Really, it would have required men with less expertise than those he had hired to pull into the alley behind her bungalow with their phony cable television van, pick the lock on her back door, then drug her and disappear out that same door, all in less than two minutes. For all his and Jerome's precautions, there were no watching eyes to record what had happened to Christine Daly.

Erik did not know the kidnappers' names. "The less you know, the better," Jerome had said, and Erik knew he was right. Just as he knew very little about the drug they'd administered to Christine, save that it would knock her out immediately and keep her out for some hours, during which time she would gradually slip into normal sleep.

"No real side effects," Jerome replied in answer to Erik's anxious questions. "She might feel a little pukey in the morning—some people do—but she'll be up and walking around in no time."

The ersatz cable van had come nowhere near Erik's home. Jerome met the kidnappers at a deserted construction site, had them transfer her to the back seat of his anonymous rented compact car, paid them the balance of their fees in cash, and then drove her himself on a winding route through Pasadena before finally arriving with her a little after three in the morning.

Now she lay in her elegant canopied bed, an unexpected fairy-tale princess with her pale face and faded red and gold USC jersey. He stood there in the half-darkness, watching as the soft golden light from her bedside lamp gently illumined her face. It would be easy, so easy to reach out and touch her, to lay his lips against the curve of her delicate cheek. Lost in the darkness of her drugged sleep, she would never know.

With a low moan he turned, the ache of his desire for her like a cramping pain through his body. Instead, he placed on the night stand his first gift to her, a bouquet of white roses, wondering if she would notice that amongst all the white, one red rose bloomed—one red rose for the love he hoped would prove triumphant...

Chapter Twelve

In my dreams I was drowning, struggling through a black sea to a dim shore that seemed to recede even as I reached out toward it. The waves broke over my head, and I slipped down, gasping, choking...

With a cough, I rolled over in bed and opened my eyes. For a few seconds I stared at the canopy of rose-hued silk without really focusing on it, and then I blinked and reopened my eyes. At first I thought this was just a bizarre continuation of my dream, but it looked real enough. Slowly I pushed myself up, groggy and just the slightest bit nauseated. I had to take several deep breaths before I felt sufficiently recovered to look around me.

I was lying in a huge four-poster bed, its canopy draped with a lush rose-colored material with the sheen and luster of silk. The room in which the bed was situated was equally huge; you could have put my entire bungalow in there with room to spare. Directly opposite the bed were three tall mullioned window that let in the soft light of a cloudy morning. Each window was hung with elegant brocade drapes in soft tones of rose, blue, and cream, shades echoed in the enormous Persian rug that covered the entire floor, with only the faintest hint of hardwood appearing at each of its edges.

Memory started to return—the dark figures in my room last night, the sting of a needle. I found the tender spot on my upper left arm with the index finger of my right hand. Yes, it was real, as was the elegant room around me.

I was immeasurably relieved to find that I still had on the shabby USC jersey and yoga pants I'd worn to bed the night before. As far as I could tell, the only ill effects I'd suffered from the kidnapping were the tenderness of my arm and a faint lingering nausea—no doubt the lingering remnants of whatever drug they had given me. And although I wasn't exactly sure what to look for, I was fairly sure that I had not been touched or molested in any way. That, apparently, had not been the motive.

With a faint moan I lowered myself from the bed—it was much higher than the narrow daybed I slept on at home—and stood, taking stock of my surroundings. The far wall to my left had been painted with an exquisite mural of what looked like an enchanted countryside of gently rolling hills, fields of flowers, and an Italian villa in the distance, all under a dreamy sky worked with billowy clouds that were faintly touched with pink. A beautifully carved table flanked by a pair of rose-upholstered chairs stood against the mural. On the table was an elegant gold-leafed lamp and one of those expensive little Bose radios.

From it I could faintly hear the sound of a violin concerto.

Past the table an arched doorway opened into another room; I made my way over to it and peered inside. It was a charming little sitting room, outfitted with a comfortable-looking armchair and matching footstool, and several tall carved bookcases filled with books. In here was another mullioned window.

Feeling bolder now, I stepped up to the window and looked out. Any thoughts I might have had of picking up the footstool or some other easily hefted piece of furniture and using it to break the glass vanished immediately. The window was fitted with narrow bars that didn't do much to block the view but were obviously very capable of keeping me trapped in here. And as far as I could tell, breaking the glass just so I could scream for help probably wouldn't do me any good, either.

The window overlooked a marble-paved loggia edged with a carved stone balustrade. To one side a set of wide, shallow steps led down to a formal rose garden, with some late blooms still lifting their heads to the half-hearted November light. After the rose garden came wide green lawns that stretched as far as I could see to either side until they were finally met with a tall edging of pine trees and Italian cypress. To my left a smaller path ended somewhere near a reflecting pool, around which weeping willows trailed their narrow branches down to the water. Directly ahead but at least several hundred yards away was some sort of gazebo or summerhouse in gray stone, almost hidden in a stand of gray-barked trees that lifted their elegant bare arms to the half-clouded sky.

It should have been a beautiful scene, but all I could do was look at it in despair. This place—whatever and wherever it was—seemed so isolated, so closed in on itself. I saw no evidence of any nearby streets or neighbors, no one who could hear my cries for help even if I did break the windows.

As I reentered the main bedroom area, I noticed for the first time the bouquet of white roses that stood on one of the carved marble-topped night stands. Moving closer, I reached out to touch one velvety petal. What sort of kidnapper would leave a vase full of roses for his victim? There had to be at least three dozen of them in the crystal urn-shaped vase, some still tightly shut, a few just beginning to open. Almost hidden amongst the sea of white buds and green accent leaves was one dark red rose, opening its brave petals like a crimson kiss.

Wondering, I stood looking at it for a long moment. I knew that red roses signified true love, while white roses could indicate reverence or humility, or love that still lay sleeping. Was this offering a message? Who could have possibly taken such desperate measures, just to leave me a bouquet of roses that stirred only questions?

Swallowing hard, trying to ignore the pounding of my heart in my breast, I looked past the roses to see another arched opening in the wall. I walked through and saw that I was in a little antechamber decorated only with a gilt mirror and matching long-legged table, on which stood a delicate orchid in a beautifully painted oriental pot. More importantly, however, I saw that opposite the mirror was a heavy wooden door with carved panels.

I pounced on the handle and tried to turn it. Locked, of course. Then I noticed that it was shut with a very businesslike deadbolt, the kind that needs a key on either side to lock it.

At last I let the panic and anger I had kept carefully in check over the past few minutes burst out, and I pounded on the door, not caring that my fists soon ached from the punishment of beating on the unyielding surface.

"Hey!" I screamed, facing the door, wondering if my unknown captor stood outside the door, listening to me carry on. The thought fueled my rage even further. "You can't do this! This is America, for Chrissake!"

Silence, of course. What had I been expecting—for someone to open the door immediately, issue an apology, and call me a cab?

"Listen, you bastards! You're committing a felony!"

Again the unanswering quiet. If anyone was listening, apparently the fact that they had committed a federal offense was not a source of huge worry.

Finally I stopped pounding on the door. My fists hurt and so did my throat. It was quite obvious that I could stand here and scream all day, and no one would heed my cries. Had I been locked in here and then abandoned?

Defeated for the moment, I turned back into the bedroom and went on to open a door on the other side of the room, a door that opened into a private bathroom.

"Bathroom," however, seemed too prosaic a word to apply to the opulent chamber which greeted me, a chamber that bore about as much resemblance to the cramped cubicle at my bungalow as a Rolls Royce did to a Yugo. It was easily the size of my living room at home, the walls, floors, and counters covered with a soft rosy marble with faint cream veining. Soft cream-colored rugs were placed strategically beside the sunken bathtub and the separate shower stall; a mirrored tray on the counter held a bottle of Évian water and a crystal glass. From the back of the door hung a plush-looking robe in a deep sapphire blue.

Despite myself, I couldn't help letting out a nervous little laugh. *Help, I'm being held captive at the Ritz-Carlton!* I thought, moving to open the bottle of Évian. I figured it was safe, since the bottle was still sealed, and besides, I was thirsty, my voice raw from shouting. Taking a few much-needed sips of water, I looked around again.

Along the ledge that ran the length of the bath was a series of potted ferns, while just above them was another window, this one of frosted glass. I could make out the shadow of more bars beyond the window—no escape that way, either. At the foot of the bath were several jars of expensive-looking bath salts and a cube of lavender-scented soap in a porcelain dish. I found all this preparation ironic, since I had never been much of a bath person. I never could see the point of soaking for hours and hours the way some women apparently did, but that might have been because I had just never had time for that kind of luxury.

I set down the crystal water glass and opened one door of the enormous Venetian glass medicine cabinet that hung over the sink. Inside were a toothbrush still in its wrapping, a new box of toothpaste, a new package of dental floss, a few other personal-care items, and apparently the full line of facial products from an extremely expensive designer. The rest of the cabinet was empty—apparently my captor wasn't about to trust me with any analgesics or other over-the-counter remedies. Curious, I opened the drawer on one side of the sink and found an assortment of new cosmetics, still in their original packaging, all from the same designer brand. Someone had obviously gone to a lot of trouble and expense to make sure I was provided for while I was here—never mind that I usually ran out the door with only mascara and lip gloss for makeup, unless I was going to work.

At the far side of the bathroom was another door. I put my hand on the knob, thinking it must be locked—what else could there be in the elegant suite that comprised my prison? But instead the doorknob turned easily, opening into the biggest walk-in closet I had ever seen. There was a light switch next to the door, and I flicked it on, bringing to life a delicate crystal chandelier that hung from the ceiling in the center of the closet.

I say "closet," but it was really a small room, complete with a compact rose-upholstered chaise lounge in the center—for reclining upon while trying to decide what to wear, I presumed. It looked like something out of a magazine, one of those glossy spreads where you were given a guided tour of the wardrobes of some of the world's richest and most spoiled women. At that moment I had to count myself among their ranks, because the room was full of clothes, all carefully organized according to color and type; one wall was made up entirely of shoes, each pair placed in its own little cedar cubbyhole. At random I pulled a chic bouclé jacket from one rack, peering inside at the label. I didn't know much about clothes—with my budget, the most designer I usually got was the clearance rack at the local discount store—but even I recognized the name of Chanel. A little awed, I hung the jacket back in its place, then looked around me again.

Placed beneath the rack that held jackets, blouses, and other shorter items was a pretty little dresser that matched the other furniture in the bedroom. I assumed it held lingerie or sweaters, items that needed to be folded. But when I pulled out the drawer, it was all I could do to keep from gasping out loud. Inside was a black velvet inset with carefully molded compartments, and against the velvet glittered a constellation of jewels.

I knew even less about gems than I knew about clothes, but I knew enough to recognize emeralds, sapphires, rubies…all set with diamonds, in improbably intricate necklaces and earrings and rings, all so glorious that at first I thought they couldn't possibly be real. I didn't want them to be real. If they were, how many hundreds of thousands—or even millions—of dollars glimmered up at me from that drawer? What kind of resources could my captor have, to conjure all this glory just for me?

My hands were shaking. I closed the drawer carefully, fearful of the treasures within. It was too much. Trying to stay calm, I told myself that at least immediate dismemberment or worse didn't seem to be on the agenda; I couldn't imagine the worst psychopath furnishing a luxurious suite with such riches if the victim weren't going to be around to enjoy them for a while. Whatever was planned for me, death didn't seem to be it, at least for now.

What I really wanted was a hot shower and a change of clothes, and since both amenities had been prepared so amply for me, I decided to go ahead and take care of myself. After a quick check of the bathroom for any obvious cameras—feeling foolish, I couldn't find any—I turned on the water and stepped into the luxury of a shower where the water pressure was just right and the hot water apparently inexhaustible. Some high-end shampoo and conditioner especially designed for curly hair had been left in the shower for me; apparently my captor had thought of everything to keep me comfortable for an extended period of time.

Except food. The nausea of earlier had passed, and I was now quite hungry, something I found a little surprising, considering the amount of food I had eaten at Randall's parents' home the night before.

Randall. Oh, God, how long would it be before he discovered I was missing? He had said he would call the next day—today—but when? There were no clocks in the bedroom or the bathroom, so I had no idea what time it was. From the light outside I guessed it was either very late morning or early afternoon, but since I had no idea how long I had slept, it was impossible to say for sure. And if he missed me, and just got my answering machine, it would probably be some time before he became truly worried. We were always playing phone tag with one another, since I was out so much and he knew not to call my cell phone unless it was an emergency.

It would be even longer before George or anyone at the restaurant missed me, because I had asked for the weekend off to finish a paper and start preparing for finals. George had granted me the time off, mostly because the restaurant was always slow the weekend after Thanksgiving anyway. Very possibly no one would notice I had vanished until I didn't show up for class on Monday morning.

The panic started to well up in me, my heart again beginning its agonized pounding. I turned off the hot water and gathered up a large soft towel and wrapped it around myself, willing the fear away. It was no use heading down that path; I had to keep my head about me, no matter what happened. For the moment, I was safe enough—no one had come to disturb me, and I had to finish preparing myself for whatever might come in the next few hours.

I stepped out of the shower and drew on the warm blue bathrobe, then looked in the cabinets under the sink and found a blow dryer with a diffuser along with some hair products, again all designed for curly hair. It was obvious that all of this had been prepared for me in particular, and not some random female college student.

With deliberate care I went through all the steps of preparing myself, from smoothing moisturizer into my skin to drying my hair. There was something almost decadent about the amount of time I was able to spend on myself, after so many years of rushing out the door to get to school or work on time. But here—well, it was obvious I wasn't going anywhere soon, so I let myself take my time with the comforting little rituals, as if by concentrating on them I could keep my thoughts away from the strangeness of my situation.

Upon reentering the wardrobe I found another smaller chest of drawers, this one filled with lingerie, all obviously new and all in my size. I tried not to think about it—how could my captor have known my *cup size*, for God's sake?—and dressed myself quickly, finding a pair of dark denim jeans that fit perfectly, along with a beautiful cashmere argyle cardigan in rich shades of emerald green and cornflower blue. A pair of dark green kitten heels seemed to finish off the outfit perfectly.

I paused for a second by the jewelry chest, fought a losing battle with my conscience, and opened up the top drawer. Surely there had to be something in there that didn't look as if it should be adorning a celebrity on the red carpet. After a bit of searching I found a pair of simple diamond stud earrings—well, as simple as a pair of multi-carat diamonds could be, anyway—and slipped them on. A gorgeous emerald winked at me from the center of the black velvet compartment, imploring to be worn, but I shut the drawer with more resolution than I felt. It was one thing to wear a pair of stud earrings, especially since I always felt naked without earrings on, but it was an entirely different matter start parading around in jewels that looked as if they should be locked in a vault surrounded by armed guards, not left in an unsecured chest of drawers. Besides, I didn't want my captor—whoever he was—to think that he could seduce me with a few flashy rocks.

A moment or so after I had shut the wardrobe door behind me, paused to fold my damp towels and rehang them on the rack, and emerged into the main bedroom, a knock came at the door that presumably opened on the main corridor. I couldn't help the sudden pounding of my heart, nor the unexpected rush of adrenaline that washed over me, but all the same I managed to take one or two deep breaths before I approached the door in the little antechamber and asked, "Who's there?" To my relief, I sounded calm and firm, not shaky and frightened as I had feared.

A male voice. "I've brought you some food. Step back from the door."

Folding my arms tightly around me, I retreated a few paces. I could hear the sound of keys rattling against the deadbolt, and then the door swung slowly inward.

A man carrying a tray covered with a domed silver lid entered the anteroom. He looked to be in his late thirties or early forties, brown-haired, conservatively but expensively dressed. His blue eyes were hard, watching me with care.

Of course I recognized him immediately. My stalker. The man I had laughingly dismissed in my conversation with Meg.

"You!"

Unperturbed, he said, "Please go on into your bedroom."

Since there didn't seem to be much point to standing in the cramped space and arguing with him, I did as he said, standing off near one of the tall windows and watching as he deposited the tray on the marble-topped side table. His manner was calm, his movements unhurried. Although he kept a close watch on me, I couldn't see anything about his manner that was immediately threatening.

"I suppose there's no point asking why you've brought me here," I said at length.

He paused, his hand resting on the handle of the silver tray cover. There was no emotion in the clear Wedgwood-colored eyes. "That's a question you'll need to ask the boss."

"The boss?"

"I'm just the intermediary, Miss Daly." He lifted the tray cover to reveal a plate of scrambled eggs, a small cut-crystal bowl of strawberries, and a stack of toast, along with a glass of orange juice.

My stomach rumbled unbecomingly. How long had it been since my last meal? Probably at least fifteen hours.

"Just following orders?" I asked, hoping that I had injected the correct amount of contempt into my tone.

He refused to be baited, however. "You'd best eat. He will see you tonight, for dinner."

"Tonight?" Despite my efforts to keep it under control, my voice let out a betraying squeak on the last syllable.

"He prefers to wait until after sunset to see you."

How melodramatic. "What, is he a vampire or something?"

The faintest twitch at the corner of his mouth. I noticed for the first time that he actually was quite attractive, in a rugged, athletic sort of way. "That might be easier to explain."

"And what the hell am I supposed to do until after sunset?"

He lifted a hand in the direction of the little sitting room. "You'll find the study well stocked with books. I suggest you find some way to amuse yourself until then." With that he stepped away from the table and moved toward the door.

Before I could react or move to stop him, he disappeared into the antechamber. I heard the lock click shut.

"Well, hell," I said softly. Part of me wanted to throw the plate of food against the locked door in a grand gesture of defiance, but I knew that would hurt no one but myself. With a resigned sigh, I approached the table and then sat down in one of the little striped chairs that flanked it.

The radio on the table played on into the silence, a delicate piano piece by Debussy. There being nothing much else I could do, I lifted the fork and took several mouthfuls of egg. They were delicious, as was the buttered sourdough toast and the strawberries. My stomach finally quieted after about five or six bites, and I finished the rest of the simple meal with a sort of aggrieved determination, since I knew I had to keep my strength up, much as I hated having to take food from these people.

After I had finished eating, I replaced the cover on the tray and then turned up the volume on the little Bose radio so I could hear it in the next room. My jailer had been right—the bookcases on both walls were filled with books, an eclectic collection of both hardbacks and paperbacks, ranging from mysteries to bestsellers to historical novels. All the sorts of books, in fact, that I enjoyed reading, although I hadn't had much time to do any kind of recreational reading for quite a while.

Well, you've got plenty of time now, I thought.

Despite my jailer's recommendation that I read to fill

up the empty hours, I couldn't help making another pass of my suite, just in case I had missed something during my initial inspection. But no—every window was covered with iron bars, and of course the door didn't budge when I tested the lock. Although sitting and quietly reading seemed to be the last thing I should be doing in such a situation, I realized soon enough that unless I wanted to spend the next six hours or so pacing around the room like a caged animal, I might as well choose a book and do what the brown-haired man had instructed.

I needed something quite thick, something that would occupy me for the next five or six hours. A fat tome on the top shelf caught my eyes; I brought it down and saw that it was a historical novel about the illegitimate daughter of King John. Good—the thing was over eight hundred pages long, and the political infighting of that much-maligned king and his familial entanglements promised enough distraction that I hoped I could concentrate on it and not my present situation. Otherwise, I'd drive myself crazy with conjecture before sundown arrived.

The afternoon ticked away slowly. With a sense of ironic amusement, I noticed the radio was tuned to USC's radio station—no huge surprise, considering it was the only classical station in the Los Angeles area. At least that told me I had to be somewhere within the station's broad-cast range, although, since that ranged from the coast to about sixty or seventy miles inland, and from Santa Barbara in the north all the way to the southern border of Orange County, there were thousands of square miles where I could be hidden.

I was able to gauge the passage of time somewhat by the station identifications at the top of the hour. And no matter how excruciating the wait, it is true that time will eventually pass, no matter how slowly it feels to those who wait. The quality of light outside the window changed slowly, ebbing down to a muted dusk of mist and low clouds. I had to lay aside my book to turn on the lamp next to my chair; I was surprised to see, once I picked it back up again, that I had gone through nearly four hundred pages.

The radio station announced it was six, then six-thirty. A few moments later came the knock at the door.

Heart pounding, I put the book down, paused briefly on the way to the door to check my hair in the mirror, then waited.

The key turned in the lock, and my jailer stood there. Past him I got a dim impression of a softly lit corridor where dark portraits and landscapes lined the walls. "If you would follow me," he said, and held the door open.

Lifting my chin in my best diva manner, I moved past him and on into the hall. He closed the door behind me and then headed down the corridor as I trailed in his wake, trying to take in some of the grandeur around me.

This was not a house—this was a mansion. We passed doorway after doorway until we came to a huge staircase with an elaborately carved banister and began our descent. A many-armed candelabra on the landing provided the only illumination, but I could see huge tapestries hanging on the walls; beneath my feet was a runner in a fantastically intricate Persian pattern.

From the main corridor that seemed to run the length of the ground floor of the home, I saw room after room opening up, all apparently furnished with the same darkly carved antiques that I had seen upstairs, and all lit by candles, their flickering golden light lending an air of unreality to my surroundings. This was not the sort of home that had ordinary chambers such as living rooms or family rooms—instead I saw drawing rooms, sitting rooms, salons, libraries.

Finally we came to a dining room dominated by a huge table of carved mahogany, a table around which were placed carved chairs with gorgeous blood-colored tapestry upholstery. The walls of the room were also painted dark red, set off by a series of tapestries that depicted medieval maidens and unicorns.

Only two places were set in that shining expanse, although candelabras cast their dancing shadows along all its length. At the head of the table a man rose from his tall carved chair, the pale half-mask on his face gleaming oddly in the shivering candlelight.

I recognized him almost immediately, although at first my mind didn't want to make the connection. But it slowly sank in as I continued to stare at him, although I wasn't sure I could make myself believe it.

My captor was the Phantom of the Opera.

Chapter Thirteen

For what felt like an eternity I could only stand there, staring at him. Only a second or two must have passed, however, because he said to my jailer, "Thank you, Jerome. You may leave Miss Daly with me now."

Beside me, Jerome nodded his head slightly and left the room without a backward glance. I remained where I was, shock rooting me in place.

The Phantom said, "If you would join me, Miss Daly?" and spread an elegant hand to indicate the seat next to his.

I finally found my voice. "Not until you tell me what I'm doing here."

"All in good time." The slightest edge of menace entered his tone, like the whisper of steel across silk. "For now I'm afraid I must insist."

Not knowing what else to do, I crossed the heavy tufted rug that covered the floor and allowed him to pull out the chair for me, then sat. He reclaimed his own seat at the head of the table, gracefully unfolded his napkin, and settled it in his lap.

I noticed that he had seated me on his left, so the uncovered side of his face was toward me. It was the same man from the Halloween party at L'Opéra, of course; his voice had told me that almost immediately, and the uncovered half of his face was familiar, the elegant features, the faint shadow of a scar high up on his cheekbone, like some remnant of a long-forgotten duel. Now, however, instead of the formal tails he had worn on Halloween, he was dressed in a black mock-neck sweater and dark pants, his skin pale against the somber garments.

"Some wine?" he inquired. "A '61 Bordeaux—quite a good year. I think you will find the nuances...interesting."

Without waiting for my reply, he poured the heavy, garnet-colored liquid from a crystal decanter into my glass. Even from where I sat I could smell the heavy richness of it, the seductive swirl of fruit from the aged grapes.

"You are full of questions, no doubt," he continued, watching me carefully. In the dim candlelight it was impossible for me to tell what color his eyes really were, and his expression was equally inscrutable.

"No doubt," I said. "Are you going to answer any of them?"

His gaze slid away from mine. "Perhaps...in time. For now, I would very much appreciate it if you would try the wine."

I replied, a bit surprised by my own boldness, "Maybe you should have a sip of mine first. After all, you poured it from a decanter, not from a bottle. Why should I trust what's in it?"

Instead of anger, my sharp tone elicited an amused chuckle. "If that concerns you, of course, Christine…I may call you Christine? We have, after all, met before."

I wanted to scream at him, *What the hell difference does it make?* but managed to keep my tone calm. "If that's what you'd like."

"Yes, Christine, I would like it very much." The caress of his voice across my name was obvious, and I shivered. He went on, "As for the other matter, it's common practice to decant a Bordeaux like this. But if it makes you uncomfortable—" And with that he reached across to my wine goblet and took a small sip, his eyes mocking me over the rim of the glass. Then, instead of setting it back down on the table, he handed it directly to me, so I was forced to take it from him. The tips of his fingers brushed mine, so quickly I barely had time to register the fact. I noticed that he still wore the gold and onyx ring on the pinky of his right hand.

He continued to watch me with that level, dark gaze, so I had no choice but to lift the heavy glass to my lips and drink. Probably most of the wine's finer points were lost on me, but I recognized a swirl of dark flavors, hints of fruit, smoky earth. The warm rush of it hit my almost-empty stomach; it had been quite some time since the light breakfast Jerome had brought me.

"It's very good," I said. "But you didn't really bring me here to discuss wine, did you?"

A pause. "No." He took a sip of his own wine, then said, "You may reassure yourself that I mean you no harm.

I'm prepared to give you anything you could possibly ask for."

"Except my freedom, I suppose." I forced myself to maintain eye contact with him, but he showed no outward sign of reaction to my words.

"'Freedom,'" he repeated. "Freedom is a highly overrated commodity, in my opinion. Here you will have every comfort you lacked in the outside world."

And how far away was the outside world, I thought, *and had it missed me yet?* I tried to force my thoughts away from that particular path—it led inevitably to Randall, and I couldn't allow myself to think of his emotional turmoil once he realized that I had seemingly vanished off the face of the earth.

"Well, we can leave aside the debate over the value of freedom for now," I said. "Maybe we should discuss the legal consequences of kidnapping? Or how about false imprisonment?"

He regarded me with an amused twitch at the left corner of his mouth. "I assure you, Christine, I'm not worried about any of that."

"No? What about breaking and entering or assault?"

With a wave of one elegant hand he brushed away the litany of offenses. "To be convicted, one first has to be caught. I have no intention of that happening."

"I'm sure that's what every criminal thinks, right before the police come knocking at the door."

At that comment he actually laughed, a laugh that under other circumstances I probably would have found attractive. It was forthright and pitched beautifully, just like his speaking voice. "I'm not in a position to tell you everything you want to know, Christine, but I will tell you this: There is no way anyone can connect me to you—just to put your mind at ease as to the imminence of my arrest. Your being here is the result of very careful planning. No one saw you taken. No one saw you brought here. And, as you probably observed from the windows of your suite, my home is quite isolated. There is no way anyone can discover your presence here. So you might as well put away this particular line of questioning—you'll discover nothing that will be of any assistance to you."

As much as I hated to admit it to myself, I had to concede him that point. Since I had been taken in the middle of the night, my next-door neighbor on one side had been away at work, and the girls who rented the house on the other had gone off to Mammoth for the long weekend. I'd seen them myself when I'd come home from work on Wednesday night; they'd just finished loading the last of the skis on the roof rack of their ancient Bronco as I parked my own car in front of the house. I was sure my captor had been equally careful about my arrival here in his home.

I was saved by making any comment by the arrival of dinner, which was wheeled in by an elderly man in evening dress who nonetheless attended to our meal quickly and efficiently, filling each of our plates with deft movements. I wasn't sure what the main dish was, but it smelled heavenly. However, I had more important things on my mind at that moment than food—I wasn't about to let this opportunity pass by. The man—who I assumed was the butler—had a pleasant face, his eyes kind. I couldn't imagine that he was in on this kidnap plot as well.

No sooner had I parted my lips to speak, however, than my captor said smoothly, "Thank you, Ennis. I'll let you know if we need anything else." And under the table I could feel him grasp my wrist in a grip of iron.

"Very good, sir," Ennis replied, turning and wheeling the dinner cart back out toward the hallway.

Not caring how much it hurt, I wrenched my arm from the man's grasp. He relinquished his grip, a satisfied half-smile on his mouth. It didn't matter now whether my wrist was free or not—I'd lost my chance to appeal to the butler for help.

"It wouldn't do you any good," the Phantom said. "Ennis was already told about your coming here. Not the particulars, of course—I told him you were Jerome's niece, who was coming to stay with us for a while." He picked up his fork, an elaborate piece of baroque sterling, then added, "And Jerome informed him that you had a tendency to delusional behavior, although you'd been managing fairly well lately as long as you kept on your medication."

Son of a bitch. "I guess you've thought of everything, haven't you?" I asked bitterly.

"As much as I could. I don't," he said softly, "much like surprises."

Yes, I could see that. As little as I knew of him, it was quite obvious he was the master here, and that he very much controlled what happened in his ordered little universe. He had about him an air of command that could only come from a lifetime of having his own way. That he thought he control me in the same way, I had no doubt. Like it or not, he was going to be in for a surprise there.

I picked up my own fork, determined that he should see nothing of my inner turmoil on my face. "What is this?" I asked, gesturing to the food on my plate.

"*Coq au vin*," he replied. "My cook definitely has a way with it. You'll find it complements the Bordeaux nicely."

And so it did, I discovered, after I took my first mouthful and let the rich, wine-laden taste roll over my tongue. It was delicious, as were the tiny new potatoes sprinkled with rosemary and the fresh-baked rolls, which were so new they let out a soft wisp of steam when opened.

He allowed me to eat for a bit, watching as he took his own measured bites of food and sips of wine. Then he said, "Tomorrow we should begin working on your music."

I stopped mid-bite, staring at him. Then I remembered myself enough to finish chewing and swallow the morsel of bread. "Excuse me?"

"Surely you didn't think that simply because you were here I would allow you to neglect your studies? You have a great gift, Christine. It would not do to let it lie fallow."

"Are you a voice coach?" I asked.

A slight pause, and then he said, "Perhaps not in the formal sense. But I have had many years of training myself."

I'll bet you have, I thought, but remained silent. How delusional was he? Did he really think he was the Phantom of the Opera?

Over the years I had been teased now and then about my name and my resemblance to the heroine of the musical, but in all my imaginings I had never considered that the similarities would attract an apparently insane recluse who believed himself to be his Erik to my Christine. And what was he really hiding behind that mask?

His secret identity, a malicious little voice in my head supplied, and despite the situation I had to keep myself from smiling. "And who is to accompany me? Or had you planned on kidnapping Randall Cagney as well?"

He froze at that, the knuckles showing white on his fist as he clenched the butter knife he had been holding. Suddenly I got the impression that if Randall had been standing there, that knife would have been plunged between his ribs. When my captor spoke, however, his voice was calm and cold. "I would appreciate it, my dear, if you would not mention that name in my presence again."

Dangerous, then, beneath the veneer of sophistication and old-fashioned charm. I should have realized that—a man who could so coldly execute a kidnapping might well not scruple at killing someone he so obviously considered his rival. No matter what reassurances he gave me as to my own safety, I knew I would have to tread cautiously.

"At any rate," he continued, "I will accompany you. I think you will find my skills more than adequate to the task."

"I look forward to hearing you," I said, the words empty politeness. What I really would have looked forward to was his falling off a cliff or being struck by lightning, but somehow I had the feeling that neither of those particular events was going to happen any time soon.

Another smile. "Perhaps."

An awkward moment passed, and then another, as I picked at my food and drank more of my wine than I had really intended to, but it was a way to keep myself occupied. Without comment he refilled my glass, then his own.

I wasn't feeling exactly tipsy—I'd eaten too much for the amount of wine I'd drunk to get me to that stage yet—but the wine did give me a sense of recklessness. "So what do you want me to call you, anyway? If we're going to be spending as much time together as you seem to think we are, 'hey you' isn't going to work for long."

"My name is Erik," he said.

For a second I stared at him, outraged that he'd hand me the Phantom's own name—how much of a simpleton did he think I was, anyway? Then I took another large swallow of the Bordeaux. "Is that the best you can do?"

One muscle along his jaw line twitched, but otherwise he seemed admirably in control. "I assure you, Christine, that is my real name. I was named for my paternal grandfather. Would you like me to show you the birth certificate?"

Too late I was starting to realize just how potent the wine really was. I set down my wine glass with exaggerated care, then replied, "I suppose that's not necessary."

He looked at me then, eyes narrowing, and said, "I think you'd better have some water." With that he stood and went to the sideboard, where a pitcher of ice water and several glasses sat on a heavy silver tray. He poured a glass and then set it in front of me, removing at the same time my half-empty wine goblet. He set it down on the sideboard and remained standing for the moment.

Part of me wanted to protest the substitution and its obvious implications, but the part of my brain that still seemed to be working semi-coherently told me the removal of the wine glass was probably a good idea. What the hell had I been thinking, anyway? Smart, Christine, very smart—another glass and I could have passed out on the dining room table then and there, and then he could have done anything he wanted to me. Shamefaced, I lifted the water glass and drank deeply, then set it down and took another piece of bread. Anything to soak up the wine that was percolating through my bloodstream.

Surprisingly, he watched me with some measure of approval. "I suppose you're not used to vintages that potent."

"No, they were fresh out of '61s the last time I was at Target," I replied, and he laughed outright at that.

It was probably the first truly spontaneous sound I'd heard from him all evening. The laughter changed his countenance as well; the complicated tightness at the corner of his mouth seemed to disappear, and I could see the laugh lines around his eye deepen for a moment. Unbidden, a memory came to me of the way he'd held me as we danced, the firmness of his touch, the subtle masculine scent I'd breathed in from his impeccable evening clothes.

It was too much. This man had kidnapped me, imprisoned me in his home, and all I could think of was how he had held me on an evening that now seemed like a lifetime ago?

With a sudden movement I pushed the chair away

from the table and stood. "I'm sorry," I said, and put my hand up to my temple, feigning a headache, "I don't feel very well. Could I please go back upstairs so I can lie down?"

All solicitude, he stepped forward and took my arm. As he stood next to me I was suddenly aware of the great difference in our heights—I barely scraped five foot five on a good day, and he had to be several inches past six feet.

"It's my fault," he said. "You probably shouldn't have had anything to drink today at all, after the—after last night."

After the drugs you gave me, I thought, but said only, "It's all right. I just want to be rested for tomorrow—for my first lesson."

He smiled down at me, apparently taking my words at face value. "Let me take you upstairs."

And I allowed him to lead me back down the main hallway and up the enormous staircase, until we were back at the carved mahogany door that opened into my suite. He produced a key from his pocket and unlocked the door, opening it into the little antechamber. It was dark immediately within, but I could see a faint glow coming from the bedroom, where I'd left one of the bedside lamps lit.

We paused there for a moment. I was again aware of how much larger he was than I, of his lean but powerful build under the dark clothes. For one frightening second I thought he was going to lean down and kiss me, but instead he stepped away from the door, then said very softly, "You have nothing to fear from me, Christine."

I said nothing, but merely bowed my head in acknowledgment of his words. Then I stepped inside my suite and pushed the door shut. There was the merest pause, and then I could hear the deadbolt clicking home. I waited for a few more minutes, but there was no other sound from the hallway, and at length I moved into my bedroom, knowing that it would be a long time before I'd be able to fall asleep.

Some time after midnight rain began to fall, but at first he didn't notice it, as the soft hiss of the rain blended with the crackle of the fire in the hearth. Christine had retired hours earlier, but he had been a nocturnal creature for too many years to try to keep to her schedule. Soon she would adjust to his.

She had surprised him. What he'd been expecting, he wasn't quite sure—tears, pleading, perhaps, but certainly not righteous anger. Possibly this was because it had been years since anyone had been angry with him—or at least shown it—but he'd never thought that a woman in such a helpless position would berate him over exactly which portions of the penal code he was violating, or would mock him over his name. Although he'd been angry at the time, angrier than she had probably guessed, as he thought over it now, he could see her side of the argument. It was obvious she thought he was mad, or at the very least obsessive to the point of delusion.

He would concede her a point on his own obsessiveness. As for the rest, it would simply be a matter of time before he won her over, made her see that he really was the only man for her. And he and Jerome had made sure that Erik would have all the time in the world to make Christine fall in love with her Phantom.

The final loose end had been tied up earlier this evening, as Christine's shabby little car disappeared from its parking place at the curb in front of her home. All it had taken was for Jerome to let certain individuals at a disreputable mechanic's in El Monte know that the car had been abandoned and was ripe for the taking. The car vanished, taken to another shop, where the VIN plate was removed and the serial numbers sanded off the engine block. Then the whole thing was sold to a wrecking yard. Now it would be only another piece of flattened metal, indistinguishable from the other hulks around it.

The car's disappearance, as well as other details he'd had the kidnappers attend to, would all point to a voluntary flight by Miss Daly. Young women disappeared all the time, after all, driven to flee because of bad relationships, job pressures, financial extremity. Christine would only be another statistic.

He was relieved that the car was gone, relieved that everything had gone smoothly thus far. Now that she was here with him, he didn't want to have to think about the outside world, worry whether anyone could possibly connect her to Erik Deitrich, heir to the Deitrich fortune. He thought not. He'd only been seen with her in public once, and that was at a crowded restaurant where he blended in with all of the other masked partygoers. He'd never used his name, and paid his bill with cash. There was no way to connect him to *L'Opera*, or the beautiful dark-haired student who had once worked there.

No, now he was free to sit here in the semidarkness and remember how her sea-colored eyes had picked up the green of her sweater, recall the gorgeous profusion of curls that spilled down her back and how the candlelight picked errant gleams of cinnabar and topaz from among their depths, savor the memory of how the Bordeaux had stained her full lips an even darker crimson. She intoxicated him by her very presence.

He doubted she would be gratified to learn that even her anger pleased him, that her sharp words were a source of amusement instead of outrage. It was all of her that he wanted, not just her beautiful form but her quick mind, her strength, her amazing talent. He'd had bodies before; now he wanted the whole woman.

He wanted to love her, but more than that—he wanted her to love him. All that was left to him now was to prove himself worthy of her love.

Chapter Fourteen

WITH A SLIGHT GROAN I ROLLED OVER, lifting a hand to my throbbing temple. Not good. Last night I might have been embellishing just a bit when I'd told Erik I had a headache and needed to lie down, but there was no need for prevarication this morning. My head felt as if someone had slipped about thirty rubber bands around its circumference and then slowly tightened them.

Still, I knew that lying in bed and feeling like hell wasn't going to help any. Moving with care, I climbed out of bed and staggered toward the bathroom in search of analgesics. It was only after I opened the pretty Venetian glass medicine cabinet and stood staring at it blankly for a moment that I remembered I hadn't seen anything remotely resembling a headache remedy in there. It figured.

The next best thing was a hot shower. I discarded the filmy nightgown I was wearing—apparently the Phantom didn't like his Christine to sleep in sweats and T-shirts—got in, and let the pulsating spray knock some of the pain away as it kneaded at my head and neck in waves of rippling heat. It did help, especially since it seemed I could stand there forever luxuriating in the massaging warmth, long past the time when the puny hot water heater at my own bungalow would have given up.

But all good things must come to an end. Eventually I got out and toweled off, then went in search of something to wear. From what I could see of the day outside, it was gray and gloomy, the landscape still wet from what must have been a fairly significant rain the night before. Luckily for me, however, Erik had invested heavily in cashmere when procuring my wardrobe, and this time I selected a nice V-neck in a soft raspberry shade and a pair of black slacks to go with the sweater. I didn't really want to admit it, but the grandeur of the house had cowed me a bit. Although there were several pairs of jeans in my new wardrobe, they seemed a bit out of place in a home that looked more like a museum than someplace where people actually lived. So the slacks—exquisitely cut wool crepe—were a compromise. I wasn't ready to start climbing into skirts and dresses quite yet.

Although I felt considerably more human than when I had first woken up, my head still throbbed faintly, and the hum of the blow dryer didn't help much. I stopped while my hair was still damp and set the dryer down on the bathroom counter, then stared at myself in the mirror. I looked pale and had dark circles under my eyes.

"Great," I muttered, searching through the drawer of cosmetics for some concealer. I wasn't about to give Erik the satisfaction of knowing that he'd apparently given me my first hangover.

While I applied spackle and the rest of the artifices that women resort to when they're feeling less than lovely, I tried hard not to think about Randall or my situation.

Unfortunately, I failed at both. I couldn't help wondering how many times he'd tried to call, or whether he'd resorted to driving past my house yet, and if he'd contacted Meg to see if she knew where I was. The thought of his increasingly frantic phone calls, the worry in those hazel eyes that were usually so lively, worry that might soon turn to actual fear—all of it combined to bring out the tears that had been lurking under the surface for the past thirty-six hours.

"Stop it," I told my reflection. "No one cares that you're sitting in here blubbering like a baby." With an angry gesture I reached up to blot my eye makeup with a tissue. Luckily the tears had started to flow before I had applied any mascara, but I was still a soggy mess and had to redo most of my previous handiwork.

The tears eventually dried up, as I had learned they always do, and settling in their place was a deep and abiding anger. How dare he? Who the hell did he think he was anyway, kidnapping me just because I fit his sick profile of the perfect woman?

I hurled a Chanel eyeshadow quad into the drawer, but luckily the container was too well-designed to break. The silly impotence of the gesture was actually what calmed me down. I could sit in here and rant and rage all I wanted, but it wouldn't change the fact that I was being held captive by a man who apparently had limitless resources and the cunning to use them as he saw fit. And although he had told me I had nothing to fear from him, I saw no real reason to believe those words. There was nothing to keep him from raping and murdering me and burying my violated body somewhere on his property. I didn't even know where I was—I could be only a few miles from home, or hidden in some secluded spot in the hills of Malibu.

No, even though he had reassured me that I would be all right, and even though he had apparently shopped for me—or at least hired someone to do so—with the same care most women would accord their own wardrobes, I could not feel safe. No woman could, in a situation where she had so little control.

It was at that inopportune time that I heard a knock coming from the door to my suite. I set down the makeup brush I had been turning over and over in my hands, and went to the door.

"Ah," I said, once I saw that it was Jerome who stood there. "The lackey."

A brief tightening of the lines at the corner of his eyes was his only response to the insult. I didn't know anything about Jerome, what his background was or how he'd come to work for Erik, but I guessed that fetching and carrying was something new to his job description.

When he spoke, however, his tone was carefully neutral. "Would you like anything in particular for breakfast?"

"I'd kill for some Tylenol."

"Anything more substantial?" he asked, refusing to rise to the bait.

Deciding it wasn't worth the effort, I abandoned the game. "Some fruit would be heavenly. And some more of that sourdough toast I had yesterday—it was wonderful." I thought for a moment, then decided, what the heck? "And some cappuccino."

"Anything else?"

Was it just me, or was there a slight twitch at the corner of his mouth? Was he laughing at me, at my presumption? "The key to the front door would be nice," I said.

"I'll have to take that up with the management," he replied. His tone was serious, his face expressionless, but I could tell he was giving me some of my own back.

"Well, let's just start with the cappuccino, then."

He gave me a slight nod, then went out, with the inevitable snick of the lock following in his wake. It was probably less than fifteen minutes before he returned with another laden tray, the cappuccino sending a drift of heavenly-smelling steam into the air.

"What time is it?" I asked, taking a slow sip of the cappuccino. The heat of it hit my stomach at about the same time the caffeine started to work itself into my depleted bloodstream. Ah, vice.

"Around ten. He wants to see you at one."

"So late?" For some strange reason, I felt oddly disappointed.

That time Jerome did smile, a little. "That's early for him. Most of the time he doesn't sleep until dawn."

"So I was right—he is a vampire."

"It might be easier if he were."

I set my cappuccino down on the marble-topped table that held the rest of my breakfast. Jerome seemed unusually friendly, for him. Maybe this was the time to ask a few questions. "So…what's with the mask, anyway? Is that just part of his Phantom obsession?"

Whatever warmth might have been in his eyes died then. "Don't ever mention the mask."

"But why—"

"Ever," he repeated.

Still persisting, I went on, "You don't expect me to believe that he's really deformed under that thing? It's a stage prop!"

With one swift gesture he grasped my arm just as I was reaching out to retrieve my mug. I think I gave a little gasp of shock, but he appeared not to notice. "This is not a game, Christine. A piece of advice—leave the mask alone if you want to survive this."

He was deadly serious, I could tell. It was only until I reluctantly said "if you say so" that he released me. I rubbed my arm a little. With my luck, I'd have a set of bruises on my bicep to match the ones Erik had left on my wrist the night before.

Jerome appeared to be wrestling something over in his head. Finally he said, the words rushed, as if he wanted to get them out before he changed his mind, "I've worked for him for seven years. Seven years. And I've never seen him without the mask. It is never discussed. Servants that gossiped disappeared."

"What, are you saying that he had them whacked or

something?" I could only hope that my sarcasm covered up the fear that lay beneath it.

He made a dismissive gesture. "Of course not. They were dismissed." Then he watched me carefully, the blue eyes vivid against his tanned skin. "But he can't very well do the same with you, can he?"

And with that he turned and walked out, leaving me with a breakfast that suddenly seemed far less appetizing than it had a few minutes ago. Thank God he'd at least left me the Tylenol; I needed the capsules now more than ever.

Much sooner than I wanted to, given what Jerome had told me only a few hours earlier, I stood outside the music room. Jerome had left me here after admonishing me to wait until Erik invited me in. Almost as an aside, he informed me that it was no use to go wandering about the house, since all the exits were guarded by closed-circuit cameras and secured by keypad locks. It made me wonder why they bothered locking the door to my suite at all, as it was quite obvious I couldn't get out of the house anyway. I had the sudden idea that perhaps they thought it would make me feel more safe.

The door to the music room stood slightly ajar, and suddenly any nervousness or fear I'd been feeling melted away to be replaced by wonder, for Erik had begun to play.

It was some fiendishly difficult Chopin polonaise; I recognized the opening notes of the piece even as I tried to recall in vain its actual opus number. But the difficulty of the work was surpassed only by the technical brilliance with which it was being played. As a music major I'd had the privilege of attending many concerts on campus and hearing all sorts of visiting virtuosos, but I hadn't heard anything to rival this.

I was no keyboard expert, but even I could recognize the combined elegance and strength of his touch, the effortless grace with which he made the notes spill out into the air. The virtuosic technique was matched by a fierce passion that seemed to imbue every note with an almost erotic intensity. Fascinated, I waited in my spot outside the door, hardly daring to breathe lest I disturb his playing. It didn't make sense. This man played like a god. Why had he hidden himself away from the world when he possessed a talent like that?

Unfortunately, the spell was broken by an ill-timed sneeze on my part. The glorious spill of notes went silent, and then he was there, still masked of course, but this time in a white shirt open at the throat.

If he was at all upset at being interrupted in such a fashion, he showed no sign of it. "Ah, Christine. Not catching a cold, I hope?"

"Just a tickle in my throat," I replied, and then stepped into the room as he opened the door wide to let me in.

Like the rest of the house, it had been furnished in heavy carved pieces, but the mood in here was lighter because of the walls, which were painted a dreamy shell pink, the color of clouds at dawn. A bank of French doors opening onto a verandah brought more light into the room, although I could only imagine what it would be like in bright sunlight; outside the sky was lowering again, the first drops of renewed rain hitting the colored pavement outside. Beyond the verandah stretched more green lawns, though the prospect was broken up slightly by a curved gravel driveway that ended at a substantial building of gray stone with a steeply pitched roof.

The music room, though large, was dominated by a Steinway concert grand situated to make the most of the natural light. In one corner stood a harp, now muffled in some kind of heavy green cloth. Against another wall was a large cabinet which I assumed must hold more instruments. I saw that a music stand had been set up for me in the curve of the piano, also that a pitcher and two glasses of water had been placed on a small table nearby.

"Perhaps this would help," he said, handing me one of the filled glasses.

I took it from him gratefully and drank. I'd been feeling dehydrated all morning—not a good thing with a long practice session ahead of me. "Much better," I said, then replaced the glass on its table.

"Well, then." He resumed his seat on the piano bench and launched immediately into scales. After a brief hesitation I joined in, singing lightly as my voice warmed up, concentrating on my breathing while at the same time making sure that the annoying tickle truly had gone from my throat.

After a series of increasingly difficult warmup exercises, he stopped suddenly. "Ready?"

"Ready?" I echoed, not sure what he meant.

With no answer except the half-smile that was visible beneath the mask, he launched into the lively introduction to Marguerite's "Jewel Song."

Perhaps he thought he would catch me off-guard, but I had practiced the thing so many times I was able to hit the opening trill right on cue. This was the key, after all, to know it so well that it came to you like breathing, that the notes swelled up and out, taking on a life that was much more than just a combination of lungs and larynx and palate. One of the girls at school had called it "the only orgasm you'll ever need," but since I didn't have any basis for comparison, I didn't know whether I agreed with her or not.

When the song ended, I turned and looked at Erik. He watched me carefully, without much expression on the half of his face I could see. Brushing away a small wave of annoyance—I thought I had done very well—I asked, "Well?"

He put a hand to his chin. "I'm thinking."

"About?"

A smile then, revealing even white teeth. "About how on earth I'm supposed to improve on perfection."

Randall had said almost the same thing to me, barely two months ago. Once again I experienced a rush of satisfaction, although this time it was followed by puzzlement. Why should I care what Erik thought of me? I knew the answer, though. Obsessive he was, definitely; dangerous, very probably; mad—quite possibly. But he was also one of the most talented musicians I had ever heard, and recognition by one's peers is the sweetest approbation one can have.

"But at the very least we can keep that magnificent instrument of yours limber," he went on. "If I had to venture a criticism, I would say that possibly you lose a little energy in the middle section. Shall we begin at 'achevons le métamorphose'?"

Then we launched into it again, and then once more, until he seemed satisfied and I could feel myself flushed with exertion and tingling with blood flowing around my lungs and throat.

"You are never more lovely than when you sing, Christine," Erik said softly, his elegant hands resting on the keyboard. I should have recognized them for what they were the first time I met him—the strong, long-fingered hands of a pianist.

I responded to compliments about my voice much better than I did to compliments about my face. Hoping my color hadn't risen too much, I asked, "Do you sing, Erik?"

"Do I sing?" he repeated, seeming a little puzzled by the question. "I had a little training, once." The masked face lifted to mine, and he sang softly, again from *Faust*,

"*Oui, c'est moi, je t'aime!*
Malgré l'effort même
Du démon moquer
Je t'ai retrouvée!"

I knew the words, of course, Faust's renewed avowal of love for Marguerite as she lay condemned in prison. But I had never expected his voice, a tenor more exquisite than any I had ever heard, almost frightening in its purity. The ache in my heart was familiar; it was the same sensation I felt when confronted by beauty in its purest form, whether it was listening to Mozart's *Requiem* or watching the moon rise over the desert. My mother had once said I had an artist's soul, and at the time I hadn't really been sure what she meant. All I knew for sure was this man had touched my heart in some way, and that frightened me. I was supposed to hate him, wasn't I? How was I supposed to feel about someone who seemed to have the soul of a devil and the voice of an angel?

Somehow without my noticing, he had stood and come to me. He reached out to my cheek, then pulled his hand away and looked at the glistening drop on his forefinger in wonder. "You're crying," he said finally.

I reached up with my own hand and wiped the tears away with a brusque gesture. "It's nothing. I'm tired, that's all."

"Christine." How was it that he always made my name into a caress? Even his speaking voice was beautiful.

"I just don't understand," I said at length, knowing that he was waiting for me to say something.

"Understand what?"

Letting out a shaky little laugh, I replied, "You, most of all. How you hide the kind of talent you have. You have everything, and yet you hide here. Why?"

For a long moment he was silent. I saw for the first time that his eyes were an elusive gray-green, but dark, like a semiprecious stone I'd seen once as a child. Moss agate, that was what my father had called it.

"One can have everything and nothing, Christine."

Again I found myself fighting to understand. There were so many shadows in his soul, that much I knew even from our brief acquaintance. How long would it take before he felt comfortable telling me anything truly important? And then I wondered why it should matter so much to me. This man had stolen me from my home, taken me away from everything that was important. Why should I care whether he confided in me or not? All I should care about was getting out of here.

But somehow I knew that he had broken down a barrier between us the moment he opened his mouth and sang those words to me. Something in my soul responded to his—I had sensed that connection on the night we first met, even though I had known nothing about him at the time. It had frightened me then; it frightened me even more now.

I don't know what he saw in my face. But he lifted his hand, reaching out to touch my cheek, and suddenly the terror surged up through me, drowning me like a riptide. *Not yet*, a voice in my mind screamed. *Not yet.*

And then I was pushing myself away from him, upsetting the music stand as I fled the room, tearing down the hallway, not knowing where I was going or what I was going to do once I got there.

All I knew was that I couldn't bear one more moment in his presence. If I had stayed, I feared that I would have lost a part of my soul forever.

Chapter Fifteen

"She won't come down, sir."

Erik tried to think of the last time he'd seen Jerome look nervous and failed. After Christine had fled from the music room, he'd let her go—followed discreetly by Jerome, to make sure she didn't wander into chambers Erik didn't want her to see…yet.

However, Jerome reported that she'd gone straight to her rooms, and that's where he had found her only a few moments later, sitting on the ground outside the locked door to her suite, knees drawn up to her chest, face pale. All she'd said, though, was, "I wondered how long it would take you to get here," before getting to her feet as Jerome had unlocked the door. She had disappeared into the suite and was now apparently refusing to come back out again.

Considering, Erik settled back in his chair. Although it was certainly in his power to have her forcibly removed from her chamber and brought down to dinner, somehow he doubted that was the correct approach. Better to let her stay alone with her anger and hope that it would burn itself out eventually. He knew he hadn't been dreaming when he saw the growing attraction in her eyes, saw the way she had responded to his music and his voice. She might fight it now—for days to come, if he knew her at all—but it was a fight he knew she would lose in the end. It wasn't all just dreams and madness; the very first time he had held her in his arms he'd felt her rouse to him, felt the rightness between them.

Apparently unnerved by Erik's continuing silence, Jerome added, "She said—and I quote, 'He's going to have to drag me down there by my hair before I'll sit down to dinner with him again.' Sir."

Did she really think he was such a barbarian as that? Well, he'd enjoy proving her wrong. Instead, he gave a brittle laugh and said, "Such an abuse of a glorious head of hair. I'd never allow that, of course…have a tray prepared and sent up to her rooms. And send Ennis in to clear her place setting away."

Jerome inclined his head. "Very good, sir. I'll see to that directly."

As Jerome went off to carry out his orders, Erik tried to resign himself to another lonely evening. It would, after all, only be another in a very long series of lonely evenings. More frustrating than most of the others, since now he at last had the woman he had dreamed of for so long living under his own roof, but now was not the time to endanger the delicate balance that existed between the two of them by giving rein to his temper. He pushed away a sudden image of himself throwing open the door to her room and finding her in the rose-canopied bed he'd had prepared for her. What would it be like, to take her by the shoulders, bring her lips to his, force the soft sweetness of her body down into the sheets, feel her move under him?

That way did lie madness. He made himself stand and go to the sideboard, where a fine unoaked chardonnay was cooling in a vintage silver bucket. Only after pouring himself a glass and taking several sips did he feel the pulse in his chest and groin begin to subside.

At that point Ennis entered the room and began to clear away Christine's unwanted place setting. He looked over to Erik where he stood by the sideboard, then asked, "I hope the young lady is feeling well?"

Erik watched the old man carefully, but he could see nothing except genuine concern in Ennis's eyes. The butler had always been the element that worried Erik the most in his whole scheme of kidnapping Christine—the man was getting on, but he certainly wasn't stupid. And strangely, what worried Erik the most was what Ennis might think of him, should he discover the truth. Jerome he trusted implicitly, and frankly, Erik didn't much care what Jerome thought. The man had seen the darker side of humanity for a good many years; Erik somehow doubted that he could do anything that would shock Jerome. But Ennis—

Ennis was the father his own should have been, Erik had to admit. It was Ennis who had taught him how to drive, Ennis who had held his head after a particularly bad experiment with a bottle of brandy, Ennis who had recommended the fencing lessons and the first computer when he could see the adolescent Erik going crazy from his enforced solitude. And it was Ennis who had watched over the rest of the household staff and made sure that no prying eyes or gossiping tongues shattered the fragile isolation Erik even then had wrapped around himself like a protective cocoon. No, he would not like to see the old man's expression if he ever discovered the true reason for Christine's tenure in the house.

"I'm afraid Christine's caught a bit of a cold," he replied at length. "She thought it would be better if she stayed in her room for a while."

"I'm sorry to hear that," Ennis said, straightening as he finished gathering up the rest of the unused silver. "Do you know if she'd like anything special? Some hot tea, perhaps?"

Hot tea seemed innocuous enough. "Certainly."

"I'll see to that and her tray right away, then. Jerome said he would take it up?"

"Yes. She—feels more comfortable with him."

Ennis seemed to accept the lie readily enough. "Poor girl. Such a pretty thing, too."

Erik hoped his tone was noncommittal when he replied, "Yes, I suppose so. She seems to do well enough on her medication, luckily."

"They do seem to work miracles these days." There was no mistaking the fondness in his eyes as he added, "It was very good of you to take her in, Erik."

There were times when wearing a mask had its distinct advantages. Erik replied, hoping his color hadn't risen too much, "Well, it was easy enough. We certainly have room to spare here."

Ennis nodded, then said, "And here I am talking when the girl's in bed with a cold. I'll see to her tray, and then bring your own dinner out."

"Thank you, Ennis." And he watched the butler leave the room, wondering when it was that Ennis had become an old man. Somewhere during his obsession of the last two decades the man's middle years had slipped away, and Erik had not even noticed. How old was Ennis now, anyway? Seventy? Seventy-five? How typical that he had never noticed until now.

Suddenly weary, he took his usual seat at the head of the table, forcing himself not to look at the newly empty place next to his, forcing himself not to think of her. Forcing himself to feel as hollow as all the empty years he had wasted, alone with his need and his despair.

Our détente lasted for three days.

The first evening I was glad to see that at least they weren't going to starve me into submission—Jerome had arrived promptly at seven with a truly lovely piece of grilled salmon, steamed vegetables, and fresh bread. He'd left it without comment, and I had to say I almost enjoyed myself as I took my meal into the little sitting room and ate as I listened to the rain fall outside the many-paned windows.

The next day was Sunday, and I didn't even bother to get out of my nightclothes—I took a long hot bath, read a good deal, listened to the radio, played with the cosmetics in my bathroom, painted my toenails, and pretty much forced myself not to think about anything. After so many years spent rushing from one place to another, I almost enjoyed my forced solitude; the little things women did to pamper themselves had never been a part of my life, and for once I didn't have to justify the wasted time.

On Monday I awoke vaguely ashamed of myself, and filled with a sort of creeping anxiety. Surely by now someone had noticed my absence—Randall might have been able to rationalize my absence over the weekend, but I never missed school unless I was ill, and since I imagined he would have gone to the bungalow to find me, he must know I wasn't at home, down with a cold or the flu. What would he do then? Would he go to the police? I had a feeling he probably would, although I wasn't sure that would do any good. I didn't see how anyone could possibly connect me with Erik—if that really was his name. I still wasn't sure I believed him.

Truth be told, I didn't know what to think about most of it. He'd had ample opportunity to force me, if that really were his intent. If this were only about sex, then why the carefully chosen wardrobe, the jewels, even the lovely room in which I was imprisoned? Why would he care whether I practiced my singing or not? And now this—this careful acquiescence to my wish not to see him again. He could have come to my room any time during the last few days and compelled me to go downstairs to be with him, but he hadn't.

Instead, I suffered the benign neglect of a long-term invalid—food was brought up at regular intervals, but otherwise I had been left to my own amusements, which were already beginning to wear thin. I had tried practicing scales, and had gone so far as to stand in the antechamber to my suite and sing pieces carefully chosen to annoy Erik if he were anywhere within earshot—ditties such as "She's Only a Bird in a Gilded Cage" and "Green Finch and Linnet Bird" from Sweeney Todd—but if he actually heard me, there was no reaction from him that I could see or hear.

By Monday evening I'd read so much that my eyes tired a little more quickly each time I picked up a book. I'd never been much of a television-watcher, more due to lack of time than anything else, but I soon found myself wishing for the mind-numbing distraction of hundreds of cable television channels. I amused myself for a few hours after dinner by trying on various items of clothing and then combining them with matching jewels from the little chest of drawers inside the wardrobe. It was all stunning, but I didn't see the point in parading around in Armani and diamonds if I really were going to be stuck in these rooms for the rest of my natural life.

I'd gone to bed early, only to be haunted by disturbing dreams like something out of a Cocteau film—long candlelit hallways, hands reaching out for me, pursuit by a nameless figure that I somehow dreaded yet desired. More than once I'd awakened in the darkness, feeling my heart pounding in my breast, breath coming in harsh gasps, not sure of where I was or what I was doing there. Then I would hear the soft classical music coming from the radio and suddenly remember. I was in Erik's house. I was his prisoner.

Once I even thought I heard his voice in the depths of the night, that yearning tenor, singing one line from *Faust* over and over again...

"Oui, c'est moi, je t'aime…oui, c'est moi, je t'aime…"

I'd sat up in bed, clutching the blankets to my chest, but all that met my ears was the deep quiet of a house in the early, early hours of the morning, that and the delicate sound of a harpsichord tinkling from the speakers of the little Bose stereo. Just another dream, another voice echoing in the darkness. And I kept telling myself that as I fell once again into uneasy sleep.

On Tuesday morning I awoke unrefreshed and more than a little irritable. Not even an extra-long shower followed by a special breakfast of eggs benedict and fresh-baked brioche could liven my spirits. I tried to engage Jerome in conversation about the weather—the rain of Thanksgiving weekend had finally given way to blue skies with only a few lingering clouds—but either he was particularly disinclined toward conversation that morning or Erik had told him to speak with me as little as possible, for he kept his answers terse to the point of rudeness and left my room as quickly as possible.

By late that afternoon I was climbing the walls and ready to sit down and have dinner with the devil himself if it meant I wouldn't have to spend another evening alone with my thoughts. I went to the door that connected my rooms to the hallway and knocked on it. Feeling rather foolish, I called out, "Hello? Anyone there? I'm waving the white flag!"

Only silence. It figured. When I didn't want Jerome showing up, then apparently he was lurking just outside the door. Now, when I was as eager to get sprung as a prisoner waiting out the last day of a ten-year sentence, no one was there. I knocked again. "Truce—really! Jerome? Hello?"

Finally the click of the key in the lock.

"Thank God," I said. "I was afraid no one was there…" And then I let the words trail off, because the man who waited on the other side of the door was not Jerome, as I had expected, but Erik himself.

"Good afternoon, Christine," he said. "Gilded cage starting to feel a bit cramped?"

So he had heard me the day before. I could feel myself blush but couldn't do much about it except return his gaze as squarely as I could and reply, "Well, you did tell me to keep up with my practice."

"So I did. You have an interesting repertoire."

I gave him a narrow look from between my eyelashes, and he smiled, daring me to rebuke him further. Instead, I just returned the smile and said, "So am I sprung?"

"Absolutely," he replied, and then stepped out of the way so I could enter the hallway.

The corridor looked different in the last light of the setting sun, which blazed through a magnificent stained-glass window at the end of the hall. The colors were richer, from the Persian runner under our feet to the mix of landscapes and portraits in their gilded frames that lined the walls. Even Erik's mask shone golden in the light, and the edges of his dark hair caught fire from the dying sun.

"Your house is stunning," I said. It was the simple truth.

For a second he looked at me, seeming a bit surprised, and then he said, "How would you like to see it from the outside?"

It seemed as if I hadn't breathed fresh air for a lifetime. "It would be heavenly," I replied.

"Well, then—" and he offered me his arm.

I hesitated just a bit, then took it. It seemed a small sacrifice when he was offering even the smallest taste of freedom.

If he noticed my reticence, he made no mention of it, for then he led me downstairs and out through the French doors of a small salon on the ground floor to the loggia I could see from the window of my sitting room, pausing only long enough for him to push some sort of code into the keypad that locked the doors. Once we were outside, he released my arm and watched as I stood on the marble pavement and opened my arms wide, as if to embrace the sunset.

"Oh, God, that feels good!" I exclaimed, taking deep breaths of the cold, clean air, reveling in the touch of the wind against my face. It was chilly enough that I knew I couldn't stand out there forever, but at that moment I wanted to.

He watched me with some amusement as the wind caught his hair, ruffling it around his face. It was heavy and thick, with the slightest wave to it—the kind of hair that a woman would want to run her hands through.

Wondering where that thought had come from, I stepped away from him and went to the edge of the steps that led down into the rose garden. Although it was almost December, there were still blooms on most of the bushes. Erik wore only a black shirt over black pants, so he would probably be even less suited to stay out here for long than I was.

I turned to look up at the house. From this vantage I couldn't get a true idea of its size, but I could see it was an immense pile of pale gray stone, done in a vaguely Norman chateau style. One section was covered in ivy, and I could see at least three fireplaces just from where I stood.

"Have you always lived here?" I asked. He seemed to be a part of this place, as integral to its structure as the stone of its façade.

He replied, eyes fixed on some point in the distance past my shoulder, "Yes...I was born here."

"Really? How...medieval!"

"Not exactly." He turned as well and looked up at the house with an unreadable gaze. "Apparently I came early. There wasn't enough time to get to the hospital."

"Better that than the back seat of a car, I suppose."

"I suppose..." he echoed.

The last of the sun disappeared behind the trees that bordered his property, and with its absence the wind seemed to rise. I shivered, and he must have noticed, for he said immediately, "It's getting cold. We should go inside."

As good as the fresh air felt, I had to agree that it was too chilly to stay outside any longer, so I followed him back into the small salon and waited as he closed the door and reentered the code into the keypad, apparently rearming the lock.

"Well, then," he said. "What would you like for dinner?"

I was surprised by that. After all, no one had really asked for my input on my meals, save that one time at the very beginning of my stay here when Jerome had inquired what I'd wanted for breakfast. The meals had all been as varied in content as they were uniform in excellence. It was like dining in a five-star restaurant every day of the week. Still, I'd been starting to crave homelier foods.

"You're going to laugh at me," I said.

He watched me carefully, the dark green eyes scanning my face. What he saw I wasn't sure. "I promise I won't laugh."

"Your chef is great—really. But we college kids usually live on simpler stuff." I took a breath and said, "So what I'd really like is an In-N-Out burger."

"A what?"

"You've never heard of an In-N-Out burger?"

A line appeared momentarily between his brows as he frowned. "I don't think so."

Well, that settled it. I didn't see how anyone could grow up in Southern California and not hear of In-N-Out—they were legendary. How sheltered a life had he led…and why?

"But I'm sure I can have my chef make us some hamburgers if that's what you'd like."

I manufactured a smile and said, "That sounds great." At least it would be a break from chicken *cordon bleu* and steak *au poivre*, if nothing else.

Odd as it seemed to me at the time, I actually enjoyed that evening. We did not eat in the forbidding red dining room, but in a smaller, cheerier chamber not far from the kitchens. I had to admit that the burgers were marvelous, better than any others I had tasted, especially accompanied as they were by a mound of freshly made french fries and a beer for him and a glass of hard cider for me. I'd never had cider before, but Erik suggested that I try it once I'd admitted that I wasn't much of a beer drinker. It was certainly tasty, crisp and fizzy, much drier than a regular sparkling apple cider.

"That's definitely more my speed," I commented after I'd had a few sips.

"It does have a fairly low alcohol content," he agreed, and again I could see the twitch at the corner of his mouth that belied some sort of secret amusement. It made me wonder how much Jerome had told him about my post-Bordeaux hangover.

Once we'd finished eating he suggested a movie. I looked at him blankly.

"A movie?" For a split-second I had a crazy image of him in his Phantom mask escorting me to the latest blockbuster at the multiplex at the Paseo Colorado shopping center.

"Yes—I'm actually quite proud of the setup. If you would follow me—"

I trailed him out of the breakfast room and down several hallways until we came to a set of double doors.

"I had this put in a year ago. I can't think now why I waited so long." And with that he flicked a light switch and led me into a theater.

Yes, a theater. Of course, it wasn't as large as a real movie theater—although in actual size it was close to some of the smaller screens I'd been to at the local multiplex. It was also furnished much more lavishly, in a vaguely Art Deco style meant to imitate the grand movie houses of the '20s or '30s. There were about twenty seats, all upholstered in dark red plush. Black lacquer sconces sent moody uplighting against the dove-gray drapes that hung on the walls.

"Wow," I breathed. I'd seen setups like this in magazines, but I'd never thought I would actually see one in real life.

I could tell he enjoyed watching my amazement. Perhaps he thought he could seduce with me with his wealth if nothing else. *It's going to take more than a private movie theater for that,* I thought, then felt a pang of guilt. He had been nothing but a gentleman to me all evening. Why did I always suspect him of the worst motivations?

Because he kidnapped you, dammit! came that little voice inside me. *All the politeness in the world can't erase that fact, can it?* I had to admit to myself that it probably couldn't, and with that thought I began to feel angry again, although oddly enough I felt angrier with Erik for thinking that the only way he could approach me was by stealing me away. Did he have that little confidence in himself? Did he really think the only way to win my favor was by coercing it? As far as I could tell, he had much more going for himself than most men—apparently limitless talent, a sharp mind, enormous wealth. What could possibly lead him to believe that he was unworthy of any affection that wasn't stolen?

The mask…

Jerome had said, *Don't ever mention the mask,* and at the time I had thought he was merely being melodramatic. I thought the mask was only a prop, something to reinforce Erik's obsession with the Phantom story, but what if it were more? What if he truly did need it?

I told myself to not be ridiculous, this wasn't the Middle Ages, or even the Victorian era in which the original Phantom story was set. These days people with disfigurements weren't hidden away, for God's sake—if anything, they were pushed out into the public eye, the subject of fundraisers and 5k runs and that sort of thing. And I'd seen documentaries where plastic surgeons performed near-miracles on people with congenital birth defects. It just didn't seem to make much sense.

"Christine?" Erik's voice broke my reverie as he stepped into a small chamber, rather like a projectionist's booth, that was located at the back of the theater.

With a guilty start I asked, "Wha - yes?"

"Any requests?"

That was a tricky one. I started desperately ticking over various films in my mind, rejecting this one for having too many love scenes, that one for being too violent, another for being too serious—it was amazing what a personal choice just picking out a movie to watch could be. "A comedy?" That seemed to be the least dangerous route, although I'd seen a few that were raunchier than I would have liked. Still, I thought I could use a good laugh.

A few moments, as I heard him rummaging through what sounded like a fairly extensive DVD collection. Then he appeared with a case in one hand and handed it to me.

I looked at the title. "*What's Up, Doc?*" I thought I recognized it as something I might have seen bits of on television when I was a kid.

"A classic, I assure you." His expression was serious, but again I thought I could catch a glint of amusement in his eyes.

"Sounds great," I replied, and handed the DVD back to him. I'd been relieved to see that it had a G rating. Nothing too terribly controversial in there, thank God.

He took the DVD from me and said, "Why don't you go ahead and sit down? I'll get this started."

So I chose a seat in the dead center of the theater, and after a few moments the lights dimmed and he came and sat down next to me. I noticed he was careful to sit on my right so that the unmasked side of his face was closest to me, although I couldn't see much of him in the darkness. The seats had the sorts of armrests that could be lifted out of the way if desired, but he kept the arm down. It seemed he was being very conscientious in maintaining a respectful distance from me.

I wasn't sure what I was expecting, but the film turned out to be hysterically funny—no one in my family had ever been much of a Streisand fan, but she was very good in it, and Madeline Kahn was hysterical. By the time the climactic chase scene rolled around and the protagonists ended up stuck inside a huge Chinese dragon as they tore all over San Francisco, I was laughing so hard the tears were rolling down my cheeks. I could hear Erik laughing beside me, too, although his reaction was a little more restrained than mine.

Once the film ended, he quickly got up and turned the lights in the theater back on, almost as if he didn't want to remain sitting there with me in the darkness. Feeling a little uncertain of myself I said, "Thank you for that. I can't remember the last time I laughed that hard."

I could hear him busying himself in the little control room. Then he replied, "I'm glad you enjoyed it." At length he emerged, and we stood there, looking at one another, feeling the awkwardness of our silence but not knowing what to do about it.

Finally I said, "It's probably getting late—"

"Of course," he said almost immediately, as if glad to seize on the opportunity to take action. "Let me take you back upstairs."

And so he led me back up to my suite. This evening the house was very softly illuminated by a few lamps here and there; the candelabras stood dark, unused. Once again I stood and waited while he unlocked my door, but this time I wasn't as uneasy as I had been before—somehow I knew that he wouldn't try to kiss me. How I felt about that, I wasn't exactly sure.

Very formally, he said, "Good night, Christine."

I said, "Good night, Erik." It was the first time I had ever called him by his name.

Then I went inside and let him lock the door behind me. I stood there for a moment, the drooping orchid my only company, trying to sort out my thoughts and failing miserably.

Still, I was beginning to understand how Persephone might have felt when she ate those six pomegranate seeds and was suddenly overwhelmed by an inexplicable sympathy for the dark lord of the underworld....

Chapter Sixteen

DETECTIVE RAOUL ORTIZ was having a bad day. Late that morning someone had reported an apparently abandoned car in the underground parking lot at the Paseo Colorado shopping center; probably the car would have gone unnoticed for several more days if not for the foul odor emanating from its trunk. Mall security called in the Pasadena police department, whose investigators discovered the body of a nude woman, bound and gagged, in the trunk. That had been bad enough—although Pasadena certainly saw its share of burglaries, domestic violence, and even gang-related shootings, actual murders were rare. Then of course the media somehow caught wind of it, and as the principal investigator on the scene, he'd been forced to make a brief statement so that the vampires—he grinned to himself—the reporters couldn't make the situation sound any worse than it already was.

Privately, Ortiz was of the opinion that the murder had taken place elsewhere and the body dumped at the mall to confuse the issue, since the shabby Toyota had been reported stolen a week earlier in Santa Ana. But that was still speculation, so he'd been able to give out only a few terse facts—that the body was that of a Latina in her early to mid-twenties, and that she'd apparently died of a single gunshot wound to the head. Probably gang-related; he'd transferred out of the LAPD four years ago so he wouldn't have to see crap like this over and over again, but no such luck on that today.

He picked up the report, sighing. On top of it all, he'd probably get an unwelcome glimpse of himself on the evening news, shining pate and all. It was amazing how he looked overweight, bald, and tired whenever he saw himself on television. That wasn't the same man he thought he saw in the mirror each morning.

"Detective Ortiz?" Officer Campbell stuck her braided head through his partially open office door. "Got time to take a missing-persons statement?"

Wonderful. A missing-persons report was second in the amount of paperwork required only to a murder-scene report, which he was in the process of filling out right now.

"What happened to Kosky?"

She rolled her big brown eyes. "MIA. Probably making a Starbucks run."

"Great, sure." Ortiz pushed the report he'd been working on off to one side of his desk and pulled out a fresh form. "Got any background?"

"Well, the guy already filled out the regular paperwork. But he wants to talk to someone in person."

"Husband?"

She shook her head. "Nope. Think it's the boyfriend. And he's got some other girl with him. A friend, I guess—they don't look related."

"Send 'em in." At the rate he was going, he'd be lucky to make it home in time for dinner tonight. Manuela was going to be ticked.

Campbell disappeared briefly and came back with a young man and woman in tow, both in their twenties, although the woman looked to be the younger of the two by several years. Good-looking kids, both of them, the young man with a nice head of sandy hair and handsome, regular features, the girl much darker and casually gorgeous in a pair of close-fitting designer jeans and a well-tailored short jacket over a low-cut tank top. Ortiz had to force his eyes upward to her face, which was worth looking at as well, with smooth olive skin and a wide, full mouth. He wondered what her heritage might be, since she didn't look Mexican to him. Brazilian?

Officer Campbell indicated that they should sit in the two chairs facing the desk, left the folder with their paperwork in front of Ortiz, and then took off.

Ortiz stood and extended his hand, first to the girl, and then to the young man. "Detective Ortiz."

"I'm Meg Garrison," the young woman said. The south of the border blood had to be on her mother's side, then.

The young man took Ortiz's proffered hand and said, "I'm Randall Cagney."

The kid's eyes looked bloodshot, and he was pale as well. Still, his grip was firm enough, and his gaze steady. It was probably stress rather than drugs, however, that gave him his somewhat haggard appearance.

"So what seems to be the problem, Mr. Cagney?"

The young man swallowed, exchanged a brief glance with Meg, then said, "It's my girlfriend, Christine Daly. She's disappeared."

"Disappeared?"

"Um, yeah. The last time I—or anyone else, I guess—saw her was Thanksgiving evening, when I dropped her off at her place after we had dinner at my parents' house in L.A. I kept trying to call her all weekend and could never get hold of her."

Ortiz took a few brief notes on a yellow pad. "Did you try going over to her house?"

"Yes—by Sunday morning I was getting really worried, so I drove over to her place." Cagney sat up a little straighter in his chair. "I didn't see her car, but I went up and knocked and then sort of walked around the house just to make sure she wasn't in the shower or something. But she wasn't there."

"Mm-hmm." Ortiz rolled his pen over between his thumb and forefinger. "Was the car there when you dropped her off on Thursday night?"

"I don't—" Then Cagney frowned, apparently thinking it through. "Yes, I'm pretty sure it was there. She usually parked it in the same place in front."

"And she wasn't in class on Monday morning," Meg supplied. "Christine never misses class unless she's on her deathbed."

"And how do you know Miss Daly, Miss Garrison?"

"We're both seniors at USC. And we work at the same restaurant here in Pasadena."

"And what restaurant would that be?"

"*L'Opéra*. Down on Green Street."

"I know it," Ortiz said, making a few more notes on the yellow pad. It was a nice place, the sort of restaurant where he'd take Manuela on their anniversary or her birthday. Who knows, he could have even seen the elusive Miss Daly there at some point.

"So anyway," Meg went on, "it was kind of weird that she didn't show up for class, but then she didn't show up for work last night, and that was totally bizarre. George said she didn't call in or anything, either."

"George is your boss?"

She nodded, shining dark hair slipping over the vibrant pink of her jacket. "And then Randall called me this morning, sounding really panicked, and we started talking, and then we decided we'd better come down here and file a report or something."

"Has Miss Daly ever disappeared like this before?" It was a standard question, but they both looked offended.

"Absolutely not—" spluttered Randall, while Meg said,

"Are you kidding? You could set a clock by Christine. She's the most responsible person I know."

Ortiz held up a hand. "Don't take it personally. I need to ask these questions to find out what's really going on."

The Cagney kid continued to look daggers at him, but Meg settled back in her chair, apparently mollified.

"So...another standard question." Ortiz lifted an eyebrow at Randall, letting him know that another outburst would be counterproductive. "Was Christine under a lot of stress? Anything that might make her want to take off for a few days?"

The two of them exchanged a glance, and then Randall said, "I don't think so. I mean, she's a senior, and she's thinking of applying to graduate school, plus she works way too many hours, but Christine's always been able to handle everything, as far as I can tell."

Meg nodded. "I don't think Christine knows how to do anything except manage everything."

Setting his pen down, Ortiz considered Meg carefully. He could tell she was worried, yes, but even more importantly, she looked puzzled, as if she couldn't possibly understand how Christine could do something as unexpected as simply disappear. "And how long have you known Miss Daly?"

"About a year. She started midyear as a junior, and we first met in music theory. I was already working at L'Opéra, so when she told me she was looking for a job I suggested she come work there, too."

"And what about you, Mr. Cagney?"

"About the same. I'm a T.A. and accompany sometimes in the upper-division voice classes."

"And you've been in a relationship with Christine for how long?"

Randall shifted in his seat, looking a little awkward. "About two and a half months."

"Any reason she would be upset with you, want to take off?"

He scowled at that, but when he spoke his tone was carefully neutral. "No. We had a great time on Thanksgiving. My whole family loved her, and I could tell she really liked them."

Oh, hell. Ortiz hated these cases. None of the obvious explanations seemed to present themselves, but he was still fairly sure it was a simple case of an overworked student cracking under the pressure and taking off for a few days or even weeks. Nine times out of ten in these cases, the missing people would reappear, usually somewhat shamefaced over what they'd put their friends and families through, but none the worse for wear.

Of course, it was the tenth case that could really be the problem. "Anything else you want to tell me about? Anything unusual going on with Christine?"

Randall shook his head, but Meg bit her lip and looked worried. Interesting.

"Miss Garrison? Is there something you'd like to tell me?"

Meg gave her companion an uneasy look, then said, hesitating over the words, "Well, Christine was sort of worried about something..."

Ortiz remained silent, watching her. Usually it was best to let the interviewee reveal her story on her own, without too much prompting.

"Christine didn't really want to talk about it, but she was sort of nervous—she thought someone might be watching her, or following her."

"What?!" Randall seemed to explode out of his chair, staring down at Meg accusingly.

"Mr. Cagney, if you could please sit back down—"

Simultaneously, Meg said to Randall, her sharp tones overriding Ortiz's words, "She told me not to say anything to you! She knew you would freak out, just like you're doing now! *Madre de dios!*" The girl's dark eyes were snapping, but she continued, her tone a little lower, "Sorry, Detective Ortiz."

"No problem," he said. "Mr. Cagney, I'll have to ask you again to sit down."

The young man glared at him for a moment, then slowly resumed his seat, his knuckles white against the arms of the chair.

"All right, then." After giving Randall one last quelling look, Ortiz transferred his attention to Meg. "So Christine thought she had a stalker?"

"Well, not in so many words, but—" Her dark, long-lashed eyes narrowed a bit, and then she said, "Okay, yeah. She said she saw this guy a couple of times on campus and got the impression he was following her."

"Do you remember if she said exactly when she saw this man?"

"Mmm...not really. I think the first time was pretty early on in the semester, like the end of September maybe? And then definitely at the autumn recital, which was mid-October."

Ortiz took rapid notes on his yellow pad. He was liking the sound of this less and less. But the first order of business was to get as many facts as possible. "Did she say anything about what he looked like?"

"A little." Meg tilted her head to one side, apparently

trying to recall exactly what her friend had told her. One long gold earring brushed against her throat as she did so, and Ortiz studiously raised his eyes once again to her face. God, the girl was distracting. "She said he had dark hair—or did she just say it was brown? Brown, dark, something like that. And she said he looked like he was in his late thirties or early forties, kind of medium height, but a good build, like he might work out or something. I think that was about it."

"Eye color?"

"Nope. I don't think she ever got close enough to tell for sure."

"And as far as you know she only saw him on those two separate occasions?"

"I'm pretty sure that was it, yeah."

Ortiz continued to make notes on his pad, although he could tell Randall was dangerously close to another outburst. To forestall any more arguments on the young man's part, he directed his next words to him. "Do you have a recent photo of Christine?"

"Yeah, actually, I do." Randall reached inside his jacket and pulled out a photo that had obviously been printed on someone's home computer. "My brother took a bunch of shots with his phone on Thanksgiving, and he gave me copies."

Giving Randall what he hoped was a reassuring smile, Ortiz took the photo and looked it over carefully. The shot was of Christine and Randall in front of a large fireplace with a heavy carved wood mantel; Randall had his arm draped around Christine's shoulders, and they were both smiling directly into the camera. The girl had a luxuriant

mass of curly dark hair that fell almost to her waist, a surprising, almost archaic look in this era of flat-ironed locks
and center parts. And she was beautiful. Possibly not as
immediately striking as Meg's flamboyant, exotic allure,
but just as lovely in her own way, with delicate, even features and large blue eyes.

"May I keep this?" Ortiz asked.

It was obvious Randall wanted to protest at first—Ortiz
could understand the young man not wanting to part with
even this small reminder of his missing girlfriend—but
then he said, "Sure. If you think it will help."

"I hope it will." Ortiz set the photo down on his yellow pad and addressed his next words to both Randall and
Meg. "At this point it's far too early to call this anything
but a missing-person case, but of course I'll continue to
investigate. I think the next step is to procure a search
warrant and contact Miss Daly's landlord so he can give
Pasadena P.D. access to her home. Maybe we'll find some
more clues there. In the meantime, don't hesitate to call
if you think of anything else—even if you're not sure it's
at all connected to Miss Daly's disappearance." He pulled
several cards out of his top desk drawer and handed one
each to Randall and Meg. "That's got both my direct line
and my pager number on it. If you think of anything else,
or have a question, just give me a call. I assume your contact info is on the report you filled out?"

They both nodded, and he glanced down at the report
just to make sure. "Good." He looked at them then, seeing the tension return to their faces, but he knew at this
point there wasn't much he could do to relieve it. "And of

course I'll contact you as soon as I have any developments in the case."

At that point Ortiz rose and extended his hand to Randall. "I know there's no point telling you not to worry. But most of the time these sorts of cases have a way of working themselves out."

Randall stood as well and took Ortiz's hand, although it was obvious he was far from satisfied with how the interview had gone. Still, his tone sounded civil enough as he said, "Thank you, Detective Ortiz."

Meg rose as well and said, "Thanks for your time, detective."

Ortiz resisted the temptation to say, *Just doin' my job, ma'am,* and instead smiled at her. "We're on it. Just try to keep your spirits up." He glanced at Randall, who was frowning again. "Both of you."

They nodded, then let Ortiz hold the door open for them to exit. He swore they couldn't have gone more than three feet down the hall before Randall started in on Meg about keeping secrets. Ortiz felt a rush of pity for her as he shut the door, then grinned to himself. As far as he could tell, that girl could probably take care of herself.

His smile faded, though, as he approached his desk and looked down at the photo of Christine. *And what of you, Miss Daly?* he thought. *Are you able to protect yourself, wherever you are?*

He had a feeling he might never find out.

For the first time in more years than he cared to count, Erik felt hope. Surely he hadn't imagined that brief moment of hesitation in Christine's eyes last night, that slightest parting of her lips before she had said good night. She was not ready yet—he wasn't going to delude himself on that point—but somehow he sensed a gradual softening in her attitude toward him, the merest hint of the beginnings of acceptance.

Certainly it had been the first "date" he'd ever had in his life—if one could call it that. However, dinner and a movie seemed to be a widely accepted form of courtship, and Christine appeared to have enjoyed herself. He smiled even now to recall her unrestrained laughter during the more manic parts of the film, laughter that didn't seem to have a trace of self-consciousness in it. Surely she wouldn't have been able to let herself go enough to react in such a way if she didn't feel able to relax—even a little—around him.

Today he'd arisen far earlier than he normally would—barely past noon—eager as he was to see her again. Before Christine, the harsh hours of daylight had held no allure for him. Darkness had always been his friend, sheltering him and keeping him secure, but he knew that Christine, unused to his nocturnal habits, was awake hours before he was, and somehow he couldn't bear to think of that time as being wasted. Perhaps in time she would adjust to his schedule, but meanwhile he could at least meet her halfway.

As he slowly mounted the stairs to her rooms, he thought of the chamber he'd had constructed all those years ago to resemble the Phantom's lair from the musical. He knew that it was far too soon to take Christine there. However much he longed to see her in that room, to hear her voice echo against its marble-lined walls, he didn't dare to upset the delicate balance between them by revealing himself as the obsessed madman she first believed him to be. No, he had to take care to keep things as normal as possible, to let her relax and come to see him only as a slightly eccentric man who, whatever his faults, truly loved her.

That realization had surprised him. He had wanted her, dreamed about her, thought of her to the exclusion of all else for so long that when he was actually confronted by the reality of her he'd been astonished to realize that she was a person in her own right, with her own quirks and awkward edges. He hadn't expected her anger when she had first confronted him, just as he hadn't expected the cheek that led her to sing those carefully chosen ditties about caged birds and whatnot. No wonder Randall had been so infatuated with her.

The thought of the boy sobered him momentarily, but he brushed the image of Randall aside. That unfortunate young man was in Christine's past. He, Erik, was her future. All that was needed was the gradual building of her trust, and the slow encouragement of the attraction he knew she felt toward him—however much she might fight it.

And here he was at her door. He hoped that in the near future he would be able to keep it unlocked, to let her share the house with him unreservedly so she would come to regard it as her only true home. But it was too soon for that. For now she must still be a prisoner, until he was sure she wouldn't try to get away.

He lifted a hand and knocked. His heart beat heavily in his chest even now at the thought of the sight of her. Even as her sweet voice bade him enter, he was still somewhat overwhelmed by the unreality of it, that his Christine was just on the other side of that door, waiting for him.

With a hand that shook a little, he placed the key in the lock and turned it. The door opened, and she stood there, her glorious hair lying loose on her shoulders, her sea-colored eyes turned almost green by the dark purple sweater she wore. Around her creamy throat twinkled a line of diamond rosettes, probably the simplest of the necklaces he had bought her, but this was the first time he'd seen her wear any of the jewels she'd been given, save that one pair of diamond studs.

Her smile was a miracle. "So," she said, her tone only slightly teasing, "what do you have planned for today?" And she stepped out in the hall to be with him.

Chapter Seventeen

IT WAS ONE OF THOSE QUIET, LOVELY DAYS, the sort that is remarkable only because of its delicate perfection. The weekend's rain was a hazy memory; when Erik led me out to his gardens, the sky was a delicate blue, etched with only the faintest high cirrus clouds. The sun warmed my face, although the westerly breeze that sent the few remaining leaves dancing on bare branches was crisp and cool.

His suggestion had been a picnic on the grounds, and since my brief foray outside the evening before had certainly not sated my appetite for fresh air, I readily agreed. At first I was surprised to see him walking so easily in the daylight—Erik had so far impressed me as a nocturnal creature—but he did not appear self-conscious. Instead he strode along next to me, fine chin lifted into the breeze, the sunlight picking out reddish lights in his dark hair, as well as the slightest traces of silver at his temples. The mask was almost blindingly white in the sun.

Our destination appeared to be the stone gazebo at one of the far edges of his property. Up close, it was fairly impressive—a large structure of fine carved marble, topped with an intricate wrought-iron roof now half-hidden by ivy, which also wound its way up the fluted columns. Benches were set in between the columns, but there were also a wooden folding table and two chairs that had been placed in the the open area at the center of the gazebo. On top of the table sat a large picnic basket, and a bottle of wine was already chilling in a silver bucket.

I looked over at Erik. "You do think of everything, don't you?"

"I try to," he replied. "Life is so much more pleasant when things go as planned, don't you think?"

"What about being spontaneous?" I asked. I was half-teasing—God knows I liked things well-planned and orderly myself, for the most part. A guy I had briefly dated my freshman year of college said my need for order stemmed from a subconscious desire to control my world, as the loss of my parents had shown me how little I actually could control.

That relationship hadn't lasted very long.

"Spontaneity has its place, I suppose," he said slowly, as if thinking over the matter with care. "But I find that the anticipation of a thing adds so much to the actual experience, once it occurs."

Those words made me look at him, considering. How long had he anticipated my presence here? And how did he feel about it, now that I was finally with him? The half of his face I could see was serious, the dark brow pulled down slightly in thought. In the bright light of midday I could see more clearly the lines etched around the corner of his eye, the slight furrow that ran from nose to mouth. Paradoxically, those signs of age made him more rather than less attractive. I wondered, not for the first time, how old he really was. Certainly a good deal older than myself. Even if our circumstances had been different—if we had met socially—I probably would not have entertained the idea of having a relationship with someone that much older than myself. It was too complicated.

But here I was, and I knew I was only fooling myself if I didn't know why. Erik had acted as a gentleman the whole time, had given me no reason to fear him—other than his means of getting me here in the first place—but I knew it was more than mere companionship he wanted. I should be glad that at least he seemed willing to wait for me to reach out to him. Exactly how long he would wait for me to make up my mind, however, remained to be seen.

Apparently nonplussed by my silence, he said, "Some riesling?" and handed me a glass filled with pale straw-colored wine.

I took it and sipped. It was light, sweeter than I had expected, with overtones of honey. Somehow it seemed to match the mild December day around us, with its impressions of clear sunlight, and warmth on leaves and vines. "That's very good," I said.

"The Germans are some of the most underrated wine-makers in the world, I find." He drank from his own glass, then set it down on the table next to the picnic basket. "Let's see what Ennis has packed for us, shall we?"

The basket contained an amazing variety of food, from another loaf of that crusty sourdough I loved so much to wonderful little pastries that turned out to be baked brie en croute. There were slices of cold smoked chicken, a fabulous tray of assorted cheeses, grapes, and strawberries. The finishing touch was a pair of crème brulées, each in its own little porcelain ramekin.

"You really are going to have to walk me all over the grounds to work this off," I said, after surveying the sumptuous spread Erik laid out on the cloth-covered table.

"It would be my pleasure," he replied. His eyes looked very green in the reflected light from the ivy-arched canopy above us.

What was it about those eyes, that voice? It would be so easy, after all, to give in to their spell, let myself be fascinated by him, let myself succumb....

I had to force my gaze from his to turn my attention to the food. *Show a little backbone!* I told myself fiercely, as I made myself pick up a piece of bread with a hand that shook a little and then made a show of selecting a piece of cheese to go with the bread. It was only after I had taken several bites and another sip of wine that I asked, "Does Ennis always pack your lunch?"

He smiled at that, as I had hoped he would. "Actually, this is my first picnic. Usually I come here at sunset, or later on in the evening. I like to watch the moon rise."

Probably it would be lovely, I thought, as I looked around. One border of trees stood very near us, and I fancied I could actually hear the slightest sound of a car going by beyond the wall that surrounded the property. Perhaps we weren't quite as isolated here as I had first thought, perhaps escape wasn't as impossible as I had feared. Up until now I had heard no hint of the world beyond Erik's property and had assumed, given the size of the grounds, that it was somewhere out in the middle of nowhere. But now, as I heard a second car go past, I realized we probably weren't as isolated as I had originally believed.

Hoping that Erik hadn't noticed my dawning realization, I took a bite of baked brie and then said, "It must be wonderful to be surrounded by so much beauty every day."

For a moment his gaze lingered on my face, and I could feel the blood rush to my cheeks. Then he said, casually enough, "In some ways, I have been blessed. Certainly my home has always been a source of comfort to me."

From this distance I could see the house in its entirety, or at least the one elevation that presented its face to us. It was enormous, done in a pseudo-Norman chateau style complete with arched mullioned windows and dark-gray imported stone. The steeply pitched roof was broken by half a dozen fireplaces.

"How old is it?"

He took another sip of the riesling before replying, his eyes fixed on the massive stone pile. "My grandfather built it in 1922. He made his fortune in steel in the teens and then moved out here from Michigan, escaping the cold winters along with everyone else, I suppose. My father was born here a few years later."

Many of the grandest homes in Pasadena had been built then, in those halcyon days when everyone thought the boom would last forever. Obviously Erik's grandfather had fared better than most in the crash that followed.

Almost as if reading my thoughts, he continued, "Luckily my grandfather didn't have much use for the stock market. First it was steel, then oil and land. Diversification was his strong suit. But it certainly served the family well."

I wondered whether I should ask the crass question, but then thought, *Oh, the hell with it.* "So how rich are you? Donald Trump rich or Bill Gates rich?"

"What, no sultan of Brunei?" His eyes laughed at me over the rim of his wine glass.

"Well, I don't see any gold-plated Rolls Royces dotting the property, so I figured you weren't that rich."

He let out a chuckle at that. "No, definitely not. As for your previous question, somewhere in between the two—but probably closer to Donald Trump if I had to hazard a guess."

The part of my brain that had to deal with monthly bill-paying took a step back and gave a few seconds of respectful silence to the concept of that kind of wealth. But then I said, "I suppose that was rude of me, to ask that sort of thing—"

"Not at all," he said smoothly. "I would have been surprised if you hadn't asked at some point. It's not as if I can take credit for most of it—the original fortune was amassed by my grandfather and then built upon by my father. I haven't done much more than maintain it. In a way, it's sort of frightening how it can pile up if you don't do much with it."

Since at last count my bank account had had exactly

$267.50 in it, I wasn't sure I could exactly relate. But at least he hadn't been offended.

Apparently noticing that I had stopped eating, he asked, "Are you ready to pack this up, then?"

"I couldn't eat another bite," I honestly replied. Everything had been fabulous, but there were limits—Ennis had packed enough for four people.

"Very good." He began to gather the half-eaten food and wrap it up, but he did it somewhat clumsily, as if he hadn't much experience with that sort of thing.

"Let me help," I offered, taking a partially wrapped hunk of cheese from him. As a waitress I certainly had plenty of opportunity to wrap up leftovers, and I made short work of the remaining food.

Once I was done, he piled everything into the basket and picked it up. "Shall we?" he asked, and I followed him out of the gazebo down a flagstone path that led back toward the house.

Our return was slow and meandering, as he detoured to show me the herb garden planted outside the kitchen, the pergola off the library that was covered in genuine grapevines—"mediocre fruit at best," he told me, "but at least it looks picturesque"—and the ornamental pool over which the willows bent, trailing their fingers in the water. A few koi moved gracefully through the jade-colored water, giving off flashes of gold and white and copper in the midday sun.

As I walked beside him, listening as he spoke of the gardens and the variety of landscapes his grandmother had had planted when they built this place, part of me wished that this was all it could be—just the two of us, enjoying this lovely home together, taking pleasure in one another's company. But that wasn't all it appeared to be, unfortunately. No matter how charming he was, how solicitous of my well-being, the ugly fact remained that he was forcing me to be here. I couldn't just walk out the front door and say, "I had a lovely time, Erik. Give me a call tomorrow and we'll have lunch."

No, he had spoiled whatever could have been between us through that one heinous act. I wouldn't lie to myself—an attraction existed between us that wasn't entirely one-sided, and I certainly couldn't say that I disliked his company—far from it. In fact, painful as it was for me to admit it, in some ways I enjoyed being with him more than I enjoyed being with Randall.

But he had taken from me the power to choose him, and that had been his one fatal blunder. Now that I knew I was somewhere still in reach of civilization, I had to at least try to escape. How and when, I had no idea, but sooner rather than later, of that much I was sure.

At length we reached the house, making our way inside through the same French doors in the small salon where he had led me outside the day before. The depths of the house seemed dim and shadowy after the bright sunlight outside, and I had to blink several times to adjust my eyes to the change.

Ennis appeared from nowhere to take the basket from Erik. "Everything to your liking, sir?"

"Wonderful, Ennis—thank you." Erik looked over at me. "Did you enjoy it, Christine?"

"It was marvelous," I said warmly, and was gratified to see Ennis smile back at me. Then I thought, Of course. Ennis. He was the only one who obviously hadn't participated in this kidnapping plot. There was nothing in his kind, still-distinguished face that showed any evidence of duplicity. Of course, Erik had apparently convinced him that I was some sort of paranoid schizophrenic who was only functional when heavily doped up with lithium, but there had to be a way for me to convince him that I was the victim in all this. I knew he would help me escape once he knew the truth.

"Very good, miss," Ennis said, then left, taking the picnic basket with him.

I looked up at Erik, hoping that my features didn't betray the turmoil I was feeling. "Would you mind if I went to my room for a while? I suppose I'm not used to that much sun after all those days inside."

"Not at all," he replied, his tone immediately solicitous. "I should have thought of that before dragging you all over the gardens—"

"Oh, I'll be fine if I just lie down for a while," I said hastily. If he were going to feel guilty over me, then at least he should feel guilty over something real and not one of my manufactured excuses.

"Of course."

Again he led up up the now-familiar staircase to my room. We paused outside as he reached in his pocket for the key; then, as he slipped it into the lock and turned it, I reached out and laid my hand on his. His fingers were slender and strong beneath mine, still warm from the lingering effects of the sun.

"Do you really think that's still necessary?" I asked softly.

He paused. The slightest tremor went through the hand holding the key, but he said nothing.

Keeping my tone still gentle, with the slightest trace of pleading, I said, "Where do you think I would go? I heard the cars going past the gazebo earlier. I could have screamed for help if I had wanted to."

Still he was silent, but I could almost feel the physical force of his gaze as he stared down me, as if he were trying to rip the truth from my mind. Then at length he asked, the words barely above a whisper, "Do you truly mean that?"

Hating myself, I forced the lie past my lips. "I do mean that. But if we're to—to be together at all, then surely you can understand why I don't want to feel like a prisoner in this place."

"Christine, I—" and then he fell silent, as if he were afraid to betray himself by speaking any further.

It was too late. I had already heard the break in his voice as he said my name, and I could feel my eyes sting with sudden tears. Damn him—why couldn't I just hate him and leave it at that? Why did I feel this overwhelming sense of betrayal? Why did I find it so hard to remember that I was the victim here?

Quickly, before I had time to react, he took my hand from his and then raised it to his mouth. His breath was warm on my skin, the feel of his lips delicate, like the brush of a butterfly's wing. Then he let go of me, and pushed the door inward.

"I can deny you nothing, it seems," he said, and suddenly his voice sounded very weary.

Not knowing what else to do, I stepped inside and gently closed the door behind me. I waited for the inevitable sound of the key turning in the lock, but it never came. After a few moments, I put my hand on the door knob. It turned easily, but I did not open the door. Instead, I leaned my head against the lintel and suddenly, foolishly, began to weep.

"You what?" Jerome glared at him, unbelieving.

"I left her door unlocked," Erik replied. Jerome's rage would have been amusing if it weren't for the fact that underneath his calm, Erik himself was a bit unnerved by the audacity of the move. Of course he had planned to take this step at some point, but not so soon, not even a week after Christine had arrived. Of course Jerome was furious, but Jerome hadn't been there, hadn't heard the faint tremor in her voice, seen the pleading in those shimmering sea-colored eyes. She had been right—how could they make any progress in their relationship if she continually thought of herself as his prisoner?

"She's trouble," Jerome said ominously.

"We knew that from the beginning," Erik said, his voice smooth, although he was beginning to be irritated. After all, he was paying Jerome to do what he was told, not offer opinions.

"I don't mean that kind of trouble. The kidnapping was a calculated risk, but it went off fine. I mean that she's too smart for her own good. And that's what gets a woman into trouble."

At that Erik laughed and was gratified to see Jerome scowl. "I would never have taken you for a misogynist, Jerome."

"Oh, I like women just fine, sir. That's not my point."

"And just what is your point?" Erik pushed his chair away from the desk and stood, going to the table by the window where his decanter of cognac sat. He poured himself a modest amount, pointedly not offering Jerome any—not that Jerome would have accepted it. Erik had never seen the man drink.

"My point is that I've seen plenty of women, both smart and dumb, get themselves into trouble. The problem with the smart ones is that they usually drag other people along with them." The man's blue eyes narrowed; his expression was not pleasant. "She's playing you, sir."

The rage welled up in him at Jerome's casually cruel words, but Erik forced himself to take a calming sip of his cognac instead of lashing out at his assistant. "You know nothing about her," he said at length, deliberately keeping his tone cold and distant.

"Maybe I don't, but I know plenty about women. They'll say and do what they have to to survive. Can't even blame them, really—they definitely got dealt a short hand out of the biological deck. But that doesn't mean I trust them—especially not one who's cornered, like Christine."

A small, hidden part of him wanted to acknowledge Jerome's statements, since the man had had far more experience of the world than he, but Erik forced those pernicious thoughts away. Christine was not like that. Jerome had not seen the look in her eyes as she made her request, and Jerome hadn't seen the easy way she had laughed and talked with him throughout that magical sunlit afternoon. Perhaps the scum Jerome had to deal with during his time with the FBI and as a private investigator soured him so much that he thought all women incapable of loyalty and compassion. Whatever the case, Jerome was obviously incapable of understanding Christine's motivations. He could not comprehend anything that was pure.

"I'm afraid you have little grasp of the situation, Jerome," Erik said at length. He was pleased to see the man's color rise slightly, his eyes narrow. But of course Jerome could not give in to his anger around Erik. "You may go now."

With that he turned to look out the window, effectively dismissing Jerome. He could hear his assistant hesitate for a moment, then say very quietly, "I'll still be watching her." But he gave Erik no time for a rebuttal, as he left immediately, closing the door with more force than was strictly necessary.

"You do that," Erik murmured, then lifted the glass of cognac to his lips once more. It would actually please him to have Jerome watch Christine and find nothing suspect. It would please him to be able to prove the man wrong, show him that his infallible knowledge of human nature wasn't so infallible after all.

It bordered on the ridiculous, really. Erik doubted very much that Jerome had ever met a woman exactly like

Christine. In fact, Erik doubted that there was another woman exactly like Christine. She was a rare treasure, from her exquisite face to her magnificent voice to the agile mind behind it all. And now she was offering that treasure to him, unbelievable as it seemed. He could still feel the pressure of her delicate hand on his, the velvet texture of her skin against his lips. The thought of her gracing his home as an honored guest and future mistress instead of a prisoner pleased him very much.

"To freedom," he said aloud, and drank again.

Chapter Eighteen

DETECTIVE ORTIZ STOOD ON THE FRONT PORCH of Christine's bungalow, waiting for her landlord to show up and let him in. The man had some unpronounceable Greek name—Ortiz had to check his notes and read through it one more time to try to get it straight. Panagapoulos. He just hoped he wouldn't mangle it too badly once the man actually got here.

The potted plants on the porch were already wilting, he noticed. Other than that, there was no real sign that the bungalow's inhabitant had been missing for a week—no papers piled on the front step, no overflowing mailbox. Probably she didn't get much, except for bills and advertising circulars.

It was quiet here, late morning on a weekday. The neighborhood consisted of other, mostly larger, bungalows built about the same time as Christine's, and a few two-story clapboard farmhouse types that had probably bridged the gap between the late 1800s and the early years of this century. Nothing here to show that anything untoward had happened to explain Miss Daly's disappearance.

A late-model Lincoln pulled up to the curb, looking distinctly out of place in the shabby working-class neighborhood. After a moment, a heavyset man in his late fifties hauled himself out of the driver's seat and came up the walk to meet Ortiz. The man did not look at all pleased to be there.

"Mr. Panagapoulos?" Ortiz extended his hand. "I'm Detective Ortiz."

Panagapoulos reached and shook Ortiz's proffered hand. His clasp was damp and clammy. A big diamond sparkled on his ring finger. "You got the warrant?"

Ortiz gladly abandoned the handshake and pulled the paperwork out of his breast pocket. Unfolding it, he handed the piece of paper to Panagapoulos so he could see it for himself. The man made a show of reading it closely, but Ortiz knew everything was in order.

"Ah, okay," the man said finally, pulling a heavy key ring out of his pants pocket. "Strange business, huh?"

"Mm-hmm," Ortiz said, trying to sound noncommittal.

Panagapoulos opened the door and pushed it inward. "Okay if I stay out here? I want to smoke."

Inwardly Ortiz cheered—nothing was more annoying than tripping over an unnecessary observer when he was trying to conduct an investigation—but he only said, "Sure, no problem. This will only take a few minutes."

Christine's landlord only gave a brief grunt in reply— he was already occupied with lighting his cigarette.

That was good enough for Ortiz. He stepped into the tiny living room, noting the seen-better-days shabbiness of the furniture, the clutter of books on the built-in shelves. A light layer of dust lay over everything, but other than that the place was scrupulously clean. A drop-leaf table to one side had obviously functioned as her computer desk; he could see one of those portable printers you used with a laptop still sitting on the table, but the computer itself was nowhere in evidence.

Nothing looked to have been disturbed—several textbooks lay stacked next to the printer, and a piece of sheet music sat open on the music stand of the tiny spinet. The roller blinds were pulled all the way down on all the windows, but if Christine truly had last been here on Thanksgiving evening, there was nothing particularly unusual about closed blinds. He didn't know too many single young women who would have gone around at night with the blinds open.

The living room opened directly into the tiny bedroom, which barely had space for a daybed and a small antique dresser. The bed was neatly made up with a faded blue and white quilt; no signs of any struggle there. He pushed aside the lace curtain she apparently used as a closet door and looked inside; the tiny closet could hold only the most meager of wardrobes, but most of the hangers were empty, signaling to Ortiz that the clothing had been taken away.

Beyond the bedroom was one of the tiniest bathrooms Ortiz had ever seen, sparkling clean except for the inevitable rust stains in the sink and bathtub. He opened the medicine cabinet but found nothing except a half-used bottle of generic ibuprofen and a mostly empty box of band-aids. Toothbrush, toothpaste, any prescriptions or cosmetics she might have used—all that was gone.

There was another door leading out of the bathroom into a small area that must have been the laundry room at one point. A few unused pipes coming out of the wall and a light square against the paint were hints of a wash basin that had probably occupied the space. Now, apparently, Christine used it for storage, as several boxes of books were stacked against one wall, and he also found a few pieces of inexpensive nylon luggage, the kind you would buy in sets at someplace like Target or Walmart. A large suitcase and a small carry-on still sat there, but it looked as if a medium-sized piece had once occupied the space between the two.

As far as he could tell, everything he'd seen so far pointed to only one plausible conclusion—the pressure had been too much, and Christine had just bolted. Where and why, he had no idea, but that wasn't really his problem.

He came back through the bedroom. As he did so, his right foot connected with a small object, sending it skittering across the hardwood floor. Immediately he squatted down, scanning the wooden surface for the source of the sound. He spotted it almost immediately and picked it up with a pair of tweezers that he pulled out of his breast pocket—it was a woman's ring, antique by the look of it, with a small oval ruby surrounded by tiny flickering diamonds in a filigree setting.

Odd. Nothing in the meager tidiness of Christine's home suggested that she would be careless with what looked like a family heirloom. That such a precious object would have been left on the floor when the rest of the house was in perfect order didn't make any sense at all. Frowning, Ortiz fished in his coat pocket with his left hand, fumbling for one of the small plastic evidence bags he carried with him at all times. Finally he pulled it out and dropped the ring inside. He'd have to ask Randall or Meg if they'd ever seen it before.

He gave the kitchen a cursory look before leaving—as he'd expected, it too was neat and tidy, with one plate and a coffee mug sitting in the wooden dish drain. Everything was in order: the refrigerator mostly empty except for a now-expired quart of milk and a couple of forlorn-looking yogurt containers, the coffee maker clean, a pair of bananas blackening in a bowl on the counter.

Except for the ring, Ortiz couldn't think of a single piece of evidence in the bungalow that pointed to anything but a planned, orderly departure by Christine. He knew he should probably just go back to his office and let Randall know that it looked as if Christine had just taken off—sorry, kid, them's the breaks. But still, that carelessly dropped ring bothered him.

Frowning, he came back out to the living room, took one last obligatory look around, but saw nothing else. With a sigh he stepped out onto the porch, where Panagapolous dropped his cigarette and ground it out on the carefully swept cement.

"Find anything?"

"Not really." Not for the first time, Ortiz was glad of the conventions that kept him from having to discuss a case in progress.

The landlord sniffed. "So what am I supposed to do with this place? The rent was due two days ago, and the girl's missing. I'm not going to hold it forever."

Just when he'd thought he'd heard it all…. Ortiz cleared his throat and said, "This is still an open case unless I say otherwise. Since this property is the site of a possible crime scene, you won't do anything with it until you hear from me or the Pasadena P.D. Got that?"

"All right." The man's small dark eyes narrowed even more. "I got bills to pay, same as everybody else."

Yeah, my heart bleeds, Ortiz thought, looking out to where the shiny Lincoln was parked at the curb. "I'll inform you if the situation changes. Until then, the property stays as it is."

Not wanting to prolong the conversation, Ortiz capped his last statement with a brisk nod of dismissal, then strode down the front steps to his own Ford Crown Victoria— really, he thought, it might as well have a big sign on the door that said "unmarked police car." Still, he was glad to heave himself in behind the wheel and get out of there. He'd had an overwhelming urge to pop Panagapolous in his fat mouth—here a girl had disappeared, a bright, beautiful, talented girl—and all the guy cared about was his lousy rent. Ortiz had seen worse over the years, but the petty small-mindedness of it still amazed him.

By the time he pulled into the parking lot behind the station, he was in a foul mood. It hadn't helped that some bastard had parked his car in Ortiz's spot—he'd been forced to park off in a distant corner and hoof it in under a sky that looked increasingly like rain. Crazy weather. Last year it had been dry as a bone, and now they were seriously heading into ark-building mode as far as he could tell.

Officer Campbell was on his tail almost the second he set foot inside the building. "Detective Ortiz—"

"What?"

She blinked her big chocolate-brown eyes at him, but Letisha Campbell had grown up in the rough end of Altadena—it would take more than a detective's bark to put her off her stride. "Meg Garrison is waiting to talk to you. I told her you were out conducting an investigation, but she said she'd wait until you got back. Should I bring her over to your office?"

"Yeah, sure. Give me a couple of minutes—I need to hit the men's room before I get into anything else."

"Sure thing, detective." She winked at him and then sauntered off.

Feeling a little more himself a few minutes later, he watched as Meg entered his office, sans Randall this time around. Today her dress was a little more subdued, as was her demeanor.

"I'm sorry to bother you, detective, but you said I should contact you if I thought of anything else, and since I was on my way in to work—"

"It's no bother, Miss Garrison," he said immediately. "What's up?"

She bit her lip. "Well, I've been thinking and think-ing about Christine. About this guy she says she saw, about anything else unusual that might have happened to her. And for a while I really couldn't think of anything, couldn't see anything that would have a connection. But then I remembered Halloween, and thought I should tell you."

Ortiz picked up his pen. "What about Halloween?"

"Well, it was a Saturday night, so George—our boss—had a big party for the evening: costume contest, dancing, that sort of thing." Meg pushed up the sleeves of her jacket in a sudden nervous gesture. "Anyway, there was this guy who paid the hostess two hundred bucks so he could sit at Christine's station."

The pen stopped scratching on the yellow pad. Ortiz looked up at Meg. "Two hundred dollars?"

"Yes. And he left Christine a huge tip—almost three hundred and fifty. She didn't think I saw it, but she got held up on her way back to the table, so I sneaked a peek. I figured a guy like that would have to be a pretty big tipper, but I wasn't really expecting that."

Who would? thought Ortiz. Then he asked, "Description?"

She hesitated. "Well, it was a costume party after all. He was dressed as the Phantom of the Opera."

Ortiz had a brief flash of Lon Chaney menacing a frizzy-haired singer; that unmasking scene had scared the crap out of him when he was a kid. "Must have been a hell of a makeup job," he said.

For a second she just looked at him blankly, and then gave a nervous laugh. "Not that Phantom of the Opera. The one from the musical—you know, with the half-mask."

"So you were able to see half his face?"

"Well, the lighting wasn't that great, but—"

"Anything would be helpful."

Meg stared off into the corner, as if concentrating on the faded urine-colored walls would help her to remember. "He had dark hair—really dark. It looked black in that lighting. Pale skin—but he could've been wearing makeup or something. And he was hot."

"Hot?"

"Okay—good-looking. Really. I could tell he was older than Christine and me, but when someone looks like that, who cares?"

"Anything more specific than that?" Ortiz felt a wave of irrational dislike for the unnamed man. Certainly no one—not even his wife Manuela—had ever referred to him as "hot."

"I don't know—he had kind of a long nose, but in a good way. I couldn't see what color his eyes were. And his mouth wasn't real full or anything, but it had a nice shape."

Apparently once Meg had categorized someone as "hot" she didn't spend a lot of time on specifics. "Approximate age?"

"Maybe forty?" The rising inflection on the last syllable telegraphed her uncertainty. "Late thirties or early forties, possibly," she amended.

"So he was the same age as the man Christine thought she saw at school?"

"I guess so. But I don't think it's the same guy."

She actually sounded certain of that fact. Ortiz leaned

forward, tapping his pen on the desktop. "What makes you say that?"

"Christine said the guy she saw at school was just medium height. I saw this Phantom guy stand up when he left, and he was pretty tall. Definitely over six feet. And Christine said the first guy had brown hair, but this guy's was almost black. Besides, if she'd thought it was the same guy she would have told me."

Great. So now Christine had two stalkers after her?

"This is the weird thing, though," Meg continued. "I thought I'd ask around at work and see if anyone else had noticed him. The other wait staff hadn't, really, because they were all swamped at their own stations. But then I talked to Jeff, one of the valets who was on duty that night, and he said he thought he remembered him—mostly because of what he was driving."

"Which was?"

"A brand-new Mercedes S600. I guess it's the top of the line. Jeff's a car nut, so he knew all about it. He said it was worth about a hundred and twenty-five thousand dollars."

Ortiz could not keep himself from letting out a low whistle. That was more than he'd paid for his first house.

"Yeah," Meg said. "We don't get too many of those at *L'Opéra*, I guess. But then Jeff said the other interesting thing about it was that it had diplomatic plates."

Eyes narrowing, Ortiz asked, "Diplomatic plates?"

"You know, whatever they put on cars that belong to ambassadors and stuff like that. Jeff said they were sweet because regular cops almost never pull over cars that have diplomatic plates on them—too much trouble." Her dark eyes widened a bit, as if she suddenly realized to whom she was speaking. "Um, sorry, detective, but that's what he said."

"It's okay, Meg. I know the drill." The unfortunate thing was, he really did. Most big-city cops had some kind of horror story about the sort of crap pulled by drivers of officially designated "foreign organization" vehicles. Technically they were supposed to abide by the rules of the road in whichever state they had residence, but officially the local police couldn't do much about it if they decided to ignore those rules.

He sighed. So Christine had two whack jobs after her, one possibly an extremely rich foreign national? "Did Christine happen to mention if this Phantom person had any kind of accent?"

"I don't think so. But we didn't get much of a chance to talk that evening—the restaurant was crazy-busy."

"Naturally." The information she'd given him had only deepened the mystery, unfortunately. Was there a connection, or was Meg only grasping at straws, trying desperately to find some sort of meaning in her friend's disappearance? He set down his pen. "Well, Meg, thanks for the update. We'll see if we can follow up on it. But without an actual license plate number it might be difficult to track down—even with a car as distinctive as the one you said this man was driving."

"Oh," she said, her expression faltering a little. It was obvious that she'd hoped her information would be of more use.

"I did want to ask you something, though," he continued, and she perked up a bit. "Have you ever seen this before?" And he produced the ring he'd found in Christine's bedroom and laid it on the desk before him.

Meg picked up the little plastic envelope and looked at the ring inside for barely a second before replying, "That's Christine's grandmother's ring."

"You're positive?"

She nodded. "I've seen Christine wear it a few times—mostly at special functions like recitals and stuff. She'd never wear it to work, of course. But I think I also saw her wear it on a chain around her neck sometimes."

"So she was careful with it?"

Giving him a condescending look, Meg said, "Well, yeah. It's not like Christine had lots of valuables. Most of her grandmother's stuff got sold off when she died, so Christine didn't have much left. She loved that ring, even if she didn't wear it that often." She frowned. "Where did you find it?"

"On the floor of her bedroom."

"Christine would never have dropped it and left it there—" She broke off, giving Detective Ortiz a narrow look. "What do you think it means?"

"I think," he said, retrieving the ring in its little plastic envelope and tucking it back in his breast pocket, "that it may be the only piece of evidence I have to show that Christine didn't just up and leave of her own accord. Nothing I could prove in a court of law, of course, but it's enough that I'm not going to treat this as a simple missing-person case any more."

Clasping her hands together, Meg leaned forward. "What are you going to do?"

I wish I knew, he thought, but said only, "Keep digging. Something's bound to turn up."

He offered his hand to Meg and she took it.

"Thanks, Detective Ortiz."

"No, thank you, Meg—I'll keep in touch."

"You'd better," she said, and went out, closing the office door behind her.

For a few moments he just sat there, turning over pieces of information in his mind, examining them the way a jeweler would a somewhat flawed jewel under his loupe. It was looking more and more as if someone had gone to considerable trouble to make it seem as if Christine had left town on her own. All he needed to know now was how.

And, more importantly, *why.*

Chapter Nineteen

SEVERAL DAYS WENT BY BEFORE I had any chance at all to speak with Ennis alone. A series of storms descended upon us, and even though I now had relatively free run of the house, I still felt imprisoned, the gardens beyond my windows now veiled in drifting rain.

Since the weather forced us inside, Erik and I spent a good deal of time in the music room, singing for one another one day, singing together the next. Music helped me take myself away—if I closed my eyes, I could try to imagine I was just in my master class, singing a duet with one of my fellow students. Of course, none of them had a voice to rival Erik's, and if nothing else it was a joy to sing with him. His repertoire was vast and varied; one moment it could be an aria from *Rigoletto*, the next a Schubert lieder, followed by snippets of Rodgers and Hammerstein or even Cole Porter, if the mood struck him. In turn I sang for him *Ach, ich fuhl's, es ist verschwunden*, Pamina's aria from Die Zauberflöte; selections from *The Merry Widow*; the delicate and lovely "Pie Jesu" from Lloyd Webber's own *Requiem*. However, we were both careful to sing nothing from *The Phantom of the Opera*. Why, I wasn't entirely sure—possibly he thought it too emotionally charged a composition, given our present circumstances. Whatever the reason, I followed his lead, although in the past I had loved to sing "Wishing You Were Somehow Here Again," given its resonances in my own life.

Late one afternoon, as the day slipped into dusk, I approached the music room to hear Erik already inside, playing Debussy's *Clair de Lune*. Not wanting to disturb him, I stood outside the door, letting the music wash over me, the rippling progression of notes flowing out and around me, reaching for its ineffable climax. Once again I felt the tears start to my eyes. How exquisitely beautiful his playing was, how effortless yet laden with emotion. I could have lingered there all evening, just listening to him, but I knew he was expecting me and so went in to him once the last chords had died away into silence.

"How did you know that was one of my favorite pieces?" I asked.

He closed the piano lid, then turned on the piano bench to face me. "I didn't. But I've always been drawn to it, despite the critics who dismiss Debussy as a composer of fluff."

"Critics are angry, bitter people," I said, smiling at him. "At least that's what Dr. Green says. 'Those who can, do. Those who can't, teach. And those who can't teach end up as critics.' I'm paraphrasing, but it was something along those lines."

"At least half the time I disagree with them, or they contradict one another anyway. I prefer to make my own decisions." His green eyes glinted at me from behind the mask. "Would you like to hear something else?"

"Some more Chopin," I said. "I love to hear you play Chopin." It was nothing more than the simple truth... and I was glad of the chance to say something to him that wasn't a lie.

And as I settled myself in a comfortable arm chair near the French doors, listening to him progress into the opening notes of the Prelude in D-flat Major, the "Raindrop Prelude," I felt once again a wave of sadness at the circumstances that forced me to lie to him, to conceal my true motives. Every smile over the past few days, every laugh that he had elicited through a pithy or sarcastic comment—to me they were just another form of betrayal. The more time I spent with him, the more I could sense myself opening to him. It wasn't fair that in many ways I felt more easy with him than with anyone else I had ever met. It wasn't fair that even now, as I watched his dark head dip toward the piano keys in utmost concentration, I had the irrational urge to walk over to him and press my lips into his wavy, slightly overlong hair.

It was growing harder and harder to distance myself from Erik. I had never been able to fully understand the mesmerizing influence of the original Phantom over his Christine, but now as I fought my own attraction to my captor, I began to sympathize with her plight. However, I couldn't allow myself to give in to it—I couldn't let him sweep me away into his dreamy world of music and luxury.

I had to get out of here, and soon. If not, I feared I would be lost forever.

The following morning I had quite a shock. For the past few days I'd been idly changing the stations on the radio in my room—even classical music had begun to pall, and the normality of the morning chatter on the local rock stations helped me feel a little more connected with the world. At that moment I was listening to the local news with half an ear before I went down to have breakfast in the little chamber where Erik and I had shared hamburgers together. He never ate breakfast with me—apparently he couldn't bring himself to be up quite that early—but usually we had lunch and the evening meal together. Today, however, he had told me he would be tied up for most of the afternoon in a conference call with several of his lawyers and one of the executive officers of his trust. I knew that would afford me the perfect opportunity to finally approach Ennis without fear of discovery, unless Jerome were prowling about. He seemed to be underfoot most of the time, although since he was Erik's personal assistant I had a feeling he would also be in attendance during the conference call.

At any rate, I was just slipping on one of my shoes when I heard my name coming out of the radio's speakers. I stiffened, the shoe dangling unheeded from my hand.

"...apparently missing since Thanksgiving evening. Christine Daly is five foot five and weighs approximately 115 pounds, with curly brown hair and blue eyes. She was last seen wearing a red sweater and black slacks.

She may be driving a faded blue '93 Honda Civic with California license plate 3MWT516. Anyone with information regarding Miss Daly is urged to contact the Pasadena P.D. at area code 626-744-4241. And now for a look at our weather…"

I managed to get the shoe on my foot and then stood up, staring at the radio. I had been in such isolation here I'd forgotten that of course Randall—and possibly Meg— would have gone to the police once they realized I was truly missing. Somehow, though, I doubted that they could have given the police enough information for them to begin to guess where I really was. While it was heartening to think that possibly the cavalry could be on its way, I couldn't count on the police for help. I couldn't count on anyone but myself.

By this time I had gotten a little more used to the rhythms of the house. Erik usually didn't emerge from his own chambers until one or two in the afternoon, and so I spent my mornings alone, idly playing on the magnificent Steinway, reading, or taking brief walks in the garden, although the weather had prevented that particular activity for the past few days. I knew that Erik employed two maids and a cook, none of whom lived on the property. Unfortunately, I couldn't really talk to the maids, since my Spanish was limited at best. All of my foreign language units had been spent learning Italian, French, and German, the common languages of opera. The cook was French, and although I had enjoyed conversing with him and letting him burnish my pronunciations, I knew he was not a reliable resource, as he seemed interested mostly in flirting with me. No, it was Ennis to whom I would have to turn for assistance.

The elderly butler was unobtrusive but omnipresent; he oversaw the maids while at the same time planning menus with Michel, going over Erik's schedule with Jerome, and directing the small army of gardeners who kept the extensive grounds lush and tidy. During the time when Erik was occupied with his conference call, I guessed that Ennis would be first planning the evening meal with the cook and then probably occupied for a few hours with the maids and the gardeners. All the better. He would be done by the time the late afternoon local news came on, and I hoped that my disappearance would have crossed over from radio to television by that time. The local media seemed to be obsessed with missing persons, weather, and unexplained murders, and so I hoped that my own missing-person report would be close to the top of the local news. If I had that obvious proof to present to Ennis, then I knew he would have to believe me, no matter what Erik might have told him about my purported mental state.

It was a very long, dull afternoon. I couldn't concentrate on a book and so went downstairs to a cozy sitting room equipped with a huge LED screen and tried to amuse myself by flipping through the hundreds of channels. Nothing caught my interest for more than a few moments, but it was better than trying to get through a book when I knew I'd keep reading the same sentence over and over. I could feel the anxiety rising in me, the sourness in my chest and at the back of my throat.

Should I really be doing this? I wondered. And, more importantly, *Can I do this?* As much as I wanted to hate Erik for what he'd done to me, I found I couldn't. There was so much about him that fascinated me, so much that grew perilously close to love. Perhaps once I was free I could finally sort out how I did feel about him.

At last the shadows began to lengthen in the trees outside, and the dark rainy day began to deepen into dusk. I looked at the clock on the wall above the television: ten minutes to five. It was now or never.

It took a bit of time for me to find Ennis. He wasn't in the kitchen, nor in the music room, where I heard the maids laughing and chattering in Spanish. Finally I located him in the red dining room, where he was rubbing the silver with a polishing cloth before laying it carefully in our customary places at the dining table: Erik at the head, me to his left.

I cleared my throat. "Excuse me, Ennis—"

He looked up from the spoon he was polishing. As always he wore an impeccable dark suit, not the tails I'd always seen butlers wear in films or on television.

"How can I help you, Miss Daly?" He had the faintest trace of a British accent, as if he'd been here so long that all but the last vestiges of the original intonation had been erased.

How can I help you, Miss Daly? That was the crux of it, after all. Could he help me? Would he?

"I'm not sure how to say this—" I began, faltering a little before his kindly dark gaze.

"As best you can," he said. "What seems to be the problem?"

The words came in a rush. "I know Erik told you that I'm Jerome's niece and that I have some sort of a mental problem, but that's just not true. He kidnapped me, brought me here because he thinks I'm the Christine to his Phantom."

One muscle in his jaw tightened, but other than that there was no reaction. When he spoke, his tone was kindly, but overly soothing, the sort of voice one would use on someone in hysterics. "Miss Daly, perhaps you are a little confused—"

"I am not confused!" I snapped. "I know it sounds crazy, but you have to believe me! Anyway, I have proof!"

He set down the spoon and polishing cloth. "What kind of proof?"

"Well, it's—I hope it's on TV. So you need to come with me and watch the news for a little bit."

Apparently too correct to cast aspersions on my sanity, he said, "If you wish it—"

"I do. Come on—it's about to start."

So he did follow me down the hall to the sitting room where I'd been watching television earlier. I picked up the remote and chose a local station at random; they all had five o'clock broadcasts. The lead story was the weather— the constant rainfall over the past few days was causing some hillsides to slip and creeks to overflow. People tended to be obsessive about rain in Southern California, probably because we usually had so little of it. After that came a piece on an officer-involved shooting in south Los Angeles, and then something about contaminated drinking water in certain sections of the San Fernando Valley. I caught Ennis watching me with a speculative look in his eyes. It was obvious he thought I was as mad as Erik had first portrayed me.

After an excruciating wait through several commercials and the weather report—more rain on the way, apparently—the anchorwoman said, just as a picture of me that must have been taken on Thanksgiving appeared on the backdrop behind her, "In other news, Pasadena police are investigating the suspicious disappearance of Christine Daly, a twenty-three-year-old Pasadena resident and senior at USC. She has been missing since Thursday evening, November 26th, and was last seen in a red sweater and black pants. She may be driving—"

I tuned out the rest; it was just a recap of what had already been said on the radio that morning. But I turned and looked at Ennis, to see what little color he had draining from his face; his cheeks looked slack and gray, his eyes dull.

Finally he said, softly, as if to himself, "Erik, how could you?"

"So you believe me?"

He made a sad gesture toward the television. "That's difficult to refute, isn't it?"

I stepped closer to him and laid a hand on his sleeve. "Please—you have to help me get out of here. Erik's busy in his office, and I know you have the codes to the keypads."

There was a deep, almost inexpressible sadness in his dark eyes. "What will you do to him?"

Something inside me twisted. The pain in Ennis's gaze was very real; obviously, Erik was much more to him than merely his employer. "Nothing, I promise," I said at last, knowing the words were true, even though I hadn't even thought that far up until that moment. "Just help me, and I promise I'll never tell the truth about where I've been."

A painful pause, as he searched my face. Apparently whatever he read there reassured him, for at length he said, "All right, Miss Daly. But hurry—I don't know how much longer his meeting will last."

With that he turned and led me out of the sitting room, down the long corridor that divided the ground floor of the house. At last it opened into a large foyer two stories tall that was fronted by an enormous double door. I had never been here before—up until now I had had no reason to come to this section of Erik's home.

My heart slammed against my ribcage in a series of crescendoing beats as Ennis began to tap the code into the keypad next to the front door. Soon, so soon—

"What the hell are you doing?"

Erik's voice lashed at us from across the room, and Ennis and I both turned to see him striding into the foyer, Jerome at his heels. The side of his face unprotected by the mask was contorted with fury.

It was as if all the blood in my body retreated from my extremities, leaving me shaking, my hands trembling. I could feel the gasps leaving my lungs, as if I couldn't possibly pull in enough oxygen to keep my adrenaline-flooded body alert.

Beside me, Ennis pulled himself up straight. He was pale, very pale, but he fixed Erik with a steady eye and said, "I'm letting your captive go, Erik."

Silence then, an eternity in which Erik stared at Ennis. Then, slowly, inexorably, that baleful gaze transferred itself to me. Somehow I was able to meet his eyes, eyes that were suddenly bleak, cold, a stranger's eyes.

Jerome began to take a step forward, but Erik put out a hand, stopping him. "Tell me, Miss Daly," he said, his tone almost impersonal. "Have you tired so soon of our hospitality? Food not to your liking? Or perhaps it was the company?"

My mouth opened—what I was going to say I wasn't sure—but Ennis spoke first.

"You can't kidnap a girl and expect her to stay with you! What were you thinking? My God!"

It was almost as if Ennis didn't exist. Erik took a step toward me, then another. He was very close, intimidating in his height and strength and the anger that seemed to seep from his very pores. "Was it lies, then?" he asked. "Everything you said to me?" And with that he grasped my arm in a grip that I knew would leave bruises.

You will not cry. You will not cry, I told myself fiercely. *No matter how much he hurts you...*

But then Ennis reached up to pull Erik's hand from me, his hand looking frail against the dark sleeve of Erik's jacket.

"Enough of your interference!" Erik snarled, letting go of my arm and grabbing Ennis's hand, pushing him away from me and to the ground.

I made some sort of shocked exclamation. Even Jerome began to move toward Ennis, but Erik appeared not to notice either one of them.

"Perhaps you were just amusing yourself with me?" he asked, and the half-masked face was very close to mine. "Was that it?"

"You can't force someone to love you!" I flung back at him. "You can't kidnap me and expect me to—to—"

"Erik." Ennis's voice sounded very weak. He still lay on the patterned marble of the floor, as if unable to regain his footing. His hoarse breathing filled the sudden silence. "Let her go. Leave her—" And his eyes closed, a sudden spasm of pain crossing his features.

Then Jerome was there, kneeling on the floor next to the fallen man. He lifted Ennis's wrist to check his pulse, then laid his ear against his chest. Then he looked up at Erik, who had seemed barely to notice. "Sir, I think he's having a heart attack."

The words took a moment to penetrate. "What?"

"I need to call 911. Okay?"

Wordlessly, Erik nodded and turned away from me, dropping to his knees beside Ennis.

I moved away from the door, watching in horrified fascination as Erik knelt there, his head bowed over the broken form of his servant. He took Ennis's hand, his whole form shaking. My God—was he weeping?

Jerome wasted no time. His iPhone was out of his pocket and into his hand in a matter of seconds. "I have a possible heart attack victim, aged seventy-four. We're at 415 Charles Street. Hurry." With that he hung up, shoved the phone back into his pocket, and began administering CPR in a smooth, practiced manner that showed he had obviously done this before. He said to Erik, in the same calm voice he had used with the 911 operator, "We're five minutes from Huntington Memorial. He'll make it."

Erik nodded, but said nothing. His back was to me; I might not have even existed.

All I could think, stupid as it might have been, was that if we were only five minutes from Huntington Memorial, then we were still in Pasadena. Not only that, but we weren't far at all from my own home. All this time, and I had never left my own city—

The minutes dragged on. In my own head I could only hear a little voice saying, *Please, please, please. Please, God, don't let him die.*

Finally the sound of sirens, coming closer, then stopping. Jerome swore under his breath. "Goddamn front gate." He got to his feet, punched a code into the keypad, then turned and looked down at Erik. "You'd better go. You don't want to be here when they come in. And take her with you."

For the first time in what seemed like hours Erik turned and looked at me. There was no expression on his face. As the windows to either side of the front door began to flash with blue and red light from the emergency vehicles, he slowly got to his feet and came toward me. Without speaking, he grasped my arm and pulled me out of the entryway, just as I heard Jerome open the front door for the paramedics.

Perhaps I could have fought him. Perhaps I could have turned and screamed for the paramedics to help me. But in the end I did neither of those things, although whether it was because I simply lacked the strength or because I just couldn't bear to subject Erik to any more anguish, I didn't know.

His silence unnerved me. On some level I would have preferred threats or verbal abuse. At least I could have defended myself against that. But he remained quiet as he dragged me back through the house and up the stairs, his grip a constant bruising force on my arm.

Only when we stopped outside my door and he began to turn the key in the lock did I finally speak. I couldn't bear it any longer. "Erik, please—"

At that he did release my arm, but only to smother my mouth with his hand. "Don't speak," he said, the words dangerously soft. "Everything that comes out of your mouth is a lie."

I tried to meet his eyes, tried to show something of the shame I felt at how things had turned out, but he only looked away. Then he opened my door and, without warning, pushed me inside with so much force that I slammed into the little decorative table, knocking the orchid in its oriental pot to the ground with a crash. I fell to my knees, the tears starting to my eyes at the sudden pain in my hip, where I had connected with the edge of the table. Behind me I could hear the inevitable snick of the key in the lock.

With that sound, final as it was, I finally began to cry, hopelessly, the sobs tearing out of my chest with such force I began to cough. I stared at the pitiful remains of the orchid on the floor, tried to gather it up as best I could, then wept even harder as a broken piece of porcelain cut the palm of my hand. At last I crawled out of the ante-chamber like a wounded animal, not bothering to turn on the light in my bedroom, barely pausing to kick the shoes off my feet as I crept into bed. My hip throbbed, but the pain was nothing compared to the ache inside. What had I done? God, what had I done?

What made it even worse was the fact that my fear over Ennis's condition was secondary to the pain I had caused Erik. I knew I would never forget the look on his face as he entered the entryway and saw me there, not if I lived to be a hundred. So much anger, to be followed by that cold remoteness—my betrayal apparently had made him retreat to a place far within himself where he wouldn't let himself be hurt again. Whether he would ever willingly come out again, I didn't know.

Dully I realized that I was fully a prisoner once more. He would never trust me again. Would I spend the rest of my life in these rooms, shut away from the world, shut away from him?

Eyes closed against the darkness, I huddled in bed as the tears came again, this time soaking my pillow. I'd keep my eyes shut forever, if it meant I wouldn't have to see his pain ever again.

Chapter Twenty

He had to get out. The empty house around him suddenly seemed suffocating, oppressive. Jerome had ridden off in the ambulance with Ennis, and not fifteen minutes ago Erik had gotten a call from his assistant, who told him that it looked as if Ennis was going to make it, even though he'd probably be in intensive care for several days. The wave of relief that washed over Erik was only temporary. Ennis would be fine—his malady of the heart had a purely physical cause. But what of the damage Christine's escape attempt had done to Erik's heart?

The downpour of earlier that evening had diminished to a light drizzle. It felt cool and friendly against the exposed side of his face, which seemed to burn with the roiling emotions he tried so desperately to suppress. Tonight he was glad of the walk from the house to the garage, glad of the chance to feel the wind and rain in his hair.

The many-bayed garage had been built by his father in the late '40s, after the war. Once it had been filled with a collection of classic and performance cars, but Erik had donated all of them to charity except for his grandfather's '33 Rolls Royce Phantom II, which he couldn't bear to part with. The car now sat in lonely splendor in the garage, accompanied only by Erik's S600 and the Range Rover he had provided for Jerome's use. Each month, Jerome took the Phantom out for a spin to make sure everything was still working properly. As much as he loved the car, Erik would never drive it. It attracted far too much attention, even in a neighborhood such as his.

The S600 was another matter. Oh, possibly it merited a second look, but the casual observer would only note it as yet another S-Class, since it was the engine that made the biggest difference between the 600 and lesser models in that same class. Now he slid into the welcoming leather seats and punched the button to open the garage door, feeling the powerful thrum of the V-12 as he turned the key over in the ignition. With a silky rumble, the car moved out into the night, down the long curved driveway, past the wrought-iron gates that protected the entrance to the property.

He had no idea of where he was going. It was enough to be away, to let the powerful car sweep him into the night, down the curving streets that hugged the arroyo. If he only thought of driving, feeling the slick roads beneath the tires, listening to the intermittent hiss of the wipers as they slicked away the light drizzle, then perhaps he wouldn't have to think of Christine, of what she had just done. Perhaps he wouldn't have to think of Ennis in an intensive care unit, with no one to visit him but Jerome. Of course Erik would never be able to go see him.

Viciously he swung the car around a hard right, hearing a slight chirp from the tires, a small tug before the traction-control device asserted itself. The car handled beautifully in the rain, of course…too well, perhaps. Possibly the best way to end all this would be to lose control, to let the Mercedes crash down into some forgotten ravine or hit a tree with such force that no one would be able to tell that the driver had only half the face of a man.

But he knew he would never do that. Thoughts of suicide had briefly crossed his mind now and then over the years, but he'd always considered that the coward's way out. No matter what agonies he might be suffering now, he knew that he would never seek to consciously end his life.

He was driving recklessly, though, taking corners much too quickly, speeding through quiet residential streets. There wasn't much chance of being pulled over; the diplomatic plates had been Jerome's idea, and they had served very well as a shield between Erik and the police over the years. The plates also saved him from the nuisance of a rash of fix-it tickets for his illegally tinted windows, windows that he'd insisted on since he was old enough to drive. They provided yet another barrier between him and the world.

How foolish of him to think he could ever let someone inside that barrier. How stupid to believe that her smiles and her laughter were genuine, were anything but a ruse intended to make him let down his guard. He thought of her pale face, the fear in her eyes as he had advanced on her. If she'd only known how close he had come to wrapping his fingers around her slender throat, ending it all then…ending the pain and the betrayal. It was only the crisis with Ennis that had stopped him from giving in to his rage.

You can't force someone to love you! she had cried. Ah, but he'd thought he could. He'd thought if he could only have her to himself for a time, let her begin to know who he was, that she would come to care for him. There were so many small things he'd noted as the days passed, little tells which had continued to reinforce his belief that she was coming to care for him. The sudden surprised laugh she gave when he said something that amused her, the warm smile with which she would greet him whenever they met for the first time during the day, her obvious admiration for his musical ability—all these had made him think that she did love him, or at least would very soon. It wasn't until now, when he had lost Christine, that he realized how much he had come to love her.

The pain rose up again, and his vision blurred, though from tears or the light mist that coated the windshield he didn't want to know. In the first throes of his anguish, as he paced the floors of his study while waiting to hear some news—any news—he had thought, *Then I'm done with her. I can always find someone else.* But the truth was, he didn't want to find anyone else. Even if he found another girl with her physical attributes, she wouldn't be Christine. No one else would have that quick uplift to her chin, the deft sense of humor that seemed to assert itself when he least expected it, the quiet acceptance of the losses she had suffered in her life. He loved her strength now as much as he had admired her beauty or her voice. And now, when he had finally understood what it was to love a woman instead of merely desire her, she had taken that love and shattered it as she had shattered the porcelain orchid pot in her room.

He had stood outside her door for a long time, listening to her wracking sobs. Part of him had wanted to go inside and take her in his arms, for she had wept for so long and so tragically that he had grown a little alarmed. But he had not allowed her tears to move him. It was her fault anyway, that Ennis was in the hospital and Erik now knew the depths of her duplicity. Finally he had forced himself to walk away, leaving her to her anguished sobbing. At some point she would cry herself to sleep—better to leave her alone to contemplate the enormity of what she had just done. That oblivion had been denied him, however, as he haunted the dark hallways of his home, waiting for the call from Jerome. When at last he had received the news, of course he felt relief, but it was overlaid with anger. Damn Ennis, anyway—what could have possibly made him side with Christine? How could he have thrown aside an entire lifetime's worth of trust, merely to help that lying girl?

She wasn't lying about the kidnapping, came a cold, still voice in his mind. *And she must have had some way of proving that to Ennis, or he would not have believed her.* Once Ennis had been convinced of the circumstances surrounding Christine's presence in the house, he would have had no choice but to help her. The man was too forthright and honorable to do anything less.

At that thought, Erik felt a strange emotion dawning in him, one that took him a moment to recognize because it was so foreign. After a pause, he realized it was shame. Yes, he actually felt shamed by what he had done to Ennis, using physical force against the man who had never shown him anything but affection and kindness. The fact that Ennis was apparently going to survive the attack did not make him Erik feel better. Instead, paradoxically, it made him feel worse. Sooner or later he would have to face Ennis and make amends for what he had done.

And Christine—God, Christine. How could he have expected her to love him, when he had just proved himself the lowest of the low—a man who, when he found he could no longer purchase love, decided to steal it instead? Perhaps she had shattered his trust in her, but how could he have ever thought she could trust him, when the foundation of their relationship was built on the quicksand of a crime? If he went to her now and begged her forgiveness, it would be too late. He had seen fear in her eyes earlier this evening, a fear that had never been there before. What could he possibly do now to show her that it had all been a terrible accident?

After driving for what seemed like hours, Erik finally came to a four-way stop and paused there for a long while. He had passed several other cars in his circuitous route along the edges of the arroyo, but there was no one at this intersection, no one to note that the driver of the Mercedes sat there, idling, for several moments. If anyone had been able to see inside the darkened windows, they would have found a man with his forehead pressed against the steering wheel as his body shook with sobs he could no longer contain. But there were no witnesses to his agony now, just as there never had been throughout the long, weary years of his life.

"This is impossible," Ortiz muttered to himself as he shuffled through the stack of papers on his desk. While it was sometimes valuable to let the news disseminate information about missing persons, most of the time all it resulted in was a morass of false leads, all of which took valuable time to chase down. He wasn't having much luck with Meg's information on the car the "Phantom" had been driving on Halloween, either. The various consulates were under no obligation to cooperate with a local police investigation, and the most he'd gotten was a series of polite "no"s in response to his questioning as to whether a given organization owned a new Mercedes S600.

There were no credit card receipts at the restaurant to identify him, no one besides Meg and the valet who even remembered his being there that night. He'd gone down and questioned the valet himself, but had gotten nothing more than what Meg had already told him. The kid had obviously been so impressed with the car that he'd paid only the barest attention to the person driving it, and so once again Ortiz was left with only Meg's sketchy description to go on.

He had to field calls from Randall at least once a day, if not more. Of course Ortiz had nothing new to give him, although once Randall had been told of the landlord's impatience to let out Christine's bungalow, he had immediately paid the delinquent rent. Apparently there had been some argument over late fees, but it seemed Randall had gotten the better of Panagapolous there. So Christine's home was safe for another month, but Ortiz was beginning to wonder whether a month would be enough time to figure out what had really happened to her.

Ortiz lifted his mug of coffee, realized it had gone stone cold, and set it back down, swearing.

"That good, huh?" Kosky remarked, pausing outside Ortiz's office, the ubiquitous Starbucks cup in his left hand. "I don't know why you keep drinking that swill, especially when you can just walk outside to the cart and get yourself a decent cup of coffee."

"I've got one kid about to graduate high school and another one needing braces," Ortiz said. "I can't afford it."

Kosky shrugged. As always, he was impeccably dressed, striped shirt and perfectly coordinated tie, the creases in his slacks so sharp it looked as if you could cut your hand on them. Ortiz at first had wondered how Kosky could afford his wardrobe on a detective's salary, until someone on the force had mentioned that Kosky came from an old-money family in Pasadena and didn't really need to work at all. He'd gotten a master's in criminal justice and thought it would be interesting to be a cop. His family had been horrified.

"Still working on the Daly case?" Kosky inquired, stepping further into the office.

"Yeah. I'm just banging my head against the wall at this point, though. All I've got is a missing girl and someone who apparently dresses up as the Phantom of the Opera on Halloween and drives a black Mercedes S600."

"Nice car."

"Thanks for the automotive review."

Kosky raised one sandy eyebrow. "Sounds like the Phantom of the Arroyo."

"What?" Ortiz set down his pen and gave Kosky a penetrating look. "What are you talking about?"

"The Phantom of the Arroyo. We used to joke about him when I was a kid."

Privately, he thought Kosky still looked like a kid. He reminded Ortiz of a younger and slightly less angular Conan O'Brien. "So what about him?"

"Just that there were sightings of a big black Mercedes with tinted windows, a car you never saw before sunset. And then there were the stories about the recluse who lived in the big gray stone mansion on Charles Street." Kosky scratched the side of his nose. "I'm not sure they're really connected or not—I mean, none of us kids could see inside the car because of the tinted windows."

"Charles Street, huh?" Ortiz tried to ignore the sudden irrational pounding in his chest and forced himself to sound casual. "Do you know what this guy's name was?"

Kosky shook his head. "Maybe I heard it once—the rumor was the guy was deformed or something and that was why he never came out. I had a few friends who used to ride their bikes by there and throw rocks at the wall, but you never saw anyone. It was just the Linda Vista version of the spooky old house everyone was afraid of but no one knew exactly why."

It was the thinnest of leads, but at this point Ortiz thought he was ready to try anything. "You're sure you can't remember the name?"

"Hell, Ortiz, that was at least fifteen years ago. Uh— Dieter? Destler? Something like that."

It wasn't much, but it was better than nothing. "Thanks, Kosky," he said.

"Glad I could be of help."

And with that Kosky left the office, as Ortiz fiddled with his pen once more. It was only a bit more of a lead than what Meg had given him, but sometimes cases were broken because of the smallest piece of information. Any fact, no matter how trivial, bore looking into.

Probably the best place to start investigating was the property tax rolls. He didn't have an address, but he'd worked with the database before and knew that he could start with a search on the street and the zip code.

It had been a while since he'd had to use that particular database, and he had to look up the the web address and passwords in the notebook he kept just for that purpose. Once he was in the database, he found that Charles Street was not a major avenue, and was comprised of approximately forty properties, so the list of owners was not very long. Anderson, Nishikawa, Longstreet, Saunders, Michelson, Deitrich...

Deitrich. That had to be it. There were no other names on the list that were at all similar. The property was listed as owned by one Erik Michael Deitrich, and apparently he had held title to it since the mid-'80s. Before that, the owner was Charles Deitrich, and before another Erik Deitrich, obviously the current owner's grandfather. But now he had the address at least—which might turn out to be the easiest part of this whole mess. Ortiz knew he had only the slimmest of leads to go on, and getting approval to go question the mysterious Mr. Deitrich might turn out to be more difficult than locating him in the first place. Still, he knew he had to try. He owed Christine Daly that much.

Chapter Twenty-One

IN MY DREAMS I COULD FEEL HIS TEARS dropping against my cheeks, hear his voice murmuring my name in broken tones. *Why, Christine, why?* Over and over I would open my mouth to reply, to do whatever I could to spare him any further agony, but no sound would emerge, only choking noises as I fought against some unseen force that kept me from speaking. Finally, gasping, I awoke in the semidarkness of early dawn, only to find that the tears on my face were my own.

With a groan, I rolled over on the bed. I lay still as I had finally collapsed yesterday evening, fully clothed, cold and aching on top of the covers. The tearstained pillow shams bore mute testimony to my anguish of the night before. The room was very quiet; I had shut off the radio yesterday afternoon before going downstairs to seek out Ennis. I had hoped that I would never see these chambers again.

The thought of Ennis made the tears start to my eyes once again. Had he survived? Was he still in an intensive care unit somewhere nearby, or had he succumbed to the weakness of his heart at last? Of course I had no way of knowing—and I could not expect Jerome to extend me the courtesy of updating me on his condition.

All your fault, all your fault, that merciless voice came from inside me. How many times had I heard psychologists and counselors tell me guilt was useless? God knows I had wracked myself with it many times before. After my parents' accident, I had convinced myself that it was all my fault, that if I hadn't asked for them to come home from that damned dinner party early so we could have a family New Year's together, then they wouldn't have been driving down that stretch of road at that particular time, only to meet with a driver who had done his celebrating early. Everyone had told me over and over that it had nothing to do with me, and eventually I had made myself believe that, but the guilt still lay there, buried perhaps, but not gone. And now it was rearing its ugly head once again.

Although my bruised hip ached in protest, I swung my legs over the side of the bed and got up. My hand stung when I placed it down to help myself to a standing position; I'd forgotten about the cut I'd gotten from the broken flower pot the night before. Ignoring the aches and pains, I went to the window, where I drew aside the curtain. The sky was still gray and heavy, although it was not raining now. Of course I couldn't see anything that gave me any helpful information. The few windows I could spy from my vantage point were still dark, and although I knew the garage with Jerome's apartment above it was located just around the corner, I could not see it from my window. No help there.

There being not much left to me, I decided to take a shower. If nothing else, the hot water would help with my bruised hip, and the cut on my hand stung enough that I knew it needed to be cleaned out. So I stood under the massaging stream of water, hoping that it would help to wash away the tears on my face as well as the ache in my heart. I knew from bitter experience that it would not be so easy, but the hot water felt good on a purely physical level, and I stood there for a long time, trying to clear my mind.

It was no good. Oh, I was able to go through the motions—intimate knowledge of grief had given me the ability to continue on with the mundanities of everyday life even when I thought I would surely go mad from the pain—but I could not keep my thoughts under control. How could I ever explain myself? How could I ever make Erik understand why I had done what I had done? What had seemed so reasonable to me at the time now seemed calculating and cruel. I had never meant to hurt him, but I was blind if I thought that betrayal and abandonment wouldn't maim him on some level I was only partially beginning to understand. At the time I had believed my only salvation lay in escape, but now, in the grim gray morning of the aftermath, I was beginning to wonder exactly what I had been trying to save.

There was no excusing what Erik had done to me. He had stolen me from my home, hijacked the life I had made for myself. No one could dispute those facts. But now I found myself trying to understand how he could have found himself driven to such an extremity. How could a man of such apparently infinite talent and wealth have ever thought that that was the only way he could have someone in his life, let alone someone as insignificant as me? Why would a man apparently so engaging and intelligent take such drastic measures?

Once again my thoughts seemed to be drawn inexorably to the mask. At first it had been easy to dismiss it as just an outward symptom of his apparent obsession with the Phantom of the Opera, but that explanation seemed far too pat now. What if he really had been born with a disfigurement so dire that not even the best surgeons money could buy had been able to correct it? What if he had hidden himself in this house all these years, waiting…for what? For the one woman who could finally see him for himself? For the woman who fit the ideal he had built up in his mind as the only companion for his solitude?

Put that way, it seemed to make a great deal more sense. Not as an excuse—oh, no, one could never excuse a capital crime—but as an explanation. Of course, it was possible I gave him far too much credit. He could be as mad as I had first thought him, a sociopath whose charm and talent hid a cunning mind that didn't think of the consequences of his actions because for him there could be no consequences…but somehow I didn't think so. There had been no mistaking the pain in his eyes when he realized I had been about to betray him and escape, just as his anguish had been obvious as he knelt to assist Ennis. His rage had been shocking, brilliant and painful as a bolt of lightning, but I didn't think it had been premeditated. The thought that I had caused him so much pain was agonizing. The realization that I had probably destroyed whatever delicate rapport had begun to develop between us was almost as painful. I couldn't hate him. I didn't even want to try anymore. Had I only attempted to flee because I couldn't bear to admit that I had come to love him?

All the hours we had spent together rose then in my mind, mocking my loneliness. Every smile, every laugh, every caressing mention of my name. I hadn't wanted to acknowledge the feelings at the time, hadn't wanted to admit to myself that every day I had become easier with him, had looked forward to seeing him. It had been easy to use my ignorance of men, of love, to dismiss everything Erik had come to mean to me. Only now, when faced with the very real prospect of a loss possibly greater than any I had yet experienced, did I realize that I couldn't bear the thought of another day without him.

The feelings I thought I had had for Randall now seemed shallow, insignificant. Perhaps I had been more attracted to the idea of being with him than to Randall himself. Oh, we got along well enough, and he was undoubtedly attractive and fun to be with, but I had to admit that I had not spent a great deal of my time over the past week or so missing him. Of course I had worried about him, wondered how he was coping with my sudden disappearance, but Erik had so filled my time and my thoughts that Randall had been pushed very much to the background.

For the first time I lifted my eyes to my reflection in the mirror. I looked a little the worse for wear—there were shadows under my eyes, and my cheeks had none of their usual color, but I had weathered the night better than I had thought. My eyes were gray this morning, cloudy to match the skies outside and the sweater I had chosen to wear, and they were very solemn.

What if it is true? I wondered. *What if he's hiding a deformity just as dreadful as the one in the book or the play?* Did I have the strength to accept it? Could I look him full in the face and not flinch? Somehow I knew I would have to, if there was to be any kind of future for us. In the musical, Christine had betrayed the Phantom by tearing the mask from his tortured features. I could only hope that Erik might understand that I would be removing the mask not to hurt, but to heal.

Of course, that idea was predicated on the assumption that he would even allow me to see him again. How deeply had the knife cut last night? How badly had I really hurt him?

By now it was full daylight beyond the windows. I turned the radio back on and moved about the room, restless to find some occupation. Not much offered itself beyond the books, none of which appealed to me. Having come to some sort of decision, now knowing what I felt I must do, I felt even more chafed by my captivity. Also, I realized that I was quite hungry—quite understandable, since of course I hadn't eaten since noon the day before, but as the time slowly slipped by, I began to wonder whether they were even going to deign to feed me.

Finally, just after the radio announced it was nine o'clock in the morning, I heard the familiar turn of the key in the deadbolt.

Jerome, of course. Unsmiling, he brought in a tray with a bowl of cereal and some toast and dropped it with a noticeable clatter on the table across from my bed. He turned back toward the door, obviously not inclined to engage me in any sort of conversation, and I stood.

"How is Ennis?" I asked, amazed that my voice actually sounded steady.

He paused, then turned partway back toward me. His face looked impassive enough, but there was cold anger far back in those blue eyes. "Recovering," he replied at length. "He should be out of ICU tomorrow."

A rush of relief went through me. At least that much could be salvaged from the horror of the night before. "Thank God," I said. Then I added, "Jerome, you know I never meant for any of that to happen—"

"Is there anything else?" he asked, cutting off my explanation. "I've got work to do."

Something inside me quailed at the thought of asking anything else of him, but I knew I must. "Please—I really need to speak to Erik. I need to explain—"

"Haven't you done enough already?" There was no mistaking the cold contempt in his voice. "He doesn't want to see you. At least he's not letting you starve—it's more than you deserve."

As I stared at him, momentarily shocked into speechlessness, he again turned and left for good this time. I could hear broken bits of pottery crunch under his heels as he exited the antechamber, and then the deadbolt turned once again.

For a long moment I remained standing, watching the closed door. And then, stupidly, I began to cry again.

"She wants to see you," Jerome said. A pause, and then he continued, "Of course I told her that was impossible."

"Of course," Erik murmured. Why would she want to see him? What could she possibly have to say? More lies, no doubt.

He was more weary than he could say. It had been the middle of the night before he returned to the estate, only to find Jerome's Range Rover already parked in the garage. Jerome had been waiting up for him, drained but politely furious. Had he no concept of the risk he had been taking? Christine had been left alone for hours—anything could have happened.

Erik hadn't bothered to point out there was very little that could have actually gone wrong; she'd been locked securely in. Short of the house burning down, he couldn't think why it mattered that she'd been left alone. After a brief inquiry into Ennis's condition, he'd sent Jerome to bed, but Erik himself was unable to sleep until almost dawn. Even then his slumber had been troubled, the usual nightmares of pain and sharp blades, although now made worse by visions of Christine standing over the operating table, her face contorted with horror at the sight of his unveiled features.

Even now he reached up briefly to touch the reassuring smoothness of the mask, so real was his memory of that dream. He tried to recall a more comforting image of Christine—perhaps from the day of their picnic, the breeze catching her glorious dark hair, soft tendrils touched with copper and mahogany blowing around her face as her eyes looked almost aquamarine in the bright sunlight. Yes, that was better. If he thought hard enough, perhaps he could also erase the way she had looked last night, the soft flush leaving her cheeks as he advanced on her, the unmistakable fear in her eyes. If only he could forget the sound of her sobbing. The sound of her pain.

Jerome regarded him expectantly, as if he thought Erik was going to issue a new set of orders regarding Christine, but for the first time in a very long while he felt adrift, rudderless. So much energy and focus had gone into planning Christine's abduction, planning her stay here, and although he had prepared for the contingency of an escape attempt along with every other worst-case scenario he and Jerome could dream up, he had let his guard down too much over the past few days. He'd been so convinced that she was warming to him, so sure she was close to returning his feelings. Now they were back to square one, with Christine once again locked up and obviously hostile, and Erik didn't know what else to do. Could he keep her prisoner indefinitely? How could he not? She had been so willing to betray him—he knew she would go straight to the authorities if she were ever freed.

Although it was barely noon, he went to the table by the window that held a decanter of his favorite cognac and poured himself a double. He lifted the glass and tossed it back, not caring for the sudden disapproval in Jerome's eyes, craving only the fire in the back of his throat and the false warmth it gave him. Perhaps it would be better if he just got very, very drunk.

"Sir—"

"Oh, the hell with it, Jerome," he snapped, then sloshed more cognac into his glass. What else did he have to do with his time, anyway?

"About Christine—"

"This changes nothing," Erik said. "Nothing. Just keep her locked up. I need time to think." He took another large swallow of cognac, then looked over at Jerome. The man appeared to have something on his mind; better to let him speak his piece and then get out. "What, Jerome?"

"I went back to see Ennis earlier this morning..." Jerome began.

"How is he doing?"

"Very much improved. I spoke with one of the nurses, and she told me he would probably be moved from ICU this afternoon."

He felt relief, of course. No thanks to him that Ennis wasn't lying in the morgue this morning instead of a hospital bed. Well, the man always had been tough. Erik tried to remember a time when Ennis had been ill enough to miss any of his duties and failed.

"Good," he said at length, and was surprised to hear a certain tremor in his own voice. God, he really was letting this get to him, wasn't he? "Make sure he has flowers for his room as soon as he gets out of ICU."

"Of course, Mr. Deitrich." Jerome removed his iPhone from his breast pocket and made a brief note.

Erik stifled a sudden impulse to laugh. At least some things never changed.

"Anyhow," Jerome continued, "Ennis was improved enough that he was able to talk with me a little. Of course he was very concerned about you—wanted to make sure you were all right."

Erik made a noncommittal sound and took another sip of cognac.

"He also wanted to make sure that I told you something about Christine—about something she said to Ennis before he agreed to help her."

Eyes narrowing, Erik took his glass of cognac and removed himself to his desk. Taking a seat, he stared at Jerome and said, "Continue."

"Ennis was very emphatic that I tell you this. He seemed—worried about her."

As well he might, Erik thought, but said only, "His concern is very touching, I'm sure. So what was this revelatory statement of Christine's?"

Jerome hesitated for a moment, as if he weren't all that eager to divulge what Christine had actually said. "He told me she had promised him that she would never turn you in—that she would never tell anyone where she had been if only he would help her escape."

Something turned over in him at those words, and he gazed at Jerome for a moment as he considered Christine's words. Had she at least cared enough that she didn't want to see Erik caught? Or had she merely lied once again to Ennis, told him what he wanted to hear so she could make her escape?

"She would have told Ennis anything to get away," he said at length, not daring to let himself hope, and Jerome nodded.

"I told Ennis the same thing. But he insisted that that was not the case, that it was obvious Christine wanted to help you in at least some small way, even if she could no longer stay here with you."

Could that really be true? Had Ennis been able to see the truth in her face as she made that promise? Once again he raged at his enforced isolation — if only he could go to the hospital now, ask Ennis to his face what he had thought of Christine's words. Of course that was impossible. Once again, he had to rely on a third party's interpretation of events — and he knew that Jerome was not disposed to be charitable toward Christine. Not that anyone could blame him.

Was it possible she had tried to spare him at least that much pain? Would a woman who cared nothing at all for him — hated him — have given him that much grace? He closed his eyes for a moment, feeling the hope rise up in him. Perhaps all was not as lost as he had thought…

"Thank you, Jerome," he said finally, deliberately keeping his tone cool. "You will make sure that Ennis knows you have told me?"

"Of course."

"Then that will be all for now, Jerome. Let me know this afternoon if Ennis is still improving."

Jerome nodded at the dismissal, face impassive, and left, closing the heavy double doors to the office behind him.

Alone once more, Erik watched the flames dance in the fireplace, although they were mostly for show. The state-of-the-art climate control system in his home kept things comfortable at all times, no matter what the conditions outside. Still, it was another dark, cloudy day, and the illusion of warmth was somehow comforting. He hoped the sudden lift of spirit he felt at Christine's words was not based on yet another illusion.

"Absolutely not," Chief Weinstock said, tossing the warrant back across his desk at Ortiz.

He'd been expecting this, but Ortiz wasn't about to give up with at least a token protest on his part. "Sir, I have several strong leads pointing to Deitrich—"

Weinstock leaned across his desk, eyes narrowing behind the half-lenses he wore in the privacy of his own office. "Ortiz, you've got dick. Hunches are all fine and good, but you're not going to get a judge to sign a warrant on a hunch. Especially not with a guy like Deitrich."

"With all due respect—"

"Do you have any idea at all who this guy is?" Weinstock stood, as if to give more weight to his words. "Calling him rich is like saying the Sears Tower is a tall building. He owns property all over town, has a controlling interest in several multinational corporations, family's been here in Pasadena forever—"

"Yet no one has ever seen him." Ortiz knew he didn't have a prayer, but went doggedly on. "At least, no one's really seen his face."

"So the guy's eccentric. With that kind of money, he can afford to be. But you go after someone like that without real evidence, and we're going to be ass-deep in lawsuits. Harassment, wrongful prosecution, pain and suffering—the guy can pay a whole army of lawyers to think up new ways to screw the Pasadena P.D. over." Weinstock took a breath, and said, "So the answer is no. No way."

It was not worth arguing anymore. Ortiz knew that Weinstock was right; as a veteran of the LAPD, Ortiz had seen what could happen when a police department got hit with a couple of successful lawsuits. It wasn't pretty. He knew that he didn't have enough on Deitrich, not by a long shot, but he also couldn't have let it go without trying. It was just a feeling, a hunch, as Weinstock had called it, but Ortiz had come to rely on his instincts over the years. They hadn't failed him yet.

"Just to make sure, refresh me a little." Weinstock's tone was a little gentler now; he could probably tell he'd beaten Ortiz down. "Any evidence at all to show that Christine Daly was forcibly abducted?"

"No, sir. No signs of forced entry at her home. No fingerprints other than hers and a couple that belonged to her boyfriend. Nothing."

"And you're saying that her connection with Deitrich is that he may have possibly attended a Halloween party at the restaurant where she worked?"

Put that way, it did sound fairly ridiculous. Ortiz sighed and said, "Yes, sir. The man dressed as the Phantom paid the hostess two hundred bucks to sit at Christine's station."

Weinstock lifted an eyebrow. "Maybe a little unusual, but she's a beautiful girl. Not really enough to go on, right?"

"Right."

Apparently satisfied that he'd made his point, Weinstock resumed his seat and said, "I'm not saying don't keep working on it. But you can understand the department's position on this. Right now I'd need the equivalent of Deitrich's fingerprints on Christine Daly's front door to sign that warrant."

"Of course, sir." Ortiz picked up the unneeded piece of paper. "Sorry to have troubled you with it."

"No trouble. I'm glad we could have this conversation."

Yeah, I'll bet, Ortiz thought. Anything where Weinstock could take him down a peg or two. The man hadn't been chief that long, and the rumor was he was a little intimidated by Ortiz's service with the LAPD before coming to Pasadena. Still, he'd hoped that personal politics wouldn't get in the way of this case—and if he had to be perfectly honest, he wasn't sure he would have signed off on the warrant if he'd been in the chief's position. There was a lot of potential for disaster here if he stepped on the wrong toes.

That rationalizing didn't keep him from being in a foul mood all the way from Weinstock's office to his own much more modest work space. Although he'd only been working on this case for a little over a week, it was starting to feel more like a month. He knew these sorts of cases came along every once in a while, cases that could take months or even years to crack. Some were never solved. But even though he knew that intellectually, it didn't make him like it any more when one came along.

He'd just seated himself behind his own desk and chucked the useless warrant into a desk drawer when Officer Campbell knocked on the door frame.

"I think I've got something for you," she announced, her dark eyes gleaming.

"Yeah, what?" Right now the only thing Ortiz wanted was a vacation. A very long vacation, preferably someplace tropical. Sunny Southern California had been anything but these past few weeks.

"Well, Officer Torres busted this lowlife last night trying to jack a car from the parking lot at Pasadena City College. Guy's been nailed before—he's still on probation from the last offense."

Ortiz gave her a disgusted look. "Yeah, and? How many car thieves do we bust every week?"

"Enough. Anyway, he's trying to make a deal seeing as he's heading right back to prison on the parole violation. I thought you should talk to him."

"What's the deal?"

"He says he jacked a car a week ago—some guys paid him to do it." She paused, obviously relishing what was coming next. "He says the car was Christine Daly's."

Chapter Twenty-Two

THE CAR THIEF WAS PROBABLY no more than nineteen, head shaved, stark bluish-black prison tattoos standing out on his knuckles and forearms. He lounged on a chair in the interrogation room, obviously trying to cover up his unease with a studied nonchalance bordering on insolence.

Ortiz had seen hundreds just like him.

"Antonio Vasquez?" he asked, dropping the kid's case folder on the table and taking a seat across from him.

"Who wants to know?"

From her corner, Campbell stirred and laid one hand on the butt of her pistol. "Watch your mouth, jerk."

"It's okay, Campbell," Ortiz said, and she settled back in her place, watching Vasquez with narrowed dark eyes. "Mr. Vasquez, I'm Detective Ortiz. Officer Campbell said you had some information relating to the Christine Daly case?"

Vasquez looked away for a moment. He could have been a handsome kid if he'd wanted to, but the gang influence had won out, from the concentration-camp hair to the spidery tattoos that covered his arms and wound their way up to his neck. "What kind of deal you gonna give me?"

"That depends. If you have information that leads us to Miss Daly's kidnapper, then we'll talk about extending your probation instead of sending you back to prison. But if it turns out you're handing me a line of crap, then it's back to Folsom—with an extra five years tacked on to your sentence."

"It's not crap, *pendejo*." Vasquez straightened up in his chair, but the improved posture did nothing to erase the hostility in his eyes. Ortiz had seen it too many times before with these kids—to them, he was a traitor. A sellout.

Ortiz decided to ignore the profanity for now. "That's for me to decide. So why don't you tell me about Miss Daly's car?"

Vasquez lifted his thin shoulders. "Seemed kind of stupid to me—the car was a piece of crap. Who'd want to jack a car older than I am? But whatever. Rigo told me he'd pay me a grand to lift it, so I did."

"Who's Rigo?"

"Guy who owns a chop shop in El Monte. Told me some rich guy gave him a bunch of money to jack the car and then take it apart and have it crushed."

Which would explain why they'd never been able to find a single trace of Christine's car. Ortiz made a few notes on his yellow pad, then asked, "Did you see the guy who gave Rigo the money initially?"

"No. Rigo told me where the car was, and then he gave me the cash after I dropped it at the shop."

"And then he scrapped it?"

Another shrug. "Guess so. I took off after I got the money."

"So where's Rigo's shop?"

Vasquez shifted in his seat, but said nothing.

Ortiz fixed him with what he hoped was a menacing glare. He tapped the kid's case folder. "Cooperation, remember? Otherwise, go directly to jail—do not pass go—"

"I tell you where his shop is, Rigo'll have his posse jump me for sure."

The kid was probably right, but since he wasn't the one who'd had contact with the guy who ordered Christine's car stolen, he was of limited use. Ortiz leaned forward. "Tell you what—if you give me the address, I'll let you warn Rigo that I'm coming over. He should be able to clean up before I get there. How about a day's notice?"

That much was true; give them even fifteen minutes' head start, and these guys were like cockroaches when you turned the light on. The shop would be cleared of any incriminating evidence long before he appeared on the scene.

Vasquez leaned back in his chair, considering. It was the best Ortiz could do, and apparently Vasquez was able to figure that out; after a moment he said, "Yeah, okay. But you don't go until tomorrow."

"Tomorrow afternoon, even." It sounded like a concession, but Ortiz had a staff meeting in the morning anyway, and this way the kid would think he was bending over backward to be accommodating.

"Okay. It's on Dodson, below Garvey. Don't know the number."

"Got a business name?"

"Rigoberto's A-1 Auto Repair. It's at the end of the cul-de-sac." Vasquez sat back up, glaring at Ortiz. "Can I have my phone call now?"

"Be my guest." Ortiz gestured Officer Campbell over. "Take Mr. Vasquez to make his phone call." He knew he didn't have to worry about Vasquez making bail and bolting; bail was almost unilaterally denied in the event of a probation violation.

He watched Campbell escort the sullen kid out of the room. Not as much as he'd hoped for, but at least Vasquez had given him a solid lead. It was more than he'd had for a few days, anyway.

Then he grinned. He was pretty sure exactly who would be the recipient of Vasquez's one and only phone call…and he had the feeling that Rigo wouldn't be exactly overjoyed to learn the police were about to come a-knocking tomorrow.

I had pleaded with Jerome each time he came to bring me food that I had to see Erik, speak with him as soon as possible. Each time I was rebuffed, and the next day began no differently—until dinnertime, when he told me that Erik would see me at nine o'clock.

At first I had just stared at Jerome, not daring to believe what he had just said. Then he added, "It looks as if Ennis will be coming home the day after tomorrow."

Well, that made more sense. Probably Erik wanted to reach some kind of a resolution before Ennis returned to the mansion. The last thing a convalescent probably needed was the atmosphere of brooding quiet that seemed to have descended upon the house.

I said, "I - I'm very relieved to hear that, Jerome. He must be making a swift recovery."

Jerome gave me a quick unreadable glance. Then, after a pause, he replied, "Oh, *Ennis* is doing very well."

And with that he departed, leaving me to brood on his words. The implication was that Erik's recovery had been anything but swift.

Nine o'clock. Luckily the announcer on the radio had given the time at the top of the hour, so I knew it was now just a little past seven. Less than two hours until I saw him again.

This could possibly be the most important meeting of my life, and suddenly I didn't want to go to face Erik in a pair of jeans and a sweater. No, the occasion called for something much more striking. If I showed him how much care I took in preparing myself to see him, maybe he would be a little more inclined to listen to what I had to say.

For the first time since I had awoken in these rooms I went to the closet of beautiful clothing Erik had provided for me and really took inventory of what was there. I had ignored the rack of evening dresses because I had not thought there was any reason to wear them, lovely as they were.

One exquisitely embroidered and beaded gown caught my eyes, but it was red and had only thin spaghetti straps to hold it up. Somehow I didn't think it was a good idea to wear red, and I had never worn something that bare. Gorgeous as it was, it just wasn't my style. And black seemed so severe, even though there were several very lovely black cocktail dresses hanging on the rack as well. I wondered why Erik had even bought them in the first place. Where could I possibly have worn all these exquisite gowns? Had he expected me to dress for dinner?

Finally I located what I had been looking for—a gown of changeable midnight blue silk, very 1950s in style, with wide-set straps accenting a deep V-neckline and a full knee-length skirt. The bodice was snug and accented my curves without being overly revealing, and the deep blue silk made my skin look porcelain pale in contrast. I found a silver pair of strappy sandals—Jimmy Choos, of course—in the shoe rack, and then nothing else would do to complete the ensemble but a string of diamond-encircled sapphires for my neck and a pair of matching drop earrings. Another sapphire in platinum and diamonds fit the ring finger of my right hand well enough.

I fought the butterflies in my stomach as I sat in front of the mirror in the bathroom, applying cosmetics with a care I had never used before. Anything to fill up the time—anything to make him want me enough to forgive me.

By the time I was done I wasn't even sure I recognized the girl in the mirror anymore—she looked as if she belonged in a different world than the slightly disheveled voice student who usually peered back at me. My curls were glossy and carefully arranged, my full lips stained a deep berry color, my eyes now a deeper blue, reflecting the color of the gown I wore. Sapphires and diamonds winked at my neck and glinted out from behind my hair. People had called me beautiful over the years, but this was the first time I truly believed them.

There wasn't much time for me to sit contemplating the girl in the mirror, however, because the next time I lifted my eyes to my reflection, I saw Jerome standing behind me.

I started, and dropped the tube of lipstick I had been holding. Then I turned on the stool to glare at him. "You shouldn't sneak up on people like that."

For a moment he said nothing, but only stared at me. "You look—different," he managed at last.

"Is that a compliment?"

"Erik will be glad to see you finally wearing some of the jewels he bought you," he said evasively. "He went to a lot of trouble picking out things he thought you would like."

I should have known Jerome would never admit to giving me a compliment. But I put one hand up to touch the sapphires that glittered against my collarbone and replied, "They're exquisite. He's been very…thoughtful."

A strange expression flickered in the back of Jerome's Delft-blue eyes. Was it my imagination, or was it a dawning respect? "No tricks this time?" he asked.

I met his gaze squarely. "No tricks. I promise. I've had a lot of time to think the past few days."

He nodded, but said only, "Then we should go. It's nine now."

Carefully, I pushed away from the dressing table and stood, following Jerome to the door, where I waited for him to unlock it. I could only hope that there would be no need to lock it ever again after tonight.

He led me to Erik's office, a room I had never been in before, although it was situated in the same wing as my chambers. Pushing the double doors inward, he announced, "She's here, sir," then gestured me inside, closing the doors behind me.

At first I had only a vague impression of a large dark-paneled room where a fire burned low in a vast marble fireplace. Besides the firelight, the only illumination came from a five-armed candelabra that sat in a far corner, its quivering flames sending odd shadows dancing around the edges of the space.

Erik stood behind the massive carved mahogany desk, a slender form in black, his profile outlined by the reddish glow of the fire. He said nothing as I approached, but merely waited until I finally paused, irresolute, at the edge of the Persian rug that fronted the desk.

Now that the moment was upon me, I found my mouth dry, my heart beginning again with its irrational pounding. Why wouldn't he speak?

The silence grew too dreadful. Finally I said, "Thank God you said you would see me."

A brief dismissive gesture. "I assure you, God had nothing to do with it."

So he was going to be difficult. Well, what had I

expected—that he would be overcome by my beauty and fling himself into my arms? "I know I did something for which there can be no apologies. But then again, so did you."

"I did?"

His voice was beautiful even when being coldly dismissive, as now. How I wanted to go to him then, feel his arms around me, feel the touch of his lips against mine. But I knew I had to go about this with great care; one misstep, and he could be lost to me forever. "By kidnapping me, you did more than commit a crime. You took away my ability to choose you for yourself." I took a step forward, then another. Now only a few feet separated us. I could feel the heat of the fire against my bare arms and neck. "Was it really so impossible, Erik? Did you really think that I couldn't possibly want you for yourself?"

At that he did turn to face me, but I could read nothing of his expression beneath the mask. "You don't know what you're talking about."

"Oh, I think I do." I looked him in his eyes, hoping he could see more of my soul than I could of his. "Didn't you feel it, that first time we met? I did, even though I didn't want to admit it to myself. When we danced, when you held me, couldn't you sense the connection?"

To his credit, he held my gaze, although I could see the thin, mobile lips tighten. "You gave little evidence of it."

"Well, what did you expect me to do? I had just met you—and I was seeing someone else at the time." My next words came out in a rush. "Of course you couldn't know that I felt your touch for hours afterward, that I heard your voice in my dreams that night. But I did. I still do."

He made no reply, but I saw his hands clench into fists at his sides.

"That's why I thought I had to run," I continued. I knew that I couldn't stop now. I had to lay everything before him, try to make him understand. "How could I let myself succumb to you? How could I give in to your plans? I thought that if I didn't get away, I'd lose a piece of my soul forever." For some reason I could feel tears start to my eyes, but I refused to let myself weep. "It wasn't until you stopped me that I realized it was too late anyway. It wasn't until I thought of how much I had hurt you that I realized I loved you."

Silence then, a silence that lengthened until I felt as if the whole world had been stretched thin as blown glass, ready to shatter at the first ungentle touch. Erik stood absolutely still, but his eyes never left my face.

"I think I know why you felt compelled to kidnap me. I think I've finally understood why you've hidden in this house, behind the mask." Again I paused to catch my breath, and for the first time I could see fear behind his eyes. "And I have to prove to you now that it doesn't matter."

And with that I reached across the gulf between us and lifted the mask from his face.

She didn't scream. She didn't faint. Her face went very pale, the stain on her lips looking almost like blood against the whiteness of her skin, but she stood her ground. The mask fell from her hand to the Persian rug.

Dear God, why wasn't she backing away, fleeing in terror, or crumpling to the ground, overcome by horror? But she did none of those things. Instead, she stepped even closer. Her hair gleamed like mahogany flame in the reflected light from the fire. The sapphires around her throat seemed to glow with their own inner incandescence. He found himself suddenly mired in quicksand, as if the wooden floor beneath his feet had turned into a swamp, and he was powerless to move or react.

"Let me love you," she said, and although her voice shook somewhat, she still looked steadily into his eyes. Before he knew what was happening, she had taken his ravaged face in her hands and brought her lips against his.

Nothing, no fevered dreams, no soul-twisting fantasies brought on by sexual deprivation, had ever matched this sensation. He had never allowed any of the women he had been with in his youth to touch his face or kiss him on the mouth, yet here was Christine doing both, unreservedly. The touch of her lips on his seemed to set his entire body on fire, as if every nerve ending had suddenly been sparked by a determined match. And now her mouth opened beneath his, and he could feel her tongue meeting his, every part of her opening to him.

He raised his hands to hold her finally, meeting the soft, slender flesh of her arms, the shocking openness of the back of her dress. She pressed her body against his, and suddenly he could smell the faint scent of roses rising once again from her hair, feel the curve of her breasts meeting his own chest, the unexpected height of her in the stiletto heels.

Surely this had to be a dream? Surely it couldn't be Christine holding him, kissing him, letting her mouth move unreservedly from his lips to his maimed cheek. But no, she was still there, still clinging to him, her heart pounding so it could be felt even through his suit jacket.

After an eternity or so she finally drew away a little, her breathing ragged. But still she looked at him with no apparent revulsion, and then she smiled, the dimple flickering at the corner of her cheek.

"You haven't said it," she commented.

He could hardly focus on what she had just said. The feel of her mouth on his was still too vivid. And how could she possibly be looking at him and smiling? "Said what?"

"I've heard it's what all women dread. Saying 'I love you' and not getting the same in return."

Was that all? Suddenly those three words sounded so inconsequential, compared to the depth of his passion for her. How woefully inadequate. "I've loved you since the moment I saw you." His own voice sounded shaken, the voice of a stranger. "And I've loved you more every day. Even when I thought you hated me." There had been a time when he thought he would have died before revealing so much of himself. But that had been a lifetime ago. That had been before Christine kissed him.

Was it only the firelight that seemed to make her eyes glisten with unshed tears? "Erik, I'm so sorry for that. I know that may not be enough, but I am sorry."

Not enough? When her kiss and unflinching regard had given him the first step toward healing a lifetime of pain? God, he should be begging her forgiveness for what he had done to her, stealing her from her life, hiding her here. But somehow, despite everything, she had still come to love him. She had found the strength to recognize the attraction between them and act upon it. If it hadn't been for her resolve, he might never have known the feel of her lips upon his.

At last he said, "Christine always leaves the Phantom."

With that she reached out and touched the scarred side of his face, brushing the tips of her fingers against the raised flesh there. Even after all these years, the nerve endings were still damaged; the feather's-touch of her fingers against the injured tissue brought on a slight pins-and-needles sensation.

Holding his gaze, she said steadily, "That was their story, Erik. This is ours."

And again she brought her mouth to his, the silk of her gown rustling against him as she held him tightly, almost as if she thought she could erase his pain by every touch, every caress. His arms tightened around her, and he let himself surrender to the flood of sensations that rushed once more over him. There was nothing in the world but her, nothing but the feel of her mouth on his, the press of her body against him. Over and over they kissed, until he thought he would surely drown in her, lose himself forever in the heat of their passion.

At length, though, they slowly drew apart, although he wasn't sure whether it was he or Christine who finally ended the embrace. He suddenly realized how naked he felt without the mask, how vulnerable. So he bent and picked it up, then made a move to replace it.

"You don't have to do that, you know," Christine said. Her glossy curls were lying in a glorious tangle over one shoulder, and her mouth looked swollen from his fierce kisses. He thought she had never been so beautiful.

He turned the mask over in his hands for a moment, watching as the firelight caught the curves and hollows, glimmering over the smooth plastic. "I've worn this mask for almost twenty years," he said. "It's a part of me still. Even though I know you don't need me to wear it, I feel as if I should." And he lifted it to his face, settling the wire that held it in place so it was covered by his hair. He managed a smile. "Besides, I'd probably shock Jerome into retirement if I went out without it."

That comment brought an answering smile to her face. "I understand, Erik. As long as you're wearing it for yourself and not for me. Because for me it doesn't matter."

He kissed her then, gently, on the cheek. "I know that now. And I thank you for it." He offered her his hand, and she took it. "Come now. I have something I want to show you."

"What's that?"

The last of my secrets, he thought, but only replied, "You'll see."

And with that he led her out of the room that had been the heart of his isolation for so many years and now, it seemed, had been the beginning of his redemption.

Chapter Twenty-Three

Erik took the candelabra from its stand in the corner of the room and gestured for me to follow him. I thought I understood why he choose to light our way with its uncertain flame, rather than turn on the harsher electric lights. Wherever he was taking me, clearly it was important to him, and he did not want to break the evening's spell with the prosaic intrusion of such modern-day inventions.

So I drifted after him in the dimly lit corridors, stumbling once on the carpet runner in those dratted stiletto heels—Erik was quick to reach out to steady me, his hand warm and strong on my bare arm. Once again the corridors slid past like something out of a Cocteau-inspired dream, but this time I was awake, and I at last knew the truth behind the mask.

In a way, I had been surprised by my own reaction, or lack thereof. Oh, I was no Victorian Christine, carefully sheltered from the ugliness of the world. If nothing else, I'd seen my share of horror movies and the elaborate excesses of today's special-effects makeup.

More than that, though, I'd been forced at a very early age to see some of the ugliest this world had to offer. When my parents had been killed in the car accident when I was fifteen, I'd had to accompany my grandmother to identify the bodies, since she had advanced diabetes and glaucoma and was legally blind by then. So even though she had stood beside me and held my hand through the whole procedure, I was the one who had to look down at the shattered faces of my parents and tell the coroner who they were. It had been a head-on collision at forty or fifty miles an hour, and the physics at work had not been kind.

Compared to that, Erik's deformity had been almost mild. Oh, there was no arguing that he had a very valid reason for hiding himself from the world, for concealing half his face behind a mask. I of course had no idea what congenital disfigurement or birth trauma he'd suffered, but the right side of his face was still crisscrossed by the scars left behind by surgeons who had obviously tried to correct those deformities. It appeared that his right eye socket had originally been located far lower down on his cheek than it was now; the skin high on his cheekbone was livid with scar tissue, and the eye socket itself was just as bad. He had no lashes on that eye, and a fine fretwork of scar tissue crossed his eyebrow and disappeared somewhere into his hairline on that side of his face. The scarring faded as it moved down toward his jaw line, and his mouth was not touched at all. To anyone else, his visage probably would have been horrific. But I knew him now, had come to realize the depth of his enormous talent and agile mind, and compared to those attributes, his scarred face was of little import.

I still felt his mouth on mine, the warmth of his breath on my cheek. I could sense the enormous pent-up passion within him. It should have frightened me, perhaps; after all, I had no real experience of men, had never gone any further with Randall than a few heated kisses. But again I was no cloistered Victorian girl, kept completely unaware of relations between the sexes. I knew exactly what Erik wanted from me, and I knew that I wanted it from him as well. The only real question lay in how long we both could wait before succumbing to our passions.

After we had descended the main staircase, Erik led me down the main corridor, on past the salon where we had once ventured out into a sunlit day—it seemed years ago now. We continued on, past a seemingly unending number of closed-off rooms, until he stopped at the very end of the corridor, where a set of carved double doors rose up before us.

He transferred the candelabra to his left hand and pulled a set of keys out of his coat pocket with his right. The key went into the lock, and he began to turn it, then said, "I don't want this to disturb you—"

"Unless you've got the remains of your last seven wives in there, like Bluebeard, I doubt that whatever is in there will bother me too much," I replied, taking care to keep my tone light.

"Nothing that bad, I assure you," he said, and I was gratified to see that he was smiling.

"Well, then—"

And he turned the key in the lock and pushed the doors open, moving ahead of me into the dark space. At first I could see nothing, but he touched the candelabra he was carrying to a similar one by the door, and then more and more as he moved throughout the room.

It was the Phantom's lair.

Or, at least as close as it could be, given that it had obviously been built into what had originally been a large room. Whatever windows the room might have had at one time were now concealed. All of the walls, the floor, and even the ceiling had been covered by black marble faintly veined with gold so that it flickered with errant sparks in the darkness. At the far side of the room was a massive gilded pipe organ, and just a few feet away from it stood a prop I recognized from the stage show: an elaborate mirror frame surrounding a mannequin dressed in Christine's lace-tiered Victorian wedding gown. I was relieved to see that she did not resemble me very much, although the long curly hair was almost exactly like mine. To one side was a replica of the Phantom's gondola, now filled with silk cushions in dark, rich hues. I couldn't remember whether that was something from the show or a detail Erik had added.

For a long moment I stood there, taking it in. About the room was a feeling of hushed anticipation. Although it was completely silent, I fancied I could almost hear the lapping of the Phantom's underground lake, just hidden around some corner. The slightest rustle of my silk cocktail dress brought a sudden rush of echoes.

Erik stood very still, having placed the candelabra on the shelf reserved for that purpose on the organ. His eyes were painfully alive behind the mask, watching me, waiting for my reaction.

I would be lying if I said the room didn't frighten me a little. The amount of work that had to have gone into producing such a faithful replica was staggering. This place was the physical manifestation of an obsession he'd clearly indulged for a number of years, and once again the fear rose up in my mind that all I was to him was this Christine, the Phantom's Christine, not a young woman who waited tables while putting herself through college, someone with an unladylike appreciation for old *A-Team* reruns, a girl who had more than once skipped a meal so that she could eat a bowl of Cherry Garcia while studying for midterms. All the million and one contradictions that made up me somehow seemed to be overshadowed by this room and what it meant. How could a man who had built this room see past his vision of who Christine should be to who I really was?

He must have seen the uncertainty in my face, because he immediately stepped closer to me and took one of my hands in his. "Don't ask me to explain," he said, "for I don't think I can, exactly. Things seem so logical when you're in the middle of the process—at the time I thought that if I were really going to be trapped in this house for the rest of my life, at least I could make one part of it feel as if it were happening someplace far away." An eloquent lift of his shoulders. "I had nothing else, you see."

And with that, I did begin to see. Oh, I had thought of myself as a lonely person, ever since the accident that transformed me from the girl who invariably got the lead in the school musicals and who, while not exactly popular, had a fairly large circle of friends, to the girl with the dead parents, the girl whom no one knew how to look in the eye. The girl who had slowly let herself drift away from almost everyone, especially after her grandmother passed away. It had been a relief to graduate, to go on to places where no one knew me, to take my own little cocoon of loneliness with me. Only Meg, through her own determined cheerfulness, and then lately Randall, had been allowed within my own isolation. But Erik had not even had that much—not the meaningless pleasantries exchanged with the checker at the supermarket, the patrons at the restaurant, or even the clerk at the DMV. All those long years he had had only himself, Ennis, and Jerome. My own life was a whirl of social activity compared to his. Could I blame him for taking whatever opportunity to escape that he could find?

I reached up to stroke his cheek, to push the heavy silver-brushed hair away from his temple. I knew I had to show him that it didn't matter to me, that I understood his compulsion, that all was still well between us. "Does the organ really work?"

The relief in his eyes was palpable. "Of course. Why go to all this trouble for a mere prop?"

"Will you play for me?"

"Of course." He released my hand very gently and went to seat himself at the organ. Then he looked up at me, and even in the dim flickering light of the candelabras

I could see the sudden glint in his eyes. "Old school, do you think?"

And with that he launched into the opening chords of Bach's *Toccata and Fugue in D Minor*. Of course it was brilliantly executed, but I found myself overcome by a fit of the giggles after only a few bars, and he stopped, lifting his hands from the keys.

"What?" Although his tone was stern, there was a tell-tale twitch at the corner of his mouth.

"I'm sorry," I said, trying to regain my composure. "I just got the sudden urge to sneak up behind you and pull off the mask, but it's a little late for that, isn't it?"

He lifted an eyebrow.

"Oh, what the hell." I reached over and lifted it from his face. Then, before he could say anything, I plopped myself down in his lap and pressed my lips against his.

It was a few moments before either of us was able to speak. His arms tightened around me, and I relaxed into their strength, the warmth of his body against mine, the subtle masculine smell of his skin and hair. I felt as if I could stay this way with him forever.

At length he murmured into my hair, his breath hot against my scalp, "You are becoming quite forward."

"Must be your bad influence," I said. "I was certainly never like this with Randall."

At those words I could feel the tension return to his body, but I spoke again before he could say anything.

"Erik, what should you care what passed between him and me? Less than what you and I have had this one night, and that's the truth. Besides, don't you understand? You've won. I can't imagine being with anyone else but you."

He pulled away from me slightly, but only so he could look me squarely in the face. I met his own scarred visage with an unflinching regard, wanting him to see how little effect it had on me.

"Do you truly mean that?" he asked. "You're willing to spend the rest of your life here—with me?"

"If you'll have me," I said. The words were light, but my tone was not. Somehow I had always known that when I found the right man—if I ever found him—I would want to be with him forever. I had never been able to understand the mindset of women who dated so frequently they couldn't keep their boyfriends' names straight.

"If I'll have you—my God, Christine, how could I want anyone but you? You, who are utter perfection, who have given me more this night than I had any reason to hope for?" His voice was ragged.

I could feel the blood rush to my cheeks, but I knew now was not the time to make my usual self-deprecating comment. What woman's heart wouldn't thrill to hear words such as those? My eyes stung with sudden tears as I said, "I love you, Erik."

"And I love you, Christine."

And again his mouth was against mine as I let the waves of passion sweep over me again, my body thrilling to his touch, my soul drowning in his.

I would gladly be lost in you forever…

The phone rang just as Ortiz was about to throw on his jacket and head out the door.

"Goddammit," he muttered, but protocol forced him to pick up the receiver. "Ortiz here."

"Hi, detective—" came the reply, and Ortiz barely stifled a curse.

"Hello, Mr. Cagney," he said, attempting to wriggle into his suit jacket while holding the receiver up to his ear. "What can I do for you today?"

"Well, I hadn't heard from you for a while, so I thought I should call—"

"Believe me, Mr. Cagney, if I had anything new to report, I would be in touch with you immediately." He should have known, after all. Here it was almost two o'clock in the afternoon; Randall usually called before twelve. Actually, the kid was showing remarkable restraint. "However, I was just about on my way out to follow a new lead—"

Randall's voice was too eager. "A new lead? Something promising?"

"Possibly, Mr. Cagney, but of course I'm not at liberty to discuss it with you until I have more facts in hand."

"Of course." A brief hesitation, then Randall said, "It's just—it's been almost two weeks, and now it's finals, and no one knows where she is—"

"I understand your frustration, Mr. Cagney," Ortiz said. Boy, do I. "However, the best you can do is wait and be patient. But I really need to get going now."

"Of course, sir." The misery was in Randall's tone was obvious. "Just keep me posted."

"Absolutely. I'll give you a call if anything changes."

With that he hung up, glad that he had only been delayed by a few minutes. Some of his previous conversations with Randall had dragged on for almost an hour as the kid went over every detail of Christine's disappearance once more, almost as if he thought he could solve it himself if he just repeated the facts enough times, retraced Christine's steps on the off-chance they might have missed something. Ortiz had long since given up trying to decide whether Randall Cagney was just a truly devoted boyfriend, or whether he had a bit of the stalker in him as well. His obsession seemed out of proportion for what really had been a fairly short-term relationship, but Ortiz knew better to say such a thing aloud.

At least today it wasn't raining, although a thin layer of cloud cover painted the sky a peculiar grayish white, with the sun a sickly yellow hue like the yolk of an undercooked egg. Ortiz headed south on Los Robles, glad at least that the afternoon traffic hadn't begun to pick up yet. For a while the neighborhoods around him grew steadily more affluent as he drove through San Marino, and then, as he crossed onto Garfield and headed south toward the 10 Freeway, they grew just as steadily seedier. By the time he got to Dodson, a scrubby little cul-de-sac a few blocks below the freeway, he was about as far from the high-rent district as you could get in the San Gabriel Valley.

Several of the businesses looked as if they had been closed for a long time, and most of the others didn't appear as if they had much time left before they closed up shop as well. It was difficult to tell whether the cars parked on the street had been abandoned or were merely in an advanced state of disrepair. Graffiti covered the fences and walls.

A real garden spot, Ortiz thought as he climbed out

of his car. He'd be lucky if the hubcaps were still in place when he got back.

Rigoberto's A-1 Auto Repair was located on the south side of the street, just about where it dead-ended into a weed-filled lot. From where he stood he could hear the sound of an air drill being operated, but other than that there didn't seem to be much activity going on at the shop.

He began to wonder whether he should have brought Kosky along with him — it was the detective's discretion as to whether to have backup with him on these routine investigations — but Ortiz had been in rougher places than this on many occasions. Besides, he had the feeling the mysterious Rigo wouldn't appreciate someone besides himself showing up, let alone a gawky, well-dressed *gringo* like Kosky.

Making sure the badge was visible on his hip, he went toward what looked like the office entrance. A bored-looking Latina sat at the battered blond-wood desk, filing her nails. She gave Ortiz a vaguely hostile look from underneath heavily mascaraed lashes and said, "*¿Qué usted desea?*"

"I'm here to see Rigo," Ortiz replied in English, and moved his jacket aside so there was no way she could miss the badge. "I'm Detective Ortiz."

Her eyes narrowed, but she got up from behind the desk — coincidentally showing off a pair of magnificent legs encased in skintight stretch jeans — and yelled back into the shop, "*Rigo! ¡La policía!*"

It took him a few minutes, but eventually Rigo slouched into the office. He was just about as Ortiz had expected:

tattooed, head shaved to stubble, thin mustache. He was also stocky and short; he made Ortiz actually feel tall.

"You Ortiz?" he asked.

Ortiz showed him the badge, and Rigo nodded.

"Yeah, Tony told me about you. Come on back."

Of course Rigo would magnanimously allow Ortiz a glimpse at the shop—he'd had more than twenty-four hours to erase any incriminating evidence. Now the bay was half-filled with a motley collection of vehicles, from someone's souped-up rice grinder—it appeared to be a Nissan Sentra under all the ground effects, spoiler, and metallic paint—to an ancient Chevy Caprice station wagon that looked as if it would shake apart the second it went over a speed bump. Ortiz guessed that Rigo had probably called in favors with family and friends to get legitimate vehicles in here. No matter. He wasn't here to investigate the chop shop anyway.

Ortiz took out his notepad. "Antonio Vasquez informed me that you paid him to lift a car about ten days ago?"

Rigo scowled. "No, man, I didn't pay him. I was just sort of, you know, the middleman. Yeah."

"Okay, so you brokered a deal. Were you aware at the time that the car belonged to a missing college student?"

"No, man, I didn't know nothing about that. This guy comes in, says he needs a car taken care of, and he asks me to handle it."

"Did you get his name?"

"Jerome."

"Jerome what?"

Again Rigo frowned, brows almost meeting. "Guy

didn't give me his last name. And he paid in cash, so I didn't ask."

"How much?"

"How much what?"

"How much did he pay you?" Ortiz could feel his teeth starting to grind together, and forced himself to stop. You couldn't make these guys tell you anything; you just had to wait and keep coaxing it out of them. If Ortiz hadn't been of Mexican descent himself, he doubted he'd have been able to get any useful information from Rigo at all.

"Five grand."

"Five grand? To steal a car that was worth barely twelve hundred? Didn't you think that was a little strange?"

"Hey, man, I don't worry about whether it's strange or not. I just worry about if the money is good."

Which apparently it had been, considering that the unknown Jerome had paid Rigo five thousand bucks and Rigo had given Tony only a grand to actually steal the car.

Ortiz decided to try another tack. "Can you describe this Jerome character?"

Rigo shrugged. "Just some *gringo*, man. Nice set of wheels, though. New Range Rover, custom rims, loaded. That shit's worth a lot."

Ortiz made a note on his pad. "So you don't remember anything about the man? Age? Hair?"

"Maybe late thirties, something like that. Brown hair—not dark, though. Couldn't see his eyes—he was wearing sunglasses."

Late thirties, brown hair. That description probably could be applied to a million men in the greater Los

Angeles area, but it still tripped Ortiz's alarms. "Would you say he was athletic-looking?"

Rigo didn't even pause to think it over. "Yeah, he looked pretty tough for a rich guy. At first I thought he was maybe a cop or something. Don't know why—just the way he looked around at things. Like he was sizing up threats." Another shrug. "But once he pulled out the cash I figured he was okay. And he was. Sweet deal, over in five. He never came back. Called once, to make sure we got the car all right."

It could just be a coincidence, but somehow Ortiz doubted it. Whoever this Jerome was, he sounded very much like the stalker Christine had spotted on campus and who Meg herself had described to Ortiz. Whether there was any connection between him and the reclusive Erik Deitrich was another thing.

"Did you happen to catch his license plate number?"

At that Rigo grinned, revealing a gold canine. "You're lucky that I notice shit like that. I wrote it down." He lifted a clipboard off a nearby workbench and started rifling through the pages. "I like to be careful—figured it couldn't hurt to have some info on him in case he tried to rat me out later."

Ortiz was trying like anything to keep from grinning. Goddamn—an actual license plate number. Surely it couldn't be that easy—

"Yeah, here it is. 6GBH271." Rigo squinted at Ortiz. "You're gonna help out Tony now, right?"

"I'll throw him a goddamn party if this works out. But yeah, he's been very cooperative. And so have you."

Rigo spread his hands, dark eyes gleaming. "Hey, just doing my part, man, like any other law-abiding citizen."

Law-abiding my ass. At this point, though, Ortiz really couldn't care less whether Rigo was chopping up the Popemobile or Air Force One. This was what he had been looking for—a real lead, a tangible piece of evidence.

He thanked Rigo and headed back to his car, its hub-caps blessedly still intact. Probably Rigo had warned the neighborhood thugs away, telling them they didn't want to screw things up for Tony Vasquez.

Before Ortiz had even cleared the cul-de-sac and headed out onto Peck Road, he'd picked up the radio and called in the license plate number. By the time he was back in the office, he should have a nice fat file on this Jerome character that he could look over at his leisure.

And after that, he thought, weaving in and out of the thickening afternoon traffic, *your ass is mine.*

Chapter Twenty-Four

I KNOW THIS MAN, ORTIZ THOUGHT, staring down at the open file in front of him. Crazy as it might sound, the owner of the much-admired Range Rover was someone Ortiz had contact with back during the time when he still worked for the LAPD. Oh, he hadn't known the man well—met him at a crime scene once, talked with him on the phone a few more times when the LAPD was coordinating with the FBI on a well-publicized case where the perpetrator had car-jacked his victim in Arizona but messily murdered her in a back alley only a few blocks from skid row in downtown Los Angeles. But Ortiz never forgot a face, and he remembered Special Agent Jerome Manning. *Ex-special agent*, he reminded himself, leafing through the dossier. Apparently Manning had quit the Bureau seven or eight years ago and gone into business for himself. But what the hell he was doing tangled up in the Daly case, Ortiz couldn't begin to imagine.

Manning's photo stared up at him from the file, impassive, just this side of handsome. It was not the sort of face to reveal any secrets.

According to the file, his current address was on Los Robles, in one of those pricey mixed-use condo/shopping developments clustered around the Paseo Colorado mall. He had a fictitious business name on file with the county: Manning Security Consulting. The address associated with the business was a Mailbox Plus mail drop only a few blocks away from the condo. The Range Rover had been purchased with cash a little over six months ago. Ortiz let out a low whistle. Apparently the security consulting business was doing well for Jerome Manning.

No wonder Rigo thought he was a cop. Ortiz flipped through the meager pages of the file, hoping he would see some kind of pattern, some kind of clue that would make sense of his connection to Christine Daly's disappearance. Unfortunately, it would take a court order for the police to investigate Manning's bank records and tax statements, and Ortiz wasn't sure he had enough evidence yet to make a strong case for that kind of invasion of privacy.

There wasn't much here. The paperwork indicated that Manning had left the FBI voluntarily and with sterling recommendations. He certainly wasn't a disgruntled ex-Bureau officer with a hate on for law enforcement in general. Obviously he had decided he could make more money working in the private sector, and apparently he had been correct. And he certainly did not seem the type to develop an obsessive interest in a local college student, no matter how beautiful and talented she might be. He was still single at forty, which was a little unusual, but not much, considering his line of work. A lot of men in that field found it easier to pursue their careers unencumbered by a family. Hell, he could even be gay, although Ortiz had definitely not gotten that vibe from him.

All of which left Ortiz with basically nothing to go on. There was also the possibility that Jerome was just the go-between, someone who had been hired to handle the kidnapping of Christine Daly. Maybe it was really Erik Deitrich who paid the bills, although Ortiz wasn't sure how he'd ever be able to prove that. Even if he had access to Manning's bank records, Ortiz was pretty sure that that sort of transaction would have been handled on a cash-only basis—possibly with funds changing hands through offshore accounts. People with that kind of money had access to all sorts of ingenious methods of subverting the government, and he'd been around long enough to know that they were hardly ever caught. The general public would probably be staggered to know how much illegal financial activity went unpunished.

It seemed the direct route would be the best here. All he could do was put an APB out on Manning's vehicle, stake out a few officers near his condo, and then wait. Manning obviously spent a good deal of time in Pasadena and its environs; hell, his condo was only a few blocks from the police station itself. Sooner or later someone would be able to tag him and bring him in for questioning. Not that Ortiz pinned all of his hopes on that, either. Interrogating an ex-FBI agent would be anything but easy.

He ran a hand through his thinning hair and sighed. *Just once*, he thought, *I'd like something about this case to be simple. Just once.*

Long experience, however, told him that his wishes weren't very likely to be granted.

Jerome put down the phone receiver and turned to face Erik. "The hospital wants to keep Ennis for another night."

"Did they say why?" Erik laid aside his newspaper and looked at Jerome with some concern. Part of him was still so buoyed up by the events of the night before that a setback like this was only mildly worrisome, but on the other hand, he did want Ennis home and safe as soon as possible.

"His blood pressure isn't quite where they want it to be, so they're keeping him another twenty-four hours just to be safe. But I'll be able to pick him up tomorrow afternoon around two."

"Well, I suppose we can survive another night without him if we must," Erik replied, but inwardly he was a little pleased. He would have another night alone with Christine at least. Now if he could just get rid of Jerome—

"I noticed that you didn't lock Christine's door last night," Jerome said, his tone somewhat ominous.

"Not necessary." In answer to Jerome's continued frown, Erik added, "We seem to have worked out our... issues. There's no need to fear another escape attempt."

For a moment it looked as if Jerome wanted to argue the point further, but then he just lifted his shoulders. "So now what?"

"So now you get the rest of the day off. I'd like to be alone with Christine."

"What about Anna and Consuelo?"

For a second Erik looked at Jerome blankly, then realized he must be talking about the maids. "Oh, give them the day off as well. With pay, of course."

"Of course. And Michel?"

He definitely needed the cook here, if only until dinner was ready. Then he, too, could get out. Erik wanted champagne tonight, to celebrate his and Christine's blossoming relationship, but which? The delicate and lovely '97 Perrier-Jouet Belle Époque, or the magnificent '90 Veuve Clicquot rosé? After a moment's deliberation, he thought he would go with the rosé. He doubted whether Christine had ever had anything like the Veuve Clicquot, and he wanted the evening to be as memorable as he could possibly make it. And to go with it? Lobster perhaps, although the rosé could stand up to a delicately roasted duck if Michel had a gentle hand with the sauce...

He realized that Jerome was still watching him, waiting for an answer. "Michel, of course. Tell him we'll be having the '90 Veuve Clicquot, and that I was thinking duck. He can take it from there."

"Very good, Mr. Deitrich. Anything else?"

"I don't think so. After you've spoken with Michel, you can go. If I need anything, I can call you on your cell."

Jerome nodded and went out, this time leaving the office doors open behind him. He probably thought there was no need to keep everything closed up, now that Christine apparently had the run of the house.

No need for secrets any longer, he thought, and he looked around his office with some wonder. Only last night they had stood by the now-cold hearth, and Christine had taken his scarred face in her hands and kissed him, healing him with her embraces. Only last night she had whispered "I love you" and smiled to hear him say it in return.

Even now he wasn't sure whether it had all been a dream, some lovely vision that would surely melt with the return of day. But no—he knew it to be true. Earlier he had heard her singing a few bars from Marguerite's aria as she went down the stairs to find herself some breakfast. Never an early riser, he had still been in bed when she went by, but just hearing her, just knowing that she was in the house and singing joyfully the morning after their declarations of love, had been enough for him. The thought that this was but the first of many such mornings filled him with such happiness he thought it might be more than he could bear. All through his wretched, lonely life he had never imagined what the love of such a woman could mean—and now that he actually had achieved it, even through all his wrongdoing and selfishness, all he could do was endeavor to make himself worthy of her— now and forever.

It had been a lovely, idyllic day. Clouds chased themselves across a deep blue sky that spoke more of March than December; although many of the trees on the property were bare, they were still elegant in their nakedness, and the grass was almost supernaturally green following all the rain. I followed Erik as he took me over the house, showing me all the rooms I hadn't yet explored—the library, the sumptuous spare bedrooms and salons, the greenhouse where apparently Ennis liked to putter with the orchids. It was if he had to put on display everything he had to offer me—as if he didn't think he was worthy enough on his own.

I didn't try to disabuse him of the notion. It would come in time—eventually he would learn that, magnificent as it was, the house and all the wealth it represented meant very little to me, compared to the strength of my feelings for him. It was enough now to be with him, to listen to the marvelous timber of his voice and see the warmth in his eyes every time he looked at me. Our love was still new and a little fragile, and I only wanted to reassure him with every glance and touch how much I really cared for him.

Perhaps I was myself a little surprised by the depth of my feelings for Erik. Only a few days ago I had tried so hard to hate him, to hate what he had done to me, but now I could not imagine what my life would be without him.

Who can say, really, what it is that causes two people to come together? Sometimes the matches that seem logical are the ones that flicker out and die quickly, while the improbable pairings endure. Although on the surface we seemed to have very little in common, save our love of music, I knew that in some ways we were both broken— he by the deformity that had shaped his very existence, I by crippling losses and the grief and isolation that had inevitably followed. We had both known despair. Was it so surprising that we had reached out to one another, hoping for some warmth in the darkness?

At the end of the afternoon, he told me that he had planned a special dinner and would like me to dress for it.

"That sounds so decadent," I replied. Who in this day and age dressed for dinner? Especially here in Southern California, where I'd actually seen people wearing jeans to the opera.

"Indulge me," he'd said, running one finger down my arm.

"For you, anything." And the words had been truer than even he could have guessed.

So at seven I appeared in the red dining room, appropriately attired in the beaded red gown I had pushed aside as too provocative the night before. The dress was so bare that all I could wear under it was a pair of bikini panties, and I had to admit it made me feel a little devilish. This time it was rubies that dripped from my throat and ears and flashed from two of my fingers. I found no need to deny myself the treasures of the jewelry chest any longer and delighted in choosing the correct pieces to go with my gown.

The room looked magnificent. It seemed as if every candelabra in the house had been forced into service to light the space, and they shimmered from the sideboards and down the center of the table. Erik rose from his place at the head of the table as I entered. He looked magnificent in a black double-breasted tuxedo, a red rose on his lapel. In the background I heard the delicate strains of a Mozart piano concerto.

"You're stunning," he said, moving to pull my chair out for me.

"So are you," I replied, although I was a little disappointed to see that he still wore the mask. How much convincing would it take to make him understand that his scars didn't matter to me?

At his left elbow was a gorgeous silver wine bucket, now filled with ice and a huge bottle of champagne. After seating me, he lifted it from the ice, holding a small towel to protect himself from the moisture.

"That is the biggest bottle of champagne I have ever seen," I remarked.

"*That*, as you put it, is a magnum of '90 Veuve Clicquot rosé. I thought you might enjoy it. Many experts say that a champagne can only reach its true potential when bottled in a magnum." He nimbly worked the cork with both his thumbs, slowly loosening it, until it popped out almost quietly, only shooting a few feet before it dropped to the Persian rug.

I assumed that this was not the sort of champagne one would waste in a spray of foam. "Was it very expensive?"

He lifted his shoulders. "I suppose. A little over 600 euros."

Six hundred—I didn't know what the exchange rate was right now, but I knew that bottle of champagne could have paid for the rent on my little bungalow. Clearly, Erik and I moved in very different worlds.

I managed a smile and said, "I'll try not to be too scared to drink it."

He gave me an answering smile and poured some champagne into the cut-crystal flute in front of me. "Don't ever be afraid. Open yourself to new experiences."

I suddenly got the feeling that he was talking about much more than just champagne, but in answer I picked up the flute and took a sip. Up until that point my chief experience with champagne had been the cheap stuff you get included with champagne brunches, and this was about as far from that as my tiny bungalow was from Erik's mansion. First of all, it was so light it almost felt as if the bubbles were just evaporating in my mouth without my even having to swallow. But with that was also a delicate fruitiness that I had not been expecting, a shimmer of black currant against my palate.

My expression must have been enough to inform Erik of my reaction, for then he said, "Impressive, isn't it? I have to say that it's one of my favorites."

"It's wonderful."

With that Michel came out, pushing the dinner cart. I supposed that Erik had drafted him to handle some of the serving duties with Ennis still in the hospital. There was an expression dangerously close to a pout on his handsome features, but he dished up the lobster bisque without comment before disappearing back into the kitchen.

I looked at Erik, who lifted an eyebrow. I had an overwhelming urge to burst into laughter, but I thought perhaps that might ruin the mood, so instead I took another sip of champagne. "Michel doesn't seem terribly happy about having to serve this evening."

"As to that—" He waved a hand. "Michel considers himself an artist. Anyone who serves food is merely the help. No offense."

"None taken." Possibly being a waitress was a

cliché—poor struggling college student has to wait tables to support herself—but the truth was that it could pay pretty well, if you worked at a good restaurant and were reasonably skilled at your job. It was certainly better than the minimum-wage retail gigs I had considered before going into waitressing.

The lobster bisque was excellent, however, as was the roast duck that followed. Throughout the meal we drank an alarming amount of champagne without seeming to really get anywhere; that was the downside (or possibly upside, depending on how one looked at it) of drinking a magnum. By the time we finished the strawberries for dessert—the only dessert one could reasonably consume while drinking champagne, according to Erik—I was feeling more than a little tipsy. It was different from the effect of the Bordeaux I had drunk in this room so many days ago, however. I felt light as the air itself, floating, the candles in the room shimmering around me with an unearthly glow.

Erik helped me to my feet, arms strong around me. We kissed then, my body crushed against his. The dress I wore was so thin it was almost as if nothing separated us, as if my bare breasts were pressed against his tuxedo jacket.

He paused then for a moment, looking down at me. I gazed back at him, flushed with desire and champagne, and it was if some flash of lightning passed between us. I could feel myself nod, and he took a deep breath. Then he lifted me into his arms and swept me out of the dining room.

I had felt his strength before, but nothing like this. It was seemingly without effort that he carried me up the stairs and down the corridor, past the entrance to my own room, all the way to the end of the hall. There we entered a chamber I had never seen before, but recognized immediately. Erik's bedroom.

It had a somber, elegant quality very different from my own pretty blue and rose rooms. A fire burned low in the hearth, and again candelabras provided the illumination, showing darkly carved antique furniture and a huge four-poster bed with coverings that looked deep blood-red in the gloom.

Once there, he set me down next to the bed. We were silent for a moment, facing each other, and then he said, "If it's too soon—"

"It's not," I said immediately. Then I reached up and lifted the mask from his face. Now, with the moment here at last, I wanted no barriers between us.

There was a long, awful second when I thought I had gone too far, when he just stared at me as if still expecting me to scream or faint or some such other Victorian nonsense. Then he pulled me against him, his mouth on mine with almost punishing force, as his hands moved up and down my body, seeking the curves of my form through the thin beaded silk.

Then his fingers found the zipper and yanked it down, the gown falling to the floor in a slither of jet and crimson. My own hands seemed to move with a life of their own as I unbuttoned his tuxedo jacket, then struggled with the tighter fastening of his dress shirt. All the while our mouths were locked together, his tongue meeting mine, the urgency building as we finally sank down onto the bed, free at last of the confines of our clothing.

His body was lean and well-muscled, pale in the flickering light of the fire. I could feel him struggle to pull the heavy bedclothes aside, even as his mouth left mine and traveled down my neck, his breath hot against my flesh until he closed on my breast.

I had never imagined such exquisite sensations. I arched against him, fingers knotting in his heavy dark hair as he brought me to the edge of ecstasy. And even then his other hand reached lower, lower...

From somewhere I could hear moaning, and then realized the sound was coming from me. I leaned back against the pillows, letting him touch me, letting him explore my body, exulting in the waves of pleasure that washed over me. And then I was boldly touching him, feeling him writhe against me, feeling the muscles of his body tense as I brought him closer and closer to release.

Finally he heaved himself on top of me. I looked up to see his face in the uncertain candlelight, a face that was half demon, half angel — I no longer knew or cared which.

"Yes," I whispered, and then he was inside me, our bodies joined in a way I had never known was possible, until the waves of ecstasy crashed over us both and pulled us away into the darkness, all knowledge of the world lost, so that there was only Erik, only me. And then there was nothing left at all.

Chapter Twenty-Five

THE INSISTENT SHRILLING OF A TELEPHONE was the first thing to brought me back to consciousness. I opened my eyes and blinked several times at the unfamiliar ceiling above me, a gorgeous expanse of coffered mahogany, nothing like the softly draped rose silk of my own canopy bed that met my gaze every morning. Beside me, Erik stirred, the scarred side of his face turned toward the wall. All I could see was an immaculate profile of aquiline nose and well-defined chin, the latter now faintly covered with dark stubble.

Blood rushed to my cheeks as I recalled the events of the evening before. Some time in the middle of the night he had awakened me, seeking my body in a moment of renewed ardor, and I had willingly gone to him once again. Now I felt tired and more than a little sore—*that's one thing the romance novels never tell you about,* I thought. But amidst the fatigue and the slight embarrassment over how easily I had fallen in bed with him, I was aware of a great contentment. I would not have wished to be anywhere else but here next to Erik, here in Erik's bed.

"Phone," I said to Erik, who seemed to be having a more difficult time waking than I had.

He groaned and rolled over toward me. "Machine'll get it," he murmured, his voice still fogged with sleep. Then his eyes opened, and he stared at me, as if registering for the first time that I was lying in bed next to him.

Sure enough, the phone stopped ringing.

I smiled at him. "Good morning."

One hand went to his face, as if he couldn't believe that he was casually facing me without the mask. Then I saw the beginnings of a wary smile in return, perhaps his first tentative realization that the mask really didn't matter very much to me. "Good morning," he replied at length. Then his gaze went to the heavily curtained windows across the room. "What time is it, anyway?"

"I have no idea." I leaned down and kissed him softly on his scarred cheek, gratified to see that this time he did not flinch. "It feels pretty late."

With that he sat up, the bedclothes slipping away from his torso. He was very pale, of course, but I found the effect pleasing nonetheless. The carefully sculptured musculature of his upper body reminded me an ancient Greek statue; apparently he spent at least some of his time working out in a home gym.

Still clutching the bedcovers about his waist, he leaned over and began reaching for something with his left hand. "Oh, Christ," he said.

"What?"

"I appear to have lost my underwear. Would you mind—" and he broke off, a faint flush of color dusting his cheekbone.

"Averting my eyes?" I asked, unable to keep from grinning. How odd he was sometimes—here we had been as intimate as two people could be, yet he couldn't bear for me to see his naked backside. I turned away, still smiling. "I promise I won't peek."

And I didn't, even though the temptation was almost irresistible as I felt him get up off the bed and then drop to his knees on the floor.

Something soft hit my arm. "What the—"

"Found yours," he said, and then, "Ah—got them."

"Is it safe now?" I asked, and then opened my eyes to see him standing there in a pair of black boxer briefs. I had to admit that they clung to his well-muscled thighs very nicely.

I didn't get to admire him for very long, however, for he went to his closet and drew on a lovely red silk dressing robe and then handed a second one to me.

"Unless you'd rather not?" he asked delicately, his gaze dropping to where my breasts were beginning to slip out from the sheet I had pulled around myself earlier.

It was my turn to blush. "Thank you," I said, taking the dressing robe from him. It was obviously Japanese, dark green with silvery cranes and bamboo leaves woven into the liquid silk. I pulled it around me, then took advantage of the relative cover it afforded to wriggle into my own underwear.

The phone chose that moment to start shrilling again. Erik muttered something under his breath and then looked over to the opposite wall, where a handsome carved mahogany clock showed the time as being a little before one in the afternoon. I could almost see him weigh the consequences of not answering the phone again, then decide that whoever it was would probably just keep calling until they reached a live person.

He crossed the room and punched a button on the multiline phone that sat on a side table there. Even the scarred side of his face looked annoyed. "Yes?"

Of course I couldn't hear who was on the other end of the phone, but it only took a few seconds for Erik's expression to transform from annoyance to worry. "He's not there? He didn't call?"

A pause while Erik listened to the reply.

"I don't have anyone here who can pick you up—yes, she's here—yes, she's fine—no, I don't think that's a good idea. Can you call a cab?"

Another long pause, during which Erik began to shake his head.

"No, I have no idea what could have happened. I just saw him yesterday, but I gave him the evening off. I'll have to have Greenburg look into it."

Frowning, Erik stood quite still as he listened to the speaker on the other end of the line.

"Yes, I know, but my hands are tied. Just get home, and then we'll try to figure out what happened."

With that he hung up the phone, his face drawn into lines of anxiety. Any afterglow from the night before had been completely erased.

Immediately I got up from the bed and went to him. "What's the matter?"

"That was Ennis calling from the hospital. Jerome was supposed to pick him up at noon, but he never showed up. I told Ennis to take a cab." He frowned. "Jerome would not forget an appointment like that."

"So what do you think happened?"

He shook his head. "I don't know. All I can hope is that he was merely in a car accident."

At first the words didn't quite register. "You hope?"

"Absolutely." He stepped away from the phone table and moved quickly across the chamber, heading for the bathroom. As he went he shrugged out of the silken dressing robe, and it fluttered to the ground in a shower of bloody fabric. "We both need to get ourselves ready. Ennis should be home very soon, and I don't want to meet him like this."

I looked down at my own dishabille and realized he was probably right. But that still didn't answer my question. "Why do you hope Jerome was only in a car accident?"

"Because," he said, and now the cloudy green eyes were more than merely anxious—they seemed almost frightened, "the alternative is so much worse." Erik reached out to brush away a stray curl from my forehead. "I'm afraid he might have been arrested."

Ortiz peered through the one-way glass to watch the man who sat alone on the other side. Unlike most suspects brought in for questioning, he did not appear at all restless. Often when a subject was left alone for any length of time he would tap his feet, drum his fingers on the arms of the chair, even get up and pace about the room.

But Jerome Manning did none of those things. He merely sat in the chair, hands resting lightly on his knees, blue eyes alert and fixed on the one-way glass. Of course he must have known that one or more persons was on the other side, watching him, and he obviously wasn't going to give anything away.

He was dressed casually but expensively in a black lamb leather jacket over a dark striped shirt and dark jeans, an ideal outfit for a night on the town. Apparently that was what he'd been up to when the two officers watching his condo caught him walking back home at around one in the morning. He'd casually informed them that he'd spent most of the evening shooting pool at the 35er on Colorado and was on foot because he didn't want to monitor the amount of beer he had to drink.

Up until the time of his arrest, he'd probably been having a pretty good evening; the officers who brought him in found several slips of paper with women's phone numbers scribbled on them in his jacket pockets. Even afterward he had seemed unruffled, asking only when he would get his phone call. No one had volunteered the information, however, and he'd spent the night in a cell by himself, since the officers on duty knew better than to put an ex-FBI agent out in the common holding area.

Ortiz's pager had gone off at around two in the morning, and he'd called in to find that Manning was already in custody. After a few moments of deliberation, Ortiz decided to hold off on seeing him until the next afternoon.

Extended time in a jail cell often worked wonders in making people more receptive to questioning, and besides, he knew he'd be more effective if he didn't have to drag himself over to the station in the middle of the night.

So now he stood here, holding a cup of the sludge that passed for coffee in the station and watching Manning from behind the one-way glass. Despite his time in a cell, the guy didn't look too much the worse for wear, except for the beginnings of some stubble on his cheeks. Ortiz scowled. It didn't seem fair that someone could spend the night in jail and still look like a candidate for the cover of *GQ*.

Kosky appeared at Ortiz's elbow and made a face at his coffee mug. "For the love of God, let me buy you a cappuccino."

"Not now, Kosky." Ortiz chewed his lower lip. This interrogation wasn't going to be easy, he knew—the guy wasn't just some loser off the street but a former government agent who'd probably forgotten more tricks about questioning suspects than Ortiz had ever known.

Shaking his head, Kosky looked through the glass at Jerome Manning. "Nice jacket," he commented.

"Did you need something?" Ortiz asked, his tone acid.

"Chief asked me to sit in on this one."

Jesus Christ, Ortiz thought, *does the guy think I'm a complete amateur?* "All right, but you stay in here. Don't interrupt unless I call you in. Got it?"

"You're the boss," Kosky replied amiably. He pulled out a chair and sat down.

With a sigh, Ortiz left the observation chamber and went out to unlock the door to the interrogation room.

Manning turned his head to watch him enter. There might have been a flicker of recognition in his eyes, but the neutral expression never changed.

"Good morning, Mr. Manning," Ortiz said, settling himself opposite Jerome on the other side of the scarred table that separated the two chairs. Ortiz placed Manning's file in front of him, brought out his ubiquitous yellow pad, and clicked his pen. "I'm Detective Ortiz.

"I know," Manning said. "You used to be LAPD. The Baumgarten case?"

"Good memory," Ortiz replied. "So do you want to tell me why you think you're here?"

"I was hoping you'd fill me in. Sure, I had a few beers last night, but I wasn't exactly being drunk and disorderly."

He should have known that Manning was not going to make this easy. "Okay, then. I've been working the Christine Daly case." Ortiz watched Manning carefully while making that statement, but the guy didn't even blink. "You hear of it?"

"I think I saw something on the news a few days ago." From all the concern in his voice, he might have been discussing an out-of-date weather report. "Any luck with that?"

"I was hoping you might tell me." Ortiz leaned forward a little, wishing he could read more from the handsome, impassive features. "A witness tells us you paid him to have Miss Daly's car stolen and then crushed. You want to explain that to me?"

Manning glanced at his watch—a Rolex, naturally. "When do I get my call?"

"Why don't you tell me about Miss Daly's car first?"

"I don't know anything about it."

"So you are stating for the record that you have no knowledge of what happened to the car?"

"I believe I don't have to tell you anything without a lawyer present."

Well, he was right there. On the other hand, Ortiz had approximately twelve more hours before Manning had to be formally charged with a crime; in these sorts of situations, Ortiz was usually looking more for reactions than actual admissions of guilt. Still, he knew he was fooling himself if he thought the former FBI agent was going to let anything important drop.

Ortiz decided to try another tack. "Do you own a 2011 Range Rover, license number 6GBH271?"

"Yes."

"You paid cash for it?"

Manning's eyes narrowed for a split second before he answered, "Yes."

"Doing well for yourself in the private security business?"

"I get along."

More than "get along," Ortiz thought, considering the guy owned a vehicle worth more than sixty grand free and clear, lived in a half-million-dollar condo, and had about ten thousand bucks' worth of watch strapped to his wrist. "And what sort of services do you provide?"

"I consult with clients on security systems for their various needs. Occasionally I've worked with high-profile individuals as a personal security consultant."

Which was just a fancy name for bodyguard. "Do your consulting services include disposing of stolen vehicles and planning kidnappings?"

The line between Manning's brows deepened momentarily, but that was his only reaction. After a pause he said, "You know you're reaching here, detective."

"Am I? Would you be interested to know that a Rigoberto Alvarez has positively ID'd you as the man who ordered the theft and disposal of one '93 Honda Civic, currently registered to Miss Christine Daly?"

Manning settled back in his chair, apparently unconcerned. "And who is this Rigoberto Alvarez?"

"He owns an automotive repair business in El Monte."

"Ah." Manning looked faintly amused. "I can guess what kind of business it is. So you're going to take his word over mine?"

Shit, Ortiz thought. The guy was right—if you put the two men in a courtroom right now and had them offer up testimony, no jury in the world would believe Rigoberto Alvarez over Jerome Manning. He hoped none of the desperation he was feeling had crept into his voice when he asked, "What reason would Alvarez have to accuse you of anything?"

A lift of the shoulders under the expensive leather jacket. "How would I know? Maybe I cut him off in traffic one day. Maybe one of my company's security systems got one of his buddies arrested. But I've never heard of the guy."

"And you would testify to that in a court of law?"

"Of course."

He's lying, Ortiz thought suddenly. Somehow he just knew—maybe Manning's responses were a little too smooth, a little too controlled. Unfortunately, there was very little he could do about it, except have him submit to a lie-detector test, and Ortiz knew there wasn't enough evidence to get departmental approval for that. All the data so far was completely circumstantial and based on hearsay from a pair of witnesses who were far from credible. Ortiz had just hoped that he might be able to get Manning to slip and say something incriminating.

No such luck, though. Clearly, the guy wasn't going to give up anything. Ortiz remembered Kosky, sitting up in the observation room and watching the whole thing and thought, *Any time you want to step in here, buddy...*

But of course Kosky had probably already realized it was a lost cause. It happened, Ortiz knew; sometimes you could just feel it in your gut that someone was guilty, but if you didn't have the evidence to back up your instincts then you were just shit out of luck. As he appeared to be here.

He hated the words even as he said them. "Well, Mr. Manning, it appears we were misled. The Pasadena Police Department sincerely apologizes for any inconvenience we might have caused you."

"No problem, detective. You had evidence you needed to investigate." Manning's face was still bland, but Ortiz couldn't help but hear the faint flicker of amusement in his voice. "Am I free to go now?"

"Of course." Ortiz stood, picking up his paperwork. "However, we may need to ask you some additional questions, so we would appreciate it if you could notify the department if you have to leave Pasadena for any length of time."

Manning stood as well, then extended a hand. "I'm sure that won't be a problem. Nice seeing you again, detective."

Talk about coals of fire, Ortiz thought, repressing the urge to punch the guy in his smug mouth. The hand he'd wanted to curl into a fist he instead extended to Manning. They shook briefly, and then Ortiz said, "Let me show you the way out."

Somehow he managed to maintain his composure until they got to the front lobby. Somehow he managed to give a barely civil farewell to Manning, who walked off jauntily toward the Paseo Colorado shopping center. Of course—his condo was only a few blocks away.

"So long, Manning," Ortiz said aloud, after he was sure the man was out of earshot. "Make sure you say hello to Christine Daly for me, you son of a bitch."

Then he turned and walked slowly back to his office, cursing Manning, the invisible Erik Deitrich, even the still-absent Christine Daly. *Right now*, he thought, *I'd be happy if I never heard of any of them again.*

But that, he reflected, as he tossed the useless Manning file onto his desktop, was just more wishful thinking. He knew no matter what, he would see this thing through to the end.

Chapter Twenty-Six

Erik watched as the taxi came to a stop at the upper-most curve of the circular drive, where the path leading to the front door ended. Of course, all he could do was wait in the shadowy foyer, not daring to allow the cab driver even the briefest glimpse of his half-masked face.

Christine did not suffer the same restrictions as he, however. As soon as Ennis emerged from the back seat and stood waiting for the driver to retrieve his valise from the trunk, she tripped lightly down the steps to meet him. Although to Erik Ennis still looked pale and drawn, there was no mistaking the sudden light in his eyes as he saw Christine come to greet him. As she took the valise from the driver, Erik could sense Ennis's gaze drawn to where he stood in the shadows, waiting for the two of them to come back into the house.

They exchanged a few words, although Erik could not hear what was said. Ennis handed the driver a couple of bills, waved off the proffered change, and began to make his slow way up the path to the front door. Christine appeared to offer her arm to steady the old man, but Ennis only smiled and shook his head at her, obviously determined to continue unaided.

Then came the moment Erik had been anticipating, yet at the same time dreading. There had been so many things he wanted to say to Ennis, apologies and explanations that he could only hope would make things all right between them, but now as he watched his butler approach he felt curiously tongue-tied. All he could manage, when Ennis crossed the threshold, was to say, "Welcome home, Ennis."

The old man looked at him then, and although the skin around his eyes was pouched and bruised-looking, the dark eyes themselves were sharp as ever. "It's good to be here, Erik," he said, and his gaze shifted to Christine, who stood off to one side, her lovely face flushed with happiness. "This was exactly the homecoming I had hoped for."

Erik wondered how much Christine had told him, and then realized she hadn't needed to say much. The mere fact of her presence here and the warmth of her gaze as she met Erik's eyes from across the room were probably enough. "Christine, let me take that valise. I'd like to help Ennis to his room."

"Oh, that's really not necessary—" Ennis began, but Erik's words cut across his.

"You've waited on me so many times over the years. Let me do this for you now."

Ennis paused, then nodded to Christine, who hurried over and handed the valise to Erik. Her fingers brushed his briefly as she did so, and again he felt a rush of desire for her. It amazed him that her merest touch could arouse such passion in him, that her continued presence only heightened his hunger for her. In the past, once he had sated his pent-up lust with the women he had bought, he had not found them all that exciting—until the passing weeks rebuilt his frustration and he needed to release the tension once again.

The flicker of the dimple at the corner of her cheek told him she had felt the same thing. Then she gave a quick glance at Ennis, obviously hoping he had not noticed what had passed between her and Erik.

"Let me just go see him settled," Erik said then, and she nodded.

"And I'll keep an ear out for the phone in case Jerome calls." Then she said to Ennis, "Would you like me to bring you something once you're all situated? Some tea? Are you hungry?"

"Such a fuss," Ennis said, but he looked rather pleased, as if he were enjoying the attention. "I still need clear liquids, but some broth would be very nice. And tea, of course."

"I'll get that started, then," she replied and went out, giving Erik a quick smile as she went.

"Such a lovely girl," commented Ennis. "Erik, I can't tell you how happy I am—"

The blood burned in his cheeks, but Erik said only, "Let me get you to your rooms. You should be resting."

Ennis gave him a knowing look but refrained from further comment, leading Erik out of the foyer to the comfortable ground-floor rooms he had occupied for so long. Erik had only been here once or twice, but Ennis's quarters hadn't changed much over the years—they were still somewhat clubby and quintessentially English, with their oxblood leather furniture and hunting prints on the walls.

After setting the valise down on the floor next to the bed, Erik went back out to the adjoining sitting room just as Ennis settled himself into an easy chair and swung his feet up on the ottoman. He sighed and closed his eyes momentarily, then opened them again, fixing Erik with a direct look.

"If you think you need to apologize, let me tell you that you don't—no, there's no use arguing with me," he added, as Erik opened his mouth to protest. "Who knows better than I what you've gone through your entire life? It was foolish what you did with Christine—very foolish."

It was amazing how the old man could make Erik feel as if he were twelve years old again. The next thing he knew, he would be shuffling his feet and pulling out the old excuses—*I didn't mean to—it was an accident—everybody always blames me—* Somehow he managed to hold on to his composure, though, waiting for Ennis's next words.

"But since it seems that you and Miss Daly have reconciled, then there's no use in self-recriminations, is there, Erik?" Ennis's tone was mild, but Erik knew from long experience that there was no point in arguing with him.

God knows he had been beating himself up enough

the past few days over what he had done to Ennis, wracking himself with guilt over the rush of anger that had made him knock the old man to his feet, berating himself about the whole terrible series of events that led to Christine's escape attempt. And now here was Ennis offering absolution.

"But my question to you now is what you plan to do next. I assume Miss Daly intends to stay here?"

What did he plan to do next? For so long he had only thought of getting Christine here, making her fall in love with him, that now, when those goals had apparently been accomplished, he was at a loss. Last night she had promised to stay with him here forever. He did not doubt her sincerity, but what exactly did her words mean? Would she forsake everything to be with him, or was she hoping to somehow integrate her former life with her new one? And if that were the case, what ramifications did those plans have for him? He cleared his throat. "We hadn't really gotten that far."

"Understandable. But you do realize that she must have family who would be worried about her?"

"She's an orphan," Erik said flatly.

"Friends, then. Coworkers and schoolmates. She had a life in the outside world, people who must have cared about her." Again that sharp look. "And we know the police are looking for her. Somehow you must find a way to resolve these issues before the two of you can go on with your lives together."

The damnable truth of it was, he knew Ennis was right. Although Erik and Jerome had planned a kidnapping of almost surgical precision, the result was not as neat as they had hoped. There were always loose ends. And somehow Erik knew that Christine, honorable as she was, would want to be as truthful as she could be in revealing her current situation. They could not have any hope of a real future together if they continually built on a foundation of lies and deceit.

"You have a lot to think about," Ennis said, his voice dry. "But time enough for that in the days ahead. I don't expect you to take care of everything immediately. But you need to give it careful consideration."

At that moment Christine came in, carrying a tray with a large soup bowl and a fine china teapot and matching cup. "Sorry it took me so long," she said. "It took me a little bit to find everything." Smiling, she added, "Your pantry is bigger than my living room."

"No trouble at all, my dear," Ennis said. "Erik and I were just having a nice chat." He allowed Christine to set the tray on his knees and fuss a bit with the napkin she had brought along. "I don't know when I've been so well taken care of—"

"I've had lots of experience," she said.

"Christine has been working as a waitress," Erik supplied, noting Ennis's slightly puzzled look.

"Well, then, I'm in expert hands, aren't I?" the butler said, then picked up the spoon and took a cautious sip of the steaming liquid.

At that moment the phone rang; Ennis had an extension in his sitting room, since it was nearly always he who took the incoming calls. Erik went to the phone table and looked at the caller I.D. Jerome's cell. Thank God.

"I need to take this," he said, lifting the phone from the receiver. "Hello, Jerome."

"Hi, boss." Jerome sounded almost cheerful, so much so that Erik wondered briefly what the hell he had been up to. "Just got back from a little overnight stay at the police station."

That had been Erik's fear all along, but Jerome didn't sound terribly concerned. "Are you all right?"

"My back's complaining a little, but I'm okay. Don't worry—they didn't get anything out of me."

Erik sighed. "So what happened?"

"Bastard Rigo ratted me out. Partly my own fault, I suppose—I really should have rented a car when I went to go see him. But it came down to his word against mine, since there's no real evidence connecting us, so they had to let me go."

The relief was almost palpable, the rush that washed over him like a wave of heat in his joints and gut. Perhaps he really would have to start believing in a God—it seemed that He had been looking out for him lately. "So where are you now?"

"At the condo. They gave me the standard line about not leaving town in case they needed to talk to me some more. And I'm noticing a patrol car parked a little way down the block, so they're keeping an eye out." Jerome paused, then added, "I don't think I'll be able to get back to the estate without them tailing me."

Damn. Still, it could have been a lot worse. "Are you sure this is a secure line?"

At that Jerome chuckled. "It's fine—we're dealing with the Pasadena P.D. here, not the CIA. They haven't got anything that can tap into a cellular transmission."

Well, as much as he could have used Jerome back here, at least the man was safe, if limited in his movements. He slept at the condo every once in a while just to show that he did maintain a residence there, and Erik suspected it was where he took any women he might be seeing, since of course Jerome couldn't bring them back to the estate.

"Good," Erik said at length. "Ennis is here, and doing very well. Christine's helping to look after him."

A pause. "So you're both—fine?"

"More than fine."

Another pause, as Jerome apparently stopped to digest that piece of information. "Well, good. Then I'll just hang out here, catch up on some movies, until we can figure out what to do next."

Erik had a feeling that Jerome was looking forward to his extended house arrest at the condo and its immediate environs. There were definitely worse places to be trapped, that was for sure. "We're working on that, Jerome," he said. "I'll keep you updated."

"Got it. Say hello to Ennis for me, and tell him I'm sorry I couldn't pick him up from the hospital."

"Given the circumstances, I think he'll understand. I'll call you as soon as something develops." With that, Erik hung up and turned to face expectant looks from both Ennis and Christine.

"Is Jerome okay?" Christine asked.

"He spent a night in jail, but he's fine—which is why he missed picking you up at the hospital, Ennis."

Ennis nodded. "I knew it had to be something like that. He's usually such a responsible person."

Of course he is—I pay him enough to be responsible, Erik thought, but made no comment. Then he said, "If you'll excuse me—"

"Is everything all right?" Christine asked. She looked concerned, as if worried that Erik had not told them everything about Jerome's situation.

"Everything's fine," he said. Action was going to need to be taken, and soon—he couldn't have Jerome's every future movement tracked by the police. "I just need to call my attorney."

And with that he exited the room, leaving Christine and Ennis to stare after him.

It was only logical, I supposed. Sooner or later Erik would have had to call in legal assistance, if only to get advice on how to proceed further. And poor Jerome—

I reflected that I never thought I'd be stringing those two words together. Still, it wasn't fair that he had the police watching his every move in the hopes he would lead them back to me. Very soon now, I would have to come clean. I was just fooling myself if I thought I could hide away from the world here forever.

Erik would not want me to do anything without consulting his lawyer first. But now, left to myself while he spoke to Mr. Greenburg, I felt frustrated, wishing I could do more than just sit and wait to be told what to do. Surely it wouldn't hurt if I just made one phone call—

Erik was on the phone, but they had more than one line here at the house, and there was an extension in the media room in which I now waited—not the same room where I had shown the news broadcast to Ennis, but a smaller chamber just a couple of doors down from the breakfast room.

Probably I should call Randall first, but I was too much of a coward to handle that confrontation right now. A call to Meg would be infinitely easier, and would accomplish the same purpose.

Without giving myself time to hesitate and back out, I lifted the receiver, pushed the button to activate the second line, and dialed Meg's cell number. Calling her at her apartment was pointless—she was hardly ever home, and even when she was there she never picked up.

The phone rang once, twice, three times. Finally it rolled over to her voicemail. I almost hung up, then thought, *Isn't this even easier?*

When I spoke, I hurried through the words. "Meg, this is Christine. Look, I can't really tell you where I am, but I just wanted to let you know that I'm safe, that everything is okay. I'll explain it to you when I get to see you, but I'm not sure yet when that will be. Just—just tell everyone I'm okay, and that they shouldn't worry anymore. And tell everyone I'm sorry if I've caused any trouble. I—" And then I paused. Better not to give any details. "I'll call you when I can."

I replaced the receiver in its cradle, shaking a little. I wasn't sure what Erik would say when I told him that I had called Meg, but surely he would understand my need to begin mending bridges, if only to let those close to me know that I was still alive and in possession of enough freedom to at least make a phone call. Perhaps it had been foolish of me, but I was beginning to see that as much as I wanted to be here with Erik, I also did not want to divorce myself completely from my previous life. I could only imagine how I would have felt if it had been Meg who had disappeared so precipitously, and I didn't want her—or Randall—to worry any more than either one of them had already.

Afterward I sat and flipped through channels for the better part of an hour, too agitated to do anything constructive. I had already seen Ennis settled into bed after he had finished his broth—the poor man needed rest in his own surroundings more than anything else, and I knew he was sleeping. Erik's call with his lawyer seemed to be going on forever, but I knew better than to go and interrupt him. Better to stay here and wait for him to call on me.

Which he did, eventually, as the day stretched into early evening and I had to reach over and flip on a light. Even behind the mask he looked grim.

"That good?" I asked.

"Only if your definition of 'good' involves listening to your lawyer lecture you about the consequences of kidnapping for the better part of two hours." Erik sighed and ran a hand through his hair. "But I eventually got him calmed down. He's coming tomorrow morning to discuss our next steps."

A little thrill of anxiety ran down my back. I wasn't sure how Erik was going to react to the fact that I had already taken a step without his knowledge. "Well, sit down and put your feet up. This is a very comfortable couch."

"Is it?" he asked vaguely. "I never spent that much time in here…"

"Obviously," I said. "The wrapper was still on the remote control."

That got a little chuckle out of him, and he sat down on the couch next to me, then put his feet up on the coffee table. It felt good to have him so close to me, to hear him sigh a little as he eased back into the cushions. "I'll have to thank Ennis for this couch the next time I see him."

For a man who had just spent a considerable chunk of time getting chewed out by his attorney, he seemed remarkably mellow. Perhaps it was having Ennis back home, and knowing that Jerome was at least safe, if not exactly accessible. Better to go ahead and tell him now — I probably wouldn't get a better opportunity. "About those next steps your lawyer mentioned —"

"What about them?" He looked over at me, the one eye I could see clearly narrowing a bit.

"Well, don't be angry, but —" Now that the moment had come, I was having a difficult time finding the words.

"Why is it that whenever someone prefaces a discussion with 'don't be angry,' it invariably means that I'm about to become very angry?"

So much for our cozy relaxed evening on the couch. I turned so I was facing him, and tucked one leg under the other to get it out of the way. The words came quickly, so that I couldn't stop myself from saying them. "I called Meg."

"You what?"

"I called Meg. It's okay—I just got her voicemail. But I wanted to let her know that I was all right, and that everything would be fine. I just felt so guilty thinking about how she and Ran—well, how worried everyone must be about me."

Silence for a moment, as I watched a muscle clench in his jaw and waited for the explosion.

His voice was very quiet. "And in your effort to assuage your guilt, did you at all think that you might be betraying your location with caller I.D.?"

Oh, shit. Stupid, Christine, stupid! Of course I hadn't—partly because I didn't have the service at home and didn't use it; it was just another one of life's little extras that I couldn't afford. I stared at him in consternation. "Oh, my God, Erik—I didn't think about that. I am so sorry—"

He glared back at me for a moment, and then, inexplicably, the corner of his mouth began to twitch. Then, shockingly, he began to laugh.

"What is so goddamn funny?" I burst out, wondering whether he really had gone mad.

"The caller I.D. on my numbers is blocked," he said. "Anyone receiving a call will just get a 'restricted number' message."

I stared at him for a moment before comprehension set in. I gasped, "Oh, that was so mean!" And then, as he continued to chuckle, I snapped, "Stop laughing!"

"But the expression on your face—"

There was nothing for it but to grab a pillow and swing it at his head. He blocked it with his arm and then snatched it from me, returning the blow. I wasn't quite as good at intercepting it, so the pillow did a sideswipe of my ear before I wrested it from his grasp. At that point he knocked it out of my hand, then pushed me down against the sofa cushions, his breath hot against my neck.

"Here?" I gasped.

"Why not? Ennis is asleep and Jerome is gone." With a casual gesture he reached up and pulled off the mask, tossing it onto the coffee table. Evidently he didn't want it getting in the way.

His touch was too irresistible. He continued to kiss me, and once again my body warmed to his. I let him make love to me there on the couch, cushions scattered and remote control knocked to the floor, the two of us like a couple of high school kids getting away with something right under their parents' noses. God knows what his lawyer would have thought if he'd known how casually I'd made my first contact with the outside world. But just then, as we reached for each other once more, the two of us were the only world that mattered.

Chapter Twenty-Seven

ORTIZ PAUSED THE TAPE, hit "Rewind," then listened to the message once again. Even somewhat distorted in its transfer from Meg's voicemail to cassette, Christine's voice was still pretty, a clear light soprano with a crispness of diction he attributed to her years of vocal training, and exhibiting none of the usual Southern California drawl. She spoke quickly, the words sounding a little rushed and breathless, but he did not detect any overt sounds of strain or fear. If anything, she sounded as if she were simply trying to squeeze in the phone call between other similarly pressing engagements.

"What the hell…?" he said aloud, then tilted back in his chair and glared up at a water spot on the ceiling tiles. It just didn't make sense—but then, when had anything in this case made sense? He had the disconcerting feeling that he was missing a vital piece of the puzzle, the one key that would suddenly turn this series of disjointed facts into a coherent whole.

Meg had called late that afternoon, apparently as soon as she had retrieved the voicemail. "I heard it ring, but I didn't pick it up because it said it was from a restricted number," she'd explained. "I only answer calls from numbers I recognize."

Restricted number. It figured. Of course they couldn't be so lucky as to have Christine calling from a phone that could be traced.

He'd asked Meg to come by the station as soon as possible so they could record the message off her voicemail, and she'd answered that was no problem. She was heading in to work at *L'Opéra* anyway, and the police station was only a few streets over from there.

"Should I call Randall?" she'd asked of Ortiz while the technician transferred the message onto a cassette.

God, no! had been Ortiz's first thought. The last thing he needed was Randall underfoot, asking unanswerable questions and generally getting in the way. But he'd said only, "I can handle that. We need to perform more analysis of the message before we let him know about this."

"Okay..." she'd replied slowly, looking a little puzzled. But apparently she'd decided that it was better not to question him about it. "Well, I hope it helps. I'm just glad to know she's all right—but if she's been okay all along, why didn't she call sooner?"

Why, indeed. *Christine, you got some splainin' to do,* he'd thought in his best Ricky Ricardo voice, but of course he'd only murmured something noncommittal to Meg and then got rid of her as soon as he could.

"Analysis" had consisted of Ortiz listening to the tape over and over again, hunting for any subtle inflections, any oddness of word choice that might indicate she was under duress of any sort. But he'd found nothing. In tone it sounded like the sort of commonplace message any girl Christine's age might have left on a friend's voicemail—except that in this case the girl leaving the message had now been missing for two weeks.

The only ambiguous element in the message had been Christine's use of the word "can't." *I can't really tell you where I am*, she'd said. Did that mean she really was being forced to keep her location a secret, or was it just a careless choice of words? And what was that bit about not wanting to cause any trouble? Had she really just gotten up and bailed out on her life for a few weeks? And if that were the case, then why the involvement of Jerome Manning and the trusty wrecking crew at Rigoberto's A-1 Auto Repair? Manning had been lying through his teeth, but the evidence linking him to the Daly case had been so scanty and circumstantial that there was no way they could have held him.

Ortiz resisted the urge to pull out the last few stalwart hairs on his head. Instead, he sighed, hit "Rewind," and listened to the tape one more time. Afterward he glanced at his watch. Good—only ten minutes to go. Then he could get the hell out of here and try not to think about Christine Daly for a few hours at least.

I'm sorry if I've caused any trouble, came her sweet, oblivious voice from the tape recorder, and Ortiz winced.

Girl, you don't know the half of it, he thought, then turned off the tape recorder. He couldn't remember the last time he'd been so happy to see six o'clock roll around.

I wasn't sure exactly what I had been expecting of Erik's attorney—I just knew that Martin Greenburg was not it. For one thing, he was fairly young, probably in his mid-thirties at best, with a strong-featured face that was more interesting than attractive. For another, he had over-long hair that brushed the edges of his collar, and instead of the typical dark suit he wore a sport coat over a pair of dark jeans, a dark blue shirt, and a wide tie that looked as if it came straight out of the bargain bin at the local vintage clothing store. He looked for all the world like the software industry's latest wunderkind—or one of the guys who staffed the help desk at school.

I could feel my eyebrows shooting up even as Erik got up from his chair and went to shake the attorney's hand. Then Erik turned toward me and said, "This is Miss Daly, Martin. Christine, this is Martin Greenburg."

Greenburg extended his hand and I took it, offering a smile and hoping that he hadn't noticed my shock.

The dark eyes that met mine were very shrewd, how-ever, and I could see the amusement dancing in them. "Ah, the infamous Miss Daly," he said.

"Martin—" Erik said, and Greenburg only smiled, then set his briefcase down on the table.

"Shall we, then?" he asked, and Erik took his seat once again.

We sat around a large mahogany table in a conference

room located to one side of Erik's private office. I had never been in there before, and had wondered, when I first saw it, at the presence of such a room in a house that never seemed to have visitors. But of course Erik's grandfather had built the house, and Erik's father had lived here as well. Presumably they had used this conference room when they hadn't wished to leave the estate to attend to business.

Greenburg didn't seem at all taken aback by Erik's mask, and so I guessed that they must have had some face-to-face dealings in the past. Likewise, Erik seemed to take Greenburg's decidedly unorthodox appearance in stride, and so I thought I had better try to do the same. He had to be good, or he wouldn't be Erik's attorney.

"I assume Erik has already told you that I am less than thrilled with the situation," Greenburg said, fixing me with a stare that clearly said he thought this was all my fault. "However, since he pays me the big bucks to keep his fat out of the fire, let's attempt to do some damage control."

"Martin—" Erik said again, but his tone was milder than I would have thought possible. "Miss Daly is certainly not responsible for my actions."

"Possibly, but your actions could get you fifteen to twenty in a federal prison. If we can make this more about her, there's a chance you can walk away with this with stories to tell your grandchildren."

Erik and I exchanged a significant glance at the "grandchildren" comment, but we both remained silent, waiting to hear what he had to say.

Lifting a heavy brow at me, Greenburg said, "So you first met Mr. Deitrich at your place of business."

"Yes. He paid the hostess so he could sit at my station."

To my surprise, the attorney slammed his hand down on the table. Erik and I both jumped. "No!" Greenburg said. "That is hearsay, Miss Daly. The hostess told you Mr. Deitrich paid to sit at your station, but you didn't actually see the transaction, did you?"

"Well, no," I replied.

"Very good. And what did you think of Mr. Deitrich?"

I shot a helpless glance at Erik. What the heck had I thought of him? That night seemed to have taken place in another life, when I stopped to think of all that had happened since then. "I thought he was interesting," I said cautiously, not wanting to invite another table-pounding.

"Just interesting? Did you find him attractive?"

God, this was excruciating. "I - I suppose I did."

"So you were attracted to him even though you were seeing someone else at the time?"

Erik interrupted, his tone a little sharper this time. "I don't really see the point here—"

"You will." Greenburg picked up his Mont Blanc pen and directed another one of those laser-beam stares at me. "Miss Daly?"

"Yes, I thought he was attractive. I was attracted to him. Satisfied?"

"Very." He scribbled a few lines on a legal pad while I stared down at my hands and absently twisted the sapphire on my right ring finger. "And did you continue to think about him after that first night?"

I lifted my shoulders. "I - I might have."

"So may I postulate that you were attracted to him, continued to think of him, and were receptive to seeing him again?"

"Well, I never really thought of it that way—"

"And that when he proposed seeing you again, you readily accepted?"

Now Erik and I exchanged incredulous looks. How the hell had he managed to jump from forcible kidnapping to a hypothetical date?

"What exactly are you driving at here, Martin?" Erik asked, his voice ominously calm.

"I am driving at keeping you out of prison, Mr. Deitrich," Greenburg replied, seemingly unruffled. "We must represent your current relationship as a natural progression of a completely normal attachment."

"Normal" and "natural" were not exactly words I would have used to describe the formative periods of Erik's and my relationship, but I'd begun to see where Greenburg was going with all this. I knew I'd have to talk to the police, and soon, and I had damn well have my story straight before I went to them.

"Yes," I said steadily, trying to ignore Erik's outraged stare. "I felt bad about it, since I was sort of dating Randall at the time, but I really wanted to be with Erik."

"Have you both lost your minds?" Erik snapped. "Or are you preparing testimony for a court in Never-Never land?"

"Erik," I said, and I looked at him steadily, willing him to go along with this. "I have to lie. There's no other way."

He held my gaze for a moment, but again his face was unreadable, as opaque as the half-mask he wore. "Martin, I can't believe you're telling her to perjure herself—"

"When she goes to the police, she'd better not be telling them the truth."

"Who said anything about going to the police?"

Greenburg set down his pen and folded his arms against his chest. "Mr. Deitrich, for all your brilliance, you can be remarkably obtuse at times."

"I have to, Erik," I said quietly, the words coming slowly as I wrestled with the dawning realization of what I must do. "Are we going to let the police trail after Jerome for the rest of his life? Are we just going to hide here and hope that no one ever finds out where I am? You know that's not possible."

He looked away from me then, and I could see the tense muscles working in his jaw and throat. "I don't want anything to happen to you," he said at length, the words barely above a whisper.

"And I don't want anything to happen to you," I returned. "So you have to let me do this."

Greenburg was looking at me with new respect. God knows what he had thought of me before. "The police will question you, Miss Daly, and they won't be happy when they find out that they've been wasting their time on an apparently false kidnapping case. Still, if you stick to your story, there's not much they can do but accept it." He transferred his stare to Erik. "And since she's not actually testifying in a court of law, no one can prosecute her for perjury. She should be fine as long as she keeps her story straight."

A long silence then, as Erik studiously looked away from us and appeared to stare at a portrait of a handsome middle-aged man that hung between the two windows on the opposite wall. The man in the portrait looked vaguely familiar, and I suddenly realized he must be Erik's father. To look at his face was to realize exactly how much damage had really been done to his son's own visage...

"And you would do this for me?" he asked at last. "Lie? Hurt your friends?"

His words made me begin to understand what my falsehoods would mean to Meg and, more importantly, to Randall. He would think that I had callously left him for another man, not caring what sort of pain and worry I might be causing him. It would be a betrayal of the worst sort, and he would never be able to know that it had all been a lie. I could feel a sudden constriction in my throat, the painful sting of tears behind my lashes. Still, I knew what I must do.

"I would do it for us," I said gently.

Greenburg cleared his throat. I could tell he was made uncomfortable by the raw emotion in the room, but he was too much the professional to do anything but say, "Then we're in agreement?"

"Yes," I said immediately, and after a moment Erik nodded.

"If it's the only way," he said.

"I assure you, it is." Greenburg slid his legal pad back into his briefcase and tucked his pen into his breast pocket. For the first time I noticed the gold wedding ring on his left hand. "And I would prefer to do it as soon as possible.

I know the police are investigating this case aggressively, and it's better to call a halt to the whole thing before they get any closer to the truth."

"Today?" I asked in a small voice. I had known this was coming, but now it seemed far too sudden.

"Today," he repeated. "Take a bit of time to compose yourself. Wait until after lunch, if that will help. But don't wait any longer than that. Here's my card." He reached into his other breast pocket and pulled out a business card. "If you start to feel as if you're in over your head, or the questioning is going in a bad direction, just tell them you need to take a break and give me a call."

I took the little piece of ivory card stock and felt a little relieved. At least I wasn't going into this completely without backup.

At that point Erik stood and came over to me, laying a reassuring hand on my shoulder and gently stroking my hair with the other. His touch calmed me even as I thrilled to it. This was what I was fighting for, after all — the chance to spend my life with him, to bring our love out of the shadows and into the light.

I reached up to touch the hand that lay on my shoulder. "With both of you in my corner, how can I do anything but succeed?" I asked, and was gratified to see Greenburg smile and feel Erik's hand tighten on mine.

At that moment, I truly did feel invincible.

Erik watched as Greenburg's BMW disappeared down the driveway, heading through the gates that had already been opened for it. While he knew intellectually that it had to be Christine who went to the police and closed the case once and for all, that knowledge didn't make this any easier. Even now his stomach felt knotted with worry, his heart already beating heavily with pent-up anxiety.

He turned away from the door and shut it. Christine stood in the foyer, elegant in the royal blue cashmere twin set and black pencil skirt he had bought her, the sapphires once again winking at her throat. She had dressed up for the meeting with Greenburg, abandoning her usual slacks or jeans.

"It's almost noon," she said, and her tone was studiously casual. "I should bring Ennis a tray, and we both need to eat something as well."

"Christine, I—" Somehow the words failed him, and he paused, trying desperately to think of something comforting, something to take away the suspicious brightness in her eyes.

"It's all right, Erik," she said. "I can do this. But I need to eat first. I can't take tests on an empty stomach, either."

Somehow that little commonplace brought a smile to his lips, and he replied, "Well, I'm sure we can find something. It's Michel's day off, but—"

"Don't worry," she said, and a little of the tension seemed to leave her mouth. "I've had to fend for myself for quite some time."

That much was true. And although she was still not familiar with the huge kitchen pantries or the oversize commercial stove, somehow she managed to make up some consommé and toast for Ennis and a pair of cheese omelets for the both of them. As he watched her breeze through these tasks, he was once again struck by the fierceness of his desire for her—not just for her body, but for her continued presence in his life. She seemed so at home here now; he couldn't imagine the house without her.

She sent him off with Ennis's tray and an admonishment to be quick or their omelets would get cold. Luckily Ennis was caught up in a broadcast of *BBC World News* and merely murmured his thanks before turning his attention to the television once more, so Erik was able to hurry back to the kitchen after only a few moments.

They took their trays to the little breakfast room off the kitchen, where the lovely view out the windows was dampened a bit by the arrival of yet another storm. But there was something cozy and companionable about sitting in the cheery little room together and eating Christine's quite excellent omelets as the rain pattered down the windows.

"Some time I'll have to return the favor," he said, gesturing toward the omelet with his fork. "I make quite a good Dagwood sandwich."

Christine raised an eyebrow. "What's in one of those, anyway?"

"Just about everything you can find in the cold-cut compartment in your refrigerator. I believe it was invented by someone who went on a midnight refrigerator raid."

"Is that when you make yours?"

"Of course. Dagwoods make excellent midnight snacks."

"'Snacks'?" She shook her head, the curls bouncing over her shoulders. "Too many snacks like that and I won't be able to fit into this skirt."

He had a difficult time imagining her any other way than she was now: slim, beautiful, perfect. Still, he'd heard that women tended to obsess over their weight even when there was really nothing to obsess over. "I wouldn't worry too much," he said, pleased by the smile his words brought to her lips.

Then her expression sobered. He knew she must be thinking of her coming appointment with the police. There was no use telling her not to worry, because he was just as worried himself. All he could do was give her a reassuring smile, reach out to touch her hand, let her know how much he loved her.

Something seemed to get through to her, for she took a deep breath and appeared to relax a little. Then she said, "And afterward—"

"Afterward?" he asked.

She made a vague gesture with one hand. "After I'm done with the police. After I come back here to be with you permanently. I've been thinking about it, and I want to finish school."

"School?" he repeated. That surprised him a little, but he knew she had worked hard and was not one to leave things undone.

"I'm so close to graduation, and I'm hoping my professors will let me make up the finals I've missed so I can go straight on to spring semester. If not, I'll have to make up those classes, but I'd still be able to graduate a year from now." She spoke quickly, her gaze turned inward.

He realized she was bringing this up now so she wouldn't have to think about the police or what she would have to say to them. "Will it be difficult for you?"

She gave a shaky little laugh. "Oh, probably. People always talk, you know. But then something else comes along and you're last week's news. At least I'd have my degree." A quick look upward through her thick lashes. "And I'd want to sing."

"We sing together all the time," he replied, knowing even as he said the words that that was not what she had meant.

"I need to try, Erik," she said. "I have to know if I'm any good."

"You know you are," he replied mechanically. What was she saying—that after all their struggles she would leave him to pursue her career?

"Don't look at me like that," she said, the desperation obvious in her voice. "I'd try for parts locally, of course. But I would always feel as if I had wasted my training if I didn't at least try."

He shouldn't be angry with her. She was facing one of the biggest confrontations of her young life, and he knew she was only trying to be honest with him, to let him know what her expectations were. But he still couldn't help but feel somehow betrayed, as if she had led him to believe that he was enough for her, and only now was telling him that he couldn't provide everything for her after all.

"Of course you must do what you feel is necessary," he said coldly, and laid down his fork on the plate.

"God, Erik, don't be like that." She clasped his hand in both of hers, forcing him to look at her directly. "I love you. I want to be with you. All I'm asking is a chance to be myself as well."

Her words shamed him. Was it fair for him to expect that she should hide her enormous talents from the world? How he could he even ask that of her? This girl…this woman—for in many ways she had shown far more maturity than he, even though two decades separated them—had given him nothing but love and healing. It was time for him to begin to give something back to her.

"I wouldn't expect you to be anything less, my dear," he said at last, and brought her hands to his lips.

She smiled at him then, the light of her happiness evident in shining eyes. He pulled her to him, holding her close, sending her his love, his reassurance. Let the world see her beauty, her astounding gifts. She would take their adulation, smile graciously, and return to him.

He had to be content with that.

Chapter Twenty-Eight

ERIK WALKED ME FROM THE HOUSE to the garage, protecting the two of us from the rain with an enormous black umbrella borrowed from Ennis. It seemed a little inconvenient to have the buildings separated by a good hundred yards or so, but I supposed it would have ruined the symmetry of the landscape to have the garage placed any closer to the house than it already was. I wished I had taken the time to change out of my black pumps and skirt into something a little more practical, but at the same time I knew I had to get this over with before I lost my nerve and retreated into the reassuring isolation of Erik's mansion.

Inside the garage it was chilly and faintly damp-smelling. But the place was spotless, the empty bays stretching on past the ones that held Erik's S600 and a spectacular vintage Rolls.

He paused next to the Mercedes and reached into his pocket, pulling out a small black device that looked like a miniature remote control.

"I have to drive that?" I asked, gesturing toward the S-Class. Up close, it was ominously shiny and sleek, exuding power even when still.

"Unless you'd rather take the Rolls—"

His tone was serious, but I could see that wicked gleam in his eyes again.

I took the little black remote from him. "Where are the keys?"

"That is the key."

"You're kidding." I looked at it a little more closely, noticing little locked and unlocked padlock icons on the buttons. "How does it work?"

"Push the unlock button."

I did as he instructed and the door unlocked as the car made a little chirping sound and the lights flashed once. "Impressive."

"You're easily impressed."

"Well, remember what I used to drive?"

He smiled at that and then pulled the door open for me. What followed was a little five-minute lesson on how to adjust the seats, use the windshield wipers, and work the climate-control system. I just hoped I'd be able to remember half of it.

It was a good excuse for us to evade discussing the real reason I had to drive the car at all, but eventually there was nothing left to show me, and he paused, looking down at me as I sat in the driver's seat.

When he spoke, his voice was very quiet. "You're sure you want to do this."

"I have to, Erik. You know I do." I reached out and touched his hand briefly, then said, "I don't want us to spend the rest of our lives looking over our shoulders."

He kept staring down at me, as if wanting to memorize my features, as if he thought he might never see me again. I couldn't imagine what must be going through his mind. "Wise Christine," he said. "Of course you are right." Then he leaned down and kissed me very gently on the forehead. "Be safe in the rain."

"I will," I replied, and let him shut the car door. I docked the key in the ignition and felt the engine rumble to life beneath me. It was frightening, having that much power at my command. Thank God it wasn't a stick—of course I had driven one most of my adult life, but adjusting to an unfamiliar gearbox was the last thing I needed right then.

I touched the button on the overhead console to open the garage door and eased my way down the drive, watching through the rearview mirror as Erik slowly lifted a hand to wave goodbye. In answer I raised my own hand briefly, then focused my attention on the road and the car around me, which felt as if it were pushing against my timid handling, yearning for someone who really knew how to drive it.

Before we had left the house, Erik had explained to me how to leave his secluded street and head into Old Pasadena. Once I was back on Colorado Boulevard and heading east I was into my own home territory, only a few blocks from *L'Opéra* and all my other familiar haunts. Since I didn't want to park the car near the police station and possibly have it be recognized, I pulled into the parking garage at the Paseo Colorado shopping center. It was still early enough on a Friday afternoon that it wasn't overly crowded, although I knew it would start to fill up in a few hours as people got off work and came looking for food and entertainment.

The second level of the parking garage was nearly deserted. I parked in a space close to the elevators and sat for a moment in the car, breathing in the pleasant scent of expensive leather upholstery. My story was simple enough—I just had to keep my nerve and not let the police fluster me, no matter what sorts of questions might be thrown in my direction.

Easier said than done, I thought, visualizing hard-faced police barking questions at me as I tried desperately to keep them from guessing the truth. My hands shook a little as I gathered up my purse and umbrella, but I forced myself out of the car, barely remembering to lock it as I headed toward the elevators. From behind me I could hear the little chirp it made as the security system armed itself. Thank God the car had more brains than I did.

Rain still fell steadily as I exited the elevators and headed through the open main square of the plaza, back toward Colorado Boulevard and over to the corner of Walnut and Garfield where the police station was located. The shopping center was sparsely populated; the rain had driven most everyone indoors. The civic center had a few more people walking about, but Southern Californians were not brave about rain, and everyone I saw was hurrying to be somewhere else.

My feet were beginning to get wet inside the impractical pumps, and I hurried along as best I could, even though I was anything but eager to reach my destination. Still, I arrived there soon enough, sooner than I would have liked. Ignoring the rain that beat down on my umbrella and the increasing dampness in my shoes, I stood outside the door for a long moment, watching as others hurried in and out. A few people cast curious glances in my direction, no doubt wondering what I was doing, standing out there in the rain.

I wondered as well, for a moment. Then I saw Erik's face in my mind—his whole face, scars and all, his cloudy green eyes warm with love. I thought of his voice, and how his mouth felt on mine. I thought of all the million and one things that made him uniquely Erik, and I remembered how much I loved him. It was for him, and us, that I did this.

Then I pushed open the door and went inside.

Officer Campbell paused significantly outside Ortiz's doorway. He knew something was up, because her dark eyes were gleaming and she could barely repress a grin.

"What is it, Campbell?" he asked. The morning had been uneventful enough; he and Kosky had been called in to investigate a burglary, but otherwise he had spent most of his time catching up on paperwork and studiously ignoring the Daly case.

"Someone to see you, detective."

He waited, not bothering to answer. Obviously Letisha wanted to take her time with this one.

She raised an eyebrow, apparently irked that he hadn't risen to her bait. "A Miss Christine Daly, detective," she said finally, and stepped aside to let a young woman enter the office.

After a few seconds in which he was certain the occasional arrhythmia he experienced was going to develop into a full-blown heart attack, Ortiz regained himself enough to say, "Please come in, Miss Daly." He looked over at Letisha, who still loitered near the doorway, obviously enjoying herself hugely. "Thank you, Officer Campbell. Can you shut the door on your way out?"

Letisha gave an irritated roll of the eyes but acquiesced in silence, closing the door after Christine had fully entered the office and taken the chair Ortiz indicated.

He continued to stare at her for a moment, as shocked by the change in her appearance as by her presence in his office itself. Gone were the shabby, worn-too-many-times clothes and the slightly frizzy hair. She wore an expensive cashmere twin set and narrow skirt, and her curly hair fell in gleaming spirals over her shoulders. Hanging from her ears and circling her neck was a matched set of sapphire and diamonds that his experience investigating high-end robberies put at no less than fifty thousand dollars, and another huge stone glittered from the ring finger of her right hand. She was absolutely stunning, and far more elegant than he could have ever imagined.

"Officer Ortiz?" she asked, extending the hand with the sapphire.

He tore his eyes away from the ring and accepted her hand. "Miss Daly—I must say that I'm a little surprised to see you." *Especially looking the way you do*, he thought. If someone had told him she'd spent the last two weeks vacationing at some European spa, he wouldn't have been surprised.

The color rose in her cheeks, obvious against her fair skin. "I'm very sorry for any trouble I've caused, detective. That's why I thought I had better come in to talk with someone."

"Well, you've had a lot of people very worried about you," he replied, although his tone was milder than he would have thought possible.

"It was—terrible of me to disappear the way I did. I realized that after I saw a story about me on the news the other day." Her manicured fingers moved restlessly on the purse she clutched in her lap—Prada, he noticed.

"So are you telling me that you left your home of your own volition? That there was no foul play involved?"

"Absolutely not, detective." Her blue eyes were wide; he noticed that they picked up some of the color of the sweater she wore. "I had been having a difficult time deciding what to do about Erik, but when he invited me to his home over the long weekend—"

"Erik?" Ortiz interrupted. "Erik Deitrich?"

"Yes," she replied, looking surprised. "Do you know him?"

"I know of him," he replied, his voice grim. Deitrich. Of course. He'd known all along that the man had to be involved in this somehow. Well, that would explain the expensive clothing and jewels, if nothing else. "How do you know him?"

"I met him at work." The smoky blue gaze slid away from his, and her full mouth pursed slightly. "We were attracted to each other right away, but it was a little awkward for me since I was already seeing Randall. But he kept calling, and we saw each other once or twice. And then when he asked for me to come over—"

"To the house on Charles Street?"

Again that widened gaze. "You know where he lives?"

Ortiz allowed himself a humorless smile. "Oh, he's been a person of interest in your case for some time. So you went to him, even though you had been seeing Randall, even though you had just spent Thanksgiving with his family?"

"It was wrong of me, I know, but I didn't know what to say to Randall—he did have a tendency to make a scene over things. I thought maybe it would just be better if I disappeared for a while."

Having been on the receiving end of Randall's persistent calls, Ortiz found himself sympathizing with her just a little. Certainly handling Randall could be difficult for someone who had trouble dealing with confrontations. But that didn't begin to excuse the hell she had put Randall and Meg through these past few weeks. "Possibly you didn't want to talk to Randall. But why didn't you at least call Meg to tell her where you were?"

"I was afraid she might tell Randall."

Again, that made sense, but Ortiz was beginning to think that her answers seemed a little too pat, a little too rehearsed. Oh, there was no mistaking the earnest tone of her voice, the pleading look in her big blue eyes, but he'd seen enough convincing acts from people who were guilty as sin to know that looks counted for very little. When he spoke, he deliberately hardened his tone. "So you're saying that you just up and disappeared for two weeks so you could cheat on your boyfriend with some reclusive millionaire?"

She winced at his question, even as her full lips thinned a little. "If you want to put it that way, yes."

"Well, we can leave it at that for now." He shifted a few papers on his desk, unearthing the Daly file. Opening it, he flipped past a few pages, just to look official—he had the facts memorized by now. "Do you know a gentleman named Jerome Manning?"

"No. Why?"

"Never heard of him?" Ortiz produced a photo and showed it to her. "Have you ever seen this man?"

She took the photo and stared down at it for a moment. "I might have seen him at school once or twice."

"Any idea why he might have been there?"

"No. I didn't even know what his name was until you said it right now."

Again he got the feeling she was lying, but he decided not to call her on it. Not yet. That there was some connection between Deitrich and Manning he was positive, but he had no proof—they'd been far too careful for that.

"So you'd be surprised to know that he was arrested in connection with the theft of your car?"

"My car?" she repeated, looking a little blank. "Did something happen to my car?"

"Yes—actually, it was stolen by a little thug named Tony Vasquez, then sold and crushed."

"Oh, my God," she said, and she did look shocked at that. "I thought it would be okay to leave it on the street— I had a street parking permit, and I figured it was so old and beat-up no one would want it anyway."

"Well, someone did. Maybe they just saw it as an easy mark since it had been sitting there for so long."

She knotted her fingers in her lap, then looked back up at him. "I don't understand—if this Tony person stole the car, why would you arrest Jerome for it?"

"Jerome." Not "Mr. Manning." A little familiar for someone she professed to have never heard of before now. Interesting, but again it was just his gut telling him she knew very well who Jerome was. "We had information indicating he had actually paid the people involved to steal the car. Unfortunately, we had to release him due to lack of evidence."

"Oh," she said awkwardly, obviously not sure how to respond.

"But what you're telling me is that you've spent the last two weeks safely with Mr. Deitrich, that you never heard of Jerome Manning, and up until now you had no idea your car had even been stolen?"

"Um, yes," she replied. Then, in a rush, "Oh, I know how terrible this all sounds. I'm not an idiot, you know. But Erik just sort of—well—"

"Swept you off your feet?" he interjected dryly.

"Yes." She leaned forward, all earnestness with her lovely features and prim-but-somehow-sexy twin set. "I—I don't have a lot of experience, Detective Ortiz. This all came up very suddenly. But my only regret is the pain I might have caused to others."

That much was true, he knew suddenly. For the first time during this interview, he heard the ring of sincerity in her voice. Oh, she was a good actress, no doubt about that—no big surprise, considering she wanted to be an opera star. But here she was speaking no more than the simple truth. Whatever might have happened—and he had a feeling he might never really know for sure—he realized that she loved this man, or at least thought she did.

What Deitrich had seen in her, he wasn't sure, aside from the fact that she was beautiful and talented. But Southern California was full of beautiful and talented girls—they flocked from all over the country to be here, after all. Somehow Deitrich had singled her out, made her the object of his interest. He supposed a girl like Christine, alone in the world as she was, would be an easy mark.

Anger flared at the unknown Erik Deitrich then, that a man with that kind of wealth and power would exert such influence over a woman as to make her forsake the few friends she had—and good friends, too, the sort who hadn't abandoned Christine but had fought to help her, to take care of her even when they had no idea whether she was even alive or dead. He felt a sudden rush of sympathy for Randall and Meg; the truth would not be easy for them once it was known.

In fact, Christine's sudden appearance had thrown Ortiz off a bit—he'd forgotten that he told Randall to come by the station when he was done at school for the day, just so he could listen to the tape of Christine's message and possibly hear something in her voice that Ortiz, as someone who didn't know her, wouldn't have been able to decipher. He thought of what might happen if Christine still happened to be here when Randall arrived, and shook his head grimly. There were some things so personal that he had no wish to be a part of them.

Suddenly weary, he said, "So your formal statement is that you were with Erik Deitrich of your own volition, and that no force or coercion was involved?"

She lifted her chin. "I told you that already. But yes, if you need a formal statement—I went with Erik of my own accord, and I accept the responsibility for whatever consequences might be involved due to my disappearance."

"The 'consequences,' as you put it, are mostly with your friends and possibly your employer, Miss Daly. And school, of course—you do realize that you missed finals, don't you?"

"Yes," she replied. "I'm hoping I can work that out. If not, I plan to repeat the semester."

"And then what?"

"We'll see." Again that defiant lift of the chin. "Erik would very much like to hear me sing professionally."

Bully for Erik, Ortiz thought, but he only said, "Well, that's very noble of him, I suppose. So the two of you have discussed a future together, then?"

"Yes." Her answer seemed a little hesitant, though, and her gaze flickered for a second to the bare ring finger on her left hand.

Not that formal yet, though? Ortiz thought. Still, even without a formal commitment it seemed that Christine had landed in clover. Here she had been struggling to get through school, living paycheck to paycheck, and now she sat across from him wearing jewels that almost certainly equaled his yearly salary. Deitrich could probably buy her a complete liberal arts college if USC proved to be difficult, so Ortiz had no doubt she would finish school one way or another. He said only, "Well, I suppose that's very good for you, Miss Daly. I hope that at some point you'll feel comfortable telling your friends exactly what happened."

His tone had been bland, but her eyes narrowed a bit at that last statement. No, she wasn't stupid, despite the big innocent eyes and the naïve act. But she was fighting for whatever vision of the future she had for herself and Deitrich, and the truth was that Ortiz could do very little if she denied ever being coerced.

"Well, Miss Daly," he said. "I must say that I'm relieved to see that you're all right. It's unfortunate that people were upset along the way, but at least we can close this case now."

He could see her visibly relax at his words, her relief palpable that this would not continue any further.

"Just one last thing—"

Wary again, she asked, "Yes?"

Ortiz reached into his desk drawer and pulled out a small plastic zipper bag. He unsealed it, and shook the ring it held out onto the palm of his hand. "Is this yours?"

The color fled her cheeks. "Where did you get that?"

"I recovered it from the floor of your bedroom when I searched the house."

She took it from him, staring at it for a moment, then sliding it onto the middle finger of her left hand. "It was my grandmother's—I can't imagine how it could have gotten there."

He thought he could imagine it very well—if she had worn it around her neck as Meg said she often did, then it would have been easy for the chain to snap as Christine was forcibly taken from her bed, and the ring to slide unheeded to the floor. However, all he said was, "At least it was found."

"Yes," she replied slowly. "I would hate for it to have been lost forever."

And you, Christine? he thought. *Are you lost forever? What is this hold Deitrich has on you?*

But then she smiled and extended her hand to him once again. "Thank you, Detective Ortiz. Thank you for all the work you've done—and I'm sorry that it was all over a misunderstanding."

"Just doing my job," he replied. It was a cliché, perhaps, but most clichés were grounded in some truth.

"Still…" she said, then paused, as if she wanted to say more but thought better of it. "May I go, then?"

"The case is closed, Miss Daly. I don't have any more questions." None that she would answer truthfully, at any rate.

She smiled again, then gathered up her purse and umbrella. And after a brief nod she went out, her expensive heels clacking on the dingy linoleum, leaving a faint trail of rose-scented perfume in her week.

Looking after Christine, Ortiz wondered whether he would ever hear of her again, or whether she would once again be lost, hidden by Erik Deitrich's wealth, blind to the pain she had caused everyone around her. She had implied that she had done it all for love. Ortiz wondered whether that would be enough.

Chapter Twenty-Nine

THE RAIN HAD STOPPED by the time I left the police station, but the day was still gloomy and threatening. It was unfortunate the rain no longer fell—after that interview I felt as if I needed a shower. Greenburg had had no problem telling me to spill all those lies, but then again, he was a lawyer; he was paid to lie convincingly. All I wanted was to get the hell out of there and back to Erik, back to the safety of his arms.

And I knew I wasn't done yet. Yes, the dreaded interview with the police was behind me, but I knew I'd have to talk to Randall, and soon. What Detective Ortiz had left unsaid had been clear enough. Randall had gone through hell the past few weeks, not knowing whether I was alive or dead. It wasn't his fault that he cared more for me than I had cared for him. How I'd ever find the right words to let him know I was sorry for his hurt, I didn't know, but somehow I'd have to try.

Then there was Meg, but I had a feeling that would be a much easier conversation. Meg had never been one to judge. Once she knew I was safe, and happy, and with someone who loved me, she would probably let the matter go.

"The hardest part's over," I told myself, as I walked as quickly as I could in those damned heels, keeping my eyes to the pavement so an unexpected crack in the sidewalk wouldn't trip me up. The expression of disappointment and suspicion in Detective Ortiz's face seemed to haunt me, even though I'd never met the man before, even though I told myself I shouldn't be concerned with what he thought of me, as long as he didn't question my story and was willing to drop the case.

By the time I got to the corner of Colorado and Garfield I was slightly winded, and my calves were beginning to ache. The pumps weren't even that high, but I still wasn't used to wearing those kinds of shoes, let alone speed-walking several blocks in them.

I had to wait for the light to change before I could cross the street. As I stood there, feeling ridiculously over-dressed compared to the two high school girls who waited along with me, I heard someone call my name.

"Christine! Hey!"

Of course I turned, looking across Garfield to the corner directly opposite me. I could feel the blood drain from my face even as my eyes met his.

Randall. I saw him staring at me in shock as well, his

face as pale as mine felt. Then the thought blazed through my mind, *Oh, God. Not here. Not like this.* I wasn't sure how I had intended to face Randall, but it wasn't on a crowded street corner, surrounded by strangers.

I turned away, but the damage was done. The light changed right after that, and I all but ran across, trying to ignore Randall's desperate voice calling my name.

Luckily for me—I supposed—I had crossed from the corner that progressed directly into the open-air mall, unlike Randall, who was stranded on the other side of the ramp that led into the underground parking structure. But that didn't stop him. I threw a quick look over my shoulder to see a hulking SUV slam on its brakes just as Randall darted across the ramp, moving against the light.

Part of my mind was screaming at me to just stop and confront him—what could he do in a crowded shopping center, after all?—but somehow the panic was more powerful, and I bolted across the plaza toward the parking garage escalators, leaving a trail of irritated shoppers in my wake. I could hear Randall still in pursuit, but once I got on the escalators I didn't dare look back to see how close he was. Luckily there was no one in front of me, and I clattered down the escalator so quickly that I broke off the heel of one of my shoes as I neared the bottom. The unexpected movement threw me off-balance, and I would have fallen if it weren't for the handrail.

With a muttered curse I kicked off the useless shoes and flung myself around the curve to the escalator leading down to the second level of the parking garage. The hose I wore began to shred on the metal of the escalator steps, but that was the least of my worries. All I could focus on was getting to the car, getting securely inside. I didn't even know what it was that frightened me so much about confronting Randall. All I knew was that I had to get out of there before he caught me.

Even as I left the escalator, I was fumbling in my purse for the little remote-control key to the Mercedes. My fingers slid over its unfamiliar surface, and I almost dropped it as I pulled it out and pushed down on the "unlock" button. The car made its reassuring little chirp as the driver's-side door unlocked itself, and I reached for the handle, almost sobbing with relief.

Then Randall's hand descended on mine, jerking it away from the car. The key fell from my fingers, clattering to the asphalt, even as he turned me around to face him.

After a two-week separation, I suppose he would have already begun to look unfamiliar to me, but the Randall who confronted me was a man I had never seen before. His face was white with fury, and his eyes were narrow, grim, his mouth pulled into a straight line. For a second he only glared at me, and then his gaze shifted past my face to look at Erik's Mercedes.

"Nice car," he commented, in a dry voice that sounded entirely unlike his own. "What, did you win the Lotto or something and then hide out so you wouldn't have to share?"

"Randall, I can explain—"

"Why don't you explain, Christine?" He made my name sound like a curse. "I'd really like to hear why the hell you just ran away from me like I was the devil!"

I forced myself to look away from his livid features and tried to see if there was any hope of assistance nearby. But even though the mall had become busier, it was obvious that not many people had made their way down to this level of the garage yet. For now, Randall and I were alone.

"Look, I was going to call you," I said, trying to keep the desperation I felt from seeping into my voice. "Randall, I'm so sorry—this isn't what I wanted—"

"What did you want? Someone to buy you a Mercedes? Did you go off and find yourself a sugar daddy or something?"

"The car's not mine," I retorted. "I borrowed it."

"Well, that makes it all better, then, doesn't it?" The hand on my wrist clenched a little tighter. "Where the hell have you been? Do you have any idea what you've put me through? Or Meg? She's been having nightmares about you!"

"I'm sorry," I said again, as the hot tears began to sting my eyes. "I never meant to hurt anyone—"

And I hadn't, that was the damnable part of it. I had been dragged into the whole mess unwillingly at the outset, and once I realized I'd begun to care for the man who had made me his prisoner, it was too late to do anything but continue on the course that had been set for me. To anyone who hadn't lived through it, I supposed it would have all seemed insane—Detective Ortiz had been almost too gentle with me, but I had seen the disappointment in his eyes. He had judged me, and found me wanting. Why the opinion of someone I had never met before and probably would never see again mattered so much, I couldn't say—possibly because his reaction was just an echo of what the world would think of me.

If Randall chose to hate me—and he had every reason to—then there wasn't much I could do about it. All I could do was try to spare him as much further hurt as I could.

"You never 'mean' to do much, do you?" he snapped. "You're more the type to just let things happen to you. So what was it this time?"

That, I felt, was patently unfair, but I forced back a sharp reply, trying to keep things from escalating into a shouting match. "I can't tell you everything, Randall—"

"'Can't,' or won't?" His hazel eyes narrowed as he took in the expensive jewels I wore, the clothing so unlike anything I had previously owned. "Who is he?"

"What does it matter? Does it change anything, you knowing who I'm with?"

"Well, call me stupid, but I'd like to know something about the man who stole my girlfriend from me." Again that bitter look in the direction of the Mercedes. "Obviously he's got a lot more to offer than I do."

"Oh, Randall," I said miserably, knowing I could never begin to explain. All he saw were the outward trappings of Erik's wealth, and I knew I didn't dare tell him of how I felt about Erik, about how my soul had somehow responded to his alone, how he had filled the emptiness that had been there ever since my parents' deaths. Better for Randall to think I had been seduced by money and security. At least that way he could dismiss me as a shallow girl who hadn't really been worthy after all, instead of someone who had instead fallen deeply in love with a man better-suited to her, both spiritually and intellectually.

It was with that resolve in mind that I finally said, "Okay, he's rich. Is that a crime?"

"Only if you use your money to take advantage of people," he replied. That look of pinched anger had never left his mouth. "I guess you just seemed like the last person to care about crap like that."

"Randall, that's really not fair—"

"Fair?" The word was practically shouted. "Was it fair for you to disappear without telling anyone where you went? Was it fair for Meg and me to lose sleep over you, thinking you were in a ditch somewhere? Maybe it was fair to make Detective Ortiz spend God knows how many hours trying to find you. You tell me."

There was so much I wanted to tell him, so much that I knew I could never divulge without endangering Erik. But faced with Randall's raw pain, I didn't know what to do. Oh, of course I had worried about how Meg and Randall were doing, hoping that I hadn't caused them too much trouble. But until now I hadn't realized exactly what they had gone through, and I was ashamed. I had waited too long to come forward. I could have saved them all days of anguish but instead had only wanted to be alone with Erik in our newfound happiness.

"No, it wasn't fair," I said quietly. "It was very selfish of me, and I apologize for that."

He did not appear mollified. "So you're sorry you made us worry, but you're not sorry you went off with this guy in the first place."

"Well, if you need to hear me say it, then yes! I'm not sorry I'm with him — is that what you wanted?"

I could see the muscles working in his jaw and neck as he struggled to rein in his anger. "Yeah, I guess that's about it," he said at length. He paused, then added, "So what does this guy look like, anyway?"

Stifling an impulse to burst out laughing, I thought, *He looks a lot like a movie star — at least half his face does.* Since I knew I could never tell Randall the truth, I said only, "Does it really matter?"

"Maybe it does."

I gave him as much as I could. "He's older than we are. He's tall, with dark hair and green eyes. Slim. Are you satisfied?"

But Randall wouldn't let it go. "Is he good-looking?"

Is he better-looking than I am? was Randall's real question, the one he probably dared not voice aloud, and at that I finally did begin to laugh. It was not a comforting sound — even to me the laughter was shrill and tinged with hysteria. "I guess I'd say he's half as good-looking as you, Randall!"

"What's so funny?" he demanded. "What the hell's the matter with you?"

"If you only knew, Randall," I gasped, "but I can't tell you — what's more, I won't tell you." And with that I bent and retrieved the remote-key from the ground as he stared at me, obviously wondering if I had lost my mind.

"What are you not telling me, Christine?" And then he focused on the key in my hand, and he frowned. "Bored with the conversation already?"

"I just don't think I have anything left to say to you," I replied, and tried not to wince at the obvious hurt in his eyes. I made a move toward the car, but his hand on my wrist pulled me back.

"Well, I still have a few things to say to you—"

Again I tried to wrench his restraining hand from my arm, but he showed no signs of letting go, and I wondered what on earth I was going to do next.

My *deus ex machina* came in the form of a mall security guard, who apparently had just descended the escalator and then spotted the two of us standing over by the car. "Hey!" he called, and began hurrying in our direction. "That guy bothering you, miss?"

Randall abruptly dropped my wrist as if it scalded him.

I turned to the security guard and said, "It's okay—I was just going. Right?" And I gave Randall a sharp look.

"Uh—right," he said. He still looked angry, an anger now overlaid with frustration, but he knew better than to say anything in front of the guard.

The security guard gave both of us a dubious look, his heavy features obviously suspicious. But he said only, "If you're sure everything's all right—"

"Oh, sure," I replied airily, more relieved than I cared to admit. I was sure Randall would never have done anything to hurt me physically, but still he had frightened me a little. I was glad to have been rescued.

The security guard didn't say anything else, but he remained close by, watching as I climbed into the Mercedes and started it up, then angled the car up the ramp toward the first level of the parking garage. Through the rearview mirror I could see Randall stand there for a moment, then hurry up the escalator the moment the guard walked off. I wasn't worried about him catching up with me, though; I reassured myself that I had gotten through the line to pay and exit long before he could have ever fallen in behind me.

Still, I kept peering in my rearview mirror as I left the parking structure, worried that an older-model black BMW would suddenly drop in behind my rear bumper in the traffic on Colorado Boulevard. But I saw nothing, and turned my gaze forward, thinking then only of Erik, not wanting to reflect on the confrontation I had just endured. For the first time in more years than I had dared count, I finally felt as if I were going home.

The rain shimmered on the mullioned windows of Erik's study, its soft pattering a counterpoint to the hissing of the fire in the hearth. After uncounted time spent wandering the halls, he had returned here, not knowing where else to wait, and so he sat in an armchair he had dragged close to the hearth, forcing his gaze away from the clock, even as he told himself that it hadn't been so long, really, since she had disappeared past the gates out onto Charles Street.

The fear he had dared not voice earlier rose from the depths of his mind—the worry that once she found herself truly free in the world, she would have no reason to return to him. Or worse, that the police would not believe her story and would hold her for questioning. With every moment that passed he tensed more, waiting for the phone to ring and Greenburg to be on the other line, telling him that Christine had been arrested for perjury after all.

But the phone remained silent, as did the great house around him; Ennis slept after his noon meal, and Jerome was still at his condo, presumably catching up on his sleep as well. Michel's shift did not even begin until after four o'clock. Erik had often been lonely in his life, but this was the first time he could recall being so utterly alone. Always before there had been someone to fulfill his every need, someone to make sure that he never lacked for any comfort.

Looking back, he realized he was appalled by the selfish creature he had been. Certainly he had had his share of suffering over his lifetime, but he had been cosseted and protected, every decision in the household made to accommodate him. He couldn't imagine what his life might have been had he been born to a poor family, born into a situation where he would have had to fend for himself.

Before Christine, he had never let himself become close to another human being, save Ennis, and that was only because Ennis refused to let Erik push him away. What had made Ennis put up with all of the self-centered demands, the complete indifference to anyone's concerns but Erik's own, Erik couldn't begin to comprehend. Only now he had the faintest glimmering of the sort of selfless love one person might have for another, and the reasons for Ennis's affection for the boy Erik had been and the man he had become. Certainly Erik had not had one-tenth that affection from his own father.

And Christine — he knew he didn't deserve her. He had planned her abduction and eventual seduction coldly, the way he had planned the financial ruin of the neighbors who had thwarted him or the corporate takeovers he had masterminded throughout the years. The plan had been for her to fall in love with him, but until it had actually happened, he had never thought about what would happen if he fell in love with her. Once it had happened, the trap in which he had thought to ensnare her had caught him instead, leaving him at her mercy. Never before had he given another person the power to hurt him—and she had hurt him, and rightfully so. He could not blame her for trying to escape, even though at the time he thought he could have killed her for wounding him in such a way. And then in place of the hurt had come the miraculous healing, her gentle touch on his ravaged face, her complete acceptance of every part of him.

If she didn't return, he knew he would have to let her go, even if it killed him. Even though she had told him repeatedly that she loved him, some part of his soul still had difficulty accepting it. Why would a woman like Christine love him—selfish, scheming, cold bastard that he was? Why would she, who could have the world at her feet, want to spend her life with a maimed half-mad recluse who could give her nothing but his unending devotion?

The ticking of the clock seemed to dig itself into his very nerve endings. He stood suddenly and walked away from the fire, pausing by the desk and looking down at the small box that sat in the middle of the blotter. If she returned, he would have something to give her to show his love, his commitment to her. If she could overlook all his flaws and still want to be with him, then he wanted her with him as his wife.

The diamond was as flawless and brilliant as Christine herself. It was not gaudily large—too big a stone would have looked awkward on her delicate hand—but it was as close to perfect as diamonds got, and he had been pleased by the effect of the stone in its antique-design platinum mounting. The thought of Christine wearing it as his wife made him tremble slightly, and he shut the ring box and replaced it on the desk.

If she returned—*when* she returned, he forced himself to think—there would be so much to plan, so much to discuss with her. Of course she must finish her degree, and then if she still wished to perform, then he would do everything he could to support her in that. Perhaps he could endow a scholarship at USC in her name; he had a feeling she would like that. He thought of all the good he could have done with his wealth over the years and shook his head. The sheer selfishness of his previous existence left him shaken. That Christine had wrought such a sea-change in him made him love her all the more. Without her, he knew he would have dwindled into an inward-turned old age, wrapped in bitterness and disdain for the world and its workings. Instead, he felt energized, ready to move forward to the next stage of his life.

If she returned, of course.

He started at the sound of a car in the driveway and moved quickly to the window, but it was only Michel in his red Audi. Was it really four o'clock already? A glance at the clock confirmed the time, and Erik could feel his heart begin to pound. It had been more than two hours since Christine left—surely the police couldn't have been questioning her this long? If she had run into trouble, wouldn't she have called Greenburg, who in turn would certainly have called Erik?

Perhaps he should go check on Ennis. The old man was really making a remarkable recovery, all things considered, but the hospital had sent home a set of post-op instructions, one of which admonished the caregiver to check on the patient every so often in case of a relapse. Ennis showed no sign of relapsing—if anything, he was already fretting about his enforced indolence, as if he thought he should already be up and about and seeing to Erik and Christine. But appearances could be deceiving, and Erik wouldn't lie to himself—he would be reassured to see Ennis doing well, and he knew that Ennis would have comforting words for him if nothing else.

But even as he turned and made for the door, he heard the sound of another car on the driveway and ran toward the window, pushing aside the heavy brocade curtains. Strange—Christine sounded as if she were going awfully fast, given her experience with the car and the wet pavement.

He looked out to see the big S-Class skid around the curve of the driveway, the car grimly gripping the pavement even under such rough handling. What the hell? When Christine had left, she had been driving the car so gingerly it looked as if it were being driven by a timid octogenarian, not a twenty-something college student.

Then he saw the reason for Christine's haste. Barely squeezing in past the closing gate was an older-model black BMW, its wipers working frenziedly in the driving rain. Obviously its driver was more experienced or at least knew his car better, for it squatted easily on the driveway's curve as it followed hard on the Mercedes' bumper.

The driver's-side door on the S-Class banged open, and Christine jumped out, running for the front door to the house. Erik barely had time to register the fact that she was both barefoot and bareheaded in the rain before he saw the door on the BMW open and Randall Cagney step out.

Cursing, Erik dropped the curtain and ran for the stairs, wondering what the hell could have happened. Of course Cagney must have followed Christine here, but how had he known she would be at the police station in the first place?

Time for that later. Now all he could think of was reaching the front door—of course he had sent Christine off without a key or the code to the front door, thinking that he would be waiting here for her return and so she could do without for now. He cursed his shortsightedness even as he pounded across the foyer and furiously typed in the code to open the front door.

It opened, and Christine fell into his arms, panting and dripping wet. "I tried to get away," she gasped, "but he just kept following me—"

And then Randall Cagney filled the doorway, pushing past the two of them to stand in the center of the entry hall. He glared at Christine as she huddled into Erik's arms, and then his eyes narrowed as he took in the half-mask.

"I don't believe it," he said at length. "You left me for the Phantom of the Opera?"

Chapter Thirty

To do him credit, Erik didn't miss a beat. He held me for a few seconds longer, gave me a reassuring hug, and set me upright. Then he raised an eyebrow in Randall's direction and said, "I take it you must be Randall Cagney?"

Randall's mouth dropped open for a second before he recovered himself enough to answer. "Yes, I'm Randall—Christine's boyfriend." There was no overlooking the emphasis he placed on the last word, and he glared from Erik to me, daring us to contradict him.

I began to open my mouth to protest, but Erik beat me to it.

"As to that," he said, "we may have a few differences of opinion. First, however, I would like to know what you're doing trespassing on my property."

"Trespassing?" Randall repeated.

"Well, yes, that's usually what one calls uninvited intrusion on one's property." Erik looked over at me, and his mouth quirked just slightly at the corner. Instead of the explosion I had been expecting, he seemed to be amused by the situation. "Perhaps you would feel more comfortable explaining your presence here to the police?"

"The police?" Randall asked, and then, swiftly, "Oh, I'd love for you to call the police. Then you can explain to them how you've been holding Christine captive here for the past few weeks."

"He has not—" I began furiously, but Erik lifted a hand.

"If that were true, why would she have come back here at all?" he inquired. "For that matter, why would she run directly to me instead of going to you?"

"I don't know—you've got her brainwashed or something—maybe she's suffering from Stockholm syndrome—"

"You have been doing your research, haven't you?" Erik drawled. "How interesting. However, perhaps we should let the police decide." He gestured down the hallway. "There's a phone in the first salon on the left. Why don't we all go down there to make the call?"

Randall's suspicious gaze shifted from Erik to me and then back again. "Great. I'd love to see you talk your way out of this one."

"Very well, then." And he led us down the hall to a large sitting room I had never been in before. It was a chilly, formal room, with fussy French antiques and a number of rosy-cheeked portraits of eighteenth-century nobility on the wall, while an enormous Aubusson rug covered the floor. The style was very different from the furnishings of the rest of the house, and I found myself wondering who had decorated the chamber.

Erik picked up the phone from the intricate ormolu table to one side of the door. "I don't suppose it's necessary to call 911 for this matter?" At Randall's hesitant head shake, Erik continued, "Do you know who was working on Christine's case?"

"Detective Ortiz," Randall replied, sounding a little numb. Obviously he was having a hard time coping with Erik's apparent nonchalance over the matter.

"Very good. Thank you."

Then Randall and I both seated ourselves somewhat awkwardly on the pair of gold-upholstered loveseats that faced one another across an inlaid coffee table, and listened as Erik dialed information for the Pasadena police department's non-emergency number and then asked for Detective Ortiz.

"Detective Ortiz? My name is Erik Deitrich." A pause, and then Erik said, "Well, it's rather awkward, but I have Randall Cagney here at my home, and he's demanding that you come out to talk to all of us. He is trespassing, but perhaps if you could come over and—ah, excellent. We'll see you in a few moments."

He hung up the phone and turned to Randall and me. "He'll be over as soon as he can. In the meantime, can I offer you some coffee? You do look a little—damp."

It was true. Although it hadn't been raining when I left the police station, partway through the drive back to

Charles Street the heavens had opened up again, and even the moment or so Randall and I had been out in the rain had been enough to dampen each of us quite a bit. My feet in their shredded hose were freezing.

"Um, sure," Randall replied, looking somewhat bemused. I'm sure he had been expecting shouting, threats—anything but a civilized offer of refreshments while we waited for the police to arrive.

Erik looked over at me, and again I could see that ghost of a smile in the corner of his mouth. "Christine, if you could let Michel know that we'll need a pot of coffee in the grand salon? And perhaps you'd like to change out of those wet things—you don't look very comfortable."

Grateful for the excuse to escape, if even for a few minutes, I nodded and slipped out of the room. I found Michel in the kitchen, standing in front of the open refrigerator door and muttering to himself in French. He started a little when I appeared, then ungraciously accepted the instructions to make coffee and bring a service for four to the grand salon. It still irritated him to have to perform the tasks that Ennis usually handled.

After that I ran upstairs to my rooms and quickly drew off the damp twin set and skirt, then pulled on a pair of jeans and the argyle sweater I had worn my first day here. My feet felt like ice, so I figured the hell with fashion and slipped on a pair of sheepskin-lined house boots. During these operations I couldn't help but wonder what Erik and Randall could possibly be saying to one another in my absence. Whatever the exchange, I was certain Erik would keep the upper hand. I had seen him passionate, angry, loving, even charming, but this was the first time I had seen Erik as a man secure in his power, used to handling difficult business transactions and legal situations. Watching Randall go up against him was rather like watching a rat terrier take on a pit bull.

By the time I returned to the salon, Michel had already come and gone, leaving the coffee behind. The delicious aroma perfumed the air, and despite the tense atmosphere in the room, I was amused to see Randall take his coffee black under Erik's watchful gaze, even though I knew he liked cream and sugar, just as I did.

"Ah, Christine," Erik said, "just in time. Feeling better?"

I nodded. "Much." I reached for a coffee cup, feeling Randall's outraged stare on me and choosing to ignore it.

No sooner had I dropped a sugar cube and stirred a dollop of cream into my cup than the buzzer sounded, indicating that someone was waiting for the driveway gates to be opened.

Erik set down his own cup and saucer. "I'd best get that," he said, and left the room.

Once he was gone, Randall said, "Who the hell is this guy?"

"According to you, he's the Phantom of the Opera," I replied sweetly, taking a sip of ambrosial coffee.

"That's not funny. What kind of sick game are you two playing?"

"It's not sick, and it's not a game," I retorted, knowing that I could never make him understand. "Anyway, he told you his name — it's Erik Deitrich."

"Yeah, that tells me a lot—" He shot me a quick, suspicious look. "How did you meet him, anyway?"

"At the restaurant." I figured it was safe to tell Randall that much. "He came to the Halloween dinner."

"Well, that makes a lot of sense," Randall began, even as I snapped,

"Do you have to be such a jerk?"

We were interrupted by the sound of a throat clearing, as Erik reentered the room, followed by Detective Ortiz. Randall and I exchanged sulky glares, then settled back on our respective loveseats, just like a couple of children caught quarreling by their parents.

Detective Ortiz caught my eye and nodded. "Good to see you again so soon, Miss Daly," he said, and I couldn't be sure whether he was serious or not.

"Coffee, detective?" Erik asked, then poured a cup for him when Ortiz nodded.

Erik sat down next to me, so the detective perforce seated himself next to Randall, facing us.

Ortiz took a sip of coffee, then said, "Your call was quite—unexpected, Mr. Deitrich."

"I can imagine," Erik said dryly. "But since Mr. Cagney was quite adamant—"

Detective Ortiz lifted an eyebrow at Randall. "What about it, Randall?" From his tone, he was not amused. Probably he had thought he was finally done with the Daly case.

"Well—look at her! She's brainwashed or something!"

Ortiz glanced over at me, one eyebrow slightly raised. Probably those steady dark eyes were contrasting my current casual appearance with the stylishly dressed woman who had been in his office only an hour or so ago, but he said only, "She looks fine to me."

"I am not brainwashed," I said. "Randall is upset that I'm with Mr. Deitrich—I understand that. But he's convinced there's no way I could possibly be here under my own free will."

Erik interposed, "We tried to point out to Mr. Cagney that Christine returned here of her own volition—but he refused to believe that. He insisted that the police be brought in."

Ortiz sighed, then took another sip of coffee. His blunt fingers looked especially large against the delicate Spode coffee cup. "Randall, I spoke with Miss Daly at length earlier this afternoon about her disappearance and her association with Mr. Deitrich. The Pasadena police department has concluded that no foul play was involved."

"Then you're wrong!"

A brief silence, during which Erik looked on with that same air of indifferent amusement and Ortiz remained sitting quite still; only a slight flaring of the nostrils indicated how irritated he really was.

When he spoke, however, it was with the same nononsense tone he had used previously. "You're entitled to your opinion, Mr. Cagney. But your opinion does not give you the right to trespass on Mr. Deitrich's property. He would be fully within his rights to press charges."

Erik lifted a hand. "I'm sure that's not necessary."

Randall transferred his outraged glare to me. "Christine—you don't have to stay here. Whatever he's made you do—"

"He hasn't *made* me do anything! Why can't you get that through your head?"

"Maybe because I just don't believe this half-assed story of yours about suddenly deciding to come stay here for a few weeks without telling anyone!"

And of course he was right…but I couldn't say that. I had to stick with the story I'd given both him and Detective Ortiz. But I also somehow knew he would hate the truth even more than the lies I'd been telling. The last thing Randall would want to hear was that I had truly fallen in love with the man who had kidnapped me. I could still barely understand it myself. All I did know was that my feelings were true, and my own. I had fought this love for Erik Deitrich, and certainly had not been brainwashed into it.

"My goodness, Randall—I hope you've handled your other breakups better than this," came Erik's voice, almost too gentle to be mocking. Almost.

"Son of a bitch—" Randall began, and started to rise from the love seat, until Ortiz clamped his hand around his wrist and pulled him back down.

"That's enough," he said. "Do you want to add assault to trespassing?"

Apparently not, for Randall subsided, glaring at both Erik and me before he finally picked up his neglected coffee and took a sip, trying to appear calm. I was sure he could have cheerfully throttled the both of us at that point.

Ortiz seemed somewhat encouraged by his silence, as he said next, "If there's nothing else—"

"I think that's covered it nicely," Erik replied.

"Although Christine and I would both be grateful if you could make sure Mr. Cagney leaves with you."

"No problem, Mr. Deitrich." Detective Ortiz set his cup and saucer down on the coffee table and stood. "Randall?"

Looking cornered, Randall finally burst out, "If everything is so normal around here, why do you wear that mask? What sick fantasy are you forcing her to act out?"

I was certain at that point the explosion would finally come. Erik was silent for a moment, staring at Randall with the sort of disinterested disgust a man might display toward a particularly unique specimen of insect that had invaded his home. "Your manners are sadly lacking, Mr. Cagney," he said at length.

At that Randall stood. Erik was the taller of the two by a few inches, but Randall was broader across the shoulders, more athletic in appearance. "Maybe they are, Mr. Deitrich," he replied, "but that still doesn't answer my question."

Detective Ortiz and I were both silent, as if this final confrontation concerned those two men alone, and we could only provide mute witness to their conflict.

"Then perhaps this will." And with that he raised his hands to lift the mask from his face.

Randall couldn't take a step back without tripping over the loveseat, but the color drained from his face even as he whispered, "Jesus Christ…"

Even Ortiz looked shaken. He had probably seen a lot of horrors in his career, but I was sure none of them could compare to the ravaged right side of Erik's face. And through it all Erik's eyes glared at the both of them, daring them to say something further, to point, to jeer—to use any and all of the means by which he had always expected to world to deride him.

I watched their reactions and wondered why I had never felt the same way. Pity, perhaps, for all the pain he must have endured, but never revulsion, never disgust. Then I realized it was because I knew him in a way they never could, knew what made him laugh, which pieces of music he liked, even which side of the bed he preferred. And I knew then that I had to show them, prove to them that Erik and I were meant to be together, no matter what the world might think of us.

Rising, I turned toward Erik, then deliberately put one hand on the scarred side of his face. "I'm here," I said, then brought my mouth up to his. I felt him go still at first in surprise, and then his arms tightened around me as I continued the kiss, our lips pressing against one another's as the seconds ticked on. Compared to most of our previous embraces, the kiss was a very chaste one, but even so Randall was looking on in shock by the time Erik and I pulled apart, and Ortiz appeared distinctly uncomfortable.

"And that," I said, "is why I'm here. Because I love him. Because he loves me. You don't have to understand it—you don't even have to accept it. But you have to leave us in peace. Can you give us that much at least?"

Even as Randall nodded dumbly, Erik raised the mask and carefully set it back in place. He said quietly, "Then I think we have nothing further to say to one another."

Detective Ortiz seemed to gain some of his composure once Erik's face was once again half-covered by the mask. "I'll make sure he doesn't disturb you again," he said, then clapped Randall on the shoulder. "Come along, Mr. Cagney. It's time we left them alone."

Randall looked from Erik to me, still with that glazed look in his eyes, as if he could not begin to comprehend what he had just seen. But at least he followed Ortiz without comment, even as Erik and I trailed along behind, to make sure they found their way to the front door. Once we were all in the foyer, Erik opened the door, and they both walked out into the wet afternoon. Randall paused for just a second on the doorstep, ignoring the rain that beat down against his bare head. His eyes met mine, and he stared at me for a moment as if he had never seen me before. Then he turned and walked slowly to the car, even as Erik closed the door behind them.

Somehow I knew I would never see Randall Cagney again.

Christmas was almost upon us, and the house was decorated for the first time since Erik was a child.

"I never felt much of a need for Christmas, until now," he told me, with unspoken meaning in his eyes.

If I had thought Erik would immediately enter the world, I was mistaken—he enjoyed the preparations for the holiday, but it was Ennis and I who brought long-unused ornaments down from the attic and who spent an obscene amount of money at Stat's in Old Pasadena for new ones. And it was Ennis who went with me to choose a tree of handsome enough proportions to decorate the second salon—the grand salon where Randall and I had had our last encounter was too fussy for me, but the second salon, with its dark wood paneling and magnificent fireplace, seemed the perfect home for the Noble fir Ennis and I selected.

It was a difficult decision, but after long deliberation I had decided to transfer to UCLA to finish out my senior year. "At least no one will know me there," I said to Erik one evening as we lingered by the fire after dinner. "It will probably take me an extra semester, but at least I'll be done."

He had agreed, although the commute concerned him. I wasn't looking forward to it, either, but at least now I didn't have to worry about rushing back to Pasadena to get in enough hours at work. And Erik, being Erik, had presented me the next morning with the keys to a brand-new Jaguar convertible—to make the commute more bearable, he explained.

"I thought perhaps the Mercedes wasn't to your taste," he said, and I just had to laugh, still somewhat bemused by the way he threw money around without even thinking twice about it.

Now the Jag sat in lordly splendor next to Erik's S-Class, with Jerome's Range Rover putting in fewer and fewer appearances. Of course Erik still required Jerome's services from time to time, and as far as I knew his payroll status never changed, but certainly he spent more time these days at his condo overlooking the Paseo Colorado than in his flat over the garage.

Now there remained only one last thing for me to do. I hovered in the foyer, waiting for the buzzer to let me know someone was waiting at the front gate. Eventually it did sound, more than ten minutes after I had expected it to. Well, some things never changed.

I tapped in the pass code to open the gates and then walked out on the front steps, lifting my hand to shield my eyes against the bright afternoon sunlight. Today was one of those rare December days of amazing beauty—we were between storms, and the sky was a deep calm blue broken up by large creamy clouds, the air cool against my face even as the sun caught my hair and warmed me. Then I saw Meg's bright yellow Mini come up the curving driveway, and I raised my hand in greeting.

The car stopped right in front of the door with a small spray of gravel, and then Meg got out, still outrageously gorgeous in a scarlet sweater with a fur collar and slim jeans. She trotted up the front steps in her high-heeled boots, then gave me a quick hug as if she'd only seen me yesterday.

"Well, you look fabulous!" she exclaimed.

"So do you," I said truthfully, because I'd never seen Meg look anything except drop-dead gorgeous.

"Oh, well," she said, waving a hand. "Okay, I am dying to see the inside of this place. Vanderbilts, eat your heart out!"

So I led her inside and let her exclaim over the antiques and the fireplaces and the general size of the place. Truly, she didn't seem at all upset with me—neither had she when I first contacted her, but Meg had always been good at being publicly polite when she had to. I hadn't been able to stop worrying about what she would say once we were alone together, but apparently all my fretting had been for nothing.

When we were finally seated in the small salon that overlooked the loggia—where Erik and I had first ventured out into the sunlight together, so many days ago—I finally found the courage to ask, "So what exactly did Randall tell you?"

"Oh, please." She shook her head and then took a sip of the espresso Ennis had brought for her. "God, I'd kill to live in a house where someone made espresso like that for me every day. Anyway—Randall was just flipping out. Who knew Mr. Mild-Mannered Accompanist had such a crazy streak? I told him he was acting nuts and that he needed to settle down. Then he started talking about how you were living with some freak who had brainwashed you into staying with him, and that's when I told him to put down the crack pipe. He got all pissed off, and so I hung up on him."

Good for you, I thought, but said nothing, instead sipping at my own café au lait.

"So then I called Detective Ortiz to get the straight scoop, since Randall had said he'd met with you and Erik as well, and he told me what was really going on." She cocked her head, her favorite gold chandelier earrings sweeping at the fur collar. "But he did tell me that Erik was, well—"

"Disfigured?" I supplied. "Deformed?" I met her dark eyes squarely. "Well, he is."

"And you don't care," she said, finishing the thought. "Well, good for you. Beauty fades, anyway."

At that I couldn't help laughing, and after a moment she joined in.

"Seriously," she said, "if he's right for you, no one else should care except you, right?"

And that was all I would get from her. No recriminations over my disappearance, no anger. I was happy, and so she was happy. If Randall wanted to agonize over the situation, that was his problem, but Meg was ready to move on.

"Meg, you may be the sanest person I've ever met in my life." I said.

"Ha—tell my mother that. She's convinced I'm completely *loca*. But whatever." The dark eyes glinted at me behind the black eyeliner and mascara. "So do I get to meet him?"

"Of course. I told him you were coming." And the announcement had met with surprisingly little resistance; Erik had only said he was glad I felt comfortable having a friend come to the house, and that of course he'd be happy to meet her.

"You should tell him it's all because of me," she whispered as we approached the music room. "If I hadn't convinced you to put on more lipstick at that Halloween party, he might never have looked at you twice."

"Your mother's right," I said fondly, realizing then how much I had missed her. "You really are *loca*."

Then we were outside the music room, and once again Erik was playing *Claire de Lune*. I could tell by Meg's sudden silence, and the dreamy look in her eyes, how impressed she was by his virtuosity. By tacit consent we both waited outside until he was finished, and then I entered, saying, "Erik, here's Meg. She really wanted to meet you."

Meg took the mask in stride, as I knew she would. She simply approached Erik at the piano and extended her hand. "Hi, Erik. It's really great getting to meet you at last."

"It was very good of you to come," he said with that grave charm I loved so much. "I know Christine has missed you very much."

"Well, next time don't let her disappear on me like that!" Meg responded, and for a second I was afraid Erik would be offended, since he hadn't any experience with Meg's airy irreverence.

But instead he simply smiled and said, "Well, you and I will both have to make sure that never happens again. Would you like to stay for dinner?"

"Absolutely!" she said, and then suddenly all three of us began chatting about music, about my decision to attend UCLA, about the upcoming holidays—anything but how I had come to live here, or what had happened to Randall Cagney.

Once again I blessed Meg for her easy rapport with people, her ability to sail through any social situation with aplomb. And I loved her even more because she obviously liked Erik very much, and approved of the two of us together. I could only hope that the rest of the world would see it that way as well.

Later that evening, after Meg had left, and Erik and I sat in companionable silence by the fire in the second salon, he turned to me and said, "Meg's a very charming girl. I hope she comes to visit often."

"Well, you two definitely make up the mutual admiration society, because she likes you very much. She asked if you had a brother."

At that he laughed. "God—I'd hate to inflict two of me on the world."

I reached out and touched his hand. "I'm glad there's only one of you, because I'm selfish and want you all to myself."

His eyes were almost the color of amber in the firelight. "I must be selfish as well, because I want you all to myself, too." Then I saw a glint of his eyes as he added, "Except for the times when I must share you with the opera aficionados of the world, of course."

I smiled then, thinking of the road ahead. There would be disappointments, no doubt—even the most successful singers met with their share of setbacks and roadblocks. But at least I would be able to go through it with Erik at my side.

"Christine?" Erik's voice was very quiet.

I pulled my thoughts back from the hazy future to look over at him. Since we were alone together, he had removed the mask, but the right side of his face was in shadow, and for a moment I could see him as he should have been. In his hand he held a small box.

My heart began to pound. I had known this was coming; it had been an unspoken agreement between the two of us almost from the very moment we had been intimate. But now that the time had come, I found myself trembling, waiting to hear his next words.

Once again I was as thrilled by the beauty of his voice as I had been the first time I ever heard him speak. He was quiet for a moment, then said, "You have brought so much to my life—so much light, so much love. You looked past the scars to the man inside. You forgave me when I couldn't forgive myself. Some part of me still thinks I have no right to ask you this—but I will." He paused, and I could see him take a ragged breath. "Christine, will you marry me?"

"Of course I will," I said, blinking back the tears that had started to my eyes as I listened to his words. "I want to share my life with you. I want your face to be the first thing I see in the morning, and the last thing I see when I lie down at night."

And then I was in his arms as he kissed me, holding me so close it was difficult to draw breath. But I didn't care—I pressed myself against him, feeling the strength of his body, taking in the warm scent of his skin, the marvelous sensation of his lips on mine. After a few moments we pulled apart, and then he smiled at me.

"You haven't even seen the ring," he said, retrieving the ring box from the hearth rug where he had dropped it.

"I got a little distracted," I replied, with a shaky laugh.

"I'm sorry," he said, but his tone was anything but contrite. Then he opened the box and slipped the ring on my finger.

It was exquisite, of course; I had expected nothing less. The delicate filigree and accent stones reminded me of pieces from my grandmother's jewelry collection.

But never before in my life had I seen a diamond that seemed to collect all the light in a room and then refract it in a thousand points of shimmering fire. It was absolutely flawless, and the most beautiful thing I had ever seen.

"It's stunning," I said, knowing even as I said them how inadequate the words were.

"Then it meets your approval?"

"Of course it does. How could any woman not love it?"

"I was afraid you might want something larger—it's only a little over four carats, after all."

Only, I thought, and then started to laugh. I couldn't help it. After a moment, Erik began to laugh, too. Then he took me in his arms again, and diamonds of any carat weight were the last thing on my mind.

We must have dozed off in front of the fireplace, for I awoke some time later, feeling the weight of Erik's arms around me, the deep rise and fall of his chest against my back as he slept.

I lay there for a long moment, comforted by his presence, the warmth of the fire, even the spicy scent of the Noble fir as it sat in splendor in a far corner of the room. The aura of contentment and peace in the room was almost palpable, and I sighed, hoping it would never end.

There would be some people would never understand. There would be those who would question and pry. But I also knew that Erik and I were meant to be together, two broken pieces who somehow made up a whole. Whatever bitterness and pain we had endured was now in the past. Now we had each other, and the future.

Then I turned so that I faced him, and he sighed and settled against me once more in sleep.

I smiled then, and kissed him very gently on his scarred cheek.

"I love you, my Phantom," I whispered.

Even in his sleep, he smiled.

The End